NFA

By

Neil Muscott

ISBN: 9781701149168
Imprint: Independently published

Characters and events in this novel are fictitious. Any similarity to real people, living or dead, is coincidental and not intended by the author.

Front cover photo by Neil Muscott
Author's photo by Neil Muscott
Book Design by IronStrikesIron

First printing November 2019
Published by Neil Muscott
1947 Dundas Street West, Unit E1
Toronto, Canada
M6R 1W5

www.neilmuscott.com

AUTHOR'S NOTE

Writing about people and events set nearly 50 years ago, I am aware of how much society has changed. To remain authentic to the time period, I have retained the sexism, racism and homophobia that was common in 1972.

TO HELEN DONNELLY

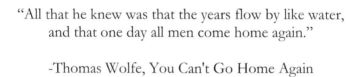

"All that he knew was that the years flow by like water,
and that one day all men come home again."

-Thomas Wolfe, You Can't Go Home Again

1972

Was he really doing this? Was he really running away from home?

Ian Musgrave stood on the small cement porch of his parent's bungalow. He pulled the front door shut and heard the lock snap home. He looked down at the house key in the palm of his hand. His fingers trembled. Once he dropped this key through the mail slot he would be locked out. He would have no choice but to go.

At his feet lay a green canvas duffle bag stuffed with a few clothes, two blankets rolled tightly and tied with a rope, and a large canteen filled with Madanon's tap water, notorious for its metallic taste. In his wallet he had less than thirty dollars; less than thirty dollars to go all the way to Vancouver and start a new life. Even he knew it was a crazy plan, but he had no choice. This was all Ian had thought about for almost a year: running away to Vancouver to start a new life. He was sixteen so legally his parents could do nothing to stop him. But he knew, deep inside, that if they caught him trying to run away, if they confronted him and told him he couldn't go, he would knuckle under and stay. His plan was crazy but staying was crazier. He couldn't take it anymore. If he stayed something would snap. He was afraid of what he would do.

Ian opened his fist and saw red lines where the key had cut into his palm. He took a deep breath, leaned down and popped the key through the mail slot. He heard a tiny metallic ring as it bounced on the tile floor. He stood up and wiped his sweaty palms on his jeans.

There was no turning back.

Ian grabbed his bedroll and draped the rope over his shoulder. He hung the canteen off his other side. He slung the duffle bag over his back and ran down the steps and out to the sidewalk. A heavy rain fell all morning, but just after noon the downpour had stopped. With no breeze, the June air hung thick and damp. A low fog had swallowed the tree tops. Ribbons of mist rose from the wet black pavement. Except for water dripping off the houses and trees, he was surrounded by silence. Ian felt like he was walking through a dream scape. Any minute he would wake up screaming, trapped in his parent's house.

He walked fast, his armpits wet, sweat beading on his forehead. This was the trickiest part of *The Plan*. He had to get from his house to the high school, Madanon Secondary School, without anyone seeing him. When Ian first got the idea to hitchhike to Vancouver, around Christmas time, he decided to leave in the spring when the school year ended. But how could he get away without being spotted? He'd have to sneak out to the highway and thumb west. Someone would see him, either walking out of town or hitchhiking, which meant his family would soon find out and try to stop him. While he started saving part of each week's allowance, he agonized over how he would actually get away.

In the late winter, things got even more complicated, when his parents announced they were moving to Steelton, a couple of hours south of Madanon. Moving day would be the morning after Ian's last exam. They had already booked a U-Haul truck for that date in June. Ian panicked. He'd have to run away before then. But that would mean missing exams and blowing his school year. His parents would be home all the time packing. How would he get out of the house without anyone seeing him carrying his things? He tossed and turned every night for a week.

Then he had an idea. One night at dinner, he told his parents he had made a mistake, he had to write one more exam a week later than the date that he had told them previously. They were furious -how could he make such a stupid mistake! But, no matter how much they yelled at him, there was nothing they could do about it. They had to move as planned because his father was starting a new job. They had already rented a house in Steelton. After hours of bickering, it was decided that his parents would leave as scheduled, but Ian would stay another week to write his last exam. Although he hoped they would leave him there by himself, his parents decided his older brother would also stay to "look after him". Then, on the evening of his last exam, his parents would drive back to Madanon to get the boys and pick up the last boxes and furniture.

Ian could hardly believe they fell for his lie. As June

approached he ran over his plans again and again in his mind, making a mental list of what he would take. Then one day after school he had another great idea. Lots of kids bussed into the school from around the region. Some traveled over an hour to get to Madanon. Ian decided that after school he'd get on the school bus that went north to White River. That meant he'd have an hour's head start before anyone even realized he was missing.

Everything fell into place. While his family packed up the household, Ian packed too; he gathered the things he needed for his trip and hid them under his bed. His brother was a few years out of school and had been working for a department store delivering furniture. He arranged to work that extra week. When moving day came, Ian helped load the truck. As his parents drove away, he felt odd. Maybe he'd never see them again. He wasn't sure exactly what would happen once he got to the west coast. In one fantasy he settled down there, living in a cottage on the ocean, starting a new life. In another version he worked for the summer and come back to Madanon in the fall. The only thing he knew for sure was this: he would never live with these people again.

For the next week, after his brother went to work, Ian pretended to study, going down to the high school every afternoon. After work his brother ate and watched TV. He resented being stuck here "baby-sitting" his kid brother. They hardly spoke, which was fine by Ian. After school he went out for coffee with his high school chums. He had decided to tell no one his plans for fear they would tell someone and his family would find out. He felt odd lying to his friends, but he knew they would be

4

amazed when they heard what he had done.

Finally, Ian's "exam day" arrived. That morning, after his brother went to work, Ian was able to pack for the first time. He took two blankets from his bed, spread them on the floor, rolled them tight, and tied them with a length of clothes line. He filled his canteen. Then he practiced carrying it all. After that he piled his stuff in the middle of the empty living room, peering out the window at the heavy rain. But, worried his brother might come home for lunch, he hid his gear in a closet. He paced around, too excited to sit still. Looking out the window, hoping the rain would let up, he kept thinking, what was he doing? This was insane. If he unpacked and waited for his parents to arrive that night, no one would ever know about his stupid fantasy.

Now, walking quickly towards the school, Ian was still terrified he would run into his brother, out making a delivery or driving around killing time with his work buddies. Every time he heard a car engine approach in the fog, he panicked, expecting his brother to drive up and confront him. He dreaded the fight that would ensue, afraid he would back down and return home. His brother would tell his parents and there would be a huge screaming fight. He peered cautiously down each side street before he crossed. Ian's heart jumped when headlights loomed out of the mist, but it was a only stranger in a car. The driver did not even look at him.

The rope from the bedroll cut into his shoulder. Ian stopped and adjusted his load, trying to get the blankets centred on his back. With each hurried step the heavy canteen banged sharply against his hip bone. The duffle bag kept sliding off his shoulder so he carried it at his side, letting it drag on the wet sidewalk. He had wanted to buy a backpack but they were too expensive. Instead he bought a cheap canvas duffle bag. Just before leaving the house, he raided the fridge, grabbing some cheese, a loaf of bread and a jar of peanut butter. As his parents were packing, he had seen his father's old hunting knife in its worn leather sheath. He swiped it, wrapped it in a t-shirt and hid it in the bottom of his bag. The idea of hitchhiking scared him. He worried about being robbed or attacked by some pervert. He wasn't sure that he had the nerve to use the knife, but still, he felt better having some way to protect himself.

Finally, Ian reached the steep city park that overlooked the high school. As he started down the wide grassy slope, he felt very exposed, so he let gravity carry him down, walking faster and faster, until he was running. He dashed across the street to the school, opened one of the heavy oak doors, and ducked inside, relieved that no one had seen him. He paused to catch his breath while his eyes adjusted the shadowy foyer, only lit by the glowing trophy case. Ian slipped the bedroll and canteen off his shoulders. Holding his gear low to the floor, he strolled quickly past the Office, afraid Mr. Farley, the VP, would spot him. But the office was empty except for the school secretary and she did not look up.

Ian went right to the study hall, a classroom set aside for students during exams. As he expected, it was nearly empty: the afternoon exams had already started. Only three other students were there, maybe preparing for tomorrow's exam or waiting to take the bus later. He didn't know them. One glanced up briefly. Ian headed to the back corner far from the door. He dumped his stuff along the wall behind the desk. He collapsed in the seat, his legs trembling from exhaustion and nerves.

So far so good. Now he had two hours to kill until the school buses came. He grabbed some old text books off a shelf at the back of the room and piled them on the desk. He opened one so it would look like he was studying. He kept his head down and tried to read, but he was too jittery: the words were just meaningless dots on the page.

Time passed slowly. One of the other students packed up and left. One put his head down on the desk and napped. A girl opened a brown paper bag and ate a sandwich. The smell of egg salad made Ian very hungry. He had not eaten since breakfast. He thought of the bread and peanut butter he had with him, but he couldn't make a sandwich here. He slipped his hand into his duffle bag and found the chunk of cheese wrapped in plastic. He ate it, looking down at an open book whenever someone walked by the door. The dry cheese made him thirsty. He decided to slip down the hall to the water fountain. Besides he had to pee.

The hallways were empty and dark and smelled of disinfectant. In the washroom mirror Ian checked his acne. He had a few small pimples in between his soft chin stubble. He touched the stubble. Pretty soon he'd need to start shaving. There was a new whitehead on the side of his nose. He squeezed it very carefully, hoping he wouldn't make it worse. He stepped back and turned his head side to side. For weeks he'd been arguing with his parents because they said his hair was getting too long. His father said he looked like a girl, but Ian thought his hair looked cool, like a rock star. Besides, it was still shorter than many of his classmates. Because he parted his hair on the side, the front was shaggy and lopsided, a big blonde mop hung over his forehead. He brushed it back: a couple of new pimples were there too. He straightened his sweater, a thick orangey-yellow pullover his mother had bought him for Christmas. He hated it, but he didn't know what else to bring in case it got cold at night when he was traveling.

On his way back to the study room, Ian paused for a second to stare at his old locker. What would his friends think when he disappeared? They'd be shocked to find out he had run away from home. After all he was known as a good student with good grades, a bit of a bookworm. Last winter he had gotten into trouble for drinking at school dances. But a lot of kids drank at dances, so no one had asked him what was wrong. Even if they had, Ian didn't think he could talk to anyone about his family. It was better like this, just getting away.

Ian returned to his seat in the back corner of the study room. Alone now, he dug in his bag and pulled out a small blue accordion-fold brochure. It opened out into a long stylized map of Canada. A red line representing the highway ran from coast to coast. Published by the federal government, it stated that 100,000 young people were traveling around, exploring Canada. They had funded a hostel in every major city and many small towns across the country. There was even one listed for Madanon. Ian had heard it was somewhere out on the highway, but he wasn't sure where. In fact, that's how he got the brochure. About a month ago, downtown after school, Ian was approached by two guys with long hair and backpacks. They asked him where the hostel was. Ian said he didn't know. He didn't want to admit that he wasn't even sure what a hostel was. They showed him the little brochure and explained that at a hostel you could crash for the night for just a couple of dollars.

"Beats sleeping on the side of a road." One of them said. "We've done that a lot." The other one nodded and chuckled.

"Where are you headed?" Ian asked.

"Montreal." One said. "Then we want to check out the east coast. We hear people are really friendly there." He added. "Not like the Prairies, eh?"

The other smiled. "We just spent the winter in Vancouver."

"I'm going to Vancouver." Ian blurted out. "I'm hitchhiking out there as soon as school is over." It was the first time he had ever said it out loud.

"Far out." The first hippie said. "Van is very cool, man."

The other grinned and nodded. "You'll really dig it."

Ian was in awe chatting with them. For years he had seen hippies on TV, on the news, in rock bands, at communes, at Woodstock and other music festivals. But this was his first time talking with two real hippies, standing right in front of him with long hair, scraggly beards, beads, and tie-dyed t-shirts.

One of them dug in his pack and handed Ian a copy of the hostel brochure. "Keep it, man," He said. "It's really handy when you're *on the road*."

"Hey." The other one said. "Have you ever read On the Road by Jack Kerouac?"

"I've heard of it." Ian lied. He had no idea who Jack Kerouac was.

"You gotta read it, man. It's a righteous book."

"Kerouac." The other nodded sagely. "Man, he's like, the guru. He went on the road way back in the fifties. Traveled all over the States. He's really the guy who started it all."

"You gotta read it," The first one repeated. "It will change your life."

"Ok, dude." The other said. "We have to split. Gotta find the hostel tonight or sleep on the side of the road."

"Thanks for this." Ian waved the little brochure. As they walked away, Ian stared after them, wondering if he could ever be that cool? He headed home, repeating the title of the book, On the road, On the road, like some kind of mantra.

Two weeks later, in the public library, Ian walked past a shelf and saw the words On the Road down the spine of a book. He pulled a worn paperback off the shelf. The cover was lemon yellow with a hodgepodge of painted images: a convertible with two guys leaning on the hood, drinking wine from a bottle, one wore a striped shirt, the other wore a beret, some black guy stood nearby playing a saxophone. There was a woman in a tight blouse dancing in front of the men. In bold black print it said: On the Road by Jack Kerouac. In smaller print: "The bible of the Beat Generation". The cover struck Ian as pretty corny, but those two hippies had said it was *the* book to read. Maybe he would read it while hitchhiking out west. He liked the idea of reading On the Road while on the road. He was going to check it out but then, on an impulse, he slipped it under his sweater and walked out of the library. He felt a little surge of adrenalin. He had never stolen anything before! It seemed like a good start to his summer. He had promised himself he was going to try new things. His life had been so dull. Now he was primed to have an adventure.

In the corner of the study room, Ian hunched over the brochure, tracing the route with his finger, from Madanon, along the north shore of Lake Superior, past Thunder Bay, Winnipeg, Regina, Moose Jaw, Calgary, then through the Rockies to Vancouver. The little map had no details. He recalled seeing an old Atlas at the back of the class room. He grabbed it and found a map of Canada across a two-page spread. Each province was a different colour. There was a dot for just about every little town along the highway. Tugging slowly, he tore the pages free. It felt weird vandalized a book but he figured a map would be helpful on the road. He was leaning over stuffing the pages into his duffle bag, when a deep male voice said.

"Ian, what are you doing here?"

Ian jerked upright. It was Mr. Greenfield, his geography teacher, standing in the doorway.

"Nothing, sir." He jumped up and walked towards him, hoping Greenfield had not seen his duffle bag and bed roll behind the desk. "I'm done with my exam and just waiting for some friends."

"Oh," Mr. Greenfield nodded. "I'm surprised to see

you here, I heard that your family was moving."

"Yeah, they are, I mean, we are moving to Steelton." Ian gestured nervously, vaguely towards the south. "I mean they are already down there. I'm leaving tomorrow. I had to write an exam. Now I'm just waiting for some friends." He was repeating himself.

"Well." Greenfield nodded and stuck out his hand. "Good luck on your new home."

"Thanks, sir." Ian shook his hand. Greenfield left.

Ian was restless now. He paced around, flipping through old text books and drawing random shapes in the blackboard dust with his finger. More and more students, done with their exams, walked past the open door, talking loudly. It was almost three. Ian started to worry again. His brother finished work at three. Usually he went straight home, but what if he decided to pop over to the school and give Ian a ride home after the exam?

Leaning to one side of the window, Ian peaked out cautiously. The school buses were already parked in the half-moon driveway. No sign of his brother. He gathered his gear and went outside to the short row of buses. Their doors were shut. There were no real lines, just a few kids milling around talking about their exams. A handful of students smoked – they were supposed to do that at the rear of the school- but it was exam week, so they didn't care. Ian saw a couple of kids that he knew who lived north of Madanon standing by one bus. He went over and stood near them. They glanced his way, probably wondering why he was there, but they continued to talk among themselves.

"Hey, Musgrave." Ian spun around. It was Joe, his lab

partner from physics class. Joe was short, very wide in the shoulders, with bulgy arms like a body builder. He had thick black hair that he wore greased down and swept back behind his ears.

Joe punched Ian on the shoulder, hard enough that it stung. "So what are you up to?"

"I just wrote an exam." Ian lied. "How about you?"

"I wrote one too. I didn't see you in there."

"I left pretty early." Ian lied again.

"You brainiacs." Joe laughed and shook his head. "I wrote 'till three and I still didn't finish." He shrugged. "I'm fucked. Hey, why are you hanging out here?"

"I'm waiting to take the bus." Ian looked around nervously.

"The bus? What for? You moving to Shite River?"

"No, I'm heading out to Vancouver to work for the summer." He blurted it out and immediately regretted it. On the other hand, it felt good to tell someone his secret.

"No shit?"

"No shit."

"Vancouver." Joe grinned. "I hear there's lots of pot and nude beaches out there. I wish I was going. What do your folks think?"

"Who cares!" Ian said angrily. "They moved to Steelton last week. I'm sick of their bullshit."

"I hear ya," Joe shook his head. "My old man is a pain in the ass." He looked at his watch. "Ok, I got to get to work." Joe worked after school stocking shelves at a grocery store. He punched Ian in the shoulder. "Keep it real, buddy." He called back over his shoulder. "Hey, bring me back a pound of that BC home grown."

The other students stopped talking and looked at Ian.

"He's just kidding around." Ian said. He had never even smoked pot, let alone bought any. "This the bus to White River, right? I'm hitchhiking out west to work for the summer. Thought I'd catch a ride, you know, to get a head start."

Other students talked about their summer jobs. Ian listened but he was distracted. It was after three. Now his brother was off work. He'd be home. What if he spotted the house key on the floor? He'd wonder what was up, where Ian was, maybe he'd drive around looking for him. Ian stood closer to the bus, so he was hidden behind the little cluster of students. Finally, the driver approached, an older man with a crew cut, heavy glasses and a drab brown, stained work shirt. He opened the door and settled in his seat. Immediately kids started to board. Ian joined the line, but as he stepped up, the driver tossed up his hand.

"Who the hell are you?" Then he pointed at Ian's gear. "What's all this stuff?"

"I'm a student here." Ian stammered. He went blank. He hadn't expected the driver to say anything. He stopped, one foot on the bus, one on the ground. His Plan was already crashing down. Then one of the boys he had been chatting with called out.

"He's with me. He's coming up to visit my family."

"Oh," the driver shrugged. "Well, stop blocking the door."

Ian shuffled down the aisle and sat behind to the boy who has spoken up. He said thanks. The boy nodded indifferently and immediately stretched out on the seat and closed his eyes. More students boarded, looking curiously at Ian as they passed. The driver still eyed him in the rear view mirror.

Ian slouched down on the hard padded seat, anxiously watching the street for his brother. *Come on, come on,* he thought, *let's get going.* Finally, with a shudder and grinding gears, the bus pulled out of the driveway. Realizing the bus would pass through downtown, Ian ducked even lower in his seat, peeking out the bottom of the window. Once they reached the fast food strip on the edge of town, the bus sped up. When it swung onto the highway, Ian sat up. His heart was pounding. He turned to look back through the dirt streaked rear window and watched as the Madanon exit sign shrank out of sight.

He had done it!

The bus was about half full. All the regulars, used to the long commute home, quickly settled in, reading, staring out the window, or napping. Ian tried to get comfortable on the hard seat. He propped his duffle bag against the window and leaned on it, but when the bus hit rough pavement his head jerked around and bumped the glass. It didn't matter. He was too excited to sleep. It started to rain again. Through the big windshield wipers he watched the wet blacktop winding between the pine trees and rock cuts. It was cold in the bus so Ian pulled his sweater from the duffle bag and put it on. He settled back again hoping the rain would stop. With the moody lighting from the dark clouds, the silent students slumped over like corpses, and the relentless swish and thump of the windshield wipers, Ian felt again like he was dreaming. He leaned back and thought about Vancouver, imagining a shining city surrounded by mountains. He figured it might take him a week or so to get there. After paying hostel fees he wouldn't have much money left, but he'd seen on TV that lots of young people lived on the beaches near Vancouver. He had seen people sleeping in tents and sitting around bonfires playing guitars and drums. It looked like fun. Ian figured he could live on a beach until he found work. If he got something that paid well, like working in a lumber camp, maybe he'd buy a motorcycle. He had imagined a thousand times how shocked and surprised his friends would be when he rode back into Madanon on a motorcycle.

Eventually Ian saw a sign for White River. They were almost there. He sat up and peered eagerly ahead. He pulled out the little blue brochure. The next hostel was in Thunder Bay. He looked at the map of Lake Superior. It was a long way away, but maybe he could still get there tonight. If not -he patted his bedroll- he'd camp on the side of the road. It would be nice, sleeping under the stars and waking up at dawn.

South of White River the rain let up. The bus slowed and turned left into a gas station parking lot. The driver left the engine running, threw open the door and stepped down to have a smoke. The regulars quickly scrambled off. By the time Ian picked up his things and stepped down, they had all walked away towards their homes. He nodded at the driver, who ignored him. He went into the gas station washroom to pee. When he came out the bus was gone.

Ian stood alone in the little parking lot. The storm clouds had blown over. It was quiet except for the sound of wind in the trees. The late afternoon sun was warm. Slinging the canteen and bedroll over his shoulders, he grabbed his duffle bag and crossed the highway to the narrow gravel shoulder. He stopped and dropped his stuff. He was sweating. He pulled off his sweater and stuffed it into his bag. He took a big drink from his canteen. The water was still cool. He waited. The pine trees rustled. A single crow flew overhead, cawing.

One car came south, slowed and turned into White River. Ian shifted his weight back and forth, nudged some gravel with his toe, wondering how long before he would get a ride. Then, in the distance, he saw a car coming north. He had never hitchhiked before. He felt oddly self-conscious as he stuck out his thumb. Was he even doing this right? Should his arm be all the way out or bent at his side? He stood up straighter and tried to smile. He hoped he looked friendly.

The car started to slow –Ian thought it was stopping- but then it turned into White River. He checked the time. It was five o'clock. His parents would be on the road from Steelton now. When they arrived around seven he was supposed to be packed and ready to go. His brother would be home from work. Ian figured he must have found the house key on the floor. What would he think? He was probably driving around Madanon looking for him. After school Ian usually went for coffee with his friends or headed over to Shanks pool hall to hang out. He never should have told Joe his plans. If Joe told his brother about seeing him at the school bus everything would be ruined.

Ian thumbed desperately at every car that passed. Some were empty except for the driver; they looked like locals going home from work. Most people stared straight ahead as if he didn't exist. A few looked right at him as they drove by, sometimes with a blank face, sometimes looking suspicious or angry. Between cars, he paced in little circles around his things. An hour passed. The temperature dropped as the wind picked up. Ian had circled his gear so many times he could see a faint path where he had walked. Sparrows played in the thick weeds along the roadside. Another short string of cars came. Ian tossed his thumb up. The driver of the last car hit his brakes and swung on to the gravel. The car stopped a ways down the road.

A ride!

Ian ran towards the car, then doubled back to scoop up his things. The brake lights were on. Ian was afraid the driver would change his mind and pull away. He ran as fast as he could, his gear banging around his legs. He grabbed the passenger door and yanked it open.

"Thanks for stopping," he panted. The driver, a middle-aged man with a round face and thick glasses, leaned sideways across the seat to talk to Ian.

"Where you headed?"

"Vancouver." Ian said.

"Well," the man nodded thoughtfully. "I'm only going as far as the turn off to Manitouwadge."

"Great. That's great." Ian shoved his stuff into the back seat and climbed in. The man checked his mirror and pulled back on the highway. Ian's heart was pounding. He was so excited that he barely heard what the man was saying – something about the storm. This is it, he thought, as he watched the trees fly past. *I'm on the road! I'm going to Vancouver!*

The driver turned out to be soft spoken and quiet. He was the manager of a grocery store. He was going in to work a night shift, to supervise a load of canned goods that was arriving soon. He didn't have much to say. He reached over and turned on the radio, it was tuned to classical music. Ian was relieved because he wasn't sure what to do if the man asked him a lot of questions. He couldn't really say, I'm running away from home, could he? Between the music and the warm sunshine on his face, he almost nodded off.

"This is my turn." The man said, stopping at a paved side road. Ian had hoped for a gas station or a corner store but there was nothing here. He dragged his gear from the back seat and thanked the man who simply nodded and turned off the highway.

Ian lugged his stuff past the intersection and dropped it on the gravel. He rubbed his face with his hands to wake up. He checked his watch: it was almost eight. By now his parents had arrived in Madanon. They'd be furious that he was missing. But what could they do? Drive around looking for him? Even if they called the police, he was already hundreds of miles away. Ian smiled. His Plan was working. At this rate he'd be in Vancouver in a few days.

But as daylight dwindled, traffic dropped off. One or two cars passed, with long gaps in between. The woods were much thicker than by White River. Up the road from

Ian was a long rock cut as tall as a house. Ian stared into the thick bush and wondered if there were bears here. He was very hungry and dug into the duffle bag for his peanut butter and bread. The loaf was misshapen but he still managed to make a lopsided sandwich, using his father's hunting knife. After the dry chewy sandwich, he was glad for the water in his canteen. He wiped the knife on some grass, put it back in the sheath and tucked it away in the duffle bag.

Time dragged. No cars appeared for over a half an hour. As it grew dark, a cool wind rose, bending the tops of the tree. It looked like it might rain again. Ian put on his sweater. He paced and started to worry. What if he couldn't get a ride? By now his parents might know where he was. Maybe they had talked to Joe or someone else who had seen him getting on the school bus. What if they called the police? For all he knew the cops were driving around now, looking for him. What if they found him here on the side of the road? How embarrassing would it be to be taken back home in a police car!

It was too dark to see into the shadowy woods. Every time Ian heard a twig break he thought it might be bear. He took the hunting knife out again. The handle was a black bone-like material; the blade was about six inches long. He undid his belt and strung it through the leather sheath, so the knife hung at his side, by his right hand. If he tugged his sweater down, only tip of the sheath showed. He touched the handle through his sweater. He felt silly. No way he could fight a bear with a knife but, somehow, he felt a little better knowing the knife was handy.

As dusk fell a cloud of mosquitoes formed around his head. He waved his hands trying to disperse them. He swatted at them when they landed on his neck and hands. Then he felt a sharp bite in his hair line. He reached up and pinched a black fly. More black flies appeared. He walked quickly back and forth, waving frantically, but as soon as he stopped moving they descended and bit his exposed skin.

There was almost no traffic now. Ian decided he should camp for the night before it was too dark to see; he hadn't thought to bring a flashlight. At least if he laid down, he could cover his head with his blanket to escape the insects. He looked around: the shoulder was too hard and the shallow ditch was full of rain water. He figured his best bet was to camp up on top of the rock cut. He'd be on higher ground, maybe there'd be less bugs and he might be a little safer from whatever lived in these woods. He picked up his things and started trudging towards the rock cut, cursing himself for not bringing bug spray. In the morning his parents or the cops would find him exhausted, covered with fly bites.

Ian heard a car coming and half turned to thumb. Before he could raise his arm the car stopped right on the pavement next to him. A woman rolled down the passenger window and smiled. The driver leaned over and nodded.

"Hey buddy, you want a lift?"

"Do I? That would be great." He didn't even ask where they were going.

The woman, who wore jeans and a sweat shirt, climbed out, then turned and got in the back seat. It was only as Ian climbed in the front, piling his gear between his legs, that he saw two small boys and an old woman in the back seat. He shut the door and the driver stepped on the gas.

"I'm Paul." A thin man with crooked teeth, he smiled, and stuck out his hand.

"I'm Ian." He was so relieved to get a ride he could hardly think.

"In the back there, that's my wife Maggie, my boys Paulie and Josh, and my mother, Gladys."

Ian half turned in his seat to nod hello. The boys were maybe five and seven years old. The older one leaned forward on the front seat.

"Are you going camping?"

"No," Ian said. "I'm going out to B.C. to work."

"B.C." the boy repeated.

"British Columbia," His father said. "Remember? That's way out west, out past the prairies." He looked at Ian. "That's a long way to go."

Ian smiled. "I guess it is. I figure I'll get there in about a week, maybe less depending on rides."

"Where you from?"

"Madanon."

"You didn't get too far today." The man chuckled.

"I just started thumbing this afternoon, after school." He hesitated. He shouldn't tell these people too much; they might report him as a runaway.

"Well," Paul said, "We aren't going very far. We was down in White River visiting Maggie's folks."

They rode in silence for a few minutes. Ian watched the endless black top passing in the headlights. He was tired but thinking that whereever they dropped him, he'd have to keep thumbing. He decided if he saw a truck stop, he'd ask Paul to let him out there. At least then he could get inside if it rained again. He hated to spend his money but he couldn't face sleeping outside. He scratched behind his ear and pinched a tiny fly.

"Black flies, eh?" Paul grinned. "They're real bad this year."

"Yeah. I didn't bring any bug spray."

Paul looked over his shoulder at his wife, then looked back at Ian.

"Look, I'm thinking if you need a place to sleep tonight, we got a couch. It's a little crowded with the boys, but you could get a sleep there."

"Aw, that's okay. I don't want to put you out."

"It's no bother," Maggie spoke for the first time. "The couch is empty, might as well use it." She chuckled. "It's nicer than sleeping in a ditch."

Ian turned to smile at her. "Thanks, that's really nice of you."

He turned back to face the road, a little lump in his throat. Total strangers were putting him up for the night.

About an hour later they swung off the highway and shortly arrived at Paul and Maggie's house, a small bungalow set back from the road in a clearing carved from the woods. Paul pulled up behind another car parked in the muddy drive. The boys jumped out and ran screaming ahead. The house was unlocked. Paul helped him carry his stuff in, while his wife guided the old lady up the wooden front steps. The porch light glowed and flickered, surrounded by a big cloud of moths.

Inside everyone kicked off their shoes by the door. The grandmother, who had not spoken a word, said goodnight and went to bed. The kids protested but followed their mother down the hall too.

"Goodnight," Maggie called from the end of the hallway. "The bathroom is down here on the left."

"Thanks," Ian said.

"Be sure to knock first." The older boy warned very seriously.

"Ok. I will. Thanks."

Ian followed Paul into the kitchen. There was a big table, the surface covered with crumbs. Beside a loaf of bread in a plastic bag, sat a chunk of butter melted on a plate, deeply mutilated by knife marks. Paul sat and lit a cigarette.

"Do you want something to eat?"

"Thanks. I'm fine." Ian still felt the heavy lump of his peanut butter sandwich.

"BC, eh? I hear it's pretty out there, with the mountains and all."

"Yeah, I'm really looking forward to seeing the mountains."

"Where's your job?"

"Well," Ian was a little embarrassed. "I don't really have one lined up, but once I get there I'll find something."

"Sure," Paul said. "I hear there's lots of work out there." But he didn't sound very confident. He butted his smoke and balanced the unsmoked half on a tin ashtray. "I have to get to bed. I start work at seven, so I'll drive you out to the highway on my way."

"What do you do?"

"Ambulance. I'm an ambulance driver." He stood up. "Maggie's a nurse. We're both on the day shift this week. Ma looks after the kids."

He showed Ian to the living room. He pointed at a sagging reddish brown couch in front of the television.

"You can sleep here."

"Thanks."

Paul went to bed. Ian sat down on the couch. It was worn and saggy. He untied his bedroll and shook out his blankets. There was one thin throw pillow on the couch. He laid down and jammed it under his head. His feet touched the arm rest. He turned sideways, trying to avoid the uneven springs. Still, it sure beat sleeping outside. When everyone else was done, Ian tiptoed down the hall and used the bathroom. It was small and littered with dirty clothes and kids toys. He had left his toothbrush in his bag but he put some toothpaste on his finger and gave his mouth a quick rinse. He washed his face and dabbed blood from a couple of black fly bites on his forehead.

Back at the couch, Ian took off his sweater, socks, and pants but he left his t-shirt and underwear on. He didn't want to be naked in the morning when the family got up. He lay down and pulled his wool blanket up to his chest. He usually read before falling asleep. He pulled out his stolen copy of On The Road. He stared at the cover again: two men with wine bottles leaned against a car watching a woman in a white blouse and tight black pants. It looked like she was dancing. A thin black man stood nearby playing a saxophone. It's kind of stupid, Ian thought. Shouldn't the cover be someone standing beside a road, alone and looking bored? There should be rain and rock cuts, peanut butter sandwiches and blackflies. Ian smiled at the thought of On The road Northern Ontario style. He dropped the book on the floor beside the couch, reached up and turned out the light. A second later he fell into a deep sleep.

Ian heard voices and the clink of dishes and silverware. He was so tired. He wanted to sleep some more.

"Hey, Buddy." Someone shook his shoulder. "Buddy."

Ian opened his eyes. Paul stood over him.

"Time to get up. We gotta roll out soon." He went back to the kitchen.

Ian sat up stiffly. Visible through the wide doorway, the entire family sat in silence at the kitchen table. The boys stared at him. He stood up and quickly slipped on his pants. He ducked down the hall to the bathroom. He wanted to take a shower but he didn't know if he should without permission. Besides it sounded like there wasn't enough time. He washed his face and held his head under the tap to wet his hair. He dried it a bit with a hand towel, then used his comb to fix his part. A big wave of hair hung over his forehead hiding his pimples and a black fly bites. He went back to the living room, put on his shirt and sweater and socks. He re-rolled his blankets and tied them tight. He stuffed On the Road back into his duffle bag.

As he entered the kitchen, the grandmother stood up, took her cup and went to the living room. She turned on the TV and sat on the couch watching some morning news program. Ian took the chair she vacated. The boys ate their cereal with deliberate smacking noises. They stared at him with wide eyes. Maggie placed a stained white mug of coffee in front of him. Paul pushed a sugar bowl over to him. He was having a smoke. Ian spooned in some sugar. The coffee was good. No one offered him breakfast. The boys finished eating and started to play fight with their spoons.

"Enough." Maggie snatched the spoons from them. She told the older boy to get ready for school. The boys went down the hall, looking back at Ian and whispering.

Paul butted out his smoke and stood up. "I have to get to work."

Ian realized he meant now. He guzzled the rest of his coffee and grabbed his things. Maggie was down the hall with the boys.

"Thanks," He called out. She waved goodbye. He nodded at the grandmother, who nodded back in silence.

When Ian came outside Paul already had the car running. He saw his breath cloud against the dim morning light and was glad he had brought his sweater. A heavy dew covered the windshield. Low clouds filled the sky. One of the boys peeked out a window, silhouetted by yellow light. Paul beeped the horn. The boy waved. It only took about ten minutes to reach the highway. Paul stopped the car before turning.

"I go south, so I guess this is the best place for you to get out."

"Thanks for everything. I really appreciated the place to stay."

"Okay," Paul nodded. "Have a good trip."

Ian climbed out and watched Paul drive away. He looked around. Nothing but bush and rock cuts. Déjà vu, he thought. But at least there were no black flies. He carried his things a little past the turn off so there would be room for cars to stop. His hair was still damp. For all his weeks of planning, he had not thought to pack a towel. He dug in his bag and rubbed his hair with a t-shirt. He ate a slice of bread and peanut butter. He picked up his canteen. The water tasted warm and stale. He had forgotten to fill it up again. He inhaled the cold fresh air and rubbed his face, trying to wake up, wishing he had had time for more coffee. A few cars exited from the side road, swinging north and south. Probably locals on the way to work. One big trailer truck roared past blowing dirt in his face.

As the sun rose higher, traffic from the south picked up. A lot of cars looked like tourists on their way out west, but that usually meant cars crowded with families and no room for him. Today Ian felt like a seasoned hitchhiker; he kept his thumb low by his hip and made friendly eye contact with each driver. Most did not look at him. Some stared as if Ian were a zoo exhibit. There were angry faces too, as if to say "look at that hippie". Ian found this funny since his hair was really not very long compared to many kids his age. Some drivers actually sped up when they saw him. Maybe they thought all hitchhikers were escaped convicts who would somehow leap on their car, drag them out and kill them.

But there were nice drivers too. A few, if their car was full, shrugged apologetically. Some pointed sideways, which Ian realized meant they were turning off the highway shortly. When one car slowed a bit, Ian saw a big family, kids crammed in the back seat. The driver smiled and threw Ian a peace sign. Ian spun around and flashed a peace sign to the retreating car. The kids in the back seat smiled and waved at him. Ian grinned. He had never made a peace sign before.

Traffic got thicker but no one stopped. Ian passed through waves of boredom and sleepiness. He paced in a circle, singing snippets of pop songs, skipping small stones across the road. When he had to pee he dashed into the edge of the woods, out of sight from the passing cars. During a wave of fatigue, he sat down on his duffle bag and thumbed but he was afraid that he looked lazy, so he stood up again. By mid-morning, he was too warm and he took his sweater off. He sniffed his arm pits. He had a little body odor and wished he had grabbed a shower.

Ian heard a horn and spun around. A car sat on the shoulder up the road. He grabbed his stuff and started to run, thinking it was a joke and the person would pull away. But the car reversed down the gravel and met him halfway. A low slung cherry red sports car. Ian opened the passenger door.

"Jump in!" The driver shouted, revving the engine. "Toss your stuff in the back." Ian shoved his things in and dropped into the low bucket seat. The driver checked his rearview mirror, popped the clutch and swerved back into the traffic.

"Where you headed, pal?"

"Vancouver." Ian turned to look at him. Late twenties, curly black hair, with a round baby face under what looked like several day's stubble. "I'm going out there to work for the summer."

"Vancouver. Far out. I can only take you to Thunder Bay today."

"Thunder Bay! That's great." Ian felt a surge of relief. Finally - a long ride! And he knew from the brochure that there was a hostel in Thunder Bay. Tonight he would have a meal, a shower and sleep in a bed.

"Name's Jack." The man stuck out his hand. Ian introduced himself. He asked if Jack was from Thunder Bay?

"Yeah. Born and raised. It's a shit hole." He laughed. "Naw, it's ok, I guess. At least the air is fucking clean. I'm just coming back from TO, went down for my bud's wedding. Hate that city, but what a blast that was. Got so wasted."

Jack leaned his head out the open window to check oncoming traffic.

"Hang on." He shouted and veered into the other lane. The engine roared as they tore past six cars. Ian felt his palms grow sweaty as the passing lane ended on a blind curve and Jack abruptly swung back into the right lane.

"Fucking traffic." Jack shouted over the wind from the open windows. "Stay home, you fucking tourists." He shouted at the rearview mirror. "You'd think they never saw a rock cut before."

"Hey, man," He lowered his voice. "You don't have any pot, do you?"

"No." Ian didn't want to admit that he had never smoked pot.

"What?" the man joked. "A hippie with no pot? Get

out of my car." He laughed. "Naw, I'm just jerking your chain." He slapped the dashboard. "Hey, so what do you think of this baby? V-8, over 300 horse."

"It's nice," Ian said.

"My old lady hates it. Says I love my car more than her." He crept up on the next line of cars. "Maybe she's right."

Even though it was a no passing zone, Jack swung into the other lane. He managed to pass half the line even with oncoming cars hurtling towards them. He swerved to safety at the last minute. Involuntarily, Ian braced his hands on the dash.

"Fuck, fuck, fuck." Jack rode the bumper of the car ahead and leaned on his horn. He shouted out the window. "Come on, come on."

Finally, on another open stretch he passed everyone. He hit the gas so hard that Ian was pressed back in his seat. The miles flew by. Jack did most of the talking, chain smoking and trying to find some tunes of the radio. Reception was terrible as they wove and dipped through the tall rocky hills that hugged Lake Superior. But the sun was out and the views of the lake were fantastic. Ian was tired, dirty and hungry, but he so excited! At this rate he'd be in Vancouver in a few days.

They stopped for gas and Jack bought him a coffee to go. Back on the road they had to catch up and pass all the same slow-moving tourists. Ian began to relax, realizing just how fast the car was. Then, in the middle of nowhere, Jack spotted another hitchhiker. He slammed on his brakes and swung to the shoulder, fish-tailing on the gravel. A tall skinny guy with a huge backpack strode over to the car. He bent down and peered in the window. He had a thin nose, long straggly brown hair and a string of black heads on his pink sunburned forehead.

"Hey man," Jack said. "Before you get in, you don't have any pot do you?"

The hiker paused, wondering what the right answer was?

"Naw, man. I'm tapped out."

"Fuck. No ride for you." Jack laughed. "Naw, I'm just jerking your chain. Get in."

"Where's he gonna sit?" Ian said.

"You get in the back." Jack said. "Just shove your shit over."

Ian climbed out, his legs a little stiff. He shoved his gear over and wedged the new guy's backpack in too. The new guy took the front seat. The rear floor was littered with empty cups and fast food wrappers. Ian worried that the rear window was blocked by their gear, but Jack leaned out his window and zoomed back into traffic.

"I'm Jack." He shouted. He jerked his thumb at Ian. "That's Ian."

"I'm Ralph."

"No pot, eh? What kind of hippies are you guys? No fucking pot." He shook his head and laughed. He reached over and fiddled with the radio. "See if you can find some fucking tunes somewhere." He checked his watch. "Christ, still a couple of hours to Thunder Bay."

Ian leaned forward to ask Ralph where he was from.

"Halifax." He said. "Going out to Van."

"Van?" Jack said.

"Vancouver." Ralph repeated.

"Vancouver," Jack shouted. "Everyone is going to fucking Vancouver. What the fuck is in Vancouver?"

Ralph grinned. "Well, I hear the pot is cheap."

"And I'm stuck in Thunder Bay where it's hard to score one damn joint."

Ralph and Jack continued to talk. To hear them Ian had to lean forward, hanging on to the back of the bucket seats. Cramped and uncomfortable, he gave up and settled back, the warm summer wind buffeting his face. Jack continued to weave in and out of traffic, passing every car he came upon. Ian wondering if he would die out here on the highway. Pretty sad, really, to die on his first day of freedom. But after a while he accepted there was nothing he could do but accept that this was where he was now. What was it the hippies said, 'Go with the flow'. He leaned back, closed his eyes and day-dreamed about Vancouver: camping on a white sand beach, swimming in the ocean, sitting around a fire while people drank wine and played guitars. He flashed on the cover of the Kerouac book; maybe it wasn't so corny.

Ian jolted awake as the car slewed onto the shoulder, gravel pinging under the wheel wells. He jerked up, thinking they had been in an accident but Jack looked back at him and shouted, "I'm picking up those two chicks." Ian twisted in his seat. Through the corner of the back window, he saw two girls walking towards the car.

"Where will they sit?" Ralph said. For a second Ian thought Jack was going to kick Ralph and him out of the car.

"One in the front, one in the back." Jack grinned. "The more the merrier."

The girls came to the passenger side window. One was tall and thin with long thin blonde hair, the other was short with black hair cut in bangs over her forehead. The tall one leaned over to peer cautiously at the three men.

"Hey girls," Jack grinned. "We're going as far as Thunder Bay, if you can squeeze in."

The blonde's eyes traveled suspiciously from Jack to Ralph to Ian.

"And how we gonna do that?"

"Easy," Jack said. "One in the back there with Ian and one up here in the front between Ralph and me". He winked. "Come on, what do you say?"

Ian felt embarrassed. The girls stepped away and spoke for a second, then the blonde leaned down and said "Yes." Ralph climbed out and folded the seat forward. The girls had no luggage with them: the blonde had a shoulder bag, the brunette had a small purse on a long strap. She climbed into the back. Ian felt awkward as she settled on his lap, leaning back against Ralph's pack. They didn't look each other in the eye. The blonde sat in the front, in the middle, hips on the transmission hump, her long legs draped over Ralph's legs, her knees touched the dashboard.

Jack looked around with a big grin. "Ok, do either of your ladies have any pot?"

"No," The blonde said. "Do you?"

"We are all shit out of luck." Jack said. He introduced himself, Ralph and Ian.

"I'm Lilly." The blonde said. "That's Julie." Julie said nothing.

Leaning far out the window to see the traffic, Jack

floored it, spewing stones as the car leapt back into traffic. The lurch threw Julie against Ian. Her head bumped the low roof of the car.

"You ok?" Ian asked.

"Yeah." She touched the top of her head. She nodded at Jack. "He seems a little wired."

"He's ok, I guess. Only another hour or so to Thunder Bay. Are you headed to the hostel?"

Julie shrugged. "Yeah, I guess."

The presence of the girls seemed to give Jack a new burst of energy. He grilled them about their travels.

"Let me guess, you're headed out to Vancouver?" Lilly explained that they were from Peterborough and headed out west to "kick around". She asked Jack for smoke. Julie leaned forward to get one too. Ian watched her as she leaned into a match to light the cigarette. She had a pale baby face, made rounder by her page boy haircut. Her hair was thick, black and shiny. Ian could smell her shampoo.

"Wanna drag?" She offered the cigarette.

"I don't smoke." Ian said.

Jack kept flirting with Lily, touching her thigh and shoulder as he talked. Ralph seemed indifferent, mostly staring out the window in silence. Julie leaned forward as she smoked, trying to join the conversation over the wind and the radio. But after a while, she tossed the butt out the window and leaned back on Ian's lap. She put one arm around his neck and wiggled a bit to settle in. Ian became very aware of her bum resting on his thighs.

"You ok?" she asked. He felt her breath on his cheek.

"Yeah, sure." He replied shyly. "You ok?"

"Your knees are a little bony," she smiled, "Hope I'm not too heavy."

"You too heavy? You have to be kidding."

"Aw, you're sweet." She wiggled again. "You're very comfortable to sit on."

"Thanks." There was an awkward silence.

With warm sunlight flooding the back seat eventually they both nodded off. When Ian woke, she was resting her head on his shoulder, breathing on his neck. He saw out the window that they were in a city now. He struggled to sit up a bit and Julie woke up.

"Where are we?" she called to the front seat.

"Welcome to beautiful downtown Thunder Bay." Jack cackled.

Julie sat up, rubbing the side of her mouth with the back of her hand. She scowled out the window. "Looks like a shit hole."

"Oh it is." Jack nodded. "but it's my shit hole. Fuck, I am tired of driving." He announced he would take them to the hostel. A few minutes later he swung into a curved driveway in front of a big sports arena. The lawn in front of the building was dotted with hitch-hikers.

"Holy shit," Jack said. "There's are a lot of you hippies wandering around."

The four of them climbed stiffly from the car. Ralph and Ian tugged their gear from the back seat. Jack revved the engine hard, making it back fire. He laughed when some of the hikers flinched. The four of them went to the driver's side to thank him.

"No problem. Thanks for keeping me awake." He floored it in reverse, laying a patch of rubber. He threw a peace sign at them and shouted with a grin, "Bring me back some pot, you lazy hippies."

"He was a nice guy." Ian said.

"Fucking perve." Lily said. "Couldn't keep his hands off me." She turned to Julie. "Next time you sit beside the creepy driver."

Ralph grabbed his backpack and walked towards the shade of a large tree. Ian picked up his gear and followed. The girls trailed along. Ralph dropped his pack.

"I'm going to see if I can find a john," he said.

"I'll come with you." Lily said. She and Ralph walked towards the arena.

Ian and Julie sat under the tree. He offered her water from his canteen. She took a swallow, then spit it out.

"Fuck, that takes like shit."

He sniffed the canteen. "Oh. that's the iron from Madanon."

"From where?"

"Madanon. It's a mining town." She said nothing. "It's so small you probably drove right by it and didn't notice."

"I hate small towns."

"Me too." He said it but he actually liked Madanon. "Where you from again?"

"Peterborough. Well near Peterborough. Nothing but assholes there.

"Sounds like a drag."

"Big fucking drag. I had to get away."

"Me too." He said. He was going to tell her about this family, but she interrupted him to ask if she could bum a smoke. She had already forgotten that he didn't smoke. When he told her again she looked annoyed and headed across the grass to a cluster of guys sitting in a circle by the arena sign. She bummed a smoke and stood there chatting. Ian could see her smiling and laughing. He sat next to his gear and waited.

She finally sauntered back and sat on his duffle bag. "When are they going to open this fucking place?"

Ian didn't understand why she was so angry. He was very happy to finally get to a hostel. He was looking forward to a meal and a shower. More hikers arrived, spreading across the big front lawn. Some sprawled in the shade of the trees, snoozing under tattered straw hats or tie-dyed bandannas. Others peeled off their shirts and lay in the sun. Four guys played hacky-sack, long hair bouncing as they kicked the little ball with the sides of their feet. Two others whipped a Frisbee back forth across the huge parking lot.

Ian could smell a little pot on the evening breeze. He stood up and looked around for Lilly and Ralph. He spotted them by a low brick wall at the edge of the parking lot. Ralph was sitting on the wall. Lilly leaned into him. They were kissing. Ralph's hands were tucked into her rear jean pockets, pressing her against him. He nudged Julie and pointed at them.

Julie gave a low chuckle. "She always was a slut."

Finally, the door of the arena opened. A man came out in jeans and t-shirt. He propped the door open with a concrete block.

"Ok, folks," He shouted through cupped hands. "The hostel is now open for business." He went back inside.

People slowly stood, gathering their things and started towards the building. Lilly and Ralph strolled back to them, looking flushed. Ralph picked up his backpack and handed his sleeping bag to Lilly, who turned to Julie.

"I'm going to thumb with Ralph tomorrow. Just for a change."

"Whatever." Julie said. "As long as we meet up in Vancouver."

"Sure." Lilly said. "I still want to go over the Island with you." She looked at Ian. "My real mom lives in Victoria. I'm going to visit her."

Julie had already grabbed her purse and walked away. Ian trotted to catch up, his canteen banging his hip.

"Hey," He touched her arm, "You ok?"

"Sure." Her eyes were very dark. She scowled as Lilly and Ralph passed them, holding hands.

"Fucking chick. I don't want to fucking travel by myself."

They took a few more steps. Ian hesitated, then blurted out. "Why don't you, uh, thumb with me tomorrow? I mean if you want to."

She stopped and stared at him. "You are sweet." She shrugged. "Sure. Let's do that." She gave him a quick kiss on the lips.

Ian had surprised himself. In high school he had barely had the nerve to ask a girl to dance, but now he had just asked a complete stranger to travel with him.

And she had said yes!

As they continued towards the building, she reached out and took his hand in her small cool fingers. But, a second later, as they entered the darkened foyer she let go. They passed a shuttered ticket booth and empty concession counters. The hallway opened into the arena: overhead there were long rows of bright arc lights. All around the edge, along boards, the cement floor was covered with mattresses. Long rows of banquet tables and folding chairs ran down the open middle area.

A line formed near a kitchen table where two people sat. Ian and Julie joined the line. When they reached the table a woman said, "Welcome to the Thunder Bay hostel. Fill out this form. The fee for the night is two dollars, which includes dinner and breakfast. Best deal in town. But if you're broke that's fine too. The feds supplement the fees."

Julie grabbed a pencil and leaned over her form. Where it asked for your name, Ian saw that she printed Mary Smith. As he leaned over his own form, he realized he shouldn't use his real name. He didn't want his family to find him. He only had a second to think so he wrote Jack Kerouac. He immediately regretted it. That was so stupid. But when they handed over the forms, the woman did not even look at them. She just tossed them on a pile. She gestured at the guy next to her.

"Ok, just pay him the fee."

"Do you have any money?" Julie asked. "Can you pay for me?"

"Sure," Ian handed the guy a five and pocketed his change.

The guy who took the money pointed over his shoulder. "Just grab yourself a mattress. There's showers over there. You'll find towels in the change room. Around eight they'll be serving food."

Julie crossed the wide cavern of the arena. Ian followed with his bag and bedroll. They circled past many empty mattresses. They all looked thin and worn; many were stained, a few were torn, stuffing bleeding at the edges. Finally, Julie picked one, dropped her purse, and lowered herself to the mattress. She laid back. Ian sat down and stretched out next to her.

"Fuck," she slapped the mattress. "This bed is hard as shit."

"It is pretty thin." He was still getting used to a girl who swore like the proverbial sailor.

She sat up and pulled a brush out of her purse. "I'm going to take a shower." He watched her walk away. This is so weird, he thought, one minute he was thumbing out west alone, now, suddenly he was hitching hiking with this girl that he hardly knew. He wasn't sure what was going on. Ralph and Lilly had been necking but Julie had only kissed him once and held his hand for a few seconds. He wasn't sure what any of it meant. Was "thumbing together" like dating? He was confused.

He sat on the edge of the hard mattress and looked around. As everyone came in from outside the line-up to check-in had grown really long. Ian tried to count the mattresses around the edge of the cavernous room. Probably over two hundred beds. That was a lot of hitchhikers.

A guy dropped his backpack on the mattress next to Ian. His sandy blonde hair hung in a tight braid all the way below his belt. The end was decorated with bits of red and yellow cloth and some beads. He nodded to Ian.

"How's it going, man?"

"Good." Ian said. "You headed to Vancouver?"

"Naw, I'm headed east." He sat on the edge of his mattress and took off his sandals. "I was down in Frisco all winter. Thought I'd head north. I've never seen Canada before. It's really nice here. How about you? Where you headed?"

"Vancouver." Ian said. "Gonna work out there for the summer."

"Cool." The man stood up and stripped off all his clothes. He was extremely thin and tanned dark brown except for his bum. Ian glanced away, a little self-conscious.

"Gotta hit the shower before dinner time." Completely naked except for some beads, he turned and walked across the polished cement floor. Ian looked around and saw a few people changing their clothes here in the open. It would take some getting used to, this hippie thing. Ian wasn't sure he could walk around naked in front of strangers.

Julie returned carrying her jeans over her shoulder. Her panties were very white against her thighs. She stood next to the mattress and shook her wet hair, fluffing it with her fingers.

"They only have little fucking towels, so I have to drip dry."

Ian noticed her top was soaking wet. It clung to her body. She wasn't wearing a bra.

"Hey," she said. "Stop staring at my tits." She giggled. "Look at you turn red. That's cute." She sat down and wrestled her jeans back on, then stood up to zip them shut. "Had to wash my top. I don't have any other clothes with me."

"Yeah." Ian said. "I noticed that you and Lily were traveling light."

"Well, sometimes you just have get the fuck out while the getting's good."

"Did you run away?" He was hoping she'd say yes. He wanted to tell her he had run away too, then maybe they could talk about their families.

"That's none of your fucking business, is it?" She snapped. "I'm gonna go find Lily." He watched her walk away, feeling confused and stupid.

Ian dug in his bag for clean socks, underwear and a t-shirt and made his way to the shower room. He took a small white towel from the pile by the door. It smelled of bleach. On a bench by the showers, he undressed. He was a little worried about being robbed, so he put his wallet inside one shoe, then piled his clothes on top of his shoes. He had no soap or shampoo with him, but on a tile ledge he saw small bars of soap like they use in cheap motels. The water was not very hot, but the pressure was good. It was his first shower in two days so he was happy for that. He tried to wash his hair with the tiny bar of soap. Not much lather and even after he rinsed, his hair felt waxy. He dried off as best he could with the small towel. He put on clean underwear, t-shirt, socks and his pants. He felt great walking back across the arena, his dirty clothes rolled under his arm. Day two - Thunder Bay. At this rate, four, maybe five days to Vancouver.

Almost every mattress was occupied now. There was a buzz of voices and laughter. Someone was singing. They had a nice voice. Here and there a few hikers clustered around one mattress. As he passed one group he smelled pot. The staff seemed laid back about it. People smiled and nodded as he passed them. This is really cool, he thought, really cool.

Julie sat on the mattress next to theirs chatting with the guy with the long braid. They were smoking a joint, keeping it cupped in their hands.

"Hey man. Toke?" The guy smiled and stuck out his hand, the last bit of the joint pinched between his fingernails.

"No." Ian said. "I'm good." He was curious but he had never smoked pot and was afraid he would do it wrong.

"Cool." Ponytail took another quick drag. "I was just rapping with your chick."

"I'm not his chick." Julie said. "We just met today."

"Yeah," Ian said. "We got a ride in the same car."

"Cool. Cool." He nodded sagely as he took in this news. He wet his finger tips and pinched the end of the joint. When it was out, he placed it in a little tin he pulled from his checked shirt. The tin was full of other little butts.

"My roach trap," he chuckled. "Hey, my name is Zane." He stuck out his hand. When Ian stuck out his hand, Zane hooked his thumb with Ian's. "Nice to meet you, brother."

Ian smiled awkwardly. He'd never done the hippie handshake before. He stuffed his dirty clothes into his duffle bag. Then he sat on the edge of the mattress. Zane sat cross legged now, his head erect, his back very straight. He tossed his braid over his shoulder.

"Look at this place," He made a wide gesture with

one arm. "This is the way it should be."

Ian looked around the cavernous arena: mattresses were mostly full, people talked and sang, the same two guys from outside now played Frisbee down the whole length of the arena, the staff carried things out to the tables.

"Can you dig the vibe, man?" Zane said, turning his wide stoned eyes to Ian. "Do you see it? All these strangers hanging out. No war, no bullshit, everyone just chilling. We're all just riding the wave."

Ian looked around again. Zane was right, it was nice. Everyone seemed relaxed and happy. "It is very cool." He almost said man, but that seemed too corny.

Across the arena a woman stepped from the kitchen with a large bell in her hand. She shook it hard. When the crowd finally quieted down, she shouted that dinner was ready.

Ian was really hungry. He jumped up. Julie walked close to him. She poked him with her elbow.

"That Zane guy is hilarious," she snickered. "Ride the fucking wave, man, ride the wave."

"Seems like a nice guy," Ian said.

"Yeah, for a flaky fucking hippie."

He wanted to say, you didn't mind smoking his pot, but he didn't want to piss her off again. All his life he had watched hippies on TV. He knew all about peace and love, sex, drugs and rock and roll. Maybe it was corny, but now that he was actually meeting them, he did like the "vibe". He felt like he was hanging out with the cool kids at school and they were accepting him.

Ian and Julie joined a line that snaked past a wide

kitchen counter. Each person was handed a plate with a scoop of potato salad, some coleslaw and two skinny hotdogs that had obviously been boiled a long time. On the end of the counter sat a big stack of white bread, already buttered. Ian grabbed two slices. He was very hungry. They found two empty chairs at the end of a long table.

"What is this bullshit?" one of the other hikers said, picking up a hotdog between two fingers. He waved it around and tossed it down in disgust.

"What do you want for two bucks?" Someone replied.

"Anything but this shit."

People laughed but continued to eat. Julie only ate a couple bites of the potato salad. She played with the coleslaw, turning it over and over with her fork. She drummed her fingers on the table and looked bored. Ian noticed the men at the table sneaking peeks at her. He looked around at the other tables. All the hitch hikers were men, except for two women who sat at the far end of one table.

People made small talk, mostly asking where people were from and where they were headed. East or West? There only seemed to be two directions. A few people had crossed paths before at other hostels. They compared notes about how long they had waited for rides. One guy asked about scoring weed. People shrugged and said they were tapped out. One of the hikers stood up and said to come see him later.

As he wandered out of ear-shot, another hiker hunched forward and whispered loudly, "I think he's a narc."

"A narc?" Someone laughed. "Naw, man, I've run into him at several hostels coming from BC. He's cool."

"Could still be a narc." The first guy said.

"Hey, you could be narc. Maybe you're just saying this shit to throw us off."

When people laughed, the guy grew annoyed.

"There's always narcs in the hostels." He argued.

"Aw, man. Chill out."

"You chill out." He stood up and walked away leaving his dirty plate on the table.

"Man," One hiker shook his head, "There's too much paranoia these days."

A few others nodded their heads sadly.

"How about you two?" The guy next to Ian spoke up. "Where are you two from?"

"I'm from Peterborough." Julie said. "I don't know where he's from. We just met today." She stood up abruptly. "I'm going to find a smoke."

As she walked away, there was an awkward silence.

"Sorry man," The hiker said. "I thought you were together."

"We are," Ian said quickly. "We met today but we're thumbing to Vancouver."

"Chicks," Another guy shrugged philosophically.

"Vancouver is nice, man." Someone down the table said to Ian. "Lots of cheap homegrown."

"Magic mushrooms too." Another said.

"Cheap smack too."

"Smack." Ian repeated the word a little uncertainly.

"Heroin." Another explained. "Stay the fuck away

from heroin."

"I don't think you have to worry too much." One hippie placed his hand on Ian's shoulder. "I mean look at this kid. Is he likely to become your local junkie?"

As several people chuckled, Ian blushed. It was true. Compared to these guys, he still looked pretty straight. His hair was not very long, certainly not for 1972. And his sweater looked like it came from Eaton's, because it had.

As they finished eating people drifted away from the tables. Ian picked up his and Julie's plates and took them back to the counter. He scraped left-overs into a garbage can and stacked the plates in the bins. There was an urn of coffee. He filled a mug. The coffee looked oily. He tasted it and added some sugar. His fingers smelled like hotdogs. He stopped by the bathroom and washed his hands. Then he went back and sat on the mattress with his coffee. Julie did not come back. Zane came along wearing cut-off jeans and a t-shirt. He sat cross legged on his mattress, dipping a tea bag in one of the white mugs.

"Herbal tea," he said. "I don't drink coffee. Makes my mind too jumpy." He stared at the tea bag as it went in and out of the liquid. Probably still stoned, Ian thought.

"Hey man, where's your lady?"

"I'm not sure." She *had* been gone a long time. Ian decided to look for her. He walked around the perimeter trying not to stare at people as he passed. Some were already asleep, curled inside their sleeping bags. A few were doing yoga. One sat cross legged in front of a lit candle, chanting softly. One woman stood, naked from the waist up, brushing her long hair. Ian looked at her, then

48

looked away, but she seemed indifferent to the people around her.

Ian found Julie sitting with a dozen people on four mattresses that were shoved together. Lilly and Ralph were there too. They nodded to him across the crowd. Julie was talking to some guy; his hair was not very long but he wore a beaded headband. Ian circled around but there was no room next to Julie so he squeezed onto the edge of the mattress opposite her. Two guys with guitars were playing some songs, mostly Beatles tunes. Occasionally people sang along. A large bottle of wine was being passed around, people holding it low so the hostel staff would not spot it. When it came to him, Ian looked around for staff, then took few big swallows.

"Hey man," the guy next to him elbowed him. "Don't hog the vino."

Ian passed the bottle, feeling the warmth in his throat and the tart aftertaste of cheap wine. He smiled and looked around. This was nice - just hanging out with a bunch of people, listening to music and drinking wine.

Ian chatted with the hikers nearest him; the usual east versus west discussion, a few sad tales of not getting a ride for over a day.

"I've had good rides so far." Ian boasted. "Of course, I was thumbing with my girlfriend." He nodded across the mattresses at Julie. He knew it was sort of a lie. They had just met today. Was she his girlfriend? He had no idea. But the guys on either side of him seemed impressed. He noticed now Julie was sitting closer to the guy with the headband. When she laughed at something he said, she touched his knee. Ian felt a pang of jealousy. When the wine came around again, he had another big slug.

Finally, around ten the overhead lights snapped off, provoking some half-hearted cheers and whistles. The big room was dark now except for long tunnels of light spilling out from the showers and kitchen areas. Ian saw a few people still working in the kitchen, washing dishes and stacking pots. Two staff sat at the registration desk. They were lit by an old floor lamp on a long extension cord. One did paperwork. The other was reading a book.

One man walked to the center of the room, cupped his hands to his mouth and shouted "Ok, everyone we are winding down for the night. The outside door is locked so you can't go out and come back in later. Believe me, it's Thunder Bay so you are not missing much. Try to get some sleep, wake-up call is seven, breakfast is at eight so you can be on the road early."

At the little party a few people announced they were going to crash. They stood up and left.

"Hey Julie. Julie." Ian called across to her. He could barely see her face in the shadows.

"What?" She sounded annoyed.

"We should go."

"Why?"

"It's getting late."

"Go if you want. I'm enjoying the music."

Ian couldn't make her go but he couldn't leave her either. When the wine came around again he raised it to his lips, but the bottle was empty. One of the guitarists left but the other one continued to play and sing softly. A couple more people drifted away. He looked around. Lilly and Ralph were gone. When did they go? Ian thought he

50

saw the guy with the headband lean towards Julie. Was he kissing her? In the dim light he could not tell.

A shadow loomed over them, one of the staff stood with his hands on this hips.

"Ok my friends." He said with a grin. "Hate to bust up the party, but it's curfew time. Your neighbours have to get some sleep."

The guitar player said they would keep it down, but the staffer was firm, "No noise after eleven. Thems the rules, folks. You'll thank me tomorrow because the seven am wake-up call will come really early." He waited while people stood up and dragged the mattresses apart. He picked up the empty wine bottle and shook it. "What, no one left me a drink?"

Ian walked over the Julie. The guy with the headband nodded at him.

"Had a good rap with your chick, man, she's very cool. You two have a great night." He walked away. Ian felt embarrassed now. Why had he been so uptight?

As they crossed the cement floor, Julie reached over and took his hand. Immediately all his jealousy dropped away.

"That was fun, eh?" Julie said.

"Yeah." He smiled at her. "I really like this," he nodded. "Everyone is so cool."

"Boy." She laughed. "You don't get out much, do you?"

"What do you mean?"

"Relax. I'm just teasing you." She squeezed his hand again.

At their bed, he busied himself rifling in his bag. He

wasn't sure what to do. She grabbed her purse.

"I'm going to brush my teeth."

While she was gone he shook out his bedroll. Only two blankets, one wool and one thinner knit throw. He remembered the stains on the mattress and decided to cover them the thin blanket and sleep under the wool because it was cold in the huge space. He flattened his duffle bag, trying to make a pillow. He felt a lump and pulled out the jar of peanut-butter and the misshapen loaf of bread. He set them on the floor. Not much of a bed. He decided to brush his teeth too. He passed Julie on the way across the floor. She reached out and touched his arm.

"You want to borrow my toothpaste?"

"Naw, I got some, thanks."

When he came back she was sitting on the edge of the bed, having a smoke. He kicked off his tennis shoes, very self-conscious about undressing in front of her. But it was pretty dark. The people on either side of them were already asleep. Meantime Julie tugged her jeans down and kicked them off. She kept her blouse on. She rolled her jeans, put them on top of the duffle bag. Ian did the same thing with his pants and his sweater. He crawled under the wool blanket still wearing his shorts and a t-shirt. He used his head to tamp down his jean-pillow. They lay on their backs a few inches apart.

"This blanket is very scratchy."

"I know," Ian felt the rough wool on his bare legs. "I wasn't sure what to bring."

"At least you brought something." Julie said. "I just grabbed my purse." She wiggled around on the hard mattress. "I had to split." She paused.

"Yeah, you said people were driving you crazy?"

"Yes. Well, just my step-dad." She slid closer to him. "He was always coming on to me."

"I'm sorry." Ian didn't know what else to say. She rolled over against him. He moved his arm and she snuggled against his chest.

"What are you sorry about? Shit happens."

"Yeah. I know." He thought for a second about his own family.

Julie rolled on one elbow and looked at him. In the dim lights he could only see the shadow of her head, the edge of her bangs. He felt her warm breath on his cheek.

"You're sweet, you know."

She leaned forward and kissed him. Her mouth was small, her lips thin and dry. They both parted lips and she pushed her tongue into his mouth and began to make a slow steady circle with it - clockwise he noticed. She leaned on him and brought one leg over his bare thighs. Her skin was cool and smooth. He began to get excited and rolled towards her. Shyly he passed his hand over her top, feeling her small breasts, through the thin material. He slipped his hand down until he touched the elastic at the top of her panties. She continued to mechanically circle his mouth with her tongue. He stroked the outside of her panties with his fingers, expecting some reaction. When she did nothing he slipped his fingers under the cloth. Her pubic hair was thick and coarse. When he found her crack it was dry and hard. He rubbed up and down with one finger, pressing his thigh against her more. He felt incredibly self-conscious and clumsy. He hoped he was doing it right. His cock was totally erect against her leg.

Were they going to have sex? He wasn't sure he could do it, here in the open where other hikers could see them. Besides Julie still felt dry. She continued grinding his mouth with her tongue. Suddenly she stuck her hand into his shorts and grabbed his cock. She started tugging on it. Too hard, he thought at first, but she pulled a few more times and he came, splashing on her hand and wrist, on his thigh and his underwear. A little moan escaped his mouth, muffled by her mouth pressed hard over his.

As suddenly as she had started, she stopped kissing him and rolled back on the mattress. She looked at her hand, then reached over and wiped it on the edge of the mattress.

He stared at her, aware of his wet sticky shorts. He was a little short of breath.

"Hard work, isn't it?" Julie said. She sat up, tugging at her top. "I'm gonna go find a smoke." She slipped on her jeans and headed across the arena towards the front desk staff.

Ian stood up, embarrassed by the wet mess in his shorts. He grabbed clean underwear from his duffle bag. He grabbed his jeans but instead of putting them on, he tossed them over his shoulder, and crossed the open space in his underwear. *No one really cares, do they?*

In the washroom he found an empty cubicle and wiped himself clean with cheap toilet paper. He put on the clean underwear and his jeans. At the sink he washed his hands. He rinsed his shorts with warm water and rung them out, but he realized there was no place by the mattress to hang them to dry. He paused for a second, then tossed his underwear in the garbage can and covered them with a few paper towels.

In the weird flickering fluorescent light, Ian pushed his mop of blonde hair aside to examine the acne on his forehead. Suddenly it hit him – he just had sex. Well, some kind of sex. He was no longer a virgin - at least not a complete virgin. He was elated but confused. Two days ago he was just a geeky kid living with his parents. He had necked with a couple of girls at house parties and school dances. Now he had a girlfriend and was thumbing to Vancouver with her. He splashed water on his face and dried himself with a brown paper towel. He crossed the arena, quiet and cavernous now, the cement floor cold on his bare feet. He wondered if they would do it again, maybe have real sex now.

Julie was sitting on the edge of the mattress smoking. He smiled at her, but she did not smile back. She butted her smoke on the floor and crawled under the blanket. He took off his jeans, placed them on top of the duffle bag, and crawled under the wool blanket. Julie lay on her back. When Ian reached out to touch her shoulder, she rolled on her side and said. "We better get some sleep. They're going to wake us up at fucking seven am."

"Yeah," Ian pulled his hand back. "Goodnight."

He lay on his back, wide wake, staring into the dark cave of the arena ceiling. He was confused. His plan -The Plan- had always been to find some work in Vancouver and likely to return to Madanon in the fall on a motorcycle. On the other hand, with everyone saying what a great place Vancouver, he was starting to think maybe he'd stay there. It sounded like a really cool place to live. But now there was Julie. She was supposed to meet up with Lilly in Vancouver and go to Victoria. Maybe he could tag along, except he really needed to find some work. His money would not last very long. He wondered if Julie would consider staying in Vancouver with him. He shook his head. This was crazy, he had just met her, still wasn't that what hippies did?

Ian had a bad night. It was cold in the arena. One blanket was not enough and Julie kept pulling it over to her side. Ian finally sat up and put on his sweater, jeans and socks. Zane, mister good vibes, snored loudly. Every time someone walked by going to the bathroom, Ian woke up. Early in the morning he woke again when he heard voices and clattering sounds from the kitchen.

At seven the overhead lights snapped on with a loud hum. Ian sat up, wondering where he was. All around the boards other hikers sat up, stretching and rubbing their eyes. Zane was already up, his backpack and neatly rolled sleeping bag sat in the center of his mattress.

Someone stepped out from the kitchen and shook the bell. People groaned and booed. The staff person shouted. "Breakfast is being served. Come and get it." They rang the bell again.

"Fuck off!" Someone shouted. That got a sleepy round of applause.

Julie's head was under the blanket. Ian pulled the edge of it back.

"Morning," He smiled. She stared at him blankly, stood up, pulled on her jeans and staggered sleepily towards the washroom.

People were already lined up for food, so Ian headed

over. Breakfast was two hard boiled eggs and two slices of toast brushed with very yellow margarine. Big tubs of peanut butter and jam sat on the table, knives protruding. On another table sat a giant dented caldron with hot water. Next to it, stacks of paper cups, instant coffee, tea bags, sugar, and powdered creamer. There were plastic jugs with some kind of orange flavored drink mix. Ian grabbed some juice and coffee and took a seat at one of the long tables.

People ate in silence. Ian watched for Julie. He wondered if he should get a plate of food for her but he wasn't sure what she liked to eat. Besides breakfast was pretty terrible. A staff member walked around with a bushel basket of oranges. Ian grabbed two for the road. He made another cup of instant coffee and dropped his plate at the kitchen window.

Back at the mattress he packed and rolled up the blankets. He went to the bathroom to wash up. He ran the water until it was very cold and filled his canteen. When he got back, Julie sitting on the mattress, clutching her knees and having a smoke.

"Did you get breakfast?" He asked, trying to sound chipper.

"Not hungry."

"They have some crappy instant coffee."

She said nothing and butted her smoke.

"Where were you?" He tried to sound casual.

"Went to find Lilly. She's still gonna hitchhike with that Ralph guy." She sounded disappointed.

"Hey man," a guy walked up to them. "Can you spare some change?" His jeans were almost white from wear, with large holes in the knees. He wore a thin dirty t-shit and hugged himself, his arms wrapped around his boney rib cage. Ian noticed he didn't have any socks, just some old tennis shoes with no laces and big holes in the toes and heels. His feet and ankles were filthy.

"I'm thumbing to New York but I got robbed a few nights ago out in Calgary. Guy took everything I own." His face was pinched and sad looking.

"Wow. That's a drag." Ian said. "I don't have any extra money. We're headed to Vancouver."

The guy continued to stare at them. "Anything would help, man, even a quarter or a dime."

"I really don't have any money to spare."

He continued to stand there. Ian had an idea.

"Hey, would you like some food? I have a loaf of bread and a jar of peanut butter." He dug in his duffle-bag and pulled out the misshapen loaf in its plastic bag and the jar of peanut butter. He handed them to the stranger.

'Thanks, man. That's righteous of you. Really." The guy clutched them to his chest and shambled along the row of mattresses begging for change.

"Poor guy." Ian said. "He's in rough shape."

"Looks like a junkie to me." Julie said.

"A junkie?"

"Yeah, didn't you see how he kept his arms hidden? So we wouldn't see the track marks?"

"I thought he was cold."

"Cold?" Julie shook her head. "Did you grow up under a rock?"

"No, I didn't." He snapped. "I'm just not as cynical as you."

"Whatever." She rolled her eyes. In silence he slung his bedroll over his shoulder and picked up the bag. He was angry –and embarrassed- because she was right. He really had led a sheltered life.

"Come on, we better get in line for the bus." At breakfast he had heard that the hostel had school buses that drove hikers to the edge of town. He wanted to get on the road.

Outside the sun was up but it was still cold enough that Ian could see his breath as he walked towards the yellow buses. One was for eastbound travelers and the other for the west. The line-up to go west was longer. Julie shivered in her jean jacket. On board, she took a window seat. Ian plunked down next to her, holding his gear between his knees. He looked around at the other travelers, in awe of the cool clothes they wore: beads and bangles, hats and bandanas, tie-dyed skirts and jeans patched with bright swathes of fabric. One guy wore a leather coat with fringes so long that they almost touched his knees. A few gave Ian a friendly nod as they worked their way to the back.

The driver started the engine. The bus lurched into motion as they pulled into the morning traffic. Ian watched the passing buildings. He caught a glimpse of Lake Superior and big lake freighters in the harbor. He felt a wave of excitement. His third day on the road. He wondered how rides would be. He wanted to get to Winnipeg today where the next hostel was located. He turned to smile at Julie but she hunched in her seat, staring coldly into space.

It didn't take long to reach the highway. As the bus

slowed to pull to the shoulder, someone at back of the bus started singing, "Hey bus driver, thank you for taking us. Thank you for taking us." Immediately a chorus of voices rose. Ian joined in too. He thought it was fun. He saw the driver's smiling face in the rearview mirror. Julie shook her head and muttered. "Fucking morons."

The hikers stumbled out of the bus with backpacks, sleeping bags and guitar cases. Ian tried to count: there were at least fifty people, mostly single males. Calling out good luck, they spread out down the road. It turned out Ralph and Lily had been on the same bus, seating at the back. Smiling and holding hands, they came over to Ian and Julie. Lily nodded towards Ian and asked Julie how her night was. She shrugged.

"Ok, I guess."

Ralph said they were going to walk all the way down the road past the crowd. "We figure it'll be easier to get rides at the end of the line."

"I'll look for you at the hostel in Winnipeg." Lily said.

"Sure. Whatever." Julie was still pissed off.

They watched Ralph and Lily saunter down the shoulder. Ian noticed that hikers were pretty close together here by the ramp.

"Maybe we should move down too?"

"Fuck that." Julie said. "If people want to walk, they can." She sat down on his duffle bag, her chin in her hands. Ian started thumbing. There was a lot of traffic, but it seemed to be mostly locals on their way to work. By mid-morning there were longer gaps between short streams of cars. Ian paced back and forth on the edge of the blacktop. Julie stretched out on the gravel, her head resting on the duffle bag. Finally, one arm over her eyes, she napped. Occasionally Ian looked over at her. He didn't understand why she was so angry today. He flashed back to the previous night on the mattress. It felt unreal - like it had never happened.

More hikers continued to arrive, climbing out of cars as they turned off the highway. A few came walking down the road from another distant exit ramp. They said there was also a backlog of hikers there too. Most just nodded as they passed, a few stopped to chat. There was a familiar pattern to the conversation: Where are you headed? Where are you from? How long have you been waiting? How are the rides? Occasionally someone told a horror story about long days spent in the middle of nowhere, sleeping on the side of the road, or being hassled by the cops.

One hiker asked if he could have a drink from Ian's canteen.

"Sure," Ian said. "It's probably warm."

"Don't matter," the hiker chugged big gulps. "Slept outside last night. Man, I am so damn thirsty." He took another long drink. Ian worried he would empty the canteen.

"You're lucky," the guy said, nodding at Julie, who still dozed. "You'll get a ride for sure."

"How's that?" Ian asked.

"The Pecking Order." He said. "People always pick up chicks first. Like one or two chicks always get a ride, then a guy and a gal." He nodded at Julie. "Then single guys thumbing. Two guys thumbing together and you're fucked. People think you're the two psychos from In Cold Blood."

"What about three girls together?" Ian asked.

The guy laughed. "That's some Penthouse Letters bullshit. You never see three chicks hitching together."

He thanked Ian for the water and headed on down the road. Ian sheltered his eyes with his hand. He could see that the line of hikers stretched right around the curve in the road. He couldn't see Lilly and Ralph. They had probably already gotten a ride.

Julie sat up suddenly. She rubbed her face and patted her jacket looking for a smoke.

"What time is it?"

"Almost noon."

"Fuck we're never gonna get out of here." She stood up and grabbed the canteen. She took a drink, then spit it out. "It's warm as piss."

Ian said nothing. At least she's standing up now so a passing driver would see her. He hoped that hiker was right about the pecking order.

Ten minutes later a big Mack truck came down the ramp to the highway. It stopped right on the ramp and the driver let out two rips on his horn. He leaned out his window and waved at them.

"Come on, come on." Ian grabbed his things and ran to the truck. Winded, he paused for a second. The huge cab towered over them. Julie jumped up on the running board. The driver had already pushed the passenger door open.

"Thanks for stopping." She shouted and climbed in. For a split second, Ian thought she would slam the door and drive off without him. He clambered up, awkwardly dragging the bedroll, duffle bag and canteen behind him.

"Toss that stuff in the back." The driver said. He was a big guy with a round beer belly that rested on the bottom of the steering wheel. There was a narrow space behind the seats with a small unmade bed and a jumbled mess of fast food cartons. Ian pushed his gear over the seat and slammed the door. It was so heavy it didn't latch the first time. He grabbed it with both hands and slammed it again.

Julie sat on to the edge of the seat with one leg draped over the center hump of the gear shift. The driver let off the brake and they chugged into action. A minute later he changed gears and they were roaring down the highway. Between the engine, the tires and the wind roaring through the driver's open window they had to shout to be heard.

"Where you headed?" Ian yelled.

"Winnipeg." The driver shouted. "How about you?"

"He's going to B.C." Julie said. "To be a lumberjack."

The driver laughed. "How about you, young lady?"

"I'm just kicking around." She nodded at Ian. "We only met yesterday."

"Oh," the driver glanced sideways at them. "Love at first sight?"

"Yeah, right." Julie laughed and rolled her eyes. "Hey, can I bum a smoke?"

"Sure. What's mine is yours." He gave a lecherous smile that bothered Ian. Still he was thrilled to finally get a ride, and all the way to Winnipeg.

Once they were up to speed, the driver rolled up his

window and stuck out his hand.

"My name is Randy." He smiled, revealing some small yellow teeth. "Go ahead. Ask me if my name is Randy." Julie hesitated. "Go ahead. Ask me."

"Ok, are you Randy?"

"I sure am. Thanks for asking." He wiggled his eyebrows like Groucho Marx.

"Oh Randy," Julie turned and looked at Ian as if to say 'what an idiot'.

Traffic thickened on long curved stretches of highway where no one could pass. Sometimes Randy would creep up on a line of cars, until it seemed like they were about touch the car ahead of them. Occasionally he'd let out a blast on his big air horn.

"Gotta push 'em." He shouted. "A lot of tourists along here. Gawkers. Me, I don't get paid by the hour. I've been doing this haul for about five years now, Winnipeg to Toronto and back, sometimes all the way to the Maritimes. It will be good to get home tonight." Randy was married with two small kids, both boys. He flipped down the sun visor to reveal a bunch of photos of his wife and kids stuck on with yellowing tape.

But being married didn't stop Randy from flirting with Julie. He would launch into a long corny joke, cracking himself up, repeating the punch line and patting her thigh. Whenever he had to change gears he managed to touch her knee. Although she made faces at Ian when Randy cracked his bad jokes, he thought she liked the attention. He noticed that Randy directed all his attention at Julie. Ian felt left out. With the hot sun shining in the cab and the steady roar of the engine, he drifted off, leaning sideways against the door, occasionally waking up when his head bumped on the window.

As they neared Kenora, Randy said, "let's stop for lunch."

"We're pretty low on cash." Ian said. He really needed to save his money for Vancouver.

"Well, then I'm buying you and your gal a burger."

"You really don't have to." Ian continued. Julie jabbed him with her elbow.

"No point in arguing. My truck, my rules." Randy wiggled his eye brows. "It's the least I can do since you are helping keep me awake."

They swung into the big parking lot of a truck stop. Randy pulled his rig in beside the other trucks. Inside they grabbed a table. Randy knew the waitress and ordered three burgers with fries. "What do you kids want to drink? Pop or coffee?"

As they ate, other truckers walking by, recognized Randy, and stopped to chat. They cast sidelong glances at Julie. Randy explained he was taking them as far as The 'Peg.

"These kids are headed to B.C. to be lumberjacks. Don't laugh, they have a chain saw back in my truck."

Randy ate very fast, let out a belch and said, "I gotta go lighten my load." He wiggled his belly free from the table and headed to the john.

"This is great, eh?" Ian said. "Randy's a nice guy."

"He's a moron." Julie said. "Notice how he's always trying to touch me?"

"Yeah. I noticed." Ian didn't say that he thought she was flirting back.

"Reminds me of my fucking step-father. I fucking hate guys like this."

But when Randy came back she smiled widely and thanked him for the burger.

Back on the highway, the sun was low in the west, flickering harshly through the endless pine trees bordering the road. Randy put on some big mirrored aviator sunglasses. Julie leaned on Ian and eventually nodded off, her head falling over on his shoulder. Randy looked over and smiled. He gave Ian a thumbs up. Ian felt good. Here he was riding in a big truck, making great time towards BC, with his girlfriend sleeping on his shoulder. At this rate he would be in Vancouver in three or four days. He day-dreamed about finding work. He knew that being a lumberjack was a stupid idea, but he wasn't sure what else he could do? Maybe he could find something in a grocery store, stocking shelves like his friend Joe. Maybe Julie could find work too. He imagined them getting a little apartment somewhere in Vancouver. Or maybe they could rent a little cabin near the ocean. It dawned on him that he might not come back at all. Maybe he'd start a new life with Julie on the west coast. With the roar of the engine and Julie warm against his side, he drifted in and out of sleep.

"Hey." Randy shouted. Ian opened his eyes. Randy grinned and pointed to a large sign: Welcome to Manitoba. "Almost home."

Sleepily, Ian looked around. The rock cuts and pines had given way to flat farm land. He drifted off again.

The truck jolted as it geared down. Ian lurched awake, his neck stiff from leaning on the door. Julie was sitting up having a smoke. They were off the highway, driving slowly through a sprawling area of factories and malls.

"Welcome to the 'Peg'." Randy said. "Where to now?" Ian sat up and rubbed his eyes. He dug in his bag and found his pamphlet that listed the hostels. He read the address to Randy.

"Uh, let's see. That's pretty much right downtown. I can't take you there. Too far out of the way." He drummed on his steering wheel. "I guess I could drop you somewhere and you could grab a bus downtown."

"Let's just keep going." Julie said to Ian. "It's still early."

Ian hesitated. "I thought you wanted to catch up with Lily in Winnipeg."

"I want to keep going." Julie said. Ian knew there was no point in arguing with her. He looked at the brochure again.

"The next hostel is west of here, in Brandon."

"Yeah," Randy said. "Brandon's about two hours west of Winnipeg. I can swing around and drop you at the turn off for Highway One."

"That would be great." Julie said. Well, Ian thought, at least every ride got him closer Vancouver.

A few minutes later Randy geared the truck down, threw on his four-way flashers and stopped, half-straddling the shoulder of the road.

"Well, kids," Randy said. "It's been a slice." He reached across and gave Ian a hearty hand shake. Ian pushed the big door open and started lowering his things to the ground.

"And for you, missy." Randy reached in the glove box and handed her an unopened pack of smokes. "Be careful. I hear they're bad for you."

"What? Get out." She smiled. "Thanks."

Randy grinned. "Ok. See that ramp, just go down there and hang a right. That's the highway to Brandon."

They climbed down from the cab. Ian had to give the door a two handed push to slam it. Randy blasted his horn as he nosed the truck back into traffic.

Julie opened the new pack and lit one of the smokes.

"He wasn't such a bad dude." She said.

"Yeah. Really nice." Ian slung his canteen and bedroll and picked up the duffle bag. He was stiff from sitting all day. They trudged down the long curved ramp to the highway. They went a little past the merge lane so cars would have room to stop. Ian dumped his stuff. The sun was over the horizon. To the west the sky glowed pink and orange. To the east it was turning a dark blue-black. The breeze was cool and smelled sweet. Traffic was steady but moving very fast. To Ian's surprise Julie started thumbing too, standing on front of him. Between cars she leaned back against him and he slipped his arm around her waist. Her head came up to his chin. The smell of her hair mingled with the summer breeze. Things are working out, Ian thought. It had been a great day. He had never felt this happy before. Still it was all so dreamlike; he was afraid he might wake up.

A police car appeared at the top of the ramp. It drove slowly past, both cops staring at them.

"Fucking cops." Julie said.

Ian glanced over his shoulder. The police car had

stopped in the right lane a little way down the highway. The rooftop flashers flicked on. For a second nothing happened, then the car slowly backed up and stopped beside them. Blinded by the flashing lights, all Ian could think was: they can't force me to go home. *They can't.* The cop on the passenger side slowly rolled his window down. He leaned over and gestured to them.

"Hey you two," he shouted. "Come over here."

"Hi officers," Ian walked over to the car. "What's up?"

"Where are you headed?"

"Vancouver." Ian said. "But tonight we're just trying to get to Brandon."

"What's your name"

"I'm Ian Musgrave." He was surprised that he had blurted out his real name.

"And you?" Julie stood back a few feet.

"My name is Jane Smith."

"Jane Smith?" The cop smirked.

"That's what I said." Julie glared at him.

The cop stared at her for a long moment. He looked at his partner who raised his brows.

"I need to see some ID from both of you."

Ian fumbled in his wallet, pulled out his student card and handed it to the cop.

"You got a driver's license?"

"No, sir." Ian said a little embarrassed. "I don't drive yet."

The cop picked up a clipboard from the seat. He wrote down Ian's name and hometown. He handed it back.

"You're a little young to be out here."

"I'm sixteen." Ian said. "I'm going out west to work for the summer."

"And you, Miss, can I see some id?"

"I don't have any."

"You don't have any ID?" Another eye roll.

"No, some asshole stole my wallet a few nights ago."

"Ok." The cop stared at her again. He clicked his pen a couple of times and wrote down Jane Smith. Next to their names he made a few notes.

"Either of you carrying any drugs with you?"

"No, sir." Ian said. Julie said nothing.

"So if I get out of the car and look in your bags over there, I'm not gonna find some pot or a couple of joints in your pockets?

"No. sir." Ian said. "I don't even smoke pot."

The cop's partner seemed bored. He was watching the traffic and tapping the wheel with both thumbs.

"Ok, just so you know, you are hitchhiking on a double highway here, which is illegal. No pedestrians are allowed down here. I could charge you right now. You need to take your things and move up that ramp to the secondary road, do you understand me?"

"Yes, sir," Ian said. "We can do that."

"Ok then." The cop stared at them again as if he was still thinking about searching their gear. Finally, he tossed the clip board on the seat. His partner stepped on the gas and they drove off.

Relieved, Ian walked over and picked up his bedroll and slug it over his shoulder.

"What the fuck are you doing?" Julie said.

"Uh, moving up the ramp." He picked up his canteen.

"Because a fucking cop told you to move?"

"Well, I don't want to get a fine."

"That's bullshit. If they were gonna fine us, they would have fined us." She waved her arms. "Look around. They're gone."

"Well, they could come back to check."

"Fuck, you are such a wimp." She spat on the road. "They're not coming back."

"I'm not a wimp. I just don't want a hassle from the cops."

Julie stuck her thumb out at a passing car. "Well, I'm not standing up there. We'll never get a ride."

Ian knew she was right. It was almost dark now. They needed to get a ride. He tossed his bedroll down and started thumbing again.

"Hey," Ian trying to make conversation. "Why did you lie to the cops, you know, about your name?"

"I don't like cops."

"But why give them a fake name? Are you in some kind of trouble?"

"That's none of your business."

They stood in silence for a minute.

"Sorry," Ian said. "I was just curious--"

"My life is none of your fucking business, so drop it, ok, drop it."

Maybe she is a runaway, Ian thought. After all she and Lilly only had their purses with them. He wanted to tell her he was a runaway too, but he knew better than to speak again.

As night fell, Ian worried that drivers would not see

them until it was too late to stop. There was only one tall lamp post at the top of the ramp. The light from it barely reached them. After another hour the traffic thinned. Ian began to eye the weeds along the road.

"Should we stop?" He finally asked. "Maybe crash on the grass until morning?"

"No way I'm spending the fucking night here." Julie stared straight ahead, jabbing her thumb at every vehicle.

"Ok." Ian shrugged. They thumbed on in silence, lit up like apparitions each time a car passed.

A half hour later, as high beams struck them, they heard a car horn. The driver slammed on the brakes and swung to the shoulder a hundred feet down the road. The car started backing up slowly until the red tail lights were very close. A woman stuck her head out the passenger window and yelled.

"Hey, do you want a ride?"

"Yes," Ian shouted. He grabbed his things. Even Julie ran to the car.

It was a two-door. The woman stepped out and flipped the seat forward.

"We're only going as far as Brandon," she said.

"That's great," Ian babbled. "We're going to Brandon."

Julie climbed in and sat behind the driver. Ian handed her his gear. He crawled in. The seat back touched his knees.

"You ok back there?" The driver said over his shoulder. He craned his neck to check the traffic, then pulled out. When on-coming headlights struck them, Ian saw the couple was older, mid to late thirties he guessed.

The man had a full head of dark hair in small curls that looked like it might a perm. The woman's sandy blonde hair also looked permed. Tiny John Lennon wire-rimmed glasses rested far down her nose. She peered over them as she turned to talk.

"So my name is Roxanne, friends call me Roxy and this" -large hoops bracelets tinkled as she gestured- "is my husband Jason. Whom do we have the pleasure to travel with?"

"I'm Ian and this is Julie."

"Welcome to our humble vehicle," she said. "So where are you kids from?"

"I'm from Madanon," Ian said. He paused for Julie to answer but she said nothing. "I'm headed out west to work for the summer." He added, half-jokingly. "Maybe in a lumber camp."

"Oh, that sounds like fun."

"And you?" Roxy nodded at Julie. "What's your story?"

"I don't have a story." Julie said.

"Oh, come now, everyone has a story."

Julie said nothing. In the darkness of the back seat, Ian reached over for her hand, but she pulled it away.

"I'm from Vancouver myself," Jason spoke for the first time. "It's beautiful there. "

"But it's no Brandon." Roxy teased.

"No," Jason chuckled. "It's no Brandon."

The woman turned sideways again. "We're both teachers at Brandon University. Jason is the head of the sociology department."

"Cool." Ian didn't know what else to say.

Roxy turned around more and rested her arms on the back of her seat. "So, how long have you two been dating?"

"Dating?" Julie snorted in the dark.

"Uh," Ian hesitated. "We just met yesterday and decided to hitchhike together."

"And you, Julie, what's your plan once you get to Vancouver?"

"I don't have a plan." Julie rifled in her bag and pulled out her smokes, but as soon as she got a cigarette to her mouth, Roxy spoke up.

"We actually don't allow smoking in our car."

"What-" Julie stopped with a lit match half way to her face.

Jason looked at them in the rearview mirror. "Sorry. I have a bad allergy to smoke." He added. "Tobacco smoke that is." He said this as if to signal that they were cool about pot.

Julie blew the match out, rolled the window down and tossed it. The unlit cigarette dangled from her lips.

"So Julie," Roxy said. "I still want to hear your plans for the summer. Are you going to work in BC too?"

"Look, Roxy," Julie pulled the cigarette out of her mouth. "I don't have any plans and I even if I did, my plans are really none of your business, are they?"

Ian stiffened. *Oh shit, please don't get us dumped on the side the road.*

"Now, now," Jason scolded, but Roxy touched her husband's arm.

"No, Jason. She's right. I am being far too inquisitive." She said over her shoulder. "I am curious to a fault."

"But," Jason added smiling in the rearview mirror. "That's what makes her a great researcher."

Ian leaned forward, eager to distract them from Julie. "What kind of research do you do?"

Roxy launched into a detailed description of her PhD thesis. Ian had a hard time following her explanation, but at least there were no more questions. Julie settled into the corner of the back seat. When headlights swept over them, Ian saw that she was staring blankly at the night sky.

When Roxy finished talking, Ian said it sounded like a lot of work. Then they all fell into a tense silence. Ian leaned back in his seat, his gear on the floor around his feet. He reached over for Julie's hand, but she pulled away again. Roxy fiddled with radio and finally settled on some CBC show where two people were discussing U.S. politics, mostly Nixon and Vietnam. Ian almost drifted off listening to the dull radio voices. He heard Jason and Roxy talking but so softly he could not make out the words over the road noises.

Shortly, as they turned off the highway for Brandon, Jason cleared his throat.

"Now," he said. "The hostel is a bit down the road here. They use an old farm, I believe. But I was just thinking if you'd like a more luxurious night, we have a spare room." He looked towards Roxanne, who quickly chimed in.

"It would be so much nicer than the hostel. You can have a shower. You must be a little, uh, musty from your travels. And in the morning we can make you a nice brunch and Jason can drop you at the highway on his way to campus."

Ian loved the idea. He leaned forward excited. "Thanks. That sounds really cool."

"No, thanks." Julie said loudly from the dark corner of the back seat.

"Why not?" Ian snapped.

"I'm going to the hostel. I told Lilly that I would look for her at each hostel."

Ian knew this was bullshit. They had no idea where Lily was. But he knew it was pointless to argue with her.

"Oh yeah, I forgot." He said to Jason and Roxy. "Julie's friend is thumbing across country too. They have to meet up tonight at the hostel." Although Jason said of course, of course, Ian knew they weren't buying this excuse. They rode on in silence.

"There's the farm house." Jason pointed to a single light off to the left. He slowed to a crawl, watching for the turn. A big sheet of plywood leaned on a post with the word Hostel painted in bright blue. Jason drove cautiously down a long driveway of hard packed dirt. He slowed, zigzagging around potholes, still hitting some. Roxy steadied herself with a hand on the dashboard. They stopped in front of a big brick farm house.

Jason jumped out and flipped the seat forward. Julie climbed out and walked away, quickly lighting her smoke. Jason reached in and helped Ian drag his gear out.

"Well." Ian felt really awkward. "Thanks for the ride."

"Sure. Good luck." Jason got back in the car. Roxy waved one hand indifferently at Ian. Jason swung the car around. Ian watched the tail lights bouncing as they drove back out to the road.

"Thank fucking Christ that's over." Julie said.

"What was wrong? They seemed nice."

"Nice!" She blew smoke. "Fucking rich nosey assholes. Who does she think she is asking me a bunch of questions?"

"I thought she was just making conversation."

'Yeah, you would." She grabbed her purse and walked away. He grabbed his stuff and ran to catch up with her.

Except for a porch light and a soft glow from a couple of windows, the farm house was dark and quiet. Ian tried the front door. It was locked. They circled around to the back door, where moths swarmed around a bare bulb. The door was locked too but the light was on. Ian leaned close to the glass. In the middle of a big country kitchen a man sat at a small wooden table. He looked up from the book he was reading. He got up slowly and hobbled to the door. He was heavy set with thick glasses. Still holding his book, he opened the door.

"You're getting in pretty late."

"We just got a ride from Winnipeg." Ian said.

"Well, you're too late to eat or shower. Everyone's crashed." He rubbed at a scraggily beard hanging from his jowly chin and walked slowly back to the table. Ian trailed after him.

"So where do we sleep?"

"Single guys are outside in that trailer by the barn. Single chicks are upstairs." He gestured with his thumb. "Couples are down that hall there, last door on the right."

"Do we register with you?"

"Just tell someone in the morning." He sat down heavily and opened his book again.

Julie followed Ian down the hall. Last door on the right. He pushed the door open. As light spilled in from the hallway he saw two sets of bunk beds shoved against opposite walls. He felt around and found the light switch. Two bare bulbs in an old brass ceiling fixture popped on.

A man and a woman lay naked on the bottom bed of one of the bunks. The woman was on top, her breasts flattened on the man's chest. They made no move to cover up.

"Woah," The man raised a hand in front of his eyes like he was staring at the sun. "That's a little bright."

"Sorry," Ian said. "We just got in."

"Me too, man, me too." The man said. He and the woman both started giggling. "Help yourself." He pointed to the other bunk.

"I'm taking the top." Julie said. She tossed her purse up, climbed the ladder and flopped on the mattress.

"Hey man," the guy in the other bunk said. "Your chick's on top, just like mine." They broke into throaty cackles again.

Ian turned off the light and closed the door. He felt his way back to the bunk bed. He was going to undress, but he was painfully aware of the couple right there. Instead he kicked off his shoes and crawled into the lower bed. It was a tight fit. These bunks were probably meant for kids. There was one thin pillow that smelled of sweat. The mattress was flat and hard. When he moved a little to get settled, the springs squeaked. When Julie shifted above him the whole bed frame swayed.

Ian lay there wide awake. He was hungry, dirty and furious. They should have gone with Jason and Roxy! Who cares if they were nosey? They could have eaten, had showers and be sleeping in some nice bedroom, instead of this bullshit.

Then the couple started to have sex. They were so close Ian could almost feel the heat coming off them. First he just heard their bed rocking, then it started banging against the wall, metal thumping plaster, faster and faster. Ian laid there hoping they would finish soon and get to sleep. The woman started with low moans, but soon her volume went up. The man made little grunts that punctuated her moans.

"Oh for fuck sakes." Julie shouted. She jumped down from the upper bunk. "I'm gonna go sleep somewhere else." She left, slamming the door behind her.

"Wait," Ian called. He sat up quickly and smacked his head -really hard- into the sharp metal frame of the bunk. Pain knifed through his forehead. He staggered out of the lower bunk, clutching his head.

"Fuck. Fuck. Fuck." The pain was worse when he stood up.

"Shit, man. Sorry about that." The man flicked a lighter and lit a cigarette. The woman still sat straddling him. He handed her the smoke. "We'll try to keep it down."

Ian grabbed his shoes. Scooping up his gear he reached for the door.

"Hey, man. Don't leave on our account." More laughter as he exited. In the hallway he hopped around pulling on his shoes.

In the kitchen, the same sleepy guy looked up from his book.

"Did you see where Julie went?"

"That chick? She went up to the women's area."

Ian looked at the stairwell. "So can I go up there?"

"No, way. It's for women only."

Ian stood in the middle the room. He let out a big sigh. His head really hurt.

"Ok then, I guess I'll move out to the trailer."

"Sorry man, the trailer is pretty much full. Besides, you can't be climbing around in there in the middle of night looking for a bed and waking every one up."

"But Julie went up there."

"Yeah, well, she shouldn't have gone up there without letting me know. You'll have to stay where you are." He gestured back down the hallway. Then he pointed at Ian's head. "Hey, did you know you're bleeding? On your forehead there?"

Ian touched his skull where he had banged the bunk and felt the wet on his fingers.

"There's some paper towels over there." The man stayed seated, holding his book. Ian grabbed a couple of thick towels and dabbed at his head. There was a big red blotch on the brown paper.

"You better get some sleep, man, They'll be making breakfast in a few hours."

Holding a towel to his cut, Ian slowly dragged his stuff back down the hallway. He pushed the door open quietly. The guy said nothing. Ian hoped they were asleep. He placed his stuff on the floor and shut the door. In the dark he felt his way back to the bunk. When he leaned over to crawl into bed, his temple and forehead throbbed. He lay on his side, facing the wall, trying to ignore the snoring. The man or the woman, he couldn't tell. The room was small and stuffy, the air smelled like sweat and sex and cigarette smoke. He tossed and turned trying to relax. He was so confused about Julie. What had he done wrong? Why was she so angry with him? Now she was sleeping in another room and he was stuck here for the night. He drifted off but woke up often to random noises: snoring, footsteps, voices, flushing toilets. Once he turned over and saw a faint glow at the window and heard the distant sound of birds. He curled up tighter and pulled the scratchy blanket over his head.

The next time Ian woke up, the couple was gone. Their stuff too. All that remained was a cracked saucer on the floor, full of cigarette butts. He heard loud voices and clattering sounds in the kitchen. He sat up carefully, avoiding the sharp metal frame. He felt a little dizzy when he stood. He touched his forehead. There was a line of crusted blood just inside his hairline. He pulled on his shoes and trudged to the kitchen.

A big woman with a mop of curly hair stood holding a coffee mug in one hand, a cigarette in the other. She greeted him.

"Hey, sleepy head, if you want breakfast, you better get out there." She hooked her thumb at the door. Ian stepped outside and saw a half dozen picnic tables placed end to end. About thirty hikers sat around the tables. He looked around for Julie. Maybe she was in the shower? Or still asleep on the second floor?

A big dented coffee urn sat on a card table. It was attached to the house by a long yellow extension cord. Ian picked up a big white mug and filled it. He took a sip and poured in some sugar. As he searched for a spoon, a thin man with a sloppy tattoo of Jesus on his forearm, handed him a plate with two hardboiled eggs and two pieces of cold toast. "There's jam and peanut butter on the tables."

Ian found a spot at the end of one table. Someone nodded and pushed the bowls of peanut butter and jam down to him. There was a spoon stuck in each bowl. He slathered jam on his toast. As he ate he listened to the usual conversations about thumbing.

"This is my third day trying to get out of here." One guy said.

"You're shitting me?" Someone replied.

"No, I'm not. The rides here are the pits."

"Didn't you hear about Brandon?" Someone called from half way down the table. "About a week ago a hitchhiker robbed some local guy. They stabbed him. That's why no one will pick anyone up."

"Did he kill him?"

"No, lucky for us. But he fucked it up big time. Hard enough to get a ride out here in red neck land."

"What happened to that guy, the one who did the robbery?"

"Nothing. They never caught him. Still out there somewhere." He made a scary face and grinned. "Watch your backs."

Down the table, someone started to sing the Doors' song Riders on the Storm. "There's a killer on the road. His brain is squirming like a toad." He drummed the beat on the table. "If you give this man a ride. Sweet family will die. Killer on the road." He raised his voice on the chorus, but no one joined in.

"Jim Morrison," Another hiker said. "Man, he was a fucking prophet."

Ian went back for more coffee. He was so tired. Still no sign of Julie. As he added sugar he stared at the house. He should go wake her up. But he recalled how angry she had been last night. Maybe it was better to wait here for her.

Back at the table, someone leaned forward.

"Hey man, what happened to your head?"

"What?" Ian reached up to touch his forehead. "Oh yeah. I cut it on a bunk bed last night."

"No shit? That's a nasty cut. You should get that looked at." The guy laughed. "Seriously, man, it makes you look fierce. You should tell people you were in a knife fight. No one will fuck with you."

"Ok, folks," The guy with the tattoo shouted from the back porch. "Breakfast is over. It's time to hit the road. As some of you know, the hostel is closed during the day" - there was some good natured booing- "I know, I know. It's a drag but that's the only way the city of Brandon would let us open a hostel. Can't have you dirty hippies crashing here all the time."

"Fuck Brandon." Someone shouted to a few cheers.

"You need to get your stuff out of the trailer and hit the road." Then he grinned. "Of course if you want to hang out all day under those lovely trees over there, we can't really stop you, can we?"

Ian went into the house. A couple of people were

washing dishes. As he started up the stairs, someone called out

"Hey! That's the women's area."

"I'm looking for Julie." He was going to say "my girlfriend" but he didn't.

"There's no one up there."

Ian went up any way. They were right: all the rooms were empty. He went back to the room where he had spent the night. Empty too.

Where the hell was she?

He dragged his things to the kitchen and asked where the shower was.

"Sorry, man, it's too late to shower," One of the dishwashers said. "The hostel is shut from nine to five. We're locking up the house in a couple of minutes."

Outside, Ian dragged his stuff around to the weedy front yard. A few hikers sat under a big willow tree smoking a joint. A few stood near a stone fire pit, chatting. He walked over to them, dropped his gear and sat on a log. He held his aching head in both hands. Where the fuck was Julie? Had she left without him? He didn't know what to do. He felt like shit. He was tired, he needed a shower, his head hurt. A few other hikers hoisted their back packs and headed out. This hostel did not provide buses, but they said the highway was only about a half hour walk away. He looked up as a car pulled in the long dirt driveway. When it stopped, he saw Julie jump out. Ian ran over to the car.

"Where the hell have you been?"

"I went to town for breakfast."

"Breakfast?"

"You were asleep. What was I gonna do? Sit around here and eat that shit they were serving?"

The driver got out of the car. It took Ian a second to recognize him - it was the guy from last night, from their room. He was taller than Ian with longish black hair, tucked behind each ear. He wore a tiny hoop earring on each side.

"Hey man," he patted Ian on the shoulder with a big grin. "You were dead asleep this morning, so I took your lady into town for breakfast."

"But -" Ian struggled, "Where's your girlfriend? The one from last night?"

"Girlfriend?" He laughed and winked at Julie, who was leaning on the car, having a smoke. "No, man, she was just some chick I was balling. I only met her last night." He made a big show of looking around. "I guess she's already hit the road."

"Hey." He pushed Ian towards the rear of the car and opened the trunk. It was stuffed with clothes, bags of food, a case of beer and bottles of wine. He put a can of beer to Ian's hands and took one for himself.

"Here, man, chill out." He popped the beer and took a swig.

Ian looked blankly at the can of beer. It was eight in the morning. He turned to Julie. "So do you want to get on the road now?"

"I'm in no hurry. I might just chill out here for the day."

"But what about Lily? I thought you wanted to catch up with her?"

"What I do is none of your business." She turned and

walked towards the farm house.

"Chicks, eh?" The guy waved his beer can. "They'll drive you crazy."

Ian walked back to his gear. He sat on the log again, turning the can of beer over and over in his hands, not sure what to do. He wanted to get going. He had to get out west and find some work. But he couldn't leave without her, could he? The gash on his head hurt. He held the cool beer can on the cut. It didn't really help, so he stuffed the can in his duffle bag. He wandered around back of the farm house looking for a place to pee. There was an old wooden outhouse. When he opened the door a few big flies swarmed his head. The fumes nearly made him vomit. He peed quickly and stepped out into the glaring sunlight.

He had to find Julie and talk. He circled back to the front yard. The car was still there but no sign of Julie or that guy. He walked over to the people under the willow tree. They were still smoking pot and talking. A couple of guys were sprawled out, snoozing, their heads on their backpacks.

"Anyone see Julie? That short girl with dark hair?"

Someone looked up, holding a joint. They held up a finger for a minute, then exhaled.

"I saw her and that dude with the car walking towards the barn." He pointed to old weathered barn and tool shed behind the farm house.

Ian circled the house and pushed angrily through the tall weeds towards the abandoned barn. He stopped in front of the doors. Had they gone in there? He leaned close to listen. Nothing. He placed his eye to a crack in the wood, but it was too dark to see. He grabbed the edge of the door and yanked on it. It moved about an inch. He leaned back and pulled harder. It was off the rails and would not budge.

If they weren't in there, where did they go?

He circled the barn. It was surrounded by abandoned fields that had grown wild. Beyond a crooked wire fence, a hundred yards away, stood a thick cluster of old, twisted apple trees. Alex thought he saw motion there in the trees. A rusty tractor sat abandoned next to the barn. Ian climbed on a stack of weathered barn boards trying to see the trees. Then he stepped up on to the big rear tire of the tractor, steading himself with one hand. He still could not see clearly. The tractor had a big sheet metal awning wielded over the seat. Ian grabbed the sharp edge and managed to drag himself up on to the top. As he stood up the sheet metal popped and shifted with his weight.

Arms outstretched for balance, Ian looked around. There, under the scrawny apple trees, he saw the guy from the car, half leaning on tree trunk, hands on his hips. His pants were down around his knees. Julie was kneeling in front of him, working his cock with her mouth and hands. Ian looked away, then looked back. The guy was patting her head, like someone would pat a dog.

Blind with rage, Ian turned quickly, almost falling off the tractor. He fell to his knees. He wanted to do something. Scream at them to stop. Run over and punch that guy. Instinctively he touched the handle of his knife. He could run over there and stab them both. But he knew he wouldn't do that. There was nothing he could do. He had to get away from them. He half slid, half fell down off the tractor, snagged his jeans and ripped a hole below one knee. He wiped orange rust stains from his hands to his jeans. He walked fast, almost running to the front of the house. He had to get out of here. He rushed over to where his gear lay under the willow tree. He was shaking with anger. He remembered the can of beer in his duffle bag and dug it out. When he popped the top, warm foam leaked out over his hand. He took a long drink.

The hikers sitting on a nearby log, watched him guzzle the beer.

"Hey man." One called out, "Want a toke?"

Ian clumsily took the joint he was offered. He had never smoked pot before but he knew to inhale and hold it. He drew in as much as he could. He only held it a second before a tickle made him cough.

"Try again. Try again." One hiker said. "That's some very dry homegrown."

Ian took another smaller toke and kept it in a little longer. He felt nothing so he dragged again.

"Oh man, don't hog that joint."

"Sorry," He whispered, trying not to exhale. He coughed. Everyone laughed.

He offered the can of beer to the guy next to him.

"Warm beer? No thanks, man. We got this." He held up a wineskin. Ian watched as the man tilted his head back and shot a stream of wine right into his open mouth. When it was his turn, Ian managed to squirt a some into his mouth; a little dribbled down his chin. No one said much. The wine and the joint circled a couple of times. One guy fingered his guitar, not really playing a tune. Ian felt a soft warmth spread through his body. He noticed the breeze on his face, and the sound the willow leaves made in the wind. The air smelled of dust and wild flowers. So this is getting stoned, he thought.

"All gone," the guy with the joint said. He licked his fingertips, pinched the end of the joint, then popped it into his mouth. "Good to the last drop." He stood up. "Hey, man, a few of us are going to walk into town and hang out, wanna join us?"

"Thanks." Ian shook his head. "But I got to get on the road."

They left their things under the tree and shambled off towards town. When he thought of Julie under the apple tree with that guy he felt angry again. But it was as if someone else was angry, as if he was watching himself through a window. This was all so weird. He shook his head and stood up. He should get going. He needed to get to Vancouver. Then he saw Julie and the guy walking towards the car.

"Hey," he shouted. "Hey! What's going on?"

He ran and caught up with them as they reached the car. Julie opened the passenger door and dug in her purse for a cigarette.

"Hey," Ian grabbed her arm. "What's going on?"

She shook off his hand and lit a smoke. "Nothing's going on."

"Nothing?" Ian shouted. "I saw you with him. I saw you."

"So what?" Julie blew smoke in his face.

"So what? What the fuck are you doing?" He fought the urge to cry. "You're with me, aren't you?"

"Fuck, what do you think? You're my boyfriend because I gave you a hand job last night?" She walked away. Before Ian could follow her, the guy came around front of the car.

"Hey man." Ian recoiled as the guy reached for him. But he threw his arm over Ian's shoulders and gave him a friendly squeeze.

"You gotta chill, man. This chick is, well, you know a little crazy." He pointed at Julie, who paced in circles a few yards away. "She's a free spirit. Like a wild horse, man. You can't tame her." He steered Ian to the rear of the car and popped the trunk again. He reached in and handed Ian another can of beer. He opened one for himself.

"Here, man. Let's drink to her." He raised his beer. "To chicks, man, they fuck you and then they fuck you up."

Ian just stared at him, holding the unopened beer in his hand. He wanted to scream, to hit the guy, to do something but he knew the guy was right. There was nothing he could do. Julie was just being Julie. He couldn't make her do anything.

The guy slugged back the rest of his beer and tossed the empty in the trunk.

"I gotta take a piss." He walked over to the shady side of the farm house and peed on the wall.

Julie came back to the car. She reached in the trunk and helped herself to a beer. She didn't look directly at Ian.

"I'm going to catch a ride with him. He's headed to Edmonton and I want to get to Regina today."

Ian said nothing. He felt deflated and stupid.

After a long silence, she asked, "You still going to Van?"

"Yeah. Sure. I gotta get some work. I'm running out of dough."

"Hey," the guy trotted up with a big grin. "We better rock and roll."

Julie tossed her purse in the front seat, climbed in and slammed the door. Before he shut the trunk, the guy handed Ian another can of beer.

"Here's another one for the road. You gotta loosen up, brother. I mean she was with you, now she's with me, tomorrow she'll be with some other guy. Life's a fucking crazy ride, man, just remember shit happens." He slapped Ian on the shoulder and jumped in the driver's seat. He revved the engine a few times and swung in a tight circle around the yard. Julie gave Ian a strange sad look as the car passed him. The guy flashed a peace sign and gunned it down the driveway. Dust flew up as the car bounced along. Then they turned and headed towards the highway. Ian stood there, a can of beer in each hand, watching them disappear.

That was it! As fast as Julie had come into his life, she was gone. He realized he didn't even know her last name. Or if Julie was even her name. None of it made sense to him. He walked back to the willow tree and plunked down on the log. He was all alone now, just the sound of the wind in the tree. He was overcome with sadness. He had to get out of here. He shoved the cans of beer inside his duffle bag, slung his gear and walked toward the highway.

As he walked all his anger returned. How could she

sleep with him, then give that guy a blow job? He walked faster. The canteen bashed against his leg. It hurt but he didn't care. The late morning sun blasted down. Sweat beaded on his forehead. At the highway he crossed to the north side. Down the road he saw some other hikers who had been here first. He knew he should walk past them before he started thumbing, but he was too tired to care. He dropped his gear and started thumbing. Traffic was steady but no one stopped.

After a while he sat down on his duffle bag and thumbed half-heartedly from where he sat. The cut on his head really started to ache. He drank from his canteen. The warm water upset his stomach. He held his head in his hands, still trying to understand what had happened. Yesterday he had been so happy, headed to Vancouver with Julie; today she was gone. It was all fucked up. And that guy with his "shit happens" – who the fuck was he? That didn't make Ian feel any better. He was so tired he decided to stretch out and grab a little nap. He lay flat on the dirt shoulder with his head on his bag. He draped one arm out over his things, his thumb up. Passing cars stirred up dust that settled on his face. He covered his eyes with his other arm.

When Ian woke up a little drool was running from the corner of his mouth. The sun glared from a cloudless sky. His face felt very hot. He knew he had gotten sunburned. He staggered to his feet and walked in a circle around his stuff. He took a mouthful of water, swished it around and spit it out. He poured more in his hand and splashed it on his face and hair. It evaporated quickly. The cut on his head stung. He had been asleep for a couple of hours. Half awake, he started thumbing again, desperate to get away. Finally, an approaching pick-up truck slowed down. It stopped on the road just past Ian. He grabbed his things and ran over. The man in the passenger seat leered out the window.

"Hey faggot, wanna suck my cock?"

"Fuck you." Ian give him the finger. The two men laughed. As they sped of Ian hurled a handful of gravel after them.

"Fucking red necks," he screamed.

Dejected he dropped his gear on the gravel and checked the time. It was almost four. He'd never get a ride. And even if he did, he wouldn't make the next hostel today. He didn't want to sleep on the side of the road somewhere. He decided to head back to the hostel. As he trudged along, he thought bitterly about Julie. She and that guy were probably already in Regina drinking beer and having sex.

The hostel had just opened, but already a lot of hikers were milling about. Some sprawled under the willow tree, others sat at the picnic tables. Ian saw some staff moving about inside the kitchen. Behind the house, a man sat a card table in the shade doing registration.

"Welcome," The man said, pushing the clip board and a pen across to Ian. "How far did you come today?"

"About ten feet." Ian said. "I was here last night. Couldn't get a ride today."

"Well, you are not alone. The locals are really steamed about last week's attack." As Ian filled out the little form, the man said. "Wow, you got a really nasty sun burn there. After you get settled see Marcie in the kitchen, we might have some sunburn cream in the first aid kit."

Ian dragged his stuff to the one of the two big trailers designated for male hikers. He climbed the metal stairs. The trailer had been gutted and lined with mattresses on the floor. There was a narrow path down the middle between the beds. Nodding to some other hikers, Ian picked a bed along the far wall. There were a few small windows high on the walls, but even with them open there was no cross breeze. The air was hot, unmoving and smelled like a locker room. He dug out some clean clothes and headed to the house to take a shower. There were three people in line. As usual people chatted about where they were from and where they were headed, east and west.

"I hear it's a bitch to get out of here."

"I've been stuck here since yesterday." Ian said. "Thumbed all afternoon without a ride." He didn't tell them he had laid down and fallen asleep.

"Man, your face is red as a tomato." One said. "That must hurt."

"It's not so bad." Ian said, "I need to get a hat."

"Well, it's gonna hurt like hell later."

When Ian turned on the shower, he realized he had no soap, no shampoo and no towel. But it didn't matter. The hot water felt so good. Someone had left a sliver of soap which he gladly used. He turned around again and again under the spray. He patted himself dry with his dirty t-shirt. He wiped steam from the mirror and checked his face. The sunburn was really bad: his face, the back of his neck, even the backs of his hands. All his exposed skin was bright red and starting to hurt.

Still damp, he pulled on his clean clothes. When he opened the door, even more people were lined up now.

"How's the hot water?" someone asked.

"Best shower ever." Ian shouted and spun in a circle. Everyone laughed.

He paused in the kitchen. A half dozen people bustled around the stove and counter.

"That smells great." He said to a very tall woman who had long braids over each shoulder.

"Beef stew." She smiled. "And fresh biscuits."

"Wow. You guys are the best."

"We try." She chuckled. "Scooch." She pushed him towards the door. "You're getting in the way. "

As Ian stepped outside, she called after him. "Hey kid, that sunburn, you better get that looked at."

Back in the trailer, he hung his dirty clothes over a nail by his mattress. Every bed was occupied now. People chatted, changed clothes, smoked and napped. The guy next to him stuck out his hand.

"Hey brother." He hooked Ian's thumb with his. "You got a real bad sunburn." He dug in his backpack and handed Ian a small jar. "Here, use this cream. It's made with aloe which is really good for burns."

"Thanks, man." Ian smeared some on his face and neck. His forehead was very tender to touch but the cream felt cool and soothing. Ian handed the jar back and went over to a small mirror that hung by the door. He leaned close to check the cut on his forehead. It looked pink and puffy but seemed to be healing.

He heard a booming voice announcing dinner was

ready and went outside to join the line. Someone handed him a bowl of beef stew and two chunky homemade biscuits. At another table there was coffee, hot water for tea and a tub of what looked like Kool-Aid. He dipped a mug into the orange drink and grabbed a seat at one of the picnic tables. He was so hungry and the stew was so good he emptied the bowl in a couple of minutes. He mopped up gravy with the last of the biscuit and wished there were seconds. He sipped his orange drink and looked around. The sun crept towards the horizon. A cool evening breeze rustled the branches over his head. He was tired and full and quietly listened to the hikers make small talk: where they were from, where they were headed; people shared stories, of good rides and bad, of places where they got stuck, of places to avoid if possible.

His thoughts drifted to Julie again. Where was she now? Off somewhere having sex with that guy. He pushed that image out of his mind, looking around the table at the hikers. He felt a sudden wave of warmth towards them. He remembered as a kid in the late sixties seeing all the hippies on TV; now here he was hanging out with them. He felt like he was part of this, whatever *this* was. He might be stuck in Brandon, but at least he wasn't alone.

The tall women from the kitchen came by gathering bowls into a bin. She called out, "If anyone would like to help with the dishes, we'd appreciate it. Many hands make light work."

Ian volunteered and soon found himself in the kitchen, in a line by a tub, drying dishes as they were handed to him. The staff was nice: asking his name, where he was from, where he was going. He found himself blurting out his story so far. Someone handed him a big mug of tea, sweetened with honey. He dried bowls and watched the evening wind ripple across the fields. It was a beautiful night. He felt that warmth again and a sense that this is where he should be.

One of the staff asked about his sunburn, saying it looked painful. When he mentioned putting some aloe cream on it, he said "that's good shit."

"You really need a hat." The women with the braids said. "Go into town tomorrow. You can probably find one at the Sally Ann thrift shop."

"Thanks," Ian said. "I'm pretty low on cash. Maybe when I get to Van, I'll track one down."

When the dishes were done, Ian took his mug of tea and wandered back to sit at the end of a picnic table. More hikers continued to straggle in from the highway. They had missed the stew and had to make do with peanut butter and jam sandwiches. No one seemed to mind. After a long day on the road, getting angry stares from rednecks, they had arrived somewhere friendly. The talk around the tables was loud, punctuated with lots of laughter. A bowl of fruit was passed around. Ian ate a banana and took an apple for tomorrow.

The tall woman from the kitchen and the guy from the registration desk came out of the farmhouse. They walked directly to the table where Ian sat. They stopped next to him, big grins on their faces. He looked up, wondering what they were going to announce. The guy held up his hands and shouted "Quiet. Quiet."

Once everyone fell silent, he said. "Folks, this is Ian. He's been stuck here for a couple of days."

Some hikers clapped and cheered. Ian felt very self-conscious, wondering what was coming next.

"Ian," The woman laid her hand on his shoulder. "We were talking about your sunburn. We don't want you to look like a lobster every day, so we are giving you a little present." From behind her back she pulled up a hat, a brown fedora with a black band. "Someone left this hat here about a week ago. I don't think he's coming back for it."

With a showy gesture she held it over Ian's head.

"In honour of the Brandon hostel, I now crown you, Ian, King of the Road." She placed the hat on Ian's head and tugged him to his feet.

The hikers burst into applause.

"The King. The King." They shouted. A couple of them stood up and made mocking bows. Ian looked around shyly at all the grinning faces.

"Aw, thanks." He smiled. He felt his eyes welling up with tears. He covered this by taking the hat off, turning it around in his hands and putting it back on again. Then he threw his thumb out like he was hitching. The hikers clapped and cheered more. The two staff slapped him on the back and headed back to the farm house.

"Thanks." He called after them. He sat back down, overwhelmed by the kindness of these strangers. He stared at his mug, feeling the unfamiliar weight of the hat on his head.

As twilight fell, hikers dispersed from the table. Late arrivals headed for the showers. A few early risers headed to bed, saying they hoped to beat the crowds in the morning. A few stopped to check out Ian's hat. He kept taking it off and putting it on again. He held it in his hands. *It was a very cool hat.*

Two hikers approached Ian and asked if he wanted to walk into town.

"We're gonna buy some beer or wine, then take a cab back."

Ian said he was too beat to walk to town, but impulsively he pulled out his wallet and chipped in on the booze run. He knew as he did it that he shouldn't. He now had less than half the money he started the trip with, and still had over a thousand miles to go to Vancouver. But he really felt like having a drink.

Ian wandered around to the front of farm house and looked west. The sun was over the horizon. The breeze had dropped. The air smelled sweet. Crickets sang loudly. But he started thinking about Julie again and his mood plummeted. It was sinking in that he would never see her again. He still didn't understand what had happened, what had he done wrong.

As darkness fell hikers gathered at the fire pit. Ian went over. Someone broke twigs for kindling, piling them in the old ashes. Others gathered some dead branches and dried weeds. One of the staff came over with some cardboard to burn. He reassured them that it was cool to have a fire. "Feel free to use the firewood." he said, pointing to a lopsided stack beside the house. "But don't burn any of the old barn boards. And make sure you knock the fire down when you are done."

Once the fire was going it attracted a few more hikers. A circle formed. People sat on logs, on wooden kitchen chairs, on blankets, and on the ground. A couple of people brought guitars and started jamming. Someone rolled a joint. When it came around, Ian toked hard. He was learning to fight the hot tickle in his throat and hold the smoke in. He really felt like getting drunk and stoned. The hikers who went to town for booze arrived back by cab. They had managed to get three large bottles of cheap wine. They joined the circle.

One made a big show of unscrewing the cap.

"Aw," he sniffed the metal. "A fine vintage. Hints of prairie rain mixed with dirty socks."

When the bottle came around, Ian took several big gulps. He started to feel pretty buzzed.

A car pulled in and parked under the willow tree. A tall older man with grey sideburns ambled over to the fire. In blue overhauls, wearing a crumpled straw hat, he looked like a farmer.

"Hey gang. I'm John. I'm working the night shift." He saw the wine bottles and winked. "I didn't see that. Just be cool, guys, be cool. Sometimes the cops swing by here at night. If they do, hide the wine. They would love to have an excuse to shut us down."

He went around to the farmhouse door. Shortly, the staff members who had cooked and done registration walked by, headed into town. A couple of hikers called out thanks.

"Don't stay up too late." One of the cooks warned. "Breakfast comes early."

The fire blazed, popping and cracking and sending sparks into the night sky. Every time the weed or the wine circled around Ian took a hit, trying to shake off his sadness. He stood up make room on the log for new arrivals and staggered a bit, bumping shoulders with other people. He felt a little out of control. There were three guitar players now. They took turns playing songs they knew, meandering from old folk songs to pop songs. When people knew the words, they joined in on the chorus. On the Beatle's Help, everyone sang at the top of their lungs. A couple of people even jumped up and danced on the edge of the shadows. Ian looked around and realized another row of hikers had joined them, standing behind the seated ones.

One of the musicians sang Cat Steven's Father and Son. The group fell very quiet as he sang. At the line "Find a girl. Settle down." Ian's chest grew tight, thinking of Julie. He was so happy to have escaped his family but it was lonely out here on his own. He tilted his head forward to hide his eyes in the shadow of his hat. When the song ended there was a round of spontaneous applause. When Ian raised his head he saw a few other hikers wiping away tears.

A few songs later someone called out a request for Me and Bobby McGee. Everyone joined in. Ian sang along quite loudly. He didn't care what anyone thought. When the line came along about "freedom's just another word for nothing left to lose" he choked up again. The guy next to him leaned forward and cried softly into his hands. Ian reached over and patted him on the back. He looked around at all the faces light by the warm fire light and saw a few guys with tears in their eyes. He felt a rush of love. Everyone here was on the road, looking for something. Or, Ian thought, running away from something.

When the song was over there was a long silence.

"To fucking Janis." Someone said.

"To Janis." The ones with the wine bottles raised them.

"And to Kris Kristofferson." Someone else called out. "He wrote it."

"To Kris." Others said. "What a great fucking song."

Ian stood up. Staggering forward, he tossed another log on the fire. As he did this one of the guitar players stood up and played Roger Miller's King of the Road. At the chorus he pointed at Ian and changed the lyric to "He's the king of the road." Hikers who had been at the table joined in, pointing at Ian each time they reached the chorus. "He's the king of the road." Ian was embarrassed but he enjoyed the attention too. To his surprise he found himself dancing around and singing loudly, "I'm the king of the road."

When the song ended everyone applauded. Ian took a drunken bow, then he staggered off in the dark to pee. He was going to find the outhouse, but instead he veered over to the edge of the field. As he peed he looked up at the night sky. He had never seen such a huge starry sky before. He was overwhelming by its beauty. The longer he stared up the more stars appeared. He felt like he was floating, drifting up in the endless points of light. *I'm just a speck of dust.* He felt peaceful but sad. He wanted so badly to be happy. Once I get to Vancouver, he thought, things will change. As he circled back to the fire, he staggered and bumped against the house. He really was fucked up. He leaned on the bricks to steady himself. From the shadows he watched the group singing around the fire and felt another rush of warmth.

In the distance a car pulled into the long driveway. It was going pretty fast, the headlight beams bounced up and down as it hit pot holes. It halted abruptly by the willow tree and three men climbed out. Back lit by the headlights, their faces were dark, but Ian saw that at least two were wearing varsity jackets, probably from the local high school football team. He knew the type - he'd seen lots of bullies in high school.

"Hey, you hippie faggots," One of them shouted. "You'd better get out of town."

One of the hikers by the fire stood up and called back.

"We're not in town, you moron."

"Fuck you." One of the jocks called back.

"Why don't you leave us alone?" One of the women called out. "We're not doing anything to you."

"Look, a talking cunt." One jock said loudly to his buddies. "Hey slut, you wanna suck my dick?"

"I would if I could find it." She called back. This drew some applause from the hippies.

"Faggot and cunts." As the three men started forward, Ian saw that one of them had a baseball bat in his hand.

Earlier he had seen a pile of bricks next to the house, left from some repairs. Without a thought, he grabbed a broken chunk of brick, took two steps forward and lobbed it like a grenade. The brick sailed high over the intruder's heads; it smacked loudly off the hood of their car. At the loud thunk they turned, confused about what had made the sound. Ian grabbed another half of brick and hurled it drunkenly at the jocks. This time it flew low, barely missed one guy's head.

"Fuck off!" Ian shouted. All the hikers turned to see who was throwing stuff. Ian grabbed another brick and ran forward into the fire light. "Fuck off and leave us alone."

"You little shit." The driver said. "I'm going to kick your ass."

"Oh yeah," Ian shouted. All his rage and frustration at the last few days came spewing out. He felt his legs shake as he waved the brick over his head.

"Come on, tough guy, I'll smash your fucking head in."

The mouthy jock hesitated.

"What's wrong, you chicken shit? You want to kick my ass?" Ian dropped the brick, yanked his jeans down and mooned the guy. "Here's my ass."

Immediately a dozen hikers stood up and mooned the jocks too. Other hikers jeered and clucked like chickens. Furious, the three jocks started forward. Suddenly a bright beam of light swept across their faces. They raised their hands to shield their eyes.

John, the night staff guy, marched rapidly forward with a big flashlight in his hand. He kept the bright light shining right in their faces.

"Ok. Ok. Break it up." He walked right up to the jocks. He was a head taller than the tallest one. "You guys better clear out. This is private property."

"So what?" one of them said.

"So you're trespassing. The cops are on their way. I'll be glad to press charges when they get here." He kept swinging the flashlight from one face to the other. "Hit any of these kids and you'll spend a night in jail." He leaned right into them. "Hit me and you'll spend a night in the hospital."

Ian and all the hikers pressed forward behind John. The jocks looked nervous.

"Come on, guys, let's split." The driver stomped back to the car. The others followed.

"Who's a faggot now?" One of the hikers yelled. Others made clucking sounds.

They jumped in the car and driver floored it backwards to turn around. His car bottomed out hard on the pot holes. One of the jocks gave them the finger but they drove off. As the car hit the paved road, they heard the tires squeal.

The hikers broke into nervous laughter and chatter.

"Holy fuck," someone asked John. "Did you really call the cops?"

"You kidding?" John turned off his flashlight, "I don't want the cops here, they'd be going through your backpacks. One bust would shut us down."

John walked over to Ian, swaying drunkenly by the fire.

"Now who's this crazy mother fucker?"

"I'm Ian." Ian said. John grabbed his hand and shook it. He was grinning but he pulled Ian into a bear hug and whispered. "Be careful, kid, you almost got your ass kicked, real bad."

"Thanks." Ian's hands were shaking. He stuffed them in his pockets. John was right. That was a stupid thing to do. But then all the hikers gathered around him, slapping his back and telling him how cool he was and how great it was when he mooned the rednecks.

"Ok, ok, kids." John shouted over the chatter. "Show's over for tonight. You guys get to bed because I'll be waking you up early." He kicked the fire apart with his boots, then dumped a bucket of water over the coals. With clouds of steam and smoke rising around him, John reminded Ian of some giant in an old fairy tale. He nodded at Ian and trudged back to the house. The group drifted away. Ian stood for a minute watching the dying embers in the fire pit. They mirrored the stars above. He felt all the fear and anger drain from his body. Suddenly he was very tired. In the dark he staggered across the farm yard to the trailer. Inside he felt his way along the wall to his mattress. He fell down on his blankets, fully clothed.

In the darkness someone called out, "Goodnight John Boy." A few people giggled.

"Good night, you hippie faggots." Someone else shouted. More laughter. After a minute of silence, someone said in a loud voice.

"Hey, king of the road. Goodnight you, crazy mother fucker." There was a lot of laughter. Ian smiled in the dark, then he was asleep.

Ian woke to the sound of other hikers moving about. He sat up and rubbed his face. He recalled the previous night. Had he really thrown bricks at some local jocks? He stood up, a little wobbly. Had he really mooned them? His hangover was all in his temples, sharp shooting pains from the cheap red wine. He grabbed his hat and staggered down the trailer steps. The sun was up but it was still chilly. A thin mist rose over the fields. He went into the house to use the bathroom. He splashed water on his face. He examined his sunburn. Two blisters on his nose, flaky peeling skin too, on his nose and forehead. He examined the gash on his forehead, healing but still painful to touch.

Back outside, breakfast was being served. Big soup bowls of watery oatmeal. He smothered it in honey and milk. He added lots of sugar to his coffee to cover the bitter taste. He squeezed into a spot at one of the tables. A few people from last night nodded at him. People were quiet, probably hung-over and tired like he was. Ian ate quickly. He decided to skip a shower. He wanted to get on the road as soon as he could to beat the line-up. He saw there was bread and peanut butter and jam laid out. He made a thick sandwich, but there was nothing to wrap it in except brown paper towels. Back in the trailer he placed the sandwich in the top of his duffle bag. He filled his canteen from the tap at the side of the farmhouse, then slung it over his side. As he picked up his bedroll and duffle bag someone called to him.

"Hey crazy man, hitting the road already?"

"Yeah. This is my third day. I have to get the fuck out of here."

"Good luck, brother. See you in Van." A couple of hikers gave him the handshake and patted him on the back.

Under the willow, some hikers sat smoking a joint.

"Hey, wanna toke for the road?"

"Naw," Ian said. "I'm still buzzed from last night."

"Watch out for those rednecks." Someone teased.

"They better watch out for me." He was surprised

how cocky he felt.

Ian enjoyed the walk to the highway. There was a cool morning breeze. Birds darted from the road side brush. He found a rhythm he liked. He was getting used to the way his canteen banged against his side. Today he would get to Regina, maybe even Calgary. Then, with luck, two more days to Vancouver. He worried about running out of money, but many hikers had mentioned crashing for free on the beaches near Vancouver.

As early as it was, a dozen hikers had already spread themselves along the shoulder. Ian nodded as he passed them, but he didn't stop to make small talk. He reached the end of the line and continued down the shoulder until he was well past the last exit ramp coming from Brandon. He plunked his things down and started thumbing. Cars came in little clusters. He kept his arm out wide. After each car passed he half turned and tossed them a peace sign, even though he knew most drivers were going too fast to see it. In the quiet gaps, he walked in circles around his stuff, singing bits of pop songs to himself. After a while he ate the orange he had brought from the hostel, wiping his sticky fingers on his jeans. When boredom set in, he skipped bits of gravel across the two lanes of blacktop. He developed a game he called White Line Curling. First he tried to land stones on the centre line. If he got one on the line, then he tried to knock it off with other stones.

The morning dragged on. By noon more hikers arrived, moving down past him to extend the line. Some stopped to talk. They had come from Winnipeg that morning. Ian warned them about how much locals hated hikers and why. He told them this was his third day here. It was a badge of honour to brag about being stuck. He felt like a seasoned hiker.

By mid-afternoon, Ian noticed that at least a dozen people were hiking behind him, standing very close together. Even if someone wanted to pick him up there was barely room for a car to pull over. He decided to move to the end of the line. He gathered up his things and marched down the shoulder. After he passed the last hiker he thought, what the hell and kept walking. When he heard a car coming, he spun around and thumbed, then continued walking. It felt good to walk after standing for so long. He had a silly fantasy about walking all the way to Regina.

He heard a car and turned to thumb. The driver made eye contact and swung over to the shoulder. Ian ran to it.

"Thanks for stopping." He tossed his stuff in the back seat.

The driver was a portly man in a suit and tie. His neck bulged over his collar.

"No problem." He sped off down the highway. "I usually don't pick up hitch hikers. Most of them are kind of lazy, eh? But I saw you walking and thought, now there's a guy who's really trying. So where you headed?"

"Vancouver to work for the summer."

"Good for you. Well, I can only take you as Virden."

"That's great." Ian had no idea how far Virden was. "Anywhere is better than being stuck in Brandon.

The man laughed. "Oh lots of people say that, even people from Brandon." He winked. "I'm from Brandon."

The man asked Ian where he was from. To his surprise, Ian found himself telling his whole story, describing his first rides, meeting Julie, riding with the trucker, losing Julie to some jerk with a car. He did not describe seeing her giving the guy blow job; he just said she flirted with this other guy. He told about the red necks coming to the hostel to beat them up, but left out how he had been drunk and stoned and throwing bricks. The man listened well, nodding and occasionally making sympathetic sounds. At Virden he pulled over to the shoulder.

"Well, you're certainly having yourself an adventure. Hope you get to Regina today."

Ian was alone again on the side of the road, surrounded by fields. He had no idea how far it was to Regina. Traffic was thin. On the good side, he was the only hiker here. After an hour he was tired and sat down on his duffle bag. He leapt up, remembering his peanut butter sandwich. He fished it out. It was flattened. Jam had squeezed out on some of his clothes. He sat back down and peeled the stale slices apart. He ate little chunks bread and jam, washing each mouthful down with warm water from his canteen. He tossed the crusts into the field. He licked his sticky fingers, then poured water over them and wiped them on his jeans.

The day dragged on. It was hot and windy. Dust coated his face. By dinner time Ian was tired and getting angry. Traffic had picked up but mostly people headed home from work he guessed. Drivers hunkered down, staring straight ahead. He tried different things to get their attention. Instead of thumbing he waved at the cars, giving them a big fake smile. He doffed his hat and threw his arms out like he was in a musical. He tossed the drivers a peace sign as they approached. Most drivers ignored him. A few gave him the finger. Once someone gave him the peace sign but they still didn't stop. Eventually Ian gave peace signs as cars approached but spun around to give the finger as they passed. He started eyeing the scraggly dried grass that bordered the shoulder. Fuck! He did not want to sleep on the side of the road tonight.

Around seven o'clock a cold wind rose. The vast wheat fields around him rippled violently. Ian saw a thin dark line on the eastern horizon. Within minutes it grew taller and darker. A major storm was rolling across the prairie towards him. Soon a tall cliff of black clouds towered overhead. Sheets of lightning flashed deep inside the clouds, followed a few seconds later by a low crackling rumble. In the distance he saw the gray haze of rainfall. The sky became dark as night as the clouds closed over him. A lightning bolt struck in the distance. Thunder cracked so loud it made him jump. He looked around and realized he was the tallest thing for miles. He laughed nervously. The wind rose violently and hurled weeds and dirt into his face. He heard a roaring sound a split second before the rain hit him.

It was a massive down pour. He tried to shelter his blankets under his duffle bag but rain was already pooling on the gravel. The duffle bag turned dark green as it got drenched. His wet clothes clung to him. His hat sagged, water ran off the brim like a tap. Shortly, the road was ankle deep in water. Passing trucks threw up huge wakes that splashed his legs. Some cars slowed down, their hazard lights flashing. As lightning struck nearby, Ian saw the tense white faces of drivers hunched over steering wheels.

Lightning struck so close the earth shook. Ian pulled off his soaked hat and looked straight up. The rain beat his face. He closed his eyes and opened his mouth. The water tasted so pure on his tongue. The line 'mana from heaven' leapt into his head. He threw his arms out, thinking: Ok, God, if you're going to kill me, now is your chance.

Suddenly, as fast as it had hit, the back edge of the storm passed over Ian. The rain stopped abruptly, like someone turning off a tap. Everything was soaked: the road, the shoulder, the fields, his gear, his clothes, his shoes. He was surrounded by puddles. He shook his hat and tried to punch it back into shape, balancing it on his canteen to dry. The traffic immediately sped up. Black clouds dominated the western sky while the east grew light and blue again. As he watched a massive rainbow formed, arcing up from the south, growing wider and more vibrant until it touched back down to the north. He had never seen such a huge rainbow before. It curved completely across the eastern sky. None of the west bound drivers knew what was happening behind them.

"Look," Ian shouted, pointing to the sky. He swung both arms like someone directing traffic. He jumped around pointing to the rainbow.

"Look," he shouted again. "A big beautiful rainbow and you idiots won't even slow down and look. Look at that! It's fucking amazing. Look."

Drivers stared at him like he was insane. Maybe he was. He stopped pointing and stood still. The rainbow shimmered for another minute or two, then it was gone. Ian turned around to look west. The storm clouds had massed along the horizon. The eastern sky was growing dark with nightfall. A cold wind continued to ruffle the fields. Ian's socks and shoes were soaked. He felt around inside his duffle bag for dry clothes, but everything was wet. He peeled off his sweater and tried to dry it. He twisted it in both hands but could only squeeze out a few drops. He spun it by the sleeves but it was still wet when he pulled it back on. Finally, he unrolled his bedroll. Both blankets felt like towels after a shower. He shook them out flat on the tall weeds next to the shoulder. One thing for sure: he would not be sleeping here tonight. Shivering, he stuck out his thumb as the next line of headlights approached.

A little after midnight Ian arrived in Regina. He had finally gotten a ride from a man in a pick-up truck. He squeezed into the cab, his wet gear crammed around his legs. It was great to get out of the cold wind. The driver chained smoked and said nothing. His radio was loud, tuned to some country station. He drove over the speed limit but on the long straight highway it made little difference. When they arrived in Regina, he suddenly stopped on a street by a strip mall and simply said, "This is it."

Ian thanked him and climbed out stiffly. The truck drove away. He had no idea where he was. He walked to a corner and looked at the street signs. He dug in his bag and pulled out the hostel brochure. It had gotten wet too. He carefully peeled the damp pages open. From the tiny map he could see that the hostel was downtown, but he wasn't sure how far away it was. He saw a bus stop. He went and sat on the bench. Maybe he could ask the bus driver for directions. But after a while he realized the buses had probably stopped for the night. He stood up, debating walking to the hostel, but even if he could find it, it would be the middle of the night: they might be full or have locked their doors.

Tired and hungry Ian crossed the street to a little strip mall. Most of the storefronts were dark. Only one place was open, called the Tasty Grill. He hesitated outside but the faint smell of hot grease made him ravenous. He decided to spend some more of his precious cash and eat.

As he opened the door a buzzer sounded. A thin man leaned over a newspaper by the cash. He looked up blankly as Ian entered. The space was long and narrow, a counter ran parallel to the grill. An older couple sat a one of the three small tables. They stared as Ian as he slumped past with his wet duffle bag and bedroll. He took a seat half way down the counter and pulled the menu from the rack. He was so hungry he could barely focus on the words. The cheapest thing was fries.

The thin man ambled over. He had very hairy arms.
"What are you having?"
"Just an order of fries." Ian said.
"That's it?" The man looked annoyed.
"Do they come with gravy?"
"That's extra."

"Ok," Ian was really hungry. "Fries with gravy. And a glass of water."

The man took a few steps, then turned.

"You got money, right?"

Ian reached in his pocket and laid some money on the table.

"Yeah. I got money."

The man scowled and walked back to the grill. He shook some frozen fries into a basket and plunged it into the hot grease. While they cooked Ian went to the bathroom. It was so small he could barely turn around to shut the door. He wanted to wash his face but the soap dispenser was empty, the nozzle caked with dried pink soap. He splashed some water on his face and stuck his head under the blow dryer but it was broken too. He wiped his face on his sleeve.

When he came out his fries were on the counter. There was a fork sitting on a single serviette. No water. He tried to get the man's attention but he never looked over. Ian leaned over the plate, shoveling the fries into his mouth. It didn't take long to finish them off. He used his finger to wipe up gravy from the edge of the plate.

All the time he ate, the couple at the table looked at him and whispered. They stood up to leave. At the cash they said something to the cook. He looked at Ian and made a comment. All three of them laughed.

Fuck you, Ian thought. He wondered if he would ever get a glass of water. He rested his elbow on the counter and leaned his head onto one hand. He started to drift off, raising his head with a start. The man had already picked up the plate and fork. He walked by and dropped the check.

"You gotta pay now. It's closing time."

"Can I get a glass of water?" The man ignored him and returned to the cash.

Ian counted his coins carefully. He paid the exact amount. Then, as an afterthought, he left a single penny for a tip.

Feeling full and warm he walked back to the intersection. Now what? It was going on two in the morning. Maybe, Ian thought, he should walk back to the highway and start hiking again. He had to do something. He couldn't sit here on a bench all night. So he loaded his gear and trudged along the street. He was still damp but here in the city, with no wind, it felt warm. The driver had come into town along this road but Ian had been half asleep and really had no idea of how far it was to the highway.

On a whim, Ian turned down a side street. It was lined with low wide bungalows, a very sixties look. He trudged along, the fries sitting heavy in his stomach. Occasionally a living room window glowed from a television. At one house there was someone standing in the kitchen window. It looked like they were washing dishes. Why were they up so late? Maybe they worked a late shift? The more Ian walked, passing house after house, the more he felt sad and lonely. Everyone had a home but him. Here he was sixteen, alone in a strange city, walking around in the dark. Back in Madanon, his friends were having a great summer, doing typical teenage things, kicking around with friends, on a date, seeing a movie or home watching TV with their families.

If he told them what he had been up to the last few days, they would be shocked. Instinctively, he knew he had crossed some line, that somehow his life would never be the same again.

Ian kept walking. He zigzagged along the residential streets, vaguely aware that he was headed in the direction of the highway. He wasn't sure he could stay awake all night hitchhiking but for now he kept putting one foot in front of another. He looked down a side street and saw that it dead-ended in a large city park. He decided to try and sleep there for a few hours. He walked into the park: a large open grassy area bordered with a few trees and a handful of benches. Across the park, there was a basketball court and, nestled by some hedges, a low brick building. Ian cut across the grass to the building. The street lamps cast a pale dream-like light on the wide empty space. As he got closer Ian smelled chlorine and saw a swimming pool behind a chain link fence. He circled the building. There were public washrooms but the doors were locked. He found a secluded area and peed against the wall.

Ian decided he would sleep there beside the building. He moved down, staying in the shadows and dropped his gear next to a row of well-trimmed hedges. He untied his blankets and shook them out. They were still a little damp but it was a warm night. Besides he had no choice. He upturned his duffle bag, dumping everything out, hoping to find something dry to wear. He felt around in the dark and touched something metal.

A can of beer! Before driving off with Julie that guy had given him two beers. He felt around and found the second can. He sat back on his blankets, leaned against the wall and opened one can. In the dark he felt the beer foam over his fingers, but he didn't care. He drank it quickly and tossed the empty under the hedge. He found a pair of dry socks, or at least drier than what he was wearing. He changed his socks and set his shoes aside to dry. He stuffed his damp clothes back into the duffle bag to make a pillow.

Ian opened the second beer, letting his mind wander to Julie again. He flip-flopped from sadness to anger and back again. He felt like crying but he could not. Maybe he was just too exhausted to care. He took a sip of the beer. It was quiet here in the park. In the distance he heard a dog bark. Further away, a siren. Someone rode by on a bicycle, wobbling and singing loudly. Ian stretched out on his blankets, leaning on his elbow. He took another drink. He dropped his head back on the duffle bag. Vancouver, he thought staring up into the dark, when he got to Vancouver things would be better.

Ian woke up briefly in the pre-dawn glow, shivering and covered with dew. He curled into a tight ball and tugged the thin blanket over his head. He woke again to a sniffing sound. He peeked from under the blanket and saw a large dog only a few feet from him, nosing around the hedges. A man stood nearby holding a paper coffee cup and smoking a cigarette. Blank faced, he stared at Ian. The dog walked a little closer to the wall, lifted its leg and pissed. The man flicked his butt into the grass and walked away. The dog followed him. Ian drifted off again.

The next time he woke, the sun was up. He tossed

and turned, trying to block the brightness with his arm. He heard a loud gas lawn mower and sat up. Far across the park a worker in brown coveralls was riding a big mower back and forth. Ian lay back. He dreaded another day of hiking. Then he heard a sharp popping sound, followed by a whisk-whisk-whisk. He sat up. The park had an automatic sprinkler system that was kicking in. Every few yards a nozzle popped up from the lawn, spraying water in wide circles. As he watched a metal sprinkler head appeared a few feet from him. Ian leapt up and dragged his stuff away just in time to avoid getting soaked. He stood there, blinking, befuddled. Two women sat nearby on a park bench with their toddlers. They looked at him suspiciously.

Well, that was that. He was up now and might as well hit the road. He made a tight roll of his blankets. He grabbed his things and rounded the corner, surprised and happy to find the men's bathroom unlocked. It was cool and dark and smelled of disinfectant. The floor was still damp from a recent mopping.

Ian peed then looked at his sunburnt face in the flickering fluorescent light. Still peeling. His nose was especially scabby. His cut was healing but still a little tender. He rubbed the stubble on his chin and leaned close to examine the little hairs on his upper lip. He had not shaved since leaving home, not that he had much facial hair. He picked up his hat, bent the brim and pulled it down over his eyes. He checked himself in the mirror. Not really a hippie but getting there. He jammed his canteen under the tap to fill it.

It took Ian almost an hour to find his way to the

highway. Between the greasy fries, the beer and a lack of sleep he felt like shit. As he reached the edge of town, houses gave way to industrial buildings. Buildings gave way to fields and, suddenly, there was the highway. He walked up the overpass to get to the westbound side. At the top of the bridge he looked east. Far off he could see a string of hikers near another ramp. Maybe that was where the hostel dropped people off. Good, he thought, I have this whole ramp to myself. But when he looked west he was disappointed to see a few hikers there too.

Ian climbed over the metal crash barrier and scrambled down an embankment. He stumbled, nearly tripping in the thick weeds. By the time he reached the bottom his shoes and pant legs were covered with burrs. He tried pulling them off but they left little patches of brown hooks on his jeans. Down the shoulder he saw two hikers, two guys standing together. He knew that he should walk past them to the end of the line, but he was tired, sweaty and hungover. Fuck it, he thought, and tossed down his gear. He took a drink from his canteen, then poured some water in his hand and splashed his face. A car whipped by so fast Ian barely got his thumb up.

Someone was shouting! He looked over his shoulder. One of the hikers down the road was shouting and waving at him. He couldn't make out the words but they sounded angry.

Ian turned to thumb at another car.

More shouting. He looked west again. A guy in a black hat was walking towards him. He walked very fast, his boots raising little clouds of dust. Ian saw he was dressed in jeans, a black t-shirt and a jean jacket. The hat came into focus: black, almost like a cowboy hat, but the wide brim was ironed flat. The guy started shouting again as he got closer. Ian's heart beat faster. Instinctively, his hand drifted down to the butt of his hunting knife under his sweater.

"Hey asshole!" The guy marched right up and shouted in Ian's face. "What the fuck are you doing cutting in line?" Ian could see the guy's flattened nose, big freckles, his angry eyes.

"Cutting in line? Fuck you," Ian snapped. "I have been here since yesterday."

"Yesterday?" The guy hesitated.

"Yeah, I got here last night and had to sleep in a fucking city park."

"Man, that's a drag." The guy took a step back. "Me and my bud just got here this morning from Winnipeg."

They both paused – *now what?*

"Yeah," Ian said. "I was in Winnipeg a couple of days ago." He nodded down the road. "Two guys? Getting rides must be brutal."

"It's the fucking shits. It's taken us a week to get here from Windsor." He nodded at Ian's stuff. "Hey man, is that water in your canteen? Can I bum a drink?"

Ian handed him the canteen. The guy was about the same height as Ian, but with a hard wiry look. His black hat was jammed over a mass of orange curls that poked out around his ears. Scraggly sideburns framed a thin freckled face with high cheek bones. The flattened nose, Ian realized, had been broken more than once.

"Thanks man." He wiped water from his chin and handed the canteen back. "My buddy and me we're going to Vancouver to visit my cousin Connie. She moved out west a few years ago."

"That's where I'm going," Ian said. "Vancouver. I'm going to try and find a job." He hesitated. "I'd love to work in a lumber camp."

"I guess you'll be heading up into the interior then?"

"Yeah," Ian said, "But I'm going to Vancouver first."

"Cool. I hear the home grown is dirt cheap in Van." He paused, then stuck out his hand. "Hey, my name's Wayne."

"Ian."

They shook hands. The normal straight hand shake. Wayne's grip was really strong. He pointed down the road. "That's my bud Tom from high school down there." He waved and the distant figure waved back. Wayne spit on the dirt. "He's a fucking idiot."

Ian thought that was a weird thing to say about a friend.

Wayne lit a smoke. "I like your hat."

"Thanks." Ian touched his fedora.

"What the fuck happened to your face? You look like you been dragged by a car."

Ian laughed. "Naw, just a really bad sunburn. I fell asleep on the shoulder of the road a couple of day ago."

A passing car slowed down and beeped its horn. The driver yelled at them.

"Faggots!"

They both turned and gave the guy the finger at exactly same time.

"Redneck assholes," Wayne said. "They're so brave in their big fucking cars."

Ian told him about the incident in at the Brandon hostel. He was surprised to hear himself bragging about throwing the bricks.

"Fuck that noise." Wayne said. "I wish I had been there." He slid his jean jacket back to reveal a big curved knife hanging under his arm in a dark leather sheath. "I won't take shit from no one."

Ian lifted his sweater a bit to show his hunting knife. He wanted Wayne know he was tough too.

"Righteous." Wayne nodded.

A few more cars zoomed by.

"You know," Ian said. "I think I will move on down past you. This corner a dead zone." He picked up his things.

Wayne walked fast. Ian had to double time to keep up. He noticed that Wayne wore cowboy boots with steel toes. The pointy caps flashed in the sunlight.

His buddy Tom stood next to two large backpacks balanced against each other. He was taller than Wayne but with sloped shoulders and a beer belly he seemed smaller. A few days scruffy beard could not hide his baby face. He wore jeans and a Rolling Stones T-shirt. There was a large stain down the front. It looked like mustard. He scowled at Ian.

"What's up?" He asked Wayne.

"This is Ian," Wayne said. "He's cool." Tom nodded. "He's headed to Vancouver too. He had to sleep in a fucking park last night."

'That's a drag." Tom said. He looked sleepy. "Hey, is that water?"

Ian handed him the canteen. Tom guzzled, water

leaking down his chin. He belched and handed it back to Ian. His face was sunburnt too.

"Look at your face, man." Wayne chuckled. "You gotta get a fucking hat."

"I know." Tom shrugged.

"Look at this guy's hat." He pointed at Ian. "He got a fucking sunburn so he got a fucking hat."

"Ok, ok, I'll get a hat." He sounded browbeaten.

Trying to shift attention away from Tom, Ian pointed at Wayne's head. "I like your hat."

"Yeah," Wayne said. He pulled the black hat off and scratched hard at his curly orange mop. "I took it off an asshole in Winnipeg. This dip shit on the street gave me some lip, so I gave him a beating and took his hat." He crushed it back on over his curls. "Kicked the shit out of that guy, eh, Tom?"

Tom nodded.

"I flattened the brim so it's like the hat Billy Jack wears." Wayne said.

"Billy Jack?" Ian said.

"You don't know Billy Jack? Oh man, you gotta see that movie." He excitedly explained the plot and how Billy Jack used karate to kick the shit out of red neck assholes. Wayne stepped back and spun, his steel-toed boot flashing close to Ian's face, making him flinch back. Wayne wobbled and had to do a two-step to keep from falling over. Ian could see this guy didn't really know karate.

A long line of cars passed. Ian realized he had not thumbed for a while.

"Well," he said. "I should get going. I think I'll walk

down past the next exit ramp."

"Hey." Wayne said, "Why don't we thumb together today?"

"Three guys?" Tom said, "Fuck. Three guys and we'll never get a ride."

"How about we take turns?" Wayne said. "Like one guy thumbs and the other two lay in the weeds there? Once some driver stops, then we all jump up."

Ian hesitated. Tom was right. No one would stop for three guys. And if they did like Wayne said and two guys hid, they'd be pissed off and drive away. Still it was nice to have someone to talk to after a couple of days by himself.

"Ok." Ian said. "I'll give it a try. We can always split up if this doesn't work." He set down his gear. "Let me thumb first."

Ian hitchhiked while Wayne and Tom sat in the wide shallow ditch beside the road. He used his friendly smile and big gestures, waving first when he saw a line of cars coming, then thumbing as they passed. The problem was Wayne. He couldn't sit still. Before long he was up, pacing around while Ian thumbed, which meant drivers saw two guys. Tom on the other hand, stretched out in the grass, put his head on his backpack and slept.

Finally, Ian said to Wayne, "Why don't you take a turn?" He went over and sat in the grass next to Tom. He was so hungry he felt dizzy.

Wayne scowled as he thumbed, keeping up a loud angry monologue as cars approached. "Come on you, dumb mother fuckers. Give us a ride." Once a car passed he turned and gave them the finger.

"Cunts." He shouted. "Fucking cunts."

Watching from the weeds, Ian thought, great, even I wouldn't stop for this guy.

When Tom took a turn he just stood there, slumped forward, looking sleepy, with his hands jammed in his jean pockets. He waited until the last minute, until the cars were right next to him, then he pulled one hand from his pocket and dangled his thumb by his side. Ian could see that was useless and soon volunteered to thumb again. He continued to force a smile as he hitched but he could see this idea of taking turns was really stupid. Any driver who slowed would obviously see there was more than one person.

For Wayne's next shift, he called to Ian "This is boring as shit. Keep me company."

Ian sat down on the shoulder, by the backpacks, hoping drivers would not see him right away. Tom went back to sleep in the weeds. Wayne paced and smoked and talked about his life back in Windsor: how his father got drunk and beat the kids; how his lame-ass teachers didn't know shit; how his girlfriend was really pretty and smart, but she had a reputation as a slut. Ian told Wayne about how he met Julie. He bragged about how cute she was and how easy it was to get rides when thumbing with her. To his surprise, he even told Wayne about how she took off with another guy after giving him a blow job.

"Chicks, man," Wayne spit on the blacktop. "First they break your balls, then they break your fucking heart."

This is weird, Ian thought, as he watched Wayne swear at passing cars. He was hanging out with a guy he would have avoided back in school, the kind of guy who beat people up after class. It was pure chance that they had met. He wasn't sure what to think of Wayne –he made Ian nervous- but still it was nice to hang out and have some company.

Traffic was steady but no one stopped. They roasted in the afternoon sun. Grasshoppers swarmed to the hot blacktop. When cars came, they whirred up in clouds, then landed again. Wayne amused himself by sneaking up and squashing them with his boots. When he got bored with that, he picked up some gravel from the shoulder and tossed stones at Tom's sleeping form.

"Come on you, fucker, wake up. Get up and do something, you fat lump." Finally, he bounced a stone off Tom's head. Tom sat up fast, snorting like he'd been having a bad dream. Wayne flicked another stone at him.

"Fuck off." Tom said.

"Fuck off." Wayne mocked. Tom rubbed his eyes and slapped his pockets until he found his smokes. He lit a cigarette, then he dug a t-shirt out of his backpack and tied it on his head like a turban. He laid back in the weeds, smoking and staring at the sky.

"This is fucked." Wayne said, tossing gravel at the grasshoppers. "We'll never get a ride. We should head into town, grab a beer and some food."

"Not me," Ian said. "I need to get to Calgary tonight."

"Ok." Wayne looked at his watch. "Let's give it another hour, then let's go get drunk."

Ian thumbed desperately, fighting waves of sadness and fatigue. He was stuck in the middle of nowhere and soon would be faced with the choice: go to town or stay out here hiking alone. If he went to town with Wayne and

Tom he'd spend more of his precious cash. At this rate he'd be broke before he reached the coast. On the other hand, if he stayed out here, he'd have nothing to eat and probably end up sleeping on the side of the road.

To his surprise, less than a half an hour later, two hippies, a man and a woman, in a VW van stopped to pick them up. Ian and Wayne grabbed their things and ran over to the van. Tom stood up and stumbled from the weeds. Two or three hikers, none of it seemed to matter to the hippies, they had already slid the side door open. The boys piled in, grinning and gushing thanks. The back of the van was crowded with a bed, a little table, a sink and cooler.

"Welcome aboard, fearless travelers." The driver shouted over his shoulder. He was naked from the waist up, very tanned, wearing a big necklace made of white and pink sea shells. The women in the passenger seat smiled at them over huge wire rimmed glasses.

"Where are you boys headed?"

When Wayne said Vancouver she launched into a speech about how cool Vancouver was. "BC home grown is the best," she said. "We still grab a pound anytime we get out there."

"We live in Calgary now." The man shouted over the roar of the engine. "It's the shits for dope."

"So ya got any pot with you?" Wayne asked.

The driver grinned and explained that they had smoked their last joint a few miles down the road. "But there's some cold beer in that cooler back there. Help yourself."

The boys scrambled for the cooler. Ian grabbed a

can and sat back on his duffle bag. He tipped the cold beer and drank half of it in one go. Wayne and Tom did the same. They looked at each other with big grins.

"Fucking, eh!" Wayne shouted. He slapped Ian on the shoulder. "You're a fucking lucky charm. I really didn't think three guys would ever get a ride."

"Beginner's luck," Ian said, but he was pleased with himself for insisting on hiking another hour. And it felt good to see Wayne happy, considering how pissed off he had been when they first met.

The driver saw a gas station-corner store combo and shouted. "I've got some wicked munchies." So he swung off the highway and ran inside. He came out with two big bags of chips. He handed one to the woman and tossed the other back to the boys. They tore it open and dove in. Wayne grabbed three more beers from the cooler. Ian leaned back. He was exhausted but ecstatic: beer, chips and a ride right to Calgary. Only a couple more days to Vancouver!

Soon Tom, a trail of broken chips down his dirty t-shirt, stretched out on the floor. A minute later he started to snore loudly. Wayne nudged him with his steel toed boot.

"You're snoring like a pig."

"Fuck off," Tom mumbled and rolled on his side.

For a moment Wayne looked as if he was going to kick Tom again, then he grinned at Ian. "What a slug. Oh well more beer for us." He grabbed another one from the cooler and crawled forward to kneel by the front seats. He started asking the couple about Vancouver, where to score dope and where to hang out. Ian leaned forward and asked about places to camp. The woman told him to check out Wreck Beach. She said he could camp there, lots of people did, although the cops came and hassled everyone once in a while.

"Plus," the driver added with wide smile, "it's a nude beach!"

"A nude beach!" Wayne repeated. He winked at Ian. "They have a fucking nude beach."

Ian smiled back. "That's great. I need a place to stay while I job hunt."

"Hey." Wayne said. "If you get stuck, you can always crash with me at my cousin Connie's place."

"Won't it be crowded with three of us?" Ian nodded at Tom.

"Connie is very cool." Wayne assured him. "She told me they have lots of space."

Ian leaned back against the backpacks and watched the western horizon in the fading light. He was hoping to see the Rocky Mountains before it got dark. Maybe he would crash with Wayne at his cousin's place, at least until he found a job. Once he was working he'd buy a tent and live rent free on a beach. That way he could save up enough money to buy a motorcycle. He thought it would be fun to ride back to Madanon in the fall and surprise his friends. He leaned his head back and drifted off.

When he opened his eyes it was dark and they were in Calgary. He sat up and peered out the window at the lights and people on the streets.

Wayne was still kneeling by the front seat, looking around excitedly.

"Hey." He called back to Ian. "They have been telling

me about the Calgary Tower. Let's grab something to eat, then go up and see the view."

"We should get to the hostel." Ian said. He didn't want to admit how little money he had left.

"Yeah, yeah, we'll get to the fucking hostel but let's see some of Calgary first. What do you say, Tom?" He nudged him with his boot. "You up for the tower?"

Tom sat up and rubbed his face. "Sure, but I'm up for some chow first."

The hippies stopped the VW at Centre Street. As the boys unloaded their gear, the driver pointed and said. "Straight down here until you reach 9th Avenue. You can't miss it. Remember: streets run north and south, avenues are east and west. Good luck in Vancouver."

"Thanks." Ian said. He felt great. In a couple of days, he'd be dipping his feet in the Pacific Ocean.

Wayne and Tom hoisted their backpacks, sleeping bags sticking up behind their heads. Ian slung his gear and they headed off down the street which seemed crowded after standing on the side of the road for a few days.

"Hey girls," Wayne yelled across to two young women. "Want to have a drink with three lonely guys?"

The women laughed but kept walking.

"Stuck up bitches." Wayne spun around. "Ok, let's find some place to eat and have a beer."

He picked a small dark looking place. A few customers sat at the counter watching a baseball game on a small TV behind the bar. One of them swiveled his stool to watch them cross the room with their gear. They took a booth at the back. The waitress took her time, wiping down the counter before she sauntered towards them. Ian was nervous. What if she asked for ID? He wasn't sure how old Wayne and Tom were. They looked older, so Ian assumed they were legal age. It would be really embarrassing to get kicked out of the bar now.

But when she got to the table all the waitress said was, "What can I get you guys?"

"Beer," Wayne said. "And something to eat."

"You want a pitcher of draft? It's cheaper than buying glasses."

"Sure," Wayne said. "And some food."

She walked away and returned shortly with a pitcher, three glasses and menus.

Ian quickly scanned the prices. Maybe he would just have fries. But he was really hungry. He had not eaten a real meal since the hostel in Brandon, so when the others ordered burger and fries, he did too.

By the time the burgers came, they had finished most of the pitcher. Wayne poured the last of it into his own glass.

"What do you say, boys? Another round?"

"Aren't we going to the hostel?" Ian asked.

"Fuck the hostel." Wayne said. "I want to go up this fucking tower."

Ian drowned his fries in ketchup. The burger really hit the spot. They drank the second pitcher more slowly. Once again Wayne sang the praises of his cousin.

"When I was a kid Connie was like a big sister to me." He said. "She moved out west about ten years ago."

"Are you going to work in Vancouver?" Ian asked.

"Don't have a fucking clue." Wayne said. "I just

wanted to take a break from Windsor. Maybe after Van, I'll head down to California and take up surfing."

"Me too." Tom said. "I hear it's really nice down around San Francisco."

Wayne laughed. "Yeah, you'll blend right in with the flower people, you fat fuck." Tom laughed but Ian noticed that he winced a little whenever Wayne rode him. The more they talked the more Ian realized that Tom had not given much thought to hitching around. It sounded like Wayne had talked him into it.

When the waitress came back to check about another jug, Ian looked at his watch. "Ok, it's after ten. We'd better get to the tower before they close."

"What are you, my mother?" Wayne said, but he agreed they should get going. Once Ian paid for the burger and his share of the beer, he had less than five dollars left. He'd get to BC broke, but at least now he had a place to crash.

Outside they walked three abreast, drunkenly bumping shoulders. The VW driver was right – the tower was easy to find. They stood at the bottom tilting their heads up to look at the bright orb at the top.

"Look at that sucker," Wayne said. "I can't wait to see the view from up there." He elbowed Ian and cackled. "I'm gonna take a piss off the top."

They entered the double glass doors, but soon as they started across the lobby with their backpacks and gear, Ian saw the woman behind the ticket counter frown at them. A security guard sat on a small chair by the elevator, he turned his head to watch them. At the counter, Ian looked over the fees and tugged on Wayne's arm.

"Hey, I'm really low on cash. I'm just going to wait down here."

"No way, man." Wayne said. "You gotta go up with us." He poked Ian in the chest. "Look, you can crash at Connie's. She's cool. Don't sweat it."

Wayne pulled out his wallet but before he could pay the fee the security guard strolled over. A tall man with close cropped salt and pepper hair, he gave them a polite smile.

"Sorry, gentlemen, you can't take those bags up with you."

"What do you mean?" Wayne said.

"No bags are allowed up to the lookout."

"What kind of bullshit is this?" Wayne said.

The guard stepped closer to Wayne. "Watch your mouth, young man."

Ian tried to intercede. "Can we leave our stuff here at the desk? We're just passing through Calgary and wanted -"

"No. There is no storage here."

"But can't we leave them here just for a few minutes?"

"Are you deaf? You can't store bags here and you can't take them up." He folded his arms as if to say, this conversation is over.

"Fuck it." Tom said. "Let's split." He started back across the lobby.

Wayne slapped a twenty on the counter. "Give me three tickets, please."

The woman did not pick up his money. She looked

nervously the guard.

"I'm paying for three people." Wayne said.

"You can't go up." The guard repeated.

"Why are you being such as asshole?"

The guard's face turned pink. "Would you like me to call the police?"

"Why? You too much of a pussy to fight me yourself?"

Ian grabbed the money off the counter and yanked on Wayne's arm.

"Come on, Wayne, let's go." Wayne shook him off.

The elevator doors opened. A group of people started to exit but hesitated when they heard the shouting.

"Come on, asshole." Wayne yelled at the guard. "You're such a tough guy in your little toy soldier outfit." The guard was furious but controlled himself.

Ian grabbed Wayne again with both hands and literally dragged him across the lobby, Wayne kept yelling at the guard.

"Come on, you up-tight cocksucker. All we wanted to do was see your shitty-ass tower."

The further they got from the desk, the louder Wayne became. Tom was already by the exit, holding the door open.

Outside, Wayne turned to kick the door. Ian yanked him off balance. Wayne's boot narrowly missed the glass.

"Fuck it!" Wayne screamed and stomped off down the street. Ian looked at Tom, who shrugged as if to say, "welcome to life with Wayne". They had to jog to catch up with him. It was a couple of blocks before Wayne slowed down. Finally, he tossed his backpack down and took out his smokes. He and Tom smoked while Ian pulled out his little hostel brochure and tried to figure out where they were. He asked a passerby and found out the hostel was only about a block away.

"Come on," Ian said. "Let's find the hostel and get some sleep." He started walking and the other two followed him. But when they got to hostel the doors were locked. A sign was taped on the inside of the glass: No one admitted after 11.

Wayne banged on the door. No one appeared. He banged some more.

"Fuck," he screamed. "What the fuck is wrong with this town?"

A guy passing on the other side of the street paused to look at them.

"What the fuck are you looking at, shithead?" Wayne shouted at him. The guy mumbled something but walked away quickly. "You'd better run away, asshole." Wayne yelled. "I'll kick your fucking head in."

"Come on." Ian said. "I slept in a park last night. Maybe there's a city park around here somewhere."

"Yeah," Tom said picking up his backpack. "let's find somewhere to crash."

They trudged along in silence. Wayne said nothing. Ian was bone tired, wishing he had headed to the hostel earlier. He hated the idea of sleeping in a park again. What if the police came and they got arrested?

Suddenly Wayne stopped and threw his hand up. "Hear that?"

"What?" Tom said.

"Listen."

Ian heard their breathing, then in the distance, a grinding mechanical sound followed by a big hollow metallic crash.

"What is it?" he asked.

"Train yards." Wayne said. "I live near one in Windsor. You know, where they switch engines and shit. Come on, let's find it." He walked in the direction of the noise. He turned with a huge grin and shouted over his shoulder. "This is great. This is great. We can jump a train right to Vancouver!"

Ian looked at Tom, who shrugged again: life with Wayne. They could barely keep up with Wayne who was now as excited as a little kid.

A few blocks later the boys came to a tall chain link fence. On the other side was a wide field of gravel covered with train tracks. Glaring white lights on high poles made a stark black and white landscape. As they looked through the fence, a massive diesel engine appeared pushing four long box cars ahead of it. The rumbling engine and clanging bell drowned out all other city noises. The earth under Ian's feet vibrated. It disappeared out of sight behind a row of tank cars on their left. A second later they heard a massive crashing sound. With a deep growl, the engine, minus the box cars, reversed back past them.

"See?" Wayne grinned. "They move cars around until they have a train full, then off it goes to BC." He slapped Ian and Tom on the shoulders. "We can grab a train and be in Vancouver tomorrow."

"But how do we get in?" Ian asked. Wayne dropped his pack and stepped back a few paces. He took a run and jumped on the fence, but only landed about half way to the top. He tried to claw his way up, but as hard as he scrambled he could not get a grip in the wire links with his boots. He dropped back to the ground, swearing. He shook his fingers. Ian was relieved. There was no way he could climb over that fence. He doubted Tom could either.

"Now what?"

"Where there's a fence, there's always a hole in the fence." Wayne marched long the fence, dragging his backpack by his side. Ian and Tom followed. Eventually the fence ran behind an old factory. Wayne led them into the narrow space between the fence and the brick wall. It was filled with bushes and small scraggly trees. Wayne pushed on. Random branches snapped back and hit Ian in the face. He heard Tom behind him cursing under his breath as they stumbled along in the dark.

"There," Wayne shouted. "I told you there'd be a fucking hole and here it is". Someone else had managed to break the wire fence free from a post. A corner was bent up in a weird curve. Wayne yanked the end of the broken fence a few times but it was bent as far as it would go. He dropped to his hands and knees and crawled through the opening.

"Give me the bags." He wiggled their gear through the opening. Ian and Tom dropped to the ground and crawled after him. By the time Ian stood up and slapped the dirt off his jeans, Wayne was standing out in the open looking up and down the tracks. He spread his arms and shouted, "Isn't this great?"

This is crazy, Ian thought. Am I really going to jump a freight train? Under the glaring white arc light, he felt exposed. He was sure they would be spotted and arrested. But there was no time to think. They heard a train coming.

"Come on." Wayne shouted and they ran after him to a small graffiti-covered shed. They ducked behind it just as the engine entered the open yard, bell clanging. It was just the engine, no train.

"So fucking cool!" Wayne shouted over the noise. He stepped out of the shadows to watch the engine pass.

"Have you ever jumped a train before?" Ian asked.

"Sure." Wayne said. "Back in Windsor, just for fun." But Ian had the feeling he was bullshitting.

Meantime Tom lit a cigarette. He plunked down on his backpack and shook his head. "I don't know, man, it looks pretty dangerous."

Ian was glad Tom had said what he was thinking.

"Aw, come on, don't be a pussy." Wayne's big grin was visible in the shadows. "Just think one ride all the way to Vancouver. Freight trains really roll. We'll be in Vancouver by tomorrow night at the latest."

"How will we know which train to get on?" Ian asked.

"All we gotta do it find one going west." Wayne dashed out into the open and looked at the sky. He ran back. "The fucking tower is there," he gestured, "so this way is west." He pointed. "All we have to do it watch for a big long fucker that is headed that way. One ride all the way to Vancouver."

Ian had to admit it sounded pretty good. He was tired of hitchhiking, of not knowing where he would sleep. He longed to just get there, to find a job and make some money. Besides, did he really have a choice? They were already in a freight yard waiting for a train. Wayne said they should be ready to run because the train might not even stop completely or only stop for a minute or two. He crushed his big black hat into his back pack. Ian stuffed his fedora into his duffle bag. Tom sat on his pack, still looking uncertain. Wayne and Ian stood in the shadow of the shed watching the cars being shunted back and forth. They heard a loud rumble coming closer. Wayne grabbed his backpack and Tom stood up, but the train was headed east. It slowed to a creep.

"See?" Wayne said. "When they slow down, bam, we jump on board."

Ian nodded but wondered if he could really jump a train, even one going that slow.

Occasionally workmen, in coveralls and bright orange safety vests, jumped down from the train cars to fiddle with switches or to unfasten a box car. When this happened the boys huddled behind the shed. Ian peeked around the corner. One man flipped a large wrench while watching another work. Suddenly the man with the wrench turned and walked towards the shed. Ian shrank back against the wall. Had he spotted them? He saw Wayne's hand drift down towards his knife. He held his breath.

But the rail worker walked right past them, unzipped and took a long pee just a few feet from them. He finished, walked back to the engine, climbed on and it went back down the tracks.

"Holy fuck," Wayne said, "That was close."

"Yeah," Ian said. "He could have pissed right on us."

The boys giggled hysterically and had to cover their mouths.

Two more long trains passed through the rail yard going east. One nearly came to a stop, then sped up again. Wayne could not stand still. In between the passing trains and engines, he ventured further and further out into the yard, standing beside the tracks, peering in both directions. Tom sat on his backpack, slumped against the shed wall, half asleep. Ian paced back and forth behind the building, fighting with his fatigue. He wondered if a westbound train would ever come by. They would probably wait all night and still end up sleeping in a park. He envied Tom who seemed to be able to sleep anywhere. Ian was afraid to nap; he wanted to be alert when a train came.

Wayne ran towards them. "Hey. Hey. Grab your shit, here comes a train. And it's moving real slow." Tom and Wayne shouldered their packs. Ian frantically slung his canteen and bedroll over his shoulders and hugged his duffle bag to his chest. They stayed in the shadow of the shed until the engine passed by. Wayne was right –the train was barely moving.

"Come on." Wayne shouted. They ran across the open gravel. Ian felt clumsy running with his duffle bag in his arms, his canteen smashing his hip. They had to cross two sets of tracks to reach the train. Ian stubbed his toe on a rail and stumbled.

Shit! He thought. *Be careful.*

By the time they reached the train it was already speeding up, far too fast to jump on board. They stood next to it, enveloped in the hammering noise of steel on steel. The caboose shot past and the noise dropped off. Tom was still panting from the run.

"Fuck." Wayne horked up and spit. Ian was relieved as they trudged back to their hiding place.

Over the next hour only two more westbound trains came. Both times they grabbed their gear and ran out to the tracks. Both times the trains were going too fast.

"This is stupid." Tom said. "The trains are too fast here."

"Aw, quit your whining." Wayne said. "There'll be a slow train. We'll get a ride all the way to Van." But Ian thought even Wayne sounded tired and uncertain.

Wayne went back out to the tracks to watch. Tom lay on his side now, hugging his backpack, his thick arm over his face. Ian sat on his duffle bag, leaning against the corrugated metal wall of the shed. He kept nodded off, jerking awake each time an engine passed or box cars crashed together.

Finally, he stood up, stiff and sore. The eastern sky looked a shade lighter. He saw the silhouettes of buildings where it had only been blackness before. Good, he thought. When the sun came up they would be too exposed. Wayne would have to give up. They could go get breakfast somewhere, drink lots of coffee and head for the highway. Three guys thumbing together would be a nightmare, but now that he was broke Ian figured he'd better stick with Wayne and take up the offer to crash at his cousin's place.

He poured some water in his palm and splashed it on his face. He stepped out and saw Wayne, a hundred yards east of the shed, leaning against a signal box. Ian stretched his back. He looked east. It would not be long until sunrise.

Wayne started waving his arms. He ran towards Ian shouting, "Here it comes. Here comes another big one and it's moving real fucking slow." He slapped Ian on the shoulders. "Come on, man, this is it. This is the one." He kicked Tom in the leg. "Come on, you fucking lump. Our train is coming."

Tom sat up, and stared at them, blinking. He rubbed his eyes with his fists, then stood up and lurched into his back pack. As soon as the engine passed, they ran into the open. Ian's heart raced. Any second he expected someone to shout, for workers to chase them, for them to get arrested. They crossed the open rail bed, then hopped over four sets of tracks to reach the train. Ian lifted his feet high as he stepped over each rail. They stopped next to the train. It was moving very slowly but loudly, tires scraping and squealing on the rails. It was mostly box cars; many empty, their doors open. Wayne started to walk beside one of the open box cars. Almost imperceptibly the train sped up. Wayne started to jog. Ian and Tom trotted behind him, single file. Ian glanced over his shoulder, saw Tom's sweaty face, his mouth hanging open. When he turned his head back, there was a gap between himself and Wayne. He ran faster to catch up.

"This one!" Wayne screamed. He pointed at an open box car. In one movement he swung his backpack off and hurled it into the open door. Ian ran faster, duffle bag clutched to his chest, terrified he would trip and fall under the train. Wayne reached up and grabbed the rusty iron handle by the door. In one leap he swung up and into the box car. Immediately, he turned and leaned out the open door, arm extended to Ian. The train had picked up speed.

"Come on." Wayne shouted waving his open hand. "Come on."

Ian pushed his duffle bag at Wayne who tossed it behind him. He reached for the same handle Wayne had used. It was inches from his hand. Wayne shouted something but he could not hear him over the roar of the train and blood pounding in his temples. His fingers snagged the handle. He grabbed it tight and jumped, but he did not get high enough. His hip slammed into the bottom edge of the open door. For a second he was hanging by one arm, his feet airborne over the flickering wooden ties. Then Wayne's fingers locked on to his wrist. Lunging backwards, he yanked Ian into the box car. Ian landed hard on his side, then scrambled around on his hands and knees to help with Tom. Terrified, he leaned out to see past Wayne's shoulder.

Wayne held the edge of the door, other arm extended, yelling at Tom.

"Run, you fat fuck, run."

Tom's face was red, contorted, his arms pumped furiously, but he could not quite catch up with the open door. Wayne leaned even further out. Instinctively, Ian grabbed his legs, afraid Wayne would fall.

Then Tom tripped and fell hard on the cinder bed. He scrambled to his feet but he was already more than a box car length behind them.

"Run." Wayne shouted.

Tom doubled over, hands on his knees. He looked

up for a second, waved one hand vaguely, like someone shooing a fly. Ian saw a flash of Tom's face, mouth open, blood on his chin.

"See you in Van." Wayne screamed. But Tom was already a stick figure disappearing in the distance. The train really rocketed now, lurching left and right, loud and hard.

Ian scrabbled back from the open door and lay flat on the dirty wood floor. He was still breathing hard, his heart racing.

I did it. I jumped a freight train.

He sat up to look at the landscape framed by the open door. Shortly, they cleared the city and crossed long stretches of pasture land. The morning sun crested the eastern horizon sending a soft golden light across the fields.

Wayne stood up and grabbed the edge of the door. He leaned far out into space.

"Fuck you, cow town!" He shouted and gave the finger to the Calgary skyline. Then he sat down with his legs dangling over the side. He turned and shouted something but Ian couldn't make out what he said. Ian moved closer but could not bring himself to sit on the edge like Wayne. He sat cross-legged near the door, holding the frame with one hand, watching fields and fences and telephone poles whip by. Wayne turned and gave him a big toothy grin.

Vancouver, Ian thought, *Vancouver.*

A few minutes later the train started to slow down. Wayne leaned out to look forward. Eventually the train was creeping along, as slow as when they first started to walk beside it. Finally, they came to a full stop; the box car lurched hard, tossing Wayne into Ian. They could hear the engine somewhere up ahead snorting like a large animal.

"What the fuck?" Wayne stood up and leaned out the door. "Maybe we're waiting for another train to pass." Ian stood up and cautiously poked his head out; all he could see was two strands of a low wire fence separating them from a wide field.

The train jerked again and they started to move backwards. After a hundred yards, they slammed to a stop. They heard some banging. The engine horn sounded twice. They heard it rumble and move away. Then silence.

"Fuck. Fuck. Fuck. We've been dumped on a siding." Wayne said. He tossed his pack to the ground and jumped down. Ian clambered down awkwardly, pulling his gear after him. They rounded the end of the box cars and ran right into a burly man in a yellow safety vest and a hard hat. He stopped and placed his hands on his hips.

"You boys lost?" he said.

"We were on this train." Wayne said.

"Well, it's not going anywhere soon." The man shrugged and continued on his way.

"Hey," Wayne yelled after him. "Where are we?"

"Middle of nowhere," The man called over his shoulder and laughed. He continued down the rails.

"Real fucking funny." Wayne called after him.

"Well," Ian said. "At least he didn't arrest us."

They walked the length of the train, about twenty empty box cars had been sided. They saw the man in the hard hat again with another man. The men fiddled with a signal box, glanced at the boys, then climbed into a yellow pick-up truck and drove down the cinder bed towards Calgary. It was quiet now except for the sound of birds somewhere in the fields.

"What do we do now?" Ian asked.

"Fuck it." Wayne said. "We'll just have to jump another train."

Ian's heart sank. He didn't want to jump another train. But looking around he realized he really had no choice. He couldn't see any roads nearby, let alone the highway.

Two tracks ran parallel to the siding. Wayne walked over to a big pile of old railroad ties, tossed his pack down, sat and lit a smoke. Ian trailed after him and sat down. He was filled with dread. The thought of jumping another train terrified him even more than before. He flashed on the image of Tom tripping. If he had fallen sideways, even a bit to the left, he would have gone under that train. Ian replayed the moment when he had jumped but didn't make the box car door. He could have died. If only he had kept hiking by himself, he might be in Vancouver by now, not sitting in the middle of nowhere trying to jump a train.

They sat and waited. The sun rose. It was very hot. Wayne grew quiet and sullen. He amused himself by tossing his big hunting knife into the dirt between his cowboy boots. Ian struggled to stay awake. A couple of large horse flies circled his head, trying to bite his neck and ears.

After an hour they heard a train coming from the west. They sat on the ties watching as it approached. It seemed far away, then suddenly it was here, roaring past them. Diesel fumes and dust buffeted Ian's face. He shielded his eyes with his forearm.

About an hour later they heard another train, this one coming from the east. They made no effort to hide. The train slowed down. Wayne stood up, one hand on his backpack. Ian stood up too. The train slowed more, then rattled to a stop.

"Let's go." Wayne grabbed his pack and ran over to the train. Ian scrambled to keep up. It was a very long train. They could hear the engine idling far down the track.

"We gotta find a boxcar." Wayne led the way past some huge black tank cars. They came to a long row of boxcars. As far as they could see, all the doors were shut.

"Fuck!" Wayne stopped and yanked on a door handle, but it was latched. A strip of dull white metal stamped with numbers and letters was wrapped around the hasp mechanism. They heard diesel engine rev louder. Suddenly the train lurched a few feet forward. Wayne followed the car. When it stopped again, he pulled out his knife and jammed the blade into the metal strip. He turned it hard, back and forth, twisting the metal band until it snapped. Ian kept looking around, worried some rail worker would see them.

"Alright." Wayne smiled at Ian as he broke the lock. He grabbed the handle with both hands and dragged the heavy door open. A bulging wall of thick cardboard loomed above them. At the bottom the cardboard was nailed to the wooden floor. A half dozen black metal bands ran horizontally across the cardboard, holding it in place.

"What the fuck?" Wayne slapped the bulging cardboard with his hand. He danced back from the train.

"Look," he pointed. "There's space at the top." Ian stepped back. He was right. The cardboard wall ended about three feet short of the top of the car.

"We can climb up there." Wayne said.

"How?" Ian shouted. "How can we get up there?"

Wayne pulled out his knife again. He reached above his head and stabbed the cardboard. He jabbed the knife in the same spot several times, making a fist sized hole. Immediately grain started to bled out, forming a puddle on the ground by their feet.

"Wheat." Wayne said. "It's full of fucking wheat. Come on. Boost me up. Cup your hands."

Ian laced his fingers together. Standing on Ian's hands, using the handle on the boxcar door to steady himself, Wayne stabbed another hole with his knife, this time just above one of the metal bands. Ian wobbled under the weight of Wayne and his backpack.

"Hold me steady." Wayne shouted.

"You're too fucking heavy."

Wayne held the knife with his teeth and used his free hand to punch at the hole he had started. He grabbed at the cardboard, then looked down and kicked the toe of his pointy boot into the first hole. Suddenly he was dangling on the cardboard wall by one hand and one toe. He snatched the knife from his mouth and chopped another hole further up. Grain poured down into his face. Wayne turned his head, spitting and swearing, but then he clenched the knife in his teeth again and dragged himself up another level.

The train lurched. Wayne lost his toe hold and nearly fell. He swore and kicked around until his boot found the hole again. The train began to creep forward very slowly, the huge wheels squealing. Ian walked beside the boxcar, dragging his duffle bag, watching Wayne stab more holes as he scaled the cardboard wall. Grunting and swearing he pulled himself over the top, disappearing from sight: head and chest, then his waist and legs. For a second, only his pointy cowboy boots stuck out.

Wayne's face, covered in wheat dust, appeared high above Ian.

"Come on, climb up."

"I can't."

"Sure you can, you fucker."

It was climb or be left behind. Ian slung the duffle bag strap over his neck. He grabbed the door handle with both hands and half leapt, half pulled himself up. He felt like he was back in gym class, trying to climb the big knotted rope, something he never did well. His feet left the ground and he twisted around in a panic. He had to get up high enough to reach the holes Wayne had carved. He got one toe on the edge of the doorway and reached way up. He jammed his fingers into one of the holes. Wheat leaked around his grip. He had to let go of the iron rung now. He strained and pulled himself up. He poked around and got his shoe into another hole. He reached up, feeling blindly for another grip.

"To the left, left." Wayne shouted. "No, no, to your right."

Ian clawed about and snagged another hole. The metal band cut into his fingers. The train bumped hard and started to pick up speed. Ian looked down and saw the ends of ties flickering below him. If he fell now it would be bad. He got a toe into another higher hole and boosted himself up. The train lurched side to side. He started to lose his grip.

"Fuck!" Ian screamed. It was climb or die. He dragged himself up one more level, clinging to the cardboard like a fly. He reached up, blindly feeling for another grip when he felt Wayne clamp his wrist in both his hands.

"Come on, buddy." Wayne shouted. "I got you."

Ian let go his other hand and clawed frantically at the top of the cardboard wall. He felt his toes slip out of the holes. He snagged the top edge of the cardboard. His fingers hurt. He had no strength left to climb. If he fell now he would die. But Wayne still had an iron grip on his wrist. Kicking and scrabbling, Wayne leaned back and dragged Ian over the cardboard edge. Face down in the wheat, Ian wiggled forward until his legs were in, then rolled over. His heart was pounding. He laughed hysterically.

"We did it!" Wayne shouted. "We did it!" He stood up and promptly banged his head on the roof of the car. "Fuck." He grabbed the top of his head with one hand and fell back down on the wheat, laughing. He leaned over and high-fived Ian.

"Vancouver, here we come." He shouted.

The train rolled really fast now, rocking and rattling in a steady rhythm. The boys sat by the door and watched the world go by. Wayne dangling his legs over the edge of the cardboard wall, the wind rippling his shaggy red hair.

Afraid to get too close to the edge, Ian used his hands to scoop out a shallow hole in the wheat. He pushed more grain up to make a backrest, then wiggled comfortably into his new bucket seat. Wayne did the same. He settled back and lit a smoke.

"This is the life, eh?" He shouted over the roar. "All the way to Vancouver on a train. We're fucking kings."

Ian grinned and nodded. Exhausted, dirty, and extremely hungry, but finally: Vancouver. He could not wait to get there and find a job. He closed his eyes and pictured a long white sand beach. He immediately fell asleep.

Ian raised his head. The sounds had changed. The train was slowing down. They both sat up. Wayne rubbed his face and stuck his head out the door.

"Can't see anything."

"Maybe we're coming into another town."

The train continued to slow, then with some screeching and a final lurch it came to a stop.

"Shit, shit, shit." Wayne shouted. "Why did we stop?"

Ian said nothing. He knew one thing: if they got dumped again, he would not jump another train. He'd rather walk to Vancouver than hang on the side of a box car again. Wayne knelt by the door and leaned out. He shouted over his shoulder.

"I don't see anything -"

With a horrendous roar another train blasted past on the next track. It was so close that Wayne instinctively jerked his head back. Light and dark flickered over them as train cars flipped past. Wheat dust swirled around them. Their boxcar shook from the pounding weight of the other train.

As suddenly as it had appeared, it was gone.

"Holy fuck." Wayne grinned. "Good thing I didn't climb down just now."

Their train grumbled back to life and they started west again. Now they knew: sometimes the train would pull over to let another train pass.

They settled back into their bucket seats.

"Man, I'm starving." Wayne shouted. "You got anything to eat?"

"No," Ian replied. "I have some water." He waved his canteen.

"I wonder if we can eat this shit?" Wayne held up a fist full of wheat. He stuck out his tongue and licked a few grains into his mouth. Ian did the same. It was like a mouth full of tiny pebbles. He worked up some spit and tried to chew. It was still too hard. He took a sip from his canteen and let the wheat float in his mouth. It got a little softer but was still too hard to eat. Plus it tasted like dirt. They both leaned forward and spit out the door. Wayne took slug of water from the canteen, gargled loudly and spit that out too.

"When we get to Vancouver, I'm going to have a steak dinner."

"Me too!" Ian smiled and nodded.

"Hey," he called over to Wayne. "What do you think happened to Tom? I mean after he fell. He looked like he was bleeding."

"Aw, who gives a fuck? He was a loser."

"Seriously, do you think he'll meet up with us in Vancouver?"

Wayne scowled. "Knowing that pussy, he's probably called his parents to pay his way home." He tossed a handful of wheat out the door. It blew away immediately. "Probably back home by now crying to his mother. I should have known it was a mistake to ask him to head out west."

"So why did you?"

"Aw." Wayne said. "I split in kind of a hurry. My dad and I got into it, a big fucking fight. He tried to punch me and I kicked his ass." Wayne smirked. "Wasn't hard since he was piss-drunk. But then my mom gave me grief, so I thought fuck it I'm going to go visit Connie." Wayne tossed more grain out the door. "I just happened to run into Tom that night and talked him into splitting. To be honest, I hardly know the guy, except to smoke a joint out back of the school."

Wayne turned to look at Ian and grinned.

"It's great to kick around with you. You're way cooler than Tom."

Ian smiled. No one had ever called him cool before.

Wayne broke into a big guffaw.

"What?" Ian said.

"I was just thinking it's a good thing I didn't kick your ass back there on the highway."

Ian grinned and nodded. "Yeah, thanks."

Now that he was safe on a train, Vancouver bound, Ian was also glad he had met Wayne. Sure, it was a little crazy, traveling with a guy that he would have avoided back home. Wayne scared him, but Ian figured his tough guy act was just that, mostly an act. And Wayne had just saved his life. Maybe twice. Of course, if not for Wayne, he would have never jumped a train. Ian laid back on the wheat. None of that mattered now. Tonight they'd be in Vancouver. All last year, day dreaming about leaving home, he had wanted an adventure. He was sure getting one now.

The train climbed continuously, a long slow grade into the Rockies. Ian stared at the mountains. They seemed close, but they were so big that it was impossible to figure out how far away they really were. The day dragged on. They both drifted in and out of sleep. There was nothing else to do. Occasionally, they stopped on a siding to let another train roar by. Sometimes they slowed down to pass through a small town. At some crossings they heard a bell clanging and saw cars lined up, waiting for the train to pass. Ian's instinct was to duck back, but Wayne leaned out the door and waved at people in their cars. The startled looks on people's faces made them both laugh.

Though it was sunny outside, the inside of the box car was dark and cool. Ian untied his blankets and spread one over his legs. He tossed the other blanket to Wayne who draped it around his shoulders like cape.

The next time Ian woke the Rockies towered all around them. Massive formations, some topped with snow; some black with dense growths of pine trees; some had tall cliffs, jagged and scarred, at the bottoms there were massive skirts of fallen stone. Occasionally Ian saw boulders the size of houses. He looked over at Wayne, who grinned and gave him a thumbs up. Now that the terror of jumping a train was past, Ian had to admit the ride was amazing!

Ian woke up mid-afternoon and noticed the train sounded different. They were still moving but something was odd. He crawled over and nudged Wayne.

"What?" Wayne sat up. "What's up?"

"Listen," Ian said, "why does it sound so different?"

Wayne crouched on his knees and stuck his head out the door.

"Holy fuck." He shouted. "Come see this."

Ian crawled to the edge of the cardboard, grabbed the door frame and leaned out. Mountain ranges and blue sky, then he looked down and felt his gut twist - they were floating in space! It took him a second to grasp what he was seeing. He looked back down the length of the train and saw they were crossing over a deep river bed on a long curved trestle bridge. The train was wider than the tracks so looking down there was nothing but a sheer drop. He felt dizzy and sat back down. Meantime Wayne was shouting yee-ha and tossing big double handfuls of wheat out the door, leaning out to watch the clouds of grain drift down into the valley. He was so excited that Ian worried he would tumble out. He shook his head –one thing for sure, the guy was fearless.

By late afternoon they were bored and very hungry. The train had not sidetracked for a while but with the steep mountain grades they were moving much slower. They had no idea where they were but Wayne continued to argue that they would make Vancouver by night time.

"Can't wait to see my cousin Connie. You'll like her. She's been out west for a few years. She's shacked up with her guy."

"You sure they won't mind me staying there?"

"Naw, don't sweat it. They knew I was thumbing out west with a buddy."

Wayne leaned forward to spit out the door. He quickly rose to his knees and pointed. "Hey! Come look at this!"

Recalling the bridge, Ian cautiously poked his head out. Looking forward he saw that the tracks curved along the side of the mountain. Most of the train was ahead of them. His eyes continued along the track past the engine. Then he saw what Wayne was pointing at.

"A tunnel!" Ian shouted

"A fucking tunnel." Wayne replied.

As they clung to the doorway, they saw the big double engines disappear into the tunnel, then car after car being swallowed, like a worm being sucked into a giant's mouth. As their car neared the hole, Ian scrambled back from the open door, his heart pounding.

Suddenly it was black. Pitch black. Ian could not see the door, Wayne, the wheat, even his own hand when he waved it right front of his face. Inside the narrow walls the screech of the train wheels was deafening. Ian shouted at Wayne but his words were lost in the roar. Wayne struck a match, cupped it with his hands and tried to look out the door. For a split second they saw a craggy rough rock wall, very close. Then the wind snuffed the match. Wayne light another one, but as soon as it sparked, it blew out. The boxcar began to fill with diesel fumes. Ian panicked. How long was this tunnel? Would they run out of air? What if the train stopped? They'd suffocate from the fumes.

In the dark, Wayne's hands clutched at Ian's

shoulder. He leaned his mouth close to Ian's ear and screamed.

"Holy fuck! It's a long tunnel." Even Wayne sounded nervous. They felt the train shudder and shake. It slowed down. Ian's breathing was short and hard. He felt sweat under his arms. *We're inside a mountain, right inside a mountain.* The air grew cold and damp. The fumes thickened. Don't stop here, Ian thought, please don't stop.

Then they burst into the open. Sunlight flooded the boxcar. They blinked and looked out at the landscape. Everything looked the same, except the mountains seemed to be mostly behind them now. To the west they saw open sky.

"We went right through a fucking mountain." Wayne slapped Ian on the shoulder and grinned. "I bet we're in B.C. now. I'm buying you a beer and steak dinner tonight."

Ian hoped Wayne was right. He tired, hungry and had never felt so grubby. Chilled from the cold tunnel, he crawled away from the windy doorway and scooped a shallow bed in the wheat. Using his duffle bag for a pillow, he curled up under his blanket, trying to get warm. As he drifted off he saw Wayne do the same, sprawled on his side by the door, his mop of red hair resting on the sun-dappled grain.

Ian woke up. He sat up, shaking some grain from his hair. He blinked. What had woken him? Then he realized: the train was not moving. It was completely silent. He scrambled to the door and looked outside. In the fading light he saw mountains, trees, rock cuts and, off to the left, a small gorge with a stream.

"Wayne," he shouted. "Hey man, we're stopped somewhere."

Wayne sat up and rubbed his face.

"What the fuck?" He crawled over the door, leaned way out and looked in both directions.

"Maybe we are just on a siding."

"Listen." Ian held up his hand. They both paused.

"What?" Wayne said.

"No engine." Ian said. "I don't hear the engine."

"Fuck. Fuck. Fuck." Wayne swung his legs over the top of the cardboard wall, rolled over and tried to lower himself down. He grunted, kicking at the cardboard to find his toe holds. He found one, lowered himself an arm's length, then dropped to the ground. He landed on his feet but fell over. He stood up, then ran to the left and disappeared.

Ian leaned out, worried the train would start up again and take off without Wayne. But a second later he was back.

"We've been fucking dumped. We're sitting on a siding, about ten box cars."

"Where are we?"

"Fucked if I know. Throw down my pack and come on down."

Ian dropped the backpack to Wayne, then his own stuff. He dangled his legs and managed to get a toe into the holes in the cardboard. He slipped down, grabbed a metal band that cut into his fingers. He tried to find another hole for his foot, his whole weight on his arms, wrenching his shoulder as he twisted sideways to look down. Finally, like Wayne, he just let go and dropped. He landed hard on his side on the cinder bed. He stood up, rubbing his shoulder.

Wayne had already shouldered his backpack.

"Come on."

Ian scrambled to catch up. He felt clumsy, trying to walk after laying on the wheat all day. They walked to the end of the box cars and around to the other side. Beside their train were three sets of tracks. Two were empty. One the far track sat a single red caboose. Wayne crossed the tracks. Ian followed. He looked up. The sky was a dark blue now, verging on black. Only the tops of the mountains glowed in the twilight sun. Ian could see his breath in the cold mountain air.

Wayne dropped his pack and climbed up a few steps to the small porch at the rear of the caboose.

"Wayne. Be careful," Ian whispered. "The train guys might be in there."

"Don't be stupid. There's no one out here." Wayne pressed his face to the little window centered high in the door. "Can't see but I bet they have a kitchen in there. Maybe some food."

He yanked on the door. Then he stepped back and kicked it a few times. It was thick and solid. Wayne unsheathed his knife and used the handle to break the glass of the tiny window. He chipped the shards from the edge of the fame, then stuck his arm in the hole. He leaned until the broken glass touched his arm pit. His face contorted as he felt around.

"Can't reach the lock." He tried a couple more times, then pulled his arm free. Bits of broken glass clung to his jean jacket. He lit a smoke, leaning on the rail of the platform.

"Maybe we should climb back up the boxcar?" Ian suggested. "We can wait until another train comes by."

"Fuck that." Wayne smoked in silence. Ian watched the darkness creep up the mountains like a rising black tide. So much for Vancouver tonight, he thought bitterly. He never should have jumped a train. If he had hitchhiked he'd be at some hostel now with food and a bed, not stuck in the fucking mountains freezing to death.

Wayne flicked his butt away and paced on the little platform.

"Fucking train." He shouted. He started kicking the door again. "Fucking cocksucker."

Ian heard Wayne's voice echo off a nearby cliff. He had never seen Wayne this angry, it was worse than when he got kicked out of the tower. Wayne took out his lighter, flicked it, then held it to wood frame of the window.

"What are you doing?"

"Gonna burn this fucker down." The wood smoked but did not catch on fire. Wayne shook his lighter, flicked it again. He kept holding the flame to the wood.

"Come on. Wayne," Ian tugged at his sleeve. "You burn this down and we'll get arrested."

"Fuck you." Wayne snarled at Ian. "Who the fuck will arrest us?" He held his lighter again under the wooden sill.

Ian climbed down to the track bed. It was almost dark. Slowly he turned in a circle. Where the hell were they? It might hours before another train came by. And who knew if it would stop or even slow down?

Then he heard a sound in the distance. It grew

closer. He realized it was a truck, a big truck. He heard it gear down. Where was it? He cocked his head and located the sound. He ran across the train tracks, stumbling, then saw a set of headlights, far down the slope to his left.

"A truck." He shouted at Wayne. "Wayne, there's a road right there."

The truck's headlights appeared. In the beams, Ian saw blacktop not that far away. Wayne jumped down from the caboose.

"That road's gotta go somewhere." He grabbed his back pack. "Come on, let's go."

In the near dark they stumbled down off the high, graded, railroad bed. They had to push through thick brush and some small pine trees. Wayne led the way, cursing under his breath. Branches snapped in Ian's face.

"Fuck," Wayne said. "I stepped in some water. Watch out!" But even as he said it, Ian stepped in a swallow ditch and felt water slosh around his ankles. His shoes and socks were soaked. They pushed on in the growing darkness. Just as Ian wondered if they were headed the right way they scrambled up a bank to the road. Ian felt the edge of the pavement under his feet. He dropped his bags. It was so dark he could barely make out the silhouette of Wayne standing next to him.

"This has got to be the highway." Wayne said. "Can't be more than one road through the fucking Rockies."

They waited in the dark for a ride. Wayne smoked. Ian dug in his duffle bag and found some dry socks, but within seconds of putting them on, they sucked water up from his shoes and grew damp. He put on his hat and rubbed his arms, trying to get warm.

They heard an engine. A big truck loomed out of the dark. The headlights blinded them. Ian instinctively stepped back, but Wayne stepped right into the road, waving both arms and shouting. The driver leaned on his horn as he swerved into the other lane. A blast of cold wind sucked around them.

"Fuck." Wayne said. "We'll be stuck here all night."

A few minutes later a car came from the other direction, going east. As soon as the headlights caught the boys, the car slowed and drew to a stop on the opposite side of the road. The driver lowered his window, but only a crack. He shouted through the opening.

"Hey, what are you doing out here?"

"What's it look like ass-" Wayne started to reply, but Ian grabbed his arm.

"We're thumbing to Vancouver." Ian said. "Where are we?"

"Revelstoke." The driver gestured back down the hill behind him. "You're only about a mile or two from Revelstoke."

"Can you give us a ride?" Ian said.

"Can't." The driver said. "Got to get home. But you could walk there in about half an hour, maybe less." He rolled up his window and drove away.

Wayne and Ian picked up their things and started walking. Wayne walked in the road. Ian could hear his boots banging the black top. He knew Wayne was still furious. The road sloped down so Ian simply leaned forward and followed the sound of Wayne's boots, keeping one foot on the pavement so he didn't stumble off in the dark and fall in a ditch. He hoped Revelstoke was as close as that guy had said. Another truck came down the mountain. When headlights appeared, Wayne stayed on the road, trying to wave him down. At the last minute the truck dodged around him. The deep horn echoed back from the mountains.

"Fuck you, mother fucker." Wayne shouted in the darkness. "Fucking cocksucker."

Eventually they saw a street light and a minute later arrived at the edge of town. They passed fast food places, all closed for the night. Cheap motels and gas stations; also closed.

"Fucking one horse town," Wayne swore. "Isn't there one god-damn place open?"

The angrier he got, the faster he walked. Ian could barely keep up. Luckily, on the other side of the road, they saw a truck stop that was open. A couple of big rigs squatted side by side in the parking lot. There was one car parked by the front door. They crossed the road and went in. Two men, the truckers Ian assumed, sat at the counter talking with an older waitress who leaned on the cash register with one elbow. They barely glanced at the boys as they entered.

Three teenage boys sat at a booth. Their table was littered with empty glasses, crumpled napkins and plates smeared with ketchup. It reminded Ian of hanging out with his buddies after school. The boys stopped talking and watched Wayne and Ian as they took seats half way down the counter. The waitress frowned at them, then slowly walked over.

"What do you guys want?"

"How about some menus?" Wayne said.

"You have any money?"

Wayne made a show of standing up and taking out his wallet. He tossed some money on the counter. "Now how about some menus."

She walked a few feet away, grabbed two dog eared menus, wrapped in thick vinyl and dropped them on the counter.

"Thanks." Ian said. Hand on her hip, she stared past them, waiting for their order. Wayne said they would have two cheese burgers, with fries and cokes. The smell of hot grease from the kitchen made Ian dizzy with hunger. His last meal had been twenty-four hours ago in Calgary. When the food came he ate too fast. Wayne also gobbled his down, taking huge bites, chewing with his mouth open. He slurped the last of his coke and deliberately smacked the glass down on the counter. The waitress, still chatting with the two truckers, looked over.

"Hey." Wayne shouted. "How about some water?" He held up a dollar bill. "Big tip if you smile." She said nothing but brought two glasses of water.

A minute later she came back and dropped the bill in front of Wayne.

"Wait a minute." Wayne said. "We're not done eating." He turned to Ian with a big grin. "What do you say? How about some coffee and a couple pieces of pie?"

Silently the waitress picked up the tab, and a few minutes later returned with pie and coffee. Wayne gave her a big fake smile. "Why thank you so much."

He grabbed his pie and spun around on his stool. He looked at the teenaged boys who had been speaking in whispers a few feet behind them.

"So," Wayne called out, "what do you do for fun in this one horse town?"

"This is it." A tall boy with sideburns said. The others laughed.

"I'd fucking kill myself if I lived here." Wayne said.

"Aw, it's not so bad." Another boy spoke. His chin was covered in pimples that he had recently been squeezing. "Sometimes we get bands in at the arena."

"Bands at the arena?" Wayne smirked. "Wow, that makes life worth living."

The boys smiled awkwardly. Ian wanted to tell Wayne to knock it off, but he knew better. He finished his pie and went to the bathroom. As he splashed water on his face, he wondered where they would sleep tonight?

On the way back he stopped to ask the truckers if they were going west. They didn't look at him. One said yes.

"Any chance my buddy and I could get a ride with you?"

"Nope." The other said.

As he walked away Ian heard one trucker say something about hating boys who looked like girls. The other snickered.

Meantime, Wayne had knelt in the booth next to the boys, leaning over to talk to them.

"What's up?" Ian asked.

"The boys here were just telling me what fun town this shit hole is, you know, what with the bands and the high school sock hop and the local hockey team." Wayne grinned sarcastically. "It's a regular fucking paradise."

Ian could see the boys weren't sure how to react.

166

Wayne made them nervous. Behind Wayne's back, Ian smiled at them and shrugged, just like Tom had done to him when Wayne was being an asshole.

The waitress walked and placed a new receipt on the counter. "We're closing soon, you have to pay up."

While Ian and Wayne gathered up their gear, the local boys left. At the cash Wayne made a show of counting his money. When he got his change he placed a dollar on the counter. When the waitress looked at it, he picked it up again, snapped it between his fingers and shoved it back in his jeans.

"Thanks for nothing." He said. Ian was a little embarrassed. He wanted to apologize but she had already walked away.

Outside, the teenagers leaned on the car in the parking lot. It was a big four door sedan. Obviously someone's family car, Ian thought.

"Hey," the tall one called out, "you want a ride?"

"Sure." Wayne said. "How about you drive us to Vancouver? Get out of this shithole while you can."

The boys laughed nervously.

"Come on," Wayne walked right up to them. "Don't be such a pussy. It's only your daddy's car."

"I have to work tomorrow." The tall boy said. "But we can give you a ride to the edge of town." He opened the back door.

"Thanks." Ian said. Any ride was better than walking. He and Wayne squeezed in the back with their gear. The three teens sat in the front side by side. Wayne flicked his cigarette butt out the window. The driver showed off, gunning it backwards, then cutting a couple of loud gravel-spewing doughnuts in the parking lot. He floored it on to the street, throwing Wayne and Ian back against the seat.

"Yee-ha," Wayne shouted. "Local boy goes crazy."

Ian scrambled upright and peered out the windows at the darkened store fronts. Funny how small towns all looked alike. Revelstoke reminded him of Madanon. Then he saw the fast food strip.

"Hey, wait a minute." He leaned forward. "Isn't Vancouver the other way? "

"Well," The driver grinned in the rearview mirror. "You like our one-horse town so much I thought maybe you'd like to walk through it again."

In one motion Wayne grabbed the guy's hair and laid the blade of his huge knife against his throat.

"You little fuck. Turn this car around." The driver took his foot off the gas and coasted to a stop in the middle of the street. Wayne jabbed the point of his knife into the driver's neck. "I mean it, you cocksucker."

"Hey." Ian grabbed at Wayne. "Take it easy man."

"Shut the fuck up." Wayne's eyes blazed.

"Come on." Wayne shouted. "Turn the fuck around."

The kid slowly pulled a u-turn. Ian's heart was pounding. In the rearview mirror, he saw the kid's terrified face.

This is fucking insane.

"Take it easy, man." The kid with the pimples said. "We were only joking."

"Shut the fuck up." Wayne waved the knife at him. They cruised back through town, past the truck stop. The lights were still on. Ian expected the kid driving to lay on the horn, to try something. But he just kept driving. Ian looked around frantically for cops, sure they'd end up in jail.

It only took a couple of minutes to reach the other end of town. The last building was some kind of auto body shop. There was one more street light just past the driveway.

"This is it." The driver said, his voice cracking. "This is the edge of town."

Ian panicked – would Wayne stab the driver and steal the car?

"Pull over. Pull over by that light." Wayne snarled. The gravel shoulder crunched beneath the tires.

"Unload our stuff." Wayne shouted. Ian jumped out the passenger side, dragging their gear to the shoulder. Wayne opened his door with his left hand, still waving the knife in the teenager's faces

"You're lucky I don't cut off your dicks, you little assholes."

"Come on." Ian shouted. Wayne stepped out and slammed the door. The driver floored it, tires squealing on the black top. They drove west into the darkness.

"What the fuck was that?" Ian shouted at Wayne. "What the fuck are you doing?" Wayne said nothing staring into the darkness where he car had disappeared. He held up his hand.

"They're coming back." He said. Ian heard it too: a racing car engine, he saw the headlights in the distance.

"Come on." He grabbed at Wayne. "Get off the road."

"Fuck that." Wayne shouted. He reached down and grabbed a handful of gravel. Under the street light, Ian looked around frantically and spotted a rock the size of baseball. He snatched it up.

The car bore down on them. It swerved to their side of the road. As the headlights lit up Wayne, he held his knife up like it was a sword. Ian held his rock up too, hoping they could see it. At the last second the car swung into the other lane and screeched to a stop.

"Assholes," The driver yelled. The pimply kid leaned over to shout. "Faggots."

"Real tough, eh?" Wayne said. "Come on, chicken shits. Get out of the car." Ian stepped forward so they could see the big rock he held. He hefted it like he was going to throw it. He flashed back to throwing the bricks in Brandon.

Wayne flicked his wrist and a piece of gravel hit the car.

"Hey." The driver said. "You're gonna scratch the paint."

"Oh poor baby, daddy won't let you borrow his car after this." Wayne ran at them. The driver gunned it a few feet, then stopped again a little way up the road.

"Fuck you." He gave Wayne the finger, then sped off. Wayne hurled stones at the retreating car.

"Little pussies." Wayne turned to Ian with a big grin. He re-sheathed his knife. "We called their bluff."

Ian watched the taillights go around the curve back into town. He was sure they would circle back again. Or worse, call the police.

"Look at you." Wayne laughed. Ian realized he was still clutching the big rock in his fist. Wayne slapped him on the back. "You're a fucking mad man."

Ian dropped the rock on the side of the road. His hands shook.

"Do you think they'll call the cops?"

"Who cares?" Wayne lit a smoke. Then, seeing how worried Ian was, he added, "Listen, that little shit head probably has a curfew. If he tells his daddy what happened he'll have to explain he gave us a ride. He won't say anything to anyone." He spit. "He'll be wetting his bed tonight."

Ian hoped he was right. Wayne paced back and forth as he smoked. Ian watched a cloud of moths around the street lamp. A few minutes passed and no police car came. But there was also no traffic, east or west. As his adrenalin faded, Ian realized he was dead tired and suggested they crash in the grassy embankment just off the road. To his surprise, Wayne said yes. They strolled a few yards into darkness and found a flat area covered in weeds. Ian unrolled his blankets. Wayne shook out his sleeping bag. They both settled, using their gear as pillows. Ian curled up sideways, pulling up his knees and tugging the thin blankets around his shoulders. Against the glow of the street light, he saw the silhouette of Wayne's face as he lay flat looking up at the stars.

"What a weird trip, eh?" Wayne said.

"Yeah." Ian blinked. "Jumping a train was pretty crazy."

"Life. I mean." Wayne rolled on his elbow and looked at Ian. "Things were so fucked up back home." He shook his head. "I really had to get away."

"Me too." Ian said.

"It's pretty cool being on the road, eh?" Wayne laid

back down. "Vancouver is going to be great. I can't wait to see Connie."

"Me too." Ian could barely keep his eyes open.

"Hey." Wayne said. "Thanks for getting my back tonight. You're way tougher than you look."

"Thanks," Ian half smiled and fell asleep.

Stiff and cold, Ian woke a couple of times to pull his blanket tighter. He sat up once when a huge truck rattled by. At dawn he woke again. A heavy dew had settled on his face. Wayne slept curled up in ball, his head inside his sleeping bag. Ian wiped his face and pulled the blanket over his head. He drifted off again, then later woke as he heard a car stop. He peeked under the edge of the blanket. A police car sat on the other side of the road. Ian lay very still, watching. The cop rolled down his window and stared at them.

This is it! Ian panicked. Those kids did tell their parents. We're going to jail. He held his breath, waiting for the cop to get out of his car. But after what seemed like forever, the cop rolled up his window and drove off.

Ian let out a big sigh. Now he was wide awake. Traffic was picking up. They should be up hiking. He stood up, stiff and sore from sleeping on the hard ground. He splashed his face and head with water from his canteen. He had not had a shower since Brandon. He was itchy from riding in the boxcar full of wheat. He rubbed his head with both hands, then dug his hat out of his bag and pulled it down over his wet hair. He decided to let Wayne sleep. He'd have better luck pretending to be a solo hiker.

An hour passed with no rides. Occasionally, Ian looked over at Wayne, snoring in a heap. He wondered what would have happened if he had not met him. Maybe he'd already be in Vancouver. On the other hand, he would not have had this whole adventure, riding a freight train through the Rockies. Wayne's temper terrified him, but so far nothing bad had really happened. With luck they'd be in Vancouver tonight. Wayne's cousin sounded nice. It would be wonderful to have shower, sleep in a real bed, maybe sit down to a nice meal with normal people. He'd get rested up and find some work. As he thumbed he daydreamed once again about living on a beach and maybe buying a motorcycle.

Wayne finally woke up. He sat up, scratched his curly hair with both hands and rubbed his face.

"What time is it?" He called out.

"About nine." Ian said. "Traffic is pretty steady."

Wayne stood up. "I gotta piss something fierce." He turned his back on the road and peed in the tall weeds. Ian walked over and did the same. He no longer cared what people thought.

Wayne dragged his gear to the shoulder and lit a smoke. "See?" He said. "I knew those kids wouldn't call the cops on us."

Ian decided not to mention the police car at dawn. Why stir him up? The worst was behind them. It was a sunny day with lots of traffic. They were bound to get a ride. It took another two hours, but finally a driver tooted his car horn and pulled to the shoulder. The boys grabbed their gear and ran to the car. By the time they reached it, the driver had stepped out. He was a short man in a dark blue suit. He wore a white shirt with no tie. He looked like he had just had his hair cut that morning.

"Hello lads," He said flashing a toothy smile. "Where you headed?"

"Vancouver." Wayne said.

"Well, this is your lucky day. I am headed right to Vancouver." He popped the trunk and gestured for them to put their stuff in. The boys shouted with happiness. Wayne hugged Ian around the shoulders.

"Buddy, you're a fucking lucky charm. A ride right to Van!"

It was a two door, a convertible but the top was up. Ian climbed in the back. Wayne sat in the front next to the driver.

"I'm Paul." The man shook hands with them. "Nice to meet you." He swung into traffic. "So off to Vancouver, eh?

Wayne explained about visiting his cousin Connie. Ian leaned forward to explain that he was going to find a job. He even joked about working in a lumber camp.

Paul laughed. "Lumber camp, eh? Not a lot of lumber camps in Vancouver."

"Well, I've got to work somewhere." Ian said.

Paul turned his head to smile at Ian. "I'm sure you will find work. Vancouver is a great city. Things are really booming there."

"Is Van your home?"

"Yes, indeed," Paul said. "I have lived and worked there for ten years now. I work for the provincial government so I get to travel some. In fact, I've been up to Banff for a conference."

"That sounds pretty cool." Ian said.

"Aw," Paul chuckled. "The work is boring, but it has some nice perks. Like this car for example. It's leased by the government." He tooted the horn. "Your tax dollars at work."

Ian could see Wayne was getting bored.

"Can I find some tunes?" He asked Paul. He fiddled with the radio. Reception crackled in and out because of the terrain. Finally, he found a rock station. Led Zeppelin was playing and Wayne cranked the volume.

"Choice!" Paul shouted. "Say, would you fellows like to smoke a joint?"

"Uh, sure," Wayne hesitated. "You're not a narc, are you?"

Paul laughed and reached across to the glove box. From under the maps he pulled out a fat joint. He licked it, stuck it between his lips and patted his pockets. Wayne whipped out his lighter. Soon they were passing the joint. It was only Ian's third time smoking dope, but he was learning. After a few tokes he felt buzzed. All the stress and craziness of last night in Revelstoke dropped away.

'This is nice shit." Wayne said.

"Home grown." Paul nodded. "A lot of nice pot in B.C."

"I wouldn't mind scoring some."

"Don't worry." Paul said. "You won't have a problem getting pot in Vancouver. Pretty much any drugs, really. Acid, mesc, peyote, magic mushrooms. Just watch out for the smack. We've got a wicked heroin problem, especially done in the Eastside."

Ian leaned back in the seat, looking out the window at the big puffy clouds. He felt great. The sun was shining, the tunes were good and they had a ride all the way to Vancouver. He realized it had only been a week since he left home. So much had happened in one week. And now, at last, Vancouver.

He leaned forward as Paul lit another joint, tuning back into the conversation.

"Hitching is a great way to see the world." Paul said. "I thumbed all over the States back in '68.

"Get out." Wayne said. "You're shitting us."

Paul leaned sideways and pulled his wallet from his hip pocket. Steering with his elbows he slipped out a photo and handed it to Wayne.

Wayne burst out laughing. "Holly shit. Look at that 'fro man. That's fucking wild." He handed the snapshot to Ian. There was Paul, the same mischievous grin, but with a huge halo of black curly hair and giant fuzzy side burns.

"That's far out." Ian handed it back to Paul, who looked at himself and laughed.

"Yeah, I decided to head down to Frisco, check out the scene. Lots of acid parties in those days. Great music. Then I hooked up with this crazy chick and we decided to go down to Mexico. Baja. The drugs were so cheap." He laughed and slapped the steering wheel. "Man, what a trip that was." He dragged on the joint again. "Then I thumbed all across the southern States, and up the east coast to New York."

"All with that chick?" Ian asked.

"Oh no. She stayed in New Mexico. We stopped at a commune and she liked it there. She was a real earth mother type, you know grow your own salad, all that shit."

Paul said he eventually ended up back in Vancouver.

"Van in the sixties." He shook his head nostalgically. "It was so sweet. Pot was cheap. Everything was mellow. Heroin was around but not like now. I lived for a while out on Wreck Beach, started doing leather work for bread, you know sandals, bags, purses, that kind of thing."

"What happened, man?" Wayne said. "You had it made." He hesitated. "No offense, but look at you now."

Paul laughed. "You mean my Mr. Clean look?" He ran his hand over his crew cut. "Shit happens, man. I met my old lady and we had a kid. I had mouths to feed. I needed to make some real coin. I ended up getting into bookkeeping. Weird, eh? Never even knew I liked math until I tried it. I went back to school and became an accountant." He seemed a little embarrassed to say it out loud. "Believe it or not, I actually like being an accountant."

Paul reached over and turned the radio down by half. "Besides man. The sixties were dead. I mean after Jimi and Janis overdosed. After fucking Manson and all that crazy shit, I realized the whole hippie thing was just so much bullshit. A pipe dream that was collapsing. It was a good time to get out."

When he paused, there was an awkward silence.

"Hey," Paul grinned. Sorry to be such a bummer. Pay no attention to the man behind the curtain. You guys are young. Have fun while you can."

Pleasantly stoned, Ian leaned back. With the warm sun and a nice breeze on his face he drifted off. He woke up when they stopped at a road side cafe.

"Come on, sleepy head." Paul said. "I'm buying you

guys lunch."

Paul insisted they have soup first.

"Soup is good for your soul." He said.

They had soup, then BLTs and fries, and several cups of coffee. The food was so good. They kept thanking Paul for the meal but he just laughed and said "What's the point of a government job for if I can't buy a meal for some hippies?"

Even though he knew Paul was joking, Ian liked being called a hippie.

Back on the highway Ian looked around. The mountains were far behind them. He could see the Vancouver skyline on the horizon. He inhaled and caught a whiff of salt air. The ocean. He could not wait to go swimming in the Pacific.

On the edge of town, Paul pulled to the shoulder and jumped out.

"Come on, give me a hand. Let's lower the top on this thing." It took a few minutes to get the convertible top folded back into the area behind the rear seat.

"Now lads," Paul said. "I insist you ride in the back seat so you can arrive in Vancouver in the style you deserve. Let me be your chauffeur." He bowed to Ian, then held the door while he climbed in. He ran around the car and did the same for Wayne. Sitting in the back seat of the convertible, the boys laughed and high-fived as Paul headed into Vancouver.

Soon they were downtown, in the late afternoon traffic. Paul drove them around, swinging by the beach, the edge of Stanley Park, past shiny office buildings. He pointed out the government offices where he worked. Ian saw the ocean glittered between buildings. Nearby mountains shone in the sun. Sidewalks were crowded with all sorts of people: business men in suits with wide lapels; guys with long hair, straggly beards, tie-died t-shirts and sandals, women in extremely short mini-dresses, with dangly earrings, headbands or huge floppy sun hats. Ian kept turning in his seat to gawk. At a red light, Wayne stood up and shouted.

"Hey girls. Looking good. We're new in town. Meet us later for a drink!"

Most women ignored him but some smiled and waved. Even Paul got into the act, beeping his horn and yelling at strangers.

"Look who I got in the back seat. Mick Jagger and Neil Young."

A few people laughed and waved at the car; someone threw them a peace sign. Ian threw one back. He could not stop smiling. He had been dreaming about this for months. The trip had been crazy but he had done it. *He had done it.* He had escaped his fucking family and arrived in Vancouver.

Finally, Paul pulled over to the curb.

"Sorry I can't drive you right to your cousins, but I have to get my ass home and see my family." He climbed out and opened the trunk. As they unloaded their gear he explained a little about where they were and how the city buses worked.

"No problem, man." Wayne said. "This was fan-fucking-tastic." He hooked thumbs and gave Paul the hippie handshake.

"Yeah. Thanks." Ian added. Paul also hooked

thumbs. He pulled Ian into a bear hug and thumped him on the shoulder. "Hang in there, kid, who knows you might be a lumberjack yet."

Before climbing into his car, Paul tucked a fat joint into the pocket of Wayne's jean jacket. "Never know when an extra joint might come in handy. Just be very careful. Simple possession will get you a couple of years in jail."

Paul waited for a gap in the traffic and pulled a U-turn. As he swung the car around he laid on the horn and threw them a peace sign.

"Holy fuck!" Wayne shouted and high-fived Ian. "We made it." He dug in his back pack and pulled out a wadded note with Connie's adress. He pointed to a corner store and said he was going to ask directions.

Standing next to their gear, Ian slowly turned in a circle. It was hard to believe he was here. Tomorrow he'd start looking for work. Then he'd get a place to live. Who knows? It was so beautiful here - maybe he'd never go back to Madanon.

Wayne dodged back through the traffic. "Ok. I got some directions. We need to catch a bus." Ian was embarrassed that he didn't even have bus fare. He already owed Wayne a lot of money for meals and drinks. They boarded a crowded bus. There were lots of people going home after work. They stared at the boys as they jostled through the crowd with their gear. After sleeping outside and jumping a train, Ian knew they were filthy. *We really are dirty hippies.* He smiled at the cliché, but worried that they actually did smell bad.

At every intersection Wayne ducked his head to look at street signs, anxiously watching for the right bus stop. A few blocks later he rang the bell and they jumped off the bus. Wayne checked his directions. They walked along another busy street, then turned down a narrow residential street filled with small wooden houses. Ian saw that Wayne was really excited to see his cousin. He stopped in front of a little blue bungalow, double checking the house number.

"This is it." He shouted and elbowed Ian. Ian stared at the place. The paint was faded and dirty. The trim around the windows was cracked and peeling. A large Canadian flag hung lopsided over the front window.

"Connie said to come around the back. They live in the basement." A pipe and wire fence surrounded the front yard, a small patch of browning grass with lots of weeds. The loose gate dangled sideways. It squeaked as they entered. Wayne led the way down a narrow space between two houses. As they passed a window, a huge dog appeared inside, barking frantically.

"Shut the fuck up!" Wayne gave the dog the finger.

The backyard was covered in concrete slabs. Weeds pushed up between them. There were lots of dog turds everywhere. Two battered garbage cans sat in one corner next to a rusty barbecue. Along the fence there was a stack of weathered plywood and warped two by fours.

Wayne skipped down a narrow set of wooden stairs that descended to the basement. He grinned at Ian, pounded on the door, and shouted in a deep voice, "Open up. It's the police."

A second later, a thin blonde woman in a baggy sweat shirt and jeans opened the door.

"Wayne, you shit! I knew that had to be you." She

grabbed his arm and pulled him into a hug. Ian waited, a little awkwardly, as she rocked Wayne side to side in her arms, her eyes closed.

"My little coz." She kissed his cheek. Then she released Wayne and turned to Ian.

"I'm Ian." He stuck out his hand but Connie grabbed him and hugged him. She was very boney and reeked of cigarette smoke. Then she held him at arm's length. She had the same toothy smile as Wayne.

"Is this cutie your high school buddy?"

"No. That was Tom." Wayne said. "This is Ian. We met on the road in Moose Jaw. We lost Tom in Calgary."

"You lost him?" Connie burst into laughter. "How the fuck do you lose someone?" She turned to Ian. "Only Wayne could lose someone." She threw her arms around both their shoulders. "Come in. Come in. Welcome to chez basement. It ain't much, but it's all we got."

Walking into the basement, Ian felt like he had entered a dimly lit cave. The low ceiling almost touched his hat. As his eyes adjusted to the darkness he saw a living room lined with fake wood panels. There was a threadbare orange couch, a couple of large chairs bleeding stuffing from their seams, and a coffee table covered with ash trays, magazines and a pizza box. A big fat candle had glued itself to the table with melted wax. Faint light bled around two small basement windows, both covered with tea towels.

"The living room." Connie gestured. They dropped their gear and followed her around the corner to the kitchen. She pointed down a narrow hallway. "That's the john on the right, if you gotta piss. The last door is our bedroom."

The kitchen felt cramped. Down one wall there was a stove, a fridge, the sink and counter, with cupboards above and below. Against the opposite wall stood an old kitchen table with a yellow Formica top. There were three mismatched chairs with stainless steel legs and vinyl padded seats. Gray tape covered a few tears and holes.

Wayne and Ian sat down.

"Larry's not home. Want some tea?" Connie put a kettle on the stove and handed them two stained enamel cups. Ian noticed something crusted on the rim of his cup. He picked it off with his thumb nail.

"It's so fucking great to see you, Wayne." She fingered his curly hair. "Little Wayne." She turned to Ian. "The last time I saw Wayne, he only came up to my boobs. Hey stand up. Stand up." She yanked Wayne up and pressed him to her chest. "See." She grinned at Ian. "He's still a little fucker." Wayne blushed. As they laughed, Ian noted the family resemblance: same boney nose. except Connie's was not broken, same high cheekbones, same big teeth and small brown eyes. They were both loud and swore a lot.

When the kettle boiled, Connie used one tea bag and moved it from cup to cup.

"Not very fancy, eh?" She said. "Larry broke our tea pot."

Over tea, as she and Wayne smoked, he told her about their travels, about jumping the train, about the Rocky Mountains and the bridge and the tunnel. Connie kept saying "wow'" and "fucking fantastic". Then Wayne told her about the kids in Revelstoke. The way he told it, it sounded like he had no choice but to the pull his knife.

"Good for you," Connie said. "Teach those little assholes a lesson."

Then Wayne described Ian picking up a big rock and aiming it at the car, Connie laughed and slapped the table.

"No, shit." She pointed at Ian. "Just look at him. He looks so innocent but he's a killer." She reached over and patted his cheek. "Thanks for taking care of my cuz. Someone has to save this asshole from himself."

Wayne blushed again. "Hey, who you calling an asshole?"

"You asshole."

Wayne laughed and gave Connie a hug.

Ian drank his tea. He had the munchies from Paul's pot and wished Connie would offer them something to eat, even some toast. He noticed white bread in a plastic bag on the table and a tub of margarine. But when she opened the fridge door to get milk for her tea, he saw it was mostly empty: a few eggs, some cracked moldy cheese, a browning head of lettuce, ketchup and a few bottles of beers.

Ian also noticed that Connie didn't look very healthy. She was so thin the bones in her wrists stuck out like knuckles. Her fingers shook as she reached for a smoke. She had a lot of whiteheads on her cheeks and a cold sore at the edge of her lip. She balanced her cigarette on the edge of the ashtray.

"Ok, cuz, I got some news too." She stood up, turned sideways and flattened her baggie sweat shirt over her belly. "I'm preggers!"

"What! That's fantastic!" Wayne jumped up and

hugged her. "Hey," he said to Ian, "I'm going to be an uncle."

"No, you dumb fuck, I'm not your sister."

"Well, what is it then?" Wayne said. "When your cousin has a baby?"

"I think," Ian said, "the baby will be your second cousin."

"That sounds about right." Connie laughed. She pointed at Ian. "Boy, he's cute and a brainiac too." She reached for her smoke. "Anyway. I'm about five months along. At least I'm not barfing as much as I was. That was a fucking nightmare. Larry was pissed off because I was up and down all the time ruining his beauty sleep."

The dog upstairs began barking loudly and leaping about, nails scraping the floor.

"Speak of the devil." Connie said. "Bet that's Larry now." She rushed off to greet him.

"Connie's so cool, eh?" Wayne said. "What did I tell you?"

"I like her." Ian said.

They heard Connie's say something, then a low male voice that sounded angry. They heard some more angry whispers, then Connie led a man into the kitchen.

"Larry." Connie made a big flourish with her thin arms. "This is my little cousin Wayne. I told you a bunch of times he was gonna visit. And his buddy Ian."

Larry was tall and lean, in jeans and a black t-shirt. His long black hair was tied back in a ponytail. He stood and stared at them. Ian felt uncomfortable under his hard gaze. Wayne stood up and stuck out his hand.

"Nice to meet you."

185

Larry gave Wayne's hand one quick yank. Ian half stood and offered his hand across the table. Larry's hand was hard and cold. Still saying nothing, he grabbed a beer from the fridge, knocked the cap off on the edge of the counter and took the chair Connie had been sitting in. He hung a canvas shoulder bag over the back of the chair. Connie ran to the other room and returned with a pop crate which she placed next to the stove.

"Here." Ian stood up. "I can sit there. Take my chair."

"Oh." She giggled as she took the chair. "Such a gentleman."

"Well, you are sitting for two."

"You told them you were knocked up?" Larry scowled. "You got a big mouth."

"Larry, he's my cousin for Christ's sake." She patted her belly. "Plus I'm showing."

Larry took a long sip from his beer. He had a thin, boney face with a pointed nose and narrow jaw. He gave a half smile and tugged a baggie filled with pot out of his shoulder bag and started rolling joints. Connie scooched closer and rubbed the back of his neck.

"Hey babe, got anything for me?"

Without looking at her, Larry slipped a thumb in his jean pocket and dropped a small folded wad of paper on the table. Connie snatched it up and disappeared into the bathroom.

The boys sat in nervous silence watching Larry roll several thin, needle like joints. His fingers were long and nimble. Ian had never seen anyone roll joints so quickly and neatly. He glanced at Wayne, who grinned, as if to say, "isn't this great?" Larry sipped his beer again, then lit one of the joints. His first toke was so long a third of the joint went down. He passed it to Wayne. When it was his turn, Ian felt like an old pro. That joint was done in two rounds. Larry lit another and finally broke the silence.

"So where are you boys from again?" As they briefly told their stories, Larry seemed to relax some. Ian was too stoned to tell. Unlike the pot he had smoked when hiking, this grass hit him hard. With every toke he felt a body rush. The top half of his brain went numb. Connie returned from the bathroom and sat down next to Larry. She took a sip of his beer. Ian noticed her eyes were shiny and her pupils dilated. She kept rubbing her arms with her hands as if she was chilled.

"So, Larry," Ian said. "What do you do for a living?"

Connie burst out laughing. "Yeah, Larry, what do you do for living?" She laughed again. Wayne laughed too but probably because he was stoned. Ian didn't know what he had said that was so funny. He had never been this stoned before.

Larry said nothing. He smiled at Ian but only with the corners of his mouth. He stared at him for what seemed like a long time. Ian squirmed under his gaze. He was really getting hungry now. As if he was psychic, Wayne said out loud: "Man, I have the munchies. Hey cuz, you got anything to eat in this place?"

Before Connie could answer, Larry sat his beer bottle down in the table, very deliberately. He pushed the pot and papers aside and leaned on his elbows.

"Here's the thing." He said. "You guys just show up out of the blue and expect to stay here-"

"Larry, I told you my cousin was coming to visit."

He scowled at Connie. She stopped talking and looked at the floor.

"I don't mind if you want to stay here for a few days. But you have to contribute to the household. I mean look around you. We can't carry anyone. Especially with Connie knocked up." Larry leaned his chair back and grabbed another beer from the fridge. "So maybe you guys can go right now and get some groceries. That'll be your contribution. I'll go buy some more beer."

Wayne stood up. "That's totally righteous, dude. Just aim us at the nearest store and we'll go get some grub."

Looking relieved Connie stood up and tossed her arm around Wayne. "See, Larry, isn't my cuz the best?"

Larry said nothing. He started to roll another joint. Connie gave them directions to a big grocery store a few blocks away. She walked them to the door, excitedly rhyming off some things she wanted.

"Eggs and bacon. And lots a bread. Bread is good. I really like toast. Oh yeah, Red Rose Tea." As they went up the basement steps, she called out "And some ice cream. Chocolate would be nice. I got a wicked fucking sweet tooth."

Outside the sun was so bright it made Ian's eyes water. He kept blinking and wiping them. He had never been this stoned before. It took concentration just to place one foot in front of the other.

"Connie is great, eh?" Wayne said as they walked.

"Very cool," Ian said. He hesitated. "Larry's a little scary. I don't think he wants us here."

"Naw. He's ok." Wayne said. "I mean he's serious, for sure, but it's his pad and we are crashing there."

A few blocks later they came to a big supermarket. Outside the store, Ian grabbed Wayne's arm. "You know I am completely broke. Like zero. I can't pay for any food."

"Hey man," Wayne grinned. "Don't sweat it. I got money. You can owe me. We gotta eat. I don't know about you but I am starving."

"I think I got the munchies." Ian said.

"No shit, Sherlock." They both giggled a little too much, then composed themselves.

Inside the store, they grabbed a cart and started walking up and the down the aisles picking up things as they saw them: spaghetti, sauce, cans of soup and beans.

In the baked goods area, Ian picked up a big loaf of sliced bread.

"This looks like it would be good for toast. Connie said she likes toast." He tossed two loaves in the cart.

"What about this?" Wayne hefted a big loaf of fresh unsliced bread in a paper bag. "There is nothing better than fresh bread with some butter." He stuck his thumb into the end of the loaf and tore off chunk of bread. He stuffed it in his mouth and chewed.

"Fuck, that's good." He mumbled, his mouth full of dough. He tore off a piece and handed it to Ian, who popped it in his mouth. As he chewed he thought, this *is* the best bread I have ever tasted. Wayne tore off another chunk.

Out of the corner of his eye, Ian noticed a middle aged woman look over at them.

"Come on." He grabbed the cart and led Wayne down another aisle. They grabbed some cereal and milk. Wayne tossed in a package of cheese.

"Grilled cheese." He said. As they went up and down the aisles, they continued to pick at the loaf of bread like it was candy. Ian had just shoved some more chewy crust in his mouth, when he saw a man standing at the end of the aisle watching them. He quickly wheeled the cart around the corner.

At the meat display Wayne grabbed some bacon. He stared at the other meats.

"We gotta get a steak." He held up package with four thick steaks. "Remember on the train, I said I wanted a steak dinner?"

Ian looked at the price tag. "Fuck, Wayne, that's really expensive."

"Fuck that." He tossed the meat in the cart. "Watch and learn." He steered the cart across the store, looking down each aisle. The one with laundry soap and cleaning products was empty. Wayne stopped half way down the aisle.

"You watch that way. I'll watch this way." Ian nodded. Wayne grabbed the steaks and tucked them inside his jean jacket, up into his armpits. He lowered his arms, elbows tucked.

"See? Free steaks!" He picked up the bacon. "Go for it. You got that big baggy sweater." Nervous, Ian looked around, then slide the bacon under his sweater. He stuck the package up to his arm pit. He had to squeeze hard with his left arm to hold it in place. He kept his arm down by his side. He could feel the cool bacon through his t-shirt.

They continued around the store, looking for tea for Connie. Meantime they had finished the entire loaf of bread.

"That was fucking fantastic." Wayne crumpled the paper bread bag and tossed it on a shelf. Then as they passed the candy area, Wayne grabbed a bag of chocolate covered nut clusters.

"Here." He reached out and yanked on Ian's pants and shoved the candy down the front of his jeans. He stepped back and started laughing.

"What's so funny?" Ian said.

"You look like you shit your pants. You need a diaper man. Get a diaper." Wayne really had the giggles. Ian pulled his sweater down, half covering the bulge. He felt awkward now, holding the bacon under his left arm, trying to hunch forward to hide the candy. When he turned around he thought he saw the same man as before, looking down the aisle at them.

"Hey man," he tugged on Wayne's arm. "Let's split. We been in here a long time."

Standing in line at the check-out, Ian was sure people were staring at them. *Everyone knows we are stealing food.* But Wayne seemed fine. He unloaded the cart on to the counter but his movements were awkward and stiff because he had to keep the steak pinned firmly under his arm. Meantime, Ian was having a hard time with the bacon. It felt like it was sliding down a little every time he moved. He was sure any second it would flop on the floor and they would be arrested for shoplifting. He tried to nudge it back up, but when the cashier saw him pushing on his sweater he pulled his hand away.

Now that the cart was empty, Wayne started to

chatter at the cashier, babbling about how they were from Ontario, visiting his cousin Connie. She was indifferent until he said Connie was pregnant.

"Oh," she smiled. "When is she due?"

"Uh, she's about five months now."

She started to talk about her own kids as she rang in each item, placing everything in paper bags. It seemed to take forever. Ian wanted to help bag the food, but he afraid to move his arm and drop the bacon.

Awkwardly Wayne pulled out his wallet while keeping his elbows tucked. When she handed him his change he dropped it and his wallet into one of the grocery bags. Smiling and repeatedly thanking her, the boys leaned forward stiffly and managed to scoop up the bags. Just as they reached the door, an angry voice called out.

"Hey you two. Stop right there."

Ian recognized him – the older man in a white shirt and tie who had been watching them. He held the crushed paper bag from the loaf of bread. He walked up and shook the bag in their face.

"You think you can come in my store and steal food?" His face was red. "You ate this bread and didn't pay for it."

"Why would we eat your fucking bread?" Wayne snarled. "We just bought all these groceries."

"You ate it. I saw you. Who knows what else you stole!"

"That's bullshit." Wayne shouted.

"You watch your language, you stinking hippie. Don't you swear in front of my customers. I'll call the police and have you arrested."

Ian knew he had to do something. Wayne was making things worse. He stepped forward between Wayne and the man.

"I'm sorry, sir. You're right, we did eat the bread. We didn't mean to steal it. We were really really hungry. We just hitchhiked here from Ontario. We haven't eaten for a couple of days. We were shopping and the bread smelled good so we ate it without thinking. I'm really sorry. We can pay now. What do we owe you?"

Ian's long winded apology seemed to catch the man off guard. Meantime, out of the corner of his eye, Ian could see Wayne was backing towards the door.

"Never mind," The man snapped. "Just get out of my store and never come back. We don't want your kind in here."

"Thank you, sir. Sorry to have upset you." Ian turned quickly, pushing Wayne ahead of him out the door.

In the parking lot, Wayne started to rant, "What an asshole! He'll call the police. Yeah right."

The man came outside and stood with his arms crossed still watching them. Wayne turned as if to shout at him-

"Wayne!" Ian snarled. "Shut the fuck up and keep walking."

Ian was surprised at himself but Wayne obeyed him. They crossed the parking lot and turned a corner. As soon as they were out of sight of the store, Ian shifted the grocery bags. The package of bacon fell to the ground. Wayne did the same, deliberately letting the steaks flop on sidewalk. They both broke into nervous giggles. They set the bags down and picked up the meat.

"Lookie that," Wayne said. "A free steak dinner."

Ian remembered the candy and tugged the bag from his jeans. The nut clusters had melted and started to stick together. He doubled over laughing. Wayne danced in a little circle and high-fived him.

"We did it, brother, we did it."

Fueled by adrenalin and hunger they hurried back to Connie's place. The big dog lunged and growled again as they slipped past the window. Holding the bags of groceries high, they marched into the kitchen, chanting: "Food, food, food, food."

Connie sat at the table, smoking. She started laughing and clapping along.

Larry came out of the bedroom, scowling. "What the fuck is all the racket?"

They plunked the groceries down on the table.

"Look what we scored," Wayne waved the steaks in the air. "Lots of red meat."

"This is for you," Ian said. He handed Connie the bag of candy. "We forgot the ice cream but we got you this instead."

"Oh man, this is great." Connie jumped up and hugged him. "Thank you." She immediately tore the bag open and shoved a chocolate nut-cluster in her mouth.

"We stole all the meat." Wayne told them how they had almost got caught shoplifting. "We'd have got busted if not for this fucker" -he pointed at Ian- "he talked the store manager out of calling the cops." He patted Ian on the shoulder. "That was a smart move considering your pants were full of stolen candy."

"Ha ha." Connie waved the bag of candy around. "Ian had chocolate covered nuts." Bits of candy flew out of her mouth as she laughed. "Get it? Chocolate covered nuts!"

Ian blushed but he felt pretty pleased with himself. Wayne was right: if not for him they would have got busted.

"Ok," Wayne grabbed the steaks again. "Let's cook these fuckers."

"Naw," Larry said. "I'm in the mood for spaghetti." He took the steaks from Wayne and tossed them in the freezer. "What do you say, babe, rustle up some spaghetti?"

"Sure thing, Lar." Connie put some water on to boil and found another pan for sauce. Wayne looked disappointed for a second but then Larry reached for the baggie and rolled more hard thin joints.

"This is great pot," Wayne said as they toked. "I'd love to score some dope. Maybe you could hook me up with your dealer."

Connie started to laugh. "Oh cuz, you are small town boy, aren't you?"

"What?" Wayne looked around baffled.

Larry squinted over the joint as he inhaled. Holding it in, he whispered, "I am a dealer."

"No shit." Wayne started to laugh. "Well, I'd still like to score."

"Here," Larry handed Wayne the joint and smirked. "That's be hundred bucks." Ian figured this was as close to joking as Larry ever came. As the joint came his way, he marveled: back in Madanon he had never even smoked pot, now here he was in Vancouver having dinner with a drug dealer.

Larry pulled four beers from the fridge and handed them around. Wayne continued to ask more questions about dope. Larry gave vague one word answers. The smell of pasta sauce made Ian very hungry. He stood next to Connie while she stirred the pasta.

"Is it done yet?"

"Not sure." Connie said.

Wayne stood up. "You know how to tell? Toss some on the wall. If it sticks, it's ready."

"Al dente." Ian said.

"What?" Wayne said.

"Al dente. That's what the Italians call spaghetti that's cooked just right."

"He's a smart guy," Connie said to Larry. "Didn't I tell you he's smart?" Larry said nothing. He scowled at Ian with his small dark eyes.

Meantime, Wayne grabbed a fork and fished a strand of spaghetti from the pot. He pinched it with his fingers and tossed it at the wall above the stove, it rolled down a little before clinging in place. It left a wet trail like a snail.

"Let me try." Ian grabbed a couple of strands and flicked his wrist but the pasta flew up at a weird angle and landed high on the wall, almost touching the ceiling,

"You throw like a girl." Wayne said.

"Like a girl?" Connie slapped Wayne's arm with the wooden spoon. She plunged her index finger right into the steaming water, snagged a strand of spaghetti and tossed it backhand across the room at the fridge door. It stuck there.

"Cool." Wayne tossed a couple of strands at the fridge too. Ian grabbed a couple more strands with the fork, but when he flicked them, they went high again, splashing on the wall above the sink.

"Hey, you fucking stoners." Larry said. "Are we gonna eat or fucking waste all this food?"

The other three looked around at all the spaghetti on the walls and started laughing.

"Sorry babe," Connie said. She grabbed a lid and tried to drain the pasta into the sink. A lot slipped over the brim. "Fuck am I high."

Using a fork, she fished it back into the pot. Soon they sat down to big piles of pasta and sauce. They ate and drank beer in silence. It was not quite the home Ian had pictured when Wayne invited him to crash at his cousin's but still, now he had a place to stay and something to eat. Life was pretty sweet. When he finished eating, Ian suddenly felt very tired. The whole week on the road caught up with him.

Larry pushed his plate back, lit a smoke and stood up. He went to the bedroom, shut the door and returned a minute later in his jean jacket with his canvas bag over his shoulder. A smoke still clenched between his teeth, he pulled the elastic off his pony tail, tugged his hair tighter and refastened it.

"I have to pop downtown for a while."

Connie threw an arm around Wayne's shoulders.

"See, Lar, didn't I tell you my little cousin was cool. And this guy." She thumbed at Ian. "He's a smart one."

Larry did not look at Ian as he said to Wayne. "You know, maybe tomorrow you can come with me. I can show you around, maybe give you a little work to do."

"That would be very cool," Wayne said.

Larry left. Connie stood up abruptly. She belched loudly and patted her bump. "I gotta crash. You boys need anything, just help yourself." She went down the hall to the bedroom and shut the door.

In the living room, Wayne said. "I got dibs on the couch." He kicked off his jeans and flopped down, using his sleeping bag for a blanket. Ian picked a corner behind the couch, unrolled his blankets and used his duffle bag for a pillow. He barely had the energy to peel off his pants. The floor was hard, but he was too tired to care.

"Connie is really nice."

"Yeah," Wayne said. "She's so cool. Can't wait to kick around with Larry tomorrow."

"Yeah." Ian mumbled. "Tomorrow…" He had no idea what kind of help Larry needed, but maybe he could make some cash too. Wayne couldn't carry him forever.

Ian woke up early with his face on the dirty carpet; it smelled of beer and cigarette smoke. He rolled over and sat up. Sunlight leaked around the small windows. Wayne was flat on his back on the couch, snoring loudly. Ian stood up slowly, slightly hungover and fuzzy headed from all the pot and beer. He had a vague memory of Larry coming home sometime during the night, walking past him in the dark. He heard someone in the kitchen and decided to get up. He slipped on his jeans and stepped into the other room.

Connie sat at the table, hunched over, gripping one end of twisted nylon stocking in her teeth. A loop was snugged around her left bicep. A few thin veins stood out on her forearm. Her boney fingers guided a needle into her skin. Her eyes rolled up to look at Ian. She tried to smile but with the nylon in her teeth, it was more of a grimace. Then she pushed down on the hypodermic. She unclenched her jaw, the nylon fell away and she shook her left arm as if it was asleep. She laid the syringe on the edge of saucer next to some cigarette butts.

Ian felt sweat on his brow. Needles always made him queasy. He sat down.

"Aw, look at your face." Connie sighed. "You didn't know I was a junkie, did you?" She gave him a thin smile and shook her head. He didn't know what to say. He had never met a junkie before, let alone watched one shoot up.

"Don't worry, kid. It's just a taste so I don't go through withdrawal. It would be too hard now that I'm knocked up." She licked the end of her finger and wiped a tiny drop of blood from her cracked and blistered skin. Only then did Ian notice several little scars in the crook of her elbow joint. She pulled the sleeve of her sweat shirt down and reached for her smokes.

"Once I pop this kid, I'm going cold turkey."

"How, uh, how long have you been addicted?"

"Oh, gosh," Connie scratched her head. "Maybe five years now. I started using after I met Larry, you know just once in a while when partying." She stood up slowly and reached for the kettle. "You want some tea?"

"Sure thing." Ian said. "Can I grab a shower? I haven't had a shower in days."

"Help yourself. There should be a clean towel in the

hall closet there."

Ian grabbed a change of clothes from his duffle bag. In the bathroom he stripped down. His jeans were very dirty but he had no other pants to wear. He sniffed his arm pits. He really did smell. Dirty hippie, he said to himself. He ran the water a long time but it never got beyond lukewarm. One well-used bar of soap lay on the shower floor. He rinsed it off. Not seeing any shampoo, he washed his hair with the soap. The towel was small and thin, but Ian didn't care. It felt so good to shower and put on clean clothes.

When he came out of the bathroom Wayne was up. Tea was ready. Connie was making toast. Wayne opened the peanut butter they had bought the day before. Connie grabbed a slice of toast and smeared it with margarine. She lifted the cracked sugar bowl with two shaky hands, tilted it over her toast and sprinkled a lot sugar on the margarine. She set the bowl down and used her finger to smear the sugar and margarine into a greasy paste.

"What?" she said when she saw Ian and Wayne staring. "I'm craving sweets."

"Next time," Wayne joked, "we'll steal some fucking jam."

"Ian can stick it down his pants." Connie giggled. "Hhhhm – crotch jam."

Ian's face grew warm.

"Look at him blush." Connie pointed. "He's so cute."

Ian ate four slices of toast and peanut butter. He took his plate to the sink. It was stacked high with dirty dishes. Judging from the crusty look and the smell, they had been there a while. He pulled the pile apart, stacking them on the stove. He started running water into the sink.

"You don't have to do that." Connie said.

"I don't mind." Ian shrugged.

"Larry's right." She cackled. "I have become a lazy bitch."

While she and Wayne smoked and gossiped about their families, Ian washed the dishes as best he could. There was a detergent bottle but it was almost empty. The dish cloth had hardened into smelly lump, but he soaked it and squeezed it a couple of times. He needed to scrape some of the plates clean. As the dishes soaked, he cleared the plates off the table and wiped up crumbs and cigarette butts. He used one of the grocery bags for garbage. He noticed that Connie had hid her needle somewhere while he was in the shower.

"Fuck, look at that!" Connie joked. "There's a table under all that shit."

Ian pointed at all the spaghetti stuck to the wall and the ceiling above the stove.

"Should I clean that up too?"

"Fuck no!" Connie laughed. "I like it. We needed some art in this room."

Ian had noticed that the only decorations in the apartment were a couple of rock and roll posters and a weird macrame thing made with thick yarn and tree branches hanging on the living room wall.

The bedroom door opened. Wearing just his underwear Larry stopped outside the bathroom. He stared at them.

"What the fuck!" He deadpanned. "Are you guys still here?"

"He's just kidding." Connie said. "Hey babe, do you want some tea?"

"Sure," Larry said. "And make me some bacon and eggs too."

"Sure thing." Connie jumped up. Larry shut the bathroom door. They heard the shower running.

"I'll fry some bacon for you boys too." Soon the pan was sizzling and popping. She forked the bacon to one side and broke some eggs into the hot grease where they spluttered loudly.

"I hate being pregnant." She nodded at the eggs. "Things like this make me want to throw up."

Larry went to the bedroom. A second later he sat at the table in jeans and a black t-shirt. It was the same thing he wore the night before. Ian noticed a sloppy blue tattoo under the dark hair on Larry's forearm. He could not make out what it was supposed to be.

"Look what Ian did," Connie gestured around. "He cleaned the place up really nice."

"Isn't that your job?" Larry said.

"I'm fucking pregnant, Larry. It was nice to have some help." She patted Ian on the head.

"Yeah, yeah." Larry gave Ian a dirty look and dug into his breakfast.

Wayne and Ian ate their bacon wrapped in a slices of white bread. Connie leaned against the counter, smoking and watching them.

"This is nice," she said. "Watching my men eat. Reminds me of back home. I had three older brothers." She said to Ian.

"Fuck." She suddenly grabbed her belly with both

hands. "I don't feel so hot. I gotta crash. Larry, you keep an eye on my cuz, ok?" She ducked into the bedroom.

Larry pushed his egg-stained plate away. He lit a smoke, then rolled a few thin joints. They smoked a couple while he drank his tea. Ian felt odd, smoking pot at breakfast. But soon he was buzzed and didn't care. Wayne made small talk, asking Larry about the types of pot common in B.C. and how sales and prices worked. Larry told him a little, but mostly gave short answers that didn't reveal much.

Ian drifted to the living room and hung his wet towel over the back of a chair. He noticed bright afternoon sunlight around the edges of the tea-towels stretched over the windows. He should get out and job hunt but he felt too stoned and laid down on the couch. He heard the big dog pacing around, its nails clicking on the floor above his head. Things were working out. He had made it to Vancouver. He had a place to stay and food to eat. It shouldn't take him long to find work and get back on his feet.

He woke up to find Wayne leaning over him, dangling the wet towel in his face. He swatted at the towel, but Wayne yanked it away.

"Come on. Get up. We're headed downtown." Larry already stood by the door in his jean jacket with his canvas bag over his shoulder. Ian jumped up and pulled his sweater over his t-shirt. He pushed his hair back off his forehead and donned his fedora. When Wayne put on his flat brimmed black hat, Larry pointed at it.

"Billy Jack." He gave one of his thin smiles.

Wayne was pleased. "Great fucking flick, eh?"

"The best." Larry said. He looked at Ian. "You ever seen it?"

"No." Ian said defensively. "But I've heard of it."

Larry shook his head as if Ian was pathetic.

"Fucking guy." Wayne said. "He's been living under a rock."

Ian had no come-back. He felt like he was back in high school, not quite cool enough to sit with the cool kids.

As they walked between the houses the dog snarled at them through the window.

"Fuck off!" Wayne shouted at it. The dog went off, barking loudly.

Larry smirked. "If that dog ever gets outside he'll eat you alive."

"No way," Wayne bragged. "I'd kick the shit out of it."

Larry shrugged and kept walking. They followed him a few blocks to a bus stop, where they waited. Ian looked at his wrist and realized he had left his watch behind. When the bus came, Wayne paid Ian's fare. They followed Larry down the aisle to the very back. They sat three abreast in the rear seat: Larry, then Wayne, then Ian. Wayne was his usual hyper self. He kept swinging his head around, taking in the view and asking Larry questions about Vancouver. Larry pulled out some sunglasses and put them on.

"You sure talk a lot." He said to Wayne. "At least your buddy knows when to shut up."

Wayne looked at little hurt but he said nothing. At one point he nudged Ian, nodded at Larry and whispered.

204

"Those are cool shades. I'm going to get some like that."

Ian noticed how older people avoided sitting near them. They would start towards the back of the bus, then see the three of them and turn to sit somewhere else. What were they afraid of? Three guys with long hair? The idea seemed so silly to Ian, but there it was: the line between the straight world and them.

Somewhere downtown Larry rang for a stop. They stepped off the bus into a crowded street. Larry strolled calmly and steadily. Wayne fell in beside him. Ian tried to walk next to Wayne, but often, when the sidewalk was narrow or crowded he had to drop back and trail along behind. He had no idea where they were or where they were headed. They walked past a lot of stores, bars and restaurants, then they arrived at a Chinese area filled with little narrow shops offering bamboo furniture, knickknacks and souvenirs; restaurants with bright red and gold signs; whole roasted ducks, glistening and dripping, hung in windows, men in white aprons stirred steaming pots, ladling noodles into bowls. Open stalls overflowed with fruits and vegetables. The streets were crowded with Chinese people carrying bulging bags of produce.

Chinatown gave way to some cobblestone streets with decorative lamps and hitching posts. Here there were restaurants, bars, a store that sold porn and a strip club. On the corner opposite the strip club, a thin woman in a hot pink mini-dress paced in front of a bar. Her straight blonde hair hung down past her shoulders.

Larry jay-walked over to her, Wayne and Ian in tow.

"Larry." She hooked one thin arm over his neck and

leaned up to kiss Larry on the mouth. Larry cupped her bum with one hand and squeezed. Ian watched this awkwardly: Wasn't Connie Larry's girlfriend?

"How's it going, babe?" Larry said.

"At least it's not raining."

Larry yanked a thumb at the boys and said. "This is Wayne and Ian. They're visiting from Ontario. This is Lilly."

Lilly looked at them blankly.

"Cool." She said as an afterthought as if there was a slight delay between her brain and her mouth.

"How was last night?" Larry said. Ian noticed that Larry always looked past her, scanning the street, eyes darting from person to person, from car to car.

"A little slow." She reached into her purse and took out a small roll of money cupped in her palm. She held it at her side. Larry took her hand. In one swift move he palmed the cash and tucked it into his jacket pocket. Just as quickly he dipped into his shoulder bag and slipped Lilly a little baggie with some pot.

"You seen Jocko around today?"

She shrugged. "Not today."

"I might see you later. I gotta show these guys around."

"Ok," she started to walk away.

"Hey, if you see Jocko, tell him to find me."

Lilly waved back over her shoulder as if to say 'whatever'.

As they started to walk again, Wayne said, "Man. She's a babe."

"Lily?" Larry shrugged. "Yeah, she's alright."

"Alright? She's fucking hot."

"You want to fuck her?" Larry paused for effect. "You can if you have twenty bucks."

"What do you mean?" Wayne started to say. "Oh yeah. I get it."

"What?" Ian tugged on Wayne's wrist.

"She's a hooker, you dork." Wayne laughed as if he had known all along. "Man, you really need to get out more." They kept walking.

A hooker? Ian thought. He couldn't get his mind around this. If Lilly was a hooker and she had given money to Larry...that means he is her pimp. So he was a drug dealer *and a pimp*. This was all so unreal. He shook his head and trotted to catch up with Larry and Wayne.

For two more hours they circled around downtown Vancouver. Several times Larry stopped to talk to women, he referred to them as "his girls". Each time they handed him some cash and he slipped them some drugs: usually pot but sometimes small packets with pills or powder. Most of the women were young, thin, wearing mini-skirts or short dresses. From a distance they really didn't look that much different than most of the young women hanging out downtown. But up close Ian saw their faces were haggard, bags under their eyes, bad acne scars under thick make-up, shaky hands. He noticed some wore long sleeves and clutched at their elbows. Seeing them, he thought of Connie that morning, shooting up at the kitchen table. He tried not to stare at them but it was hard. He had only seen prostitutes portrayed on TV shows. Maybe he was still stoned from that morning's pot, but it all felt very dream like.

Wayne, on the other hand, stared openly at the women. The more women they talked with the bolder he became. He tried to flirt, commented on their looks, whistling, telling them how hot they were. The women ignored him, quickly trading money and drugs with Larry.

As they walked away from one, Larry said. "You talk too much. Knock it off."

"I'm just trying to get some pussy." Wayne said.

"These girls work for me. Give me some cash and you can have all the pussy you want."

"Hey, I don't have to pay for pussy." Wayne bragged.

Larry replied. "One way or another, everyone has to pay for pussy."

Wayne guffawed at this line. Ian thought of Connie and felt embarrassed by this exchange.

In between seeing "his girls", Larry sold drugs to people they ran into on the street. In the early evening most of them seemed to know Larry.

"Hey man," A skinny guy with mutton chop sideburns stopped Larry. "How's it hanging?"

They hooked thumbs. The man glanced nervously at Wayne and Ian.

"These guys are cool." Larry said. Wayne grinned and nodded. Ian nodded and said, "Nice to meet you."

Stepping into the doorway of an abandoned store front, Larry sold the guy a small bag of pot. As they walked away, Larry slugged Ian hard in the shoulder.

"What the fuck was that? Nice to meet you. This isn't a fucking church social."

Wayne laughed as Ian rubbed his shoulder.

"And you." Larry poked Wayne in the chest with a

boney finger, "Don't be grinning like a fucking idiot. This is serious shit. You hang out with me, you gotta look tough."

Shortly Larry sold drugs to two guys on a corner. As he made the deal, Wayne folded his arms and gave them a stern scowl. Ian wasn't sure what to do so he pulled his hat lower over his eyes. He scowled too and shoved his hands in his pockets. Still, it was hard to look tough in an orange pull-over sweater.

Night fell. They continued to walk. Ian wasn't quite sure where they were but he started to recognize some places so he knew they were circling all around Vancouver. Along Hastings everyone seemed to know Larry. They ran into a few more of Larry's "girls", swopping money for drugs. Wayne and Ian knew better than to smile and talk. They stood close by as Larry did his business.

One women with blank dead eyes looked over at them and asked Larry. "Who are your friends? Do you want me to blow them?"

"These fags?" Larry said. "Don't waste your time. They got no bread."

As the night continued, things got weirder. The streets grew crowded and Larry began to sell pot to strangers. Contemptuously, he called them "weekend hippies" and explained they had more money than sense. As he passed people he said in a low sing song voice, "Pot. Looking for pot? Pot." Occasionally someone would respond and Larry made a sale. With strangers, he usually stepped into the doorway of a storefront or ducked down an alley out of sight. He told Wayne and Ian to stay put.

"Fucking keep your eyes open. If you see a cop, whistle real loud, then split. Walk away, but split up. Go different directions. Fucking pigs can't follow all of us."

So whenever Larry disappeared with a buyer, the boys stood guard. Wayne played it very casual, leaning on a wall, having a smoke. Ian was so nervous he could barely stand still. The whole evening was freaking him out. His mouth was so dry he didn't think he could whistle if he needed too. He walked a few feet away and looked up and down the busy street. He saw a police car passing slowly on the other side of the street. Terrified, he rushed over to Wayne.

"Cops."

"Stay cool, man. Pretend you're talking to me." Wayne dragged on his smoke and watched the cop car over Ian's shoulder. "He's not even looking this way." A minute later the police car turned a corner and was out of sight.

"See?" Wayne said. "Nothing to worry about. The pigs are fucking stupid."

Ian was relieved when Larry reappeared and they started walking again. Still he couldn't stop his feeling of panic. What the hell was he doing here, hanging out with a pimp and drug dealer? Wayne made him nervous, but Larry really scared him. His shoulder still hurt from that punch.

Around midnight, Wayne said they should quit for the night and go for a beer. "I'll buy the first round."

"No," Larry said, "You don't make dough sitting around drinking. Besides you gotta stay sharp. Still lots of cops and loonies around." But he didn't hesitate to pull out a joint from his pocket and smoke them up behind an arcade. After the joint they got the munchies. Larry led them to a grimy all night doughnut shop. It was crowded. Larry told them to grab a table in the back corner. Soon he joined them with three coffees and a half dozen doughnuts. Larry insisted on sitting with his back to the wall. He only took a couple of bites of one doughnut, then dropped it on the table and lit a smoke. No wonder he's so skinny, Ian thought. The coffee was very bitter with an oily sheen. Ian grabbed the sugar container and dumped some in. He stirred it and took a sip. Still bitter. He added more sugar.

"Have some coffee with that sugar." Wayne teased.

"Look at you." Ian said. Wayne had eaten three of the six doughnuts already.

"What?" His chin was covered in powdered sugar.

"You got the munchies bad."

"Do not." Wayne said, but he reached for the last doughnut and started to giggle.

"Knock it off." Larry spoke as if they were misbehaving kids. He drank his coffee in silence. His face was blank but his eyes constantly scanned crowd, the front door and the sidewalk. A police cruiser stopped out front. The cop called someone over who had been sitting on a newspaper box. Larry immediately stood up and headed to the men's room, taking his shoulder bag with him.

While he was gone, Wayne dusted sugar and crumbs off his face and lit a smoke.

"This is so cool, eh?" He smiled at Ian. "I mean, did you see the cash he's raking in? And those chicks? Man, I want some of that pussy!"

"Yeah." Ian forced a small smile. Everything that was weirding Ian out seemed to make Wayne happy. Only a week or so ago, Ian had been a quiet high school student, who liked science, now he was walking around with a drug dealer meeting hookers. This didn't feel right. But he was completely broke and needed a place to stay. If he left Connie and Larry's apartment, where would he live? On the street? He remembered how sad and lonely he had been that night in Regina. He didn't want to sleep in parks. Besides, he had no money, how would he eat? Tomorrow, he thought firmly, I'll start job hunting. As soon as I find work and get some money, I'll split and get my own place.

The rest of the night, Larry led them in wider and wider circles. When the bars closed, drunken crowds filled the streets.

"It's the witching hour." Larry said. "When people get drunk, they buy a lot of shit."

Now Larry sold to little clusters of drunk guys. Occasionally the conversation would lead to other drugs. Anything more than handing off a couple of joints and Larry would take the buyers into the shadows. He warned the boys to stay sharp.

"If anyone tries to rip me off, you come running."

"Fuck yeah," Wayne said. "We got your back."

Ian recognized something in Wayne's tone. He was bored walking around and probably hoped a fight would start. Ian tried to imitate Wayne's tough guy pose. He shoved his hands in his jeans, slouched against the wall, his fedora way down. He had no idea what he would do if trouble started. He hadn't been in a fight since grade eight. And even that had been more of a shoving match. He felt silly trying to look tough, like a kid playing cops and robbers.

A little after three it started to rain, a warm steady drizzle. They ducked into a doorway and waited. It kept raining and the crowds thinned out. Larry said "Ok, let's split." They walked to a stop and caught a bus. There were very few passengers but they still went straight to the back seats. Ian felt light-headed from the pot and jittery from all the coffee and sugar.

"That was so fucking cool," Wayne said. "Did we pass the audition?"

"You're getting the hang of it." Larry said. "At least you stopped acting like fucking idiots."

"So," Wayne said. "When is pay day?"

Larry gave one of his thin non-smile smiles. He took a little brown envelope from his jacket pocket. He opened it and tapped into his calloused palm three very tiny purple pills, each one about the size of a BB.

"This is your reward for tonight. Hold out your hands." Larry placed one purple pill in each of their palms. He immediately popped the third pill into his own mouth.

Ian stared at the tiny pill.

"What is it?"

"Purple Microdot." Larry said. When Ian looked puzzled, he said. "Acid. LSD. Guy owed me some money and gave me 100 tabs instead. Take it. It's pretty good shit."

"Excellent." Wayne placed the pill on his tongue.

"Been a while since I dropped acid."

Ian didn't want to admit he had never taken acid. He carefully pinched the tiny pill from his palm. It stuck to the end of his finger. He licked it into his mouth. He tasted nothing. He swallowed a couple of times but still wasn't sure if it had gone down his throat or if it was still in his mouth. He was nervous – the only thing he knew about LSD was from watching cop shows on TV where stoned people freaked out and ended up in straightjackets. Or they jumped off buildings thinking they could fly. He rested his hands on his knees and tried not to panic. Larry and Wayne seemed completely unconcerned about taking acid.

Wayne was chatty as always. He tried to get Larry to talk about the girls they had met that night, about how that worked and what kind of money he made from them, but Larry only gave one word answers, or no answer at all. The bus moved slowly, picking up a few late night partiers and people who were obviously headed home from odd work shifts.

"I'm starting to feel a little buzz," Wayne said. "How about you?"

Ian shrugged. "Nothing yet."

He began to wonder what the big deal was about acid. He felt a little buzz but that might be from the pot, he couldn't tell. He saw that it was raining harder now. He watched the water dribble down the outside of the bus window. But then he noticed rain was also running down the inside of the glass. Must be a leaky window. He reached out to touch the water drops but the window was cool and dry to his palms. Weird! He could clearly see water running down the inside of the window. But when he touched the glass it was dry. In fact, now rain water had formed a puddle by his feet. Rain continued to run down the inside of the bus window. He placed one hand flat on the glass. The rivulets split apart, flowing on either side of his fingers. He slapped the glass with his other hand trying to catch the water. It dodged out of the way. He slapped his hands a couple more times but the water moved sideways every time.

"Hey," Wayne said. "What you doing, killing flies?"

"Catching the rain." Ian said. He realized how stupid that sounded and started to giggle.

"I think that acid has kicked in." Wayne said with a grin. Larry looked at Ian like he was an idiot. Ian noticed for the first time that Larry's skin had a yellow waxy sheen. As he stared the yellow glow grew brighter, floating in the air around Larry's head.

"You got a halo." He said.

"What?" Larry said.

"I've never done acid before." Ian wanted to explain but putting words together was really hard.

"Just go with the flow." Wayne said.

"Yeah," Ian nodded. "Yeah." He looked back at the water running down the window. The Flow. Yeah. The Flow. He nodded sagely. He watched the tiny dribbles zigzag down the pane. They touched each other and merged. The water drops started to form letters, to spell out words. Ian could clearly see the words forming, but just as he was about to read them, they dissolved into rain drops again. He knew the rain had a really important message for him. But the harder he concentrated the sooner the words melted.

He tapped Wayne on the knee and pointed at the window.

"I'm reading the rain," he said.

Wayne laughed. "Man, you are getting fucked up."

Ian watched Wayne talk to Larry. He could hear their voices but the words were hard to understand. He noticed that Wayne's lips were large and rubbery. Occasionally, as he talked, his tongue fell out of the side of his mouth, yet this didn't seem to interfere with his speech. Freaked out, Ian looked away. An older woman, a few seats away, clutched her purse and stared at them. As Ian stared back, her face turned into thick white bread dough. The dough under her eyes started to sag until Ian could see the bones of her eye sockets. Terrified her eye balls would fall out, he looked back at Larry and Wayne and saw that their eyeballs were also protruding out of the sockets. Don't panic, he thought. He looked down at the floor between his legs, taking deep breaths. He could feel his lungs in his chest, like wet sponges being squeezed.

"Hey! Hey!" He heard Wayne's voice. He looked up. Wayne and Larry stood by the rear door of the bus. "Come on, stoner, it's our stop."

Ian jumped up and followed them off the bus. The rain pelted down hard now. As soon as he thought the word 'hard', the rain drops turned into little stones. They stung as they struck his face. He pulled his hat down and tried to shield his face with his hands. His skin hurt as the rain drops struck him. He worried the rain would cut his skin. At the same time he became aware of his legs; the

216

muscles in his thighs were pumping like an engine. It felt good, really good. Focused on the rhythm of his legs, he forgot about the rain. The three of them walked side by side in the middle of the deserted street. Ian liked the slap of their shoes on the wet pavement. He started snapping his fingers to the rhythm. Wayne joined in. They sped up, walking faster, snapping faster, walking faster, snapping faster, until the two of them were running down the street, way ahead of Larry.

Winded, giggling they stopped to wait for Larry. Ian blinked and looked around. He was under a street lamp staring up at the cone of white light, watching big rain drops fall through it. They left long trails like shooting stars. Ian reached his hands up, trying to catch one.

"Hey fuck-head." Larry shouted. "Come on. We're home."

Ian looked around. He was standing in front of the little bungalow. Larry and Wayne were already inside the fence waving at him to come. He shook his head. Had he and Wayne just run down the street snapping their fingers? Had that really happened? It didn't seem like something Wayne would do. But they had done it. Or had they?

Ian followed the other two into the narrow dark space between the houses. He heard the big dog bark. Dread washed over him. Ian looked at the window. The dog's head was there by the glass, skull-like, eyes glowing in the dark, blood dripping from its fangs. Terrified, Ian tried to run but he bumped into Wayne in the dark.

Downstairs in the apartment, everything seemed normal again. Ian hung up his hat and pulled off his rain-soaked sweater. They went into the kitchen. Bleary-eyed, Connie came out of the bedroom in thin pink, terry-towel bathrobe. She stopped and stared at them for a second.

"Oh my," she grinned. "Look at those eyes. What did you boys get into?"

"We dropped some purple microdot on the way home." Larry explained.

"It's his first trip." Wayne pointed at Ian who nodded and smiled.

"Oh, poor little acid virgin." Connie patted Ian's, cheek. He felt a calm white energy flow from her hand into his brain. She said to the others. "Try not to fuck too much with his head." She pecked Larry on the cheek. "I have to crash. The baby is making me feel like shit again."

"Whatever." Larry concentrated on rolling a joint.

"I'm starved." Wayne said. He shoved bread in the toaster. Every time someone moved Ian saw they left little ghost images behind, like they were moving faster than light. Larry lit a joint.

"You can eat while on acid?"

"Fuck," Wayne said. "I can eat when I'm stoned on anything."

"Here," Larry offered the joint to Ian. "It'll take the edge off. "

Ian took a toke but the smoke felt like fire in his lungs. He coughed it up.

"Don't waste it." Larry looked disgusted and took the joint back.

Meantime, Wayne tossed toast on a plate and smeared it with margarine. It smelled so good. Ian stood up and put more bread in the toaster. He had to really concentrate to do this. Everything he touched seemed to stick to his fingers, like his skin was made of glue. He had another hit from the joint; this time he managed to hold it in his lungs. His toast popped. He plated it and started to spread peanut butter on it. He realized it was not peanut butter. It was actually thick brown oil paint. He started to push it around with the knife, painting a face. He made an amazing likeness of Wayne. He had no idea he had this hidden talent. He was a fucking genius. He could make a lot of money doing paintings on toast. He would become famous for this. He pushed the peanut butter around more, trying to get the eyes just right.

"Hey. Hey." Wayne was snapping his fingers in front of Ian's face. Sparks flew from his fingertips. "You gonna eat that toast or what?"

Ian looked down. There was a slice of toast buried under a thick coat of peanut butter. There was no face, no painting, nothing but a huge mess of peanut butter. Ian dropped the knife and picked up the toast with both hands. He took a big bite. It tasted good, but it was so much work to chew it. Inside his skull he heard his jaw bone grind and squeak. He kept chewing and chewing but could not bring himself to swallow the huge gummy mess. He spit it on his plate.

"Gross." Wayne said.

"Where's Larry?" Ian asked.

"He crashed a long time ago." Wayne shook his head. He pointed at Ian's plate again. "Man, that's gross."

Ian tried another mouthful of toast, determined to eat, but as soon as he started to chew, it felt like he was choking. He stood up quickly and spit. The half-chewed lump landed on the table beside the plate. The sight of the wet mouthful on the table almost made him throw up.

"Too much." Ian said. "This is too much. I gotta crash."

"Yeah" Wayne said. "You are toast." He started giggling. "Get it? Toast!"

Ian followed Wayne to the dark living room. Wayne flopped on the couch and turned on the radio. Ian crawled down to his blankets on the floor and curled up in a ball.

"This is fucking great, eh?" Wayne said. "A place to crash, free dope. This is so cool." As Wayne spoke Ian saw the words come out of his lips inside little balloons, like in a cartoon. They floated up, glowing slightly, and drifted around the room.

"Cool." Ian said. The single word also came out of his mouth in a bubble that floated up and bounced along the ceiling. He watched as it bumped along. Then it burst and he heard the word cool again as if his voice was floating in space.

All night he alternated between nightmares and insomnia, both heavily steeped in acid. He dreamt of drowning, of knives, of running down blood-soaked alleys in Gastown. He woke up shaking and lay awake staring at the ceiling. In the dark he saw little floating dots that soon became stars, as if he was looking right through the house at the night sky. But then he heard footsteps in the narrow space between the houses. He knew it was the same person who had chased him down the alley in Gastown. The footsteps stopped by the window. Ian tried to make himself small, covering his eyes with his sweaty hands. He heard the killer breathing right outside the window. He peaked between his fingers. An blood shot eyeball pressed at the gap around the dirty tea towel. He sat up to scream, then realized the breathing he heard was only Wayne snoring. He laid back down and tried to see the stars again but they had vanished. He could see nothing but black empty space. He drifted into sleep.

Ian woke up early. Tiny waves of sunlight vibrated around the basement window. He was still stoned. He covered his face with a t-shirt but could not get back to sleep. No one else was up yet. He slipped quietly into the bathroom and splashed water on his face. The kitchen light was still on. The air smelled of cigarette smoke and rotting garbage. He decided to step outside and clear his head. He grabbed his hat and shoes and tip-toed up the stairs. The sunlight hurt his eyes. He pulled his hat down low. There was nowhere to sit in the back yard so he walked around to the front. He tensed up walking by the window but the dog did not appear. There was a big motorcycle parked in the middle of the front lawn.

Ian stood on the sidewalk in front of the house. It was a beautiful warm sunny day. In the distance he heard church bells. He decided to take a walk. He headed off in the direction he and Wayne had gone to find the grocery store. At the end of the street he turned right. His brain felt like it was packed in thick cotton. He strolled slowly, forcing one leg to step in front of the other. A few people were outside, mowing their lawn, washing their cars, playing with their kids. Ian stared at them as he passed. He felt like he was watching a movie about the suburbs, about average people. A couple of weeks ago he had been part of that world, the straight world. Now he was smoking pot and dropping acid, hanging out in Gastown, living with a drug-dealing pimp and his junkie girlfriend. It seemed like overnight he had become a hippie. But was he a hippie? He didn't know.

He meandered along, taking a couple more turns, thinking it would be great to get a coffee. Then he realized he didn't have any money, not even enough for a cup of coffee. Another block and Ian hit a wall. He was exhausted. He needed to get back to the apartment and grab some more sleep. He turned around but at the end of the block he was not sure which way he had come. He had paid no attention to street signs. He tried to concentrate but he was too thick-headed to remember which way he had turned. All the houses looked the same. He took a side street and walked a couple of blocks. This felt wrong. He backtracked and went the other way but still could not recall where he had walked before. He saw someone washing their car, but when he got close he saw it was not the same person he had passed before. At each corner he paused. Everything looked familiar but completely strange. He was lost on a sunny Sunday morning. He couldn't ask for help because he didn't even know the name of the street where Connie and Larry lived.

In the middle of another block Ian stopped in a panic. Then he looked across the street. There was the motorcycle on the front lawn in front of the little faded bungalow. He was back. He was even relieved to hear the dog bark as he slipped between the houses. He tip-toed down the back stairs into the darkness hoping he could lay down again without waking Wayne up. But everyone was up now, sitting at the kitchen table, drinking tea and eating toast.

"Where the hell were you?" Larry said.

"I went for a walk," Ian said. "to clear my head."

"You were gone a long fucking time." He sounded suspicious.

"I, I got lost," Ian admitted.

Wayne and Connie burst out laughing.

"Lost?" Wayne said. "Man! You are fucking hilarious when you get stoned. Lost in the middle of the day."

"Lost?" Larry still sounded skeptical. "Don't ever fucking wander off again without telling me."

"Aw," Connie said. "Don't pick on the poor little acid head." She handed him a cup of tea and tussled his hair. "I thought maybe you went to church." She spun Ian to face the others. "I mean, look at this guy. Doesn't he look like he's on his way to church? Can't you see him singing in the choir?"

"It's that fucking sweater." Wayne said. "It's so Eaton's catalogue."

"It is from Eaton's." Ian said. "My mother bought it for me." This made Wayne and Connie laugh even more.

Larry stood up. "Ok, choir boy, get your shit together, we gotta get going."

Ian hurried to the bathroom and ran water over his head. He tried to dry his hair with the crusty hand towel, but gave up. In the kitchen he gulped down more of his tea. In the living room, he pulled his hat over his damp hair. Before they left, Connie ran out of the kitchen and handed Ian a peanut butter sandwich.

"Look at me," she laughed. "I'm fucking June Cleaver,

sending little Beaver off to school."

Waiting at the bus stop Ian took a bite of the sandwich, but the taste of peanut butter made him gag. He remembered choking the night before. Wayne slapped him on the back. Ian leaned over and spit a gooey mouthful on the sidewalk.

"For fuck sakes, stop that." Larry pointed at the sandwich. "Throw it away."

There was no garbage can nearby so Ian tossed the sandwich into the gutter. Within seconds a few pigeons landed and started fighting over it. The bus came. Larry led them to the back seats. On the way downtown, Ian kept nodding off, slumping sideways until his head hit the window and he jerked upright.

The second night downtown Ian felt like he was having a long sleepy déjà vu. As tired as he was, he noticed Larry had a rough schedule. He met certain girls at certain times. The conversations were pretty much the same: some banal chitchat, then money and drugs exchanged hands. Tonight Ian looked more closely at the women. Most of them were in pretty rough shape. Some wobbled on their high heels, obviously stoned. Behind their sometimes sassy banter their eyes were often sad, frightened or dead looking. Some hid cuts and bruises behind thick make-up. Many were extremely thin, ribs showing where their tops were pulled up to expose a bare midriff. Although it was a warm night, a few wore long sleeves to hide track marks. One clutched her elbows tightly to her body. Again it made Ian think of Connie in the kitchen.

In between "the girls", Larry met with his regular

buyers. A few times he stopped at dimly lit bars and rundown hotels. He told Wayne and Ian to wait outside. Weak from hunger and lack of sleep, Ian sat down on the curb and stared at the dirty pavement between his feet. Wayne paced around impatiently, cupping his hands over a dirty window to see into the bar.

"Fuck," he said. "We need to get in on this action. We need to make some coin."

We? Ian said nothing. He did not want to deal drugs. He wanted to find a job and get on with his life.

Later, sitting in the doughnut shop, Wayne asked Larry, "So, how are we working out?"

"Ok," Larry said. "I think you boys hanging around keeps things cool. I mean sometimes an asshole tries to short me, but not so much when they see three of us. Last year two guys jumped me and took my stash. They laid a pretty bad beating on me. Broke my jaw." He reached up and touched his thin chin. When he pushed it side to side, it made a loud popping sound.

"Well, they better not fuck with us, eh?" Wayne elbowed Ian.

Ian nodded but thought, really, what could he do? The idea of getting jumped freaked him out. Starting tomorrow he'd wear his knife again. He had taken it off on the freight train because it poked into his side when he was sleeping. He bummed some change from Wayne and got another coffee. No matter how much sugar he added, he still felt sleepy.

Back out on the street, he stumbled after Larry and Wayne. The night dragged on. They walked, they waited, they smoked joints. Wayne and Ian stood watch while

Larry made deals in dark alleys. It rained. They got wet. It stopped raining and they dried out some. Then it rained again. Ian's shoes were squishy when he walked. Larry came away from one encounter a little more excited.

"That was fucking sweet." He almost smiled. "That guy just bought two lids off me." Ian had no idea what a lid was, but Larry was very pleased. To celebrate, he took them to a bar in Gastown and bought them beers and fries with gravy.

"So," Wayne said after they ate. "Do you think we could get some bread sometime, you know for helping out?" Ian saw that Wayne was a little nervous asking about money.

"Bread?" Larry stared blankly at Wayne for what seemed like a long time. "You mean like pay?"

"Yeah. For being your lookouts."

"Lookouts?" Larry scowled and leaned forward on the little bar table. "It's your second fucking day here and you think you're hot shit. You don't know jack about how this works. And you're living at my place for free. You got some money for rent?"

"No, but-" Wayne started to say.

"Fuck no!" Larry said. "Basically, I'm carrying you. A free place to crash. And you get drugs for free. You have to do more before I pay you shit. Lookouts are a fucking dim-a-dozen." He picked up his beer and took a drink.

In the uncomfortable silence, Ian mopped up gravy with the last of his fries.

"Well, I'm up for it, man." Wayne said. "Give me more to do, and I'll do it."

"What about your buddy?" Larry said.

"Sure." Ian said. "I can do more." But he had no idea what that meant.

Larry took out his wallet and tossed a ten-dollar bill at Wayne. After a second's hesitation, he dropped another one in front of Ian. "There's some walking-around money."

"Thanks," Ian mumbled. He stuffed the ten in his pocket. Wayne snatched his money from the table. He snapped it between his index fingers.

"Sweet." He grinned and ordered more beer.

They came out on the street after closing time. It was raining really hard. They stood under the awning of a clothing store but when the rain did not let up, Larry finally said,

"Fuck it. Let's call it a night."

Once they were sitting at the back of the bus, Larry pulled out the little envelope and gave Wayne and Ian each a hit of acid. Ian stared at the little dot in his palm. After last night he wasn't sure he wanted to do acid again. But he was afraid to say no to Larry. Wayne didn't hesitate, making a show of placing the little pill on his tongue. Ian licked his finger tip, touched the acid and placed in his mouth. He noticed Larry did not take a hit this time. As Ian waited for the acid to kick in, he told himself tonight would be different. After all he knew what to expect, he'd control it more, not get so paranoid. Now that he had dropped it, he had to admit he was curious what would happen on his second trip.

Soon Ian noticed intensified colours creeping into people's faces and hands. The windows slowly took on an odd blue glow. Tonight he wasn't caught off guard by the melting and distortion like the night before. Watching rivulets of rain run down the window, he concentrated as they twisted and turned. If he thought hard enough he could made them flow where he wanted them. He focused harder and the rain began to spell out words. He knew the words were profound, an important message he needed to know but just as he was about to grasp what was being spelled, the letters dissolved back into rain. Rather pleased with himself he told Wayne.

"I am writing with the rain."

"You are one brainy acid head." Wayne laughed. Larry gave Ian an annoyed look.

On the short walk home the damp summer air smelled really good. Ian stopped under a street lamp and inhaled deeply. As he did he felt the air become liquid, a glowing blue syrup that flowed into his lungs. He watched it fill his body. It seeped into his spine, and flowed up to his brain where it opened like a flower petal. It exploded there. He gasped at the beautiful fireworks inside his skull. When he exhaled a beautiful blue cloud floated out of his lips and drifted away into the night sky. Ian smiled up at this amazing blue cloud.

LSD is amazing! he thought, but as they walked between the houses, he felt the same dread as the previous night. He knew the dog was there, he could hear it breathing between huge fangs. He willed himself to stare straight head. *Don't look. Don't look. Don't look.* He felt so relieved to clear the window and make it to the basement door.

Once inside Larry headed off to bed. Full from the burger and fries, Wayne didn't need to eat. There was an old TV in the corner of the living room. Wayne dragged it closer to the couch and found one station showing a late movie, an old 1950's science fiction movie. He sprawled on the couch to watch it. Ian changed into some dry clothes but he was still chilled. He lay down on the floor and wrapped himself in his blankets. Shivering, he curled up in a ball. He lay in the corner behind the couch in the dark, listening to the movie like it was a radio play. He could vividly picture every scene, enhanced by the acid. It was like he was walking around the movie set. Sometimes he was a character in the film, completely lost in the action until he moved and found he was laying on the basement floor tripping out. It took him a while to realize the movie had ended. He heard the TV's white noise mixed with Wayne's snoring. The glow from the TV made the ceiling glow a weird white-grey. As Ian stared, it moved in waves, like water. Then he realized he was under water, laying in the bottom of a pool, watching the surface. He started to choke and drown. Panicking, he closed his eyes and grabbed at the dirty carpet with his hands, willing himself back to reality. A kaleidoscope of colors rushed past his eyes like he was on some ship hurtling through space. He really wanted to sleep but could not, too stoned, too much coffee. He curled into a tighter ball and waited for the acid to wear off. By the time he drifted into sleep, a ghostly dawn light was seeping around the basement windows.

Sounds from the kitchen woke him. Ian smelled eggs frying and was suddenly ravenous. He pulled on his jeans –still damp- and stepped into the kitchen. He could feel the tension in the room. He said good morning but the others said nothing.

Connie offered to make him eggs but as soon as she cracked them into the pan, she rushed to the bathroom. Through the thin door, he could hear her throwing up. Eventually, she came out, wiping her mouth on the sleeve of her robe.

"Fuck, I feel like shit." She rested one hand on Larry's shoulder. "You got something for me?"

Looking disgusted, Larry said, "I told you to have an abortion."

She leaned heavily on the chair. "Well, it's too late for that now, isn't it, asshole?"

Ian tensed. He thought Larry was going to slap her. Instead he fingered in his jacket pocket and tossed some pills on the table.

"Knock yourself out, bitch."

"Fuck you, Larry." Connie said. She popped two pills, leaning over to drink water from the kitchen tap. She went back to the bedroom slamming the door.

"What a cunt." Larry said. Wayne said nothing to defend his cousin. He kept his eyes lowered, busying himself rolling a fat joint from Larry's stash. He lit it and they passed it around in silence. Ian was afraid to ask what the pills were. He quickly ate his eggs and toast; he could tell Larry wanted to get going. Between the residual acid buzz and the fat joint the edges of the world seemed ragged, like everything was made from paper that had been torn up and hastily glued together again.

Just before they headed out, Ian remembered his knife. He threaded his belt through the sheath until the knife hung by his right side. When he tugged the sweater down only the tip of the sheath showed. He thought the knife would make him feel better but now that he was wearing it, the big knife just made him nervous.

Day three and already things felt a little routine. They followed Larry around as he dealt with his girls and his regular buyers. In between they walked all over downtown Vancouver, from Gastown to Stanley Park. They even jumped in a cab and circled around by the university where Larry made a quite a few sales. Larry spoke contemptuously about the students, calling them "little rich kids who want to be cool." Back downtown, he maintained a steady saunter, nodding to passing heads, speaking quietly from the corner of his mouth. "Pot? Looking for some pot?" Every so often someone would take him up on the offer. Ian and Wayne stood around as he made random sales.

When they stopped for coffee and doughnuts, Wayne continued to fish for details about buying and selling. Larry seemed to be relaxing with them a bit but still gave guarded answers. He admitted that most of his dealing was small time stuff.

"Kids partying, weekend hippies." He said. "They want to toke up and pretend they were at Woodstock." Ian had noticed that most sales were a few joints, the occasional dime bag, maybe some acid. Larry hinted that he was working on some larger scores.

"I need to expand my business." He picked at his top teeth with his thumb nail.

"Cool." Wayne said. "Whatever you need me to do, I'm your guy."

Larry said nothing and lit another smoke.

Even after coffee and doughnuts, Ian was bagged. No amount of caffeine and sugar could clear his brain of the wet cotton feeling. He noticed his fingers shaking as he dumped more sugar into the swill. He was glad to get back on the street; at least walking burned up some of his anxiety.

Around midnight things got weirder. Larry announced he had some new girls to see.

"New?" Wayne asked.

"Yeah, I'm working with some new birds starting tonight. A guy owed me a lot of bread from a pot shipment I set up last year. He paid me in pussy."

Larry led them down through an industrial park. They had never walked this route before. They emerged by a highway, then crossed beneath some big concrete underpasses. In the murky darkness, Ian felt the same panic he had when walking near the window with the angry dog. A wino suddenly lurched out of the shadows in front of them. Instinctively, Ian's hand moved to the handle of his knife. The guy staggered past them. Ian saw that Wayne had also reached for his knife. Although Wayne made Ian nervous, if they got jumped he figured Wayne was the best guy to have around.

Further along they came upon a dozen women walking back and forth along the curb. Larry told them to wait there. He crossed the street and located one of the girls he was looking for. He huddled with her by a low cement wall. She smoked a cigarette while Larry leaned close to talk into her ear. She nodded a few times as he spoke. Finally, he handed her something and walked away. He waved the boys over. They followed him past a few other women.

Ian tried not to stare at their tight tops and short skirts. Some skirts were so short that he could see their underwear. One woman wore no underwear. Ian could see her pubic hair as she sauntered past. She turned to stare at him and he looked away, embarrassed. Cars slowly cruised along the dark street. As soon as one stopped, one of the women would trot over, exchange a few words and climb in. It was all so unreal. Ian thought of his friends back in Madanon, living with their parents, working a summer jobs, borrowing the family car to go on dates, while Ian was here doing this – whatever the fuck this was!

Along the underpass Larry tracked down and talked with five more women. Each time he made Wayne and Ian wait across the street, as though he didn't trust them to know his business. As they watched from a distance, one woman seemed to argue with Larry. She started to walk away. He grabbed her arm. When she struggled he slapped her face.

"Hey," Ian turned to Wayne. "Did you see that? He just slapped her."

"So what?" Wayne said. "He's gotta keep them in line, eh?" He poked Ian in the chest. "It's none of your business what Larry does. Keep your fucking mouth shut."

Ian stepped back. Had Wayne just threatened him? He had already noticed how Wayne acted different around Larry, tougher, meaner; probably trying to impress him. Ian stared at his feet, wondering what to do.

Looking pissed, Larry crossed the street.

"Come on." As he breezed past, Wayne fell in beside him.

Ian was still stunned. This was crazy. What was he doing here? He should split. But it was the middle of the night. Where could he go? He had what –less than ten dollars- and all his stuff was back at the apartment. He wasn't even sure he could find his way there on his own. Tomorrow he had to clear out. He could try and live on one of those beaches, but Vancouver had been so rainy. He'd need to get a tent. Did he have enough to buy one? He felt trapped, really trapped.

"Hey fuck-head." Wayne shouted. He and Larry were already half a block away. Ian ran to catch up. Sullenly, he fell in behind them. He noticed that Wayne had even started walking like Larry: silent and menacing, his arms stiff at his sides. Tomorrow, he promised himself, tomorrow I'll move out.

Back downtown, Larry led them down an alley behind some dilapidated buildings.

"I need to make a stop here at a squat where some junkies crash."

Larry knocked on a door at the back of what looked like an abandoned warehouse.

"Wait out here?" Wayne said.

"Naw." Larry said. "Come in with me. This crew is sketchy as fuck. You never know what they'll try."

The door opened a crack, revealing one blood-shot eye. Larry said a few words and they stepped inside. The door clicked shut behind them. It was extremely dark. As his eyes adjusted, Ian saw a few skeletal people seated around a packing crate dotted with candle stubs, spoons and needles. Larry tapped one guy who stood up. They went over by the broken window to talk. Wayne stood, staring openly at the junkies as they shot up. Ian found it hard not to stare too, like driving past a car crash. Someone leaned close to the candle. In the dim flickering light he could see their forearm was covered with festering sores. He turned and started to step away but realized that a couple of the lumps in the shadows were not garbage but people passed out on the floor. He saw an open window and walked towards it, but a horrible smell made him stop. The whole corner of the room was covered with piss and shit. Turds floated in a shallow puddle. Ian looked down and realized he had stepped in the pee. He started to gag. He covered his mouth and walked quickly back to the packing crate. One of the junkies had fixed and had fallen over backwards. A couple others had nodded off sitting up, their legs crossed. The other junkies didn't seem to care; they waited anxiously for their turn with the needle.

When Larry was done, he led them outside. Ian gulped in big mouthfuls of summer air, hoping he wouldn't throw up. As they walked towards the East Hastings, Wayne asked.

"That go ok?"

"It's like shooting fish in a barrel." Larry said. "None of this fucking nickel and dime shit on the street. Their old dealer got busted so I'm taking over. Just one drop off every couple of days and a nice big chunk of cash. Easy money, as long as they all don't fucking OD and die."

"Fucking junkies." Wayne said. He laughed as if he

had told a joke.

That night ended the same as the previous two. Once the street traffic died down, Larry announced they were headed home. On the bus he offered the acid again. Ian hesitated, but in many ways taking acid had become the best part of his day. Once he was stoned he was distracted and could stop thinking about what he had witnessed that night. He noticed, once again, that Larry didn't take any acid. Occasionally Ian noticed Larry staring at him. As the acid kicked in Ian felt a weird vibe. Larry looked more and more like a vampire. His face turned as pale as plaster. A blue tinge crept into his lips. Little fangs protruded from his mouth. Ian looked away, when he looked back a trickle of blood ran from Larry's mouth. Horrified, Ian turned to stare out the bus window, but when he looked back he saw that Larry and Wayne looked so much alike he couldn't tell them apart. He realized that they were both vampires. From the bus stop to the apartment, he walked behind them, filled with dread because he knew that they were planning to kill him. They kept looking back over their shoulders at him. He could not hear what they said, but occasionally he heard his name as they discussed stabbing him and cutting him up. Larry told Wayne they would feed the pieces to the crazy dog upstairs.

But as soon as they went into the basement, Connie came out briefly with her toothy smile. Ian felt so good seeing her. He was relieved when Larry followed her back to the bedroom. Wayne said he was hungry and decided to make spaghetti. Ian was too stoned to eat. But as the pasta cooked they took turns fishing out strands and tossing them at the wall, adding to the giant art work that Connie liked. Ian started throwing them at the ceiling too. This made Wayne laugh. He tossed some up there too. A few minutes later the boys broke into hysterical giggles when they realized they had tossed almost the entire pot of spaghetti on the walls and ceiling. Wayne decided to eat some toast instead.

Meantime Ian watched the wet pasta on the ceiling. It changed into a nest of writhing worms. He knew they were going to drop on him, so he retreated to the living room. He lay down and wrapped himself in his blankets. He tried to sleep but he felt worms creeping up his legs. He bolted upright, grabbing at his feet. Half asleep, Wayne told him to knock it off. Ian wrapped himself tighter in the blankets. He decided that Larry was just waiting for him to fall asleep so he could come out and kill him. Terrified he laid awake until after sunrise, then he had nightmares about junkies leaning over him, trying to jab needles into his eyes.

Ian woke up exhausted and depressed. He found the other three at the table, eating in silence, except when Larry and Connie sniped at each other. Over tea and toast, Ian tried to psych himself up to tell them he was going to look for work, but Larry was in such a shitty mood Ian was afraid of speak up. He recalled Larry slapping that woman the previous night. He couldn't count on Wayne to back him up and Connie seemed out of it. Ian figured she had already done her morning fix. So he said nothing about job hunting. He was furious with himself. He was so stupid leaving home with no real plan, then blowing all his cash before he even got to Vancouver. Now here he was, broke, sleeping on the floor, hanging out with assholes like Larry and Wayne. When the joint circled the table he toked really hard, trying to shake his foul mood. He didn't even have time to grab a shower before Larry said they should hit the road.

This third day went by in a blur of sameness. They walked for hours, waiting and watching while Larry dealt with his girls, his regulars and complete strangers. They spent some time in the business district, cruising past some high end restaurants and night clubs. Larry told them heroin was becoming so popular that even "suits" were wanting to try it, just to prove they were cool. But dealing to clean cut men in suits and ties ratcheted up Larry's paranoia.

"I fucking hate this." He admitted as they ambled back to Gastown. "I need to set up some proper scores instead of this nickel and dime shit."

Ian was getting used to seeing people shoot up anytime and anywhere. In the squats, in alleys, on park benches. He had learned to "be cool" and not stare, but he was still freaked out around junkies. Later that night as he waited for Larry to make a deal in an alley, he turned his head and saw a guy slouched sideways in an abandoned doorway. From the corner of his eye, Ian watched a shaky hand clutching the needle, jabbing repeatedly, trying to find a vein. After three or four tries, the needle connected. As he pushed down on the fix, the junkie raised his head and looked right at Ian. It was a kid, about his own age, maybe even younger. Ian turned away, thinking once again that he had to get away from all this.

The only break from walking and waiting was when Larry wanted a coffee break. Always exhausted, Ian sucked back two or three coffees thick with sugar. Meanwhile Wayne continued hounding Larry to let him deal.

"It makes sense, man." Wayne said. "Double your territory, double your profits. You know I can do it, man. Plus, I'm not going to take any shit from anyone."

"I'll think about it." Larry said. "But what about your buddy?" He nodded at Ian. "Who's gonna buy from him?

Wayne broke into a laugh. "Yeah, he doesn't scream buy dope from me, does he?"

Larry gave one of his thin smirks.

"Maybe that's a good thing," Ian said defensively. "No one would suspect me."

"No one would approach you either." Larry said. He picked his front teeth with his thumb nail and blew smoke from his nostrils. "Still not sure what to do with this one. He's useless as tits on a bull." His eye lids narrowed as he stared at Ian. "On the other hand, he's a pretty young thing. What do you say, choir boy? You any good at hand jobs? Would you blow a guy for $20 bucks?"

"Fuck off." Ian said.

Wayne burst out laughing. "He's just jerking your chain."

"I don't know." Larry give a sly wink. "There's a lot of old dudes who like to fuck young boys. We could make some serious cash on Choir Boy's ass."

"Look at your face!" Wayne guffawed and thumped Ian on the shoulder. "He's got your goat. Come on." He stood up. "This pot's not going to sell itself."

The rest of the night Ian fretted about what Larry had said. He wasn't convinced he was kidding. He pimped girls, so why not boys? No way Ian would ever go down on someone, even for money. Larry couldn't force him to do that. Or could he? He wanted to believe that Wayne would stand up for him, but Ian could see how badly he wanted to work for Larry. And it was obvious that Larry didn't need two lookouts. All night, as he followed them around, Ian tried to talk himself into leaving, but if he split, he'd have no place to sleep, no food, and no money. He heard that the cops were cracking down on hippies sleeping in the open, busting people for vagrancy. If they had any pot on them they were screwed. Even a joint or two meant prison time for possession.

No, Ian needed to get a job first. But how could he do it? He was with Larry and Wayne every minute of every day. Half the time he was fall-down exhausted and the other half, he was stoned. He thought about saying no to the free acid, but he was afraid of Larry's reaction. He thought about trying to palm the acid and pretend he was stoned, but Larry always watched him so closely. Ian wasn't sure that he could fake being stoned. And, by the end of the day, he really felt like getting stoned to distract himself from the things he witnessed. But every morning he woke up feeling like shit and wishing he had not done it.

Ian's days and nights started to blur together into one long weird trip. He woke exhausted, usually still buzzing from the acid. Tea, toast and a couple of joints. Connie either throwing up or fighting with Larry, her bloody needle often resting on the edge of an ashtray or a dirty saucer. Downtown they walked endless hours, the same route, the same regulars, the same nerve-racking ventures into dark alleys and abandoned warehouses. Short breaks in the same dingy doughnut shop. Larry and Wayne talked more and more about the scene, ignoring Ian who tried to stave off his fatigue by drinking bad coffee loaded with sugar. When the street traffic died down, the night ended with a bus ride home and an acid trip.

Ian kept trying to control the acid, but it was impossible to predict. The hallucinations were so real. Often he was terrified by what he was seeing, struggling like someone in a nightmare who couldn't wake up. On the other hand, sometimes the acid gave him some type of pleasant hallucination, where he was distracted and happy. But often that good experience collapsed around him. Reality could not be trusted. The hardest thing was being around Larry when he was tripping. Ian was afraid of him and being stoned made it worse. He was relieved to get back at the apartment. Once Larry crashed, Ian could relax. Wayne was a funny stoner who never seemed to have a bad acid trip. He could eat huge meals when stoned and never had a problem sleeping. But after a few more days in Vancouver, Ian had to admit that he found Wayne boring. He could only talk about three things: drugs, chicks and music. Ian had heard all of his stories. Watching Wayne launch into another long animated tale about some fight he had in high school, made Ian miss his high school pals. He missed hanging out after school. He even missed going to school. He missed reading. He used to read a lot. Since leaving home, he had not read anything. The only book he had with him was On the Road. A couple of times, late at night, he had pulled it out, hoping to distract himself. But stoned on acid the words were impossible to decipher, just little dots of ink that danced across the page like some strange hieroglyphics. Ian found himself staring at the cover. Why should he read some book by an old beatnik who had died years ago? It seemed pointless. Instead Ian lay awake most of each night, stoned, out of control and feeling trapped.

One night a few days later, as he and Wayne waited at the mouth of an alley, they heard Larry shout loudly. "Fuck you!"

Wayne bolted into the dark, his knife already out. Ian ran after him.

Larry held a guy against the wall by the lapels of his jacket.

"You fuck. Don't ever try to burn me again." He slammed the guy back into the brick wall a couple of times. As soon as he let go the guy dashed towards the street.

"Want me catch him?" Wayne waved his knife. "I'll give the fucker something to write home about."

"No, let's split. I thought I saw some cops circling the block."

Ian was relieved. He firmly believed that Wayne would knife someone if Larry told him to. Back on the street, Larry stopped to light a smoke. His fingers shook.

"You guys did good. Come on. I'll buy you a beer." In the bar, he explained that the guy said he wanted to buy a half pound of pot, but tried to rip him. "Fucker had a couple of twenties wrapped around a wad of newspaper. This is the fucking bullshit I have to put up with dealing on the street."

"See," Wayne said, "That's why you need to have me dealing. Put me out there and in a week everyone would know don't fuck with Wayne."

Larry didn't say yes but he didn't say no. They quickly polished off their beers and headed back on the street. The rest of the night, every chance he had, Wayne pushed Larry to let him deal too. Meantime, Ian could not shake his jitters. Seeing Wayne with his knife drawn freaked him out. Sooner or later something bad would happen and he'd be in the thick of it. He had to get away, but how?

The next day Ian managed to sleep until mid-afternoon. Sleepily he staggered into the kitchen. Larry and Wayne had already eaten. They were smoking a joint. Connie was still in bed. Larry said she'd been up all night with backaches and nausea. As Ian made toast, Larry stood up.

"We're heading out." He tossed a couple of twenties on the table. "You stay here today, ok? Go get some groceries. Ask Connie what she needs. Maybe help her clean up this dump a little."

"Sure. Sure thing." Ian said. He knew there was no point in arguing with Larry. In fact he was relieved to get a day off. Wayne didn't seem surprised by the decision to leave him behind. He and Larry had obviously been talking. They grabbed their hats and left.

Ian sat and ate his toast. He stared at the cash laying

in the middle of the messy table. This was his chance. He could take the money and split. But where to? He'd have to find somewhere to crash tonight. Maybe in a park or on a beach but how could he avoid Larry and Wayne? They wandered all over downtown. If he ran into them, well, he didn't even want to think about that. Or maybe he should go job hunting! When walking around, he had spotted a youth employment office. Maybe he could get there and back without running into Larry and Wayne. He knew their routine pretty well. But he was still ragged from the acid and so tired. He left his half eaten toast and stumbled back to the living room. He sprawled on the couch where Wayne always slept. It was old and sagging, yet it felt so good after sleeping on the floor for almost two weeks. He fell asleep immediately.

When he woke up, he heard Connie in the kitchen.

"Hey, there's the sleepy head." She said as he wandered in. She poured him some tea. Her needle was on the table, the tip resting on the edge of her ashtray. "I knew you were here cause I heard you snoring.

"Really?" Ian smiled. "I didn't know I snored."

"Well, you do, buddy. Like a chain saw."

He asked how she was doing?

"Ok, I guess." She rubbed her bump. "This baby is trying to fucking kill me." She smeared margarine on toast and poured sugar on it. "Well, really what's killing me is not doing any smack." She laughed, showing her large stained teeth. "I mean, yeah I'm doing a little but that's just because I can't go cold turkey while I'm preggers. But as soon as this thing pops, I'm kicking for good." She said it very firmly but she had said it so many times that Ian doubted she would ever quit. He poured some sugar in his tea and worked up his nerve to ask.

"So, how did this happen? Like all this?" He gestured at the grungy kitchen with garbage on the floor, dirty dishes and the crusty spaghetti stuck to the walls.

"You mean getting hooked, Larry and all that?" She picked up a slice of toast with both shaky hands and managed to take a bite. "Ha. We don't have time for that story. Let's just say never start doing heroin. I mean I came to Vancouver to get away from my parents. Well, first I moved to Lethbridge, Alberta. You ever been there? You ain't missing much. I was waitressing in this dumpy burger joint. It was ok, I mean lots of old farmers who liked to look down your top or grab at your ass, but that usually meant a good tip." She pushed the greasy half eaten toast away from her, wiped her fingers on her jeans and grabbed a smoke. "But I was so fucking bored. I heard Van was nice. So I moved here and got a job waitressing. I was waiting on tables and hanging out, going to parties. This was, uh, about five years ago. Van is great party town then. People were really laid back. Pot was so fucking cheap." She paused to re-light her smoke. "Then I met Larry, you know, he's a pretty good looking dude. I was hanging with him, buying my pot from him, you know nothing serious." She stirred her tea and raised it to her lips. Her fingers trembled so hard the tea slopped onto the table.

"Fuck." She wiped the table with the sleeve of her robe. "I'm a fucking mess." She dragged on her smoke.

"Anyway, one day Larry had some smack. We were with a bunch of people and everyone was shooting up, so

I tried it." She stared at her mug. "I got hooked. At first I was getting it for free from Lar, but then he started bitching that it was not free and I should pay for it." She leaned down and blew on the tea. "I ended up owing Larry a lot of bread. One day he said maybe I could bring in some extra cash, you know working downtown." She tapped her smoke on the ashtray and looked straight at Ian, who tried not to look shocked.

"Yeah. I know. What can I say?" She looked away quickly. "I'm a fucking junkie."

She pointed at her belly.

"And now this asshole turns up."

"Is it Larry's?" He regretted blurting it out.

Connie sighed. "To be honest. I'm not sure. And neither is Larry, which is why he's being such a prick. But he damn well better take care of it because I am not going to end up on welfare. Fuck that shit." She leaned close and grabbed Ian by the ear.

"Promise me one thing, choir boy. Promise me you'll never try heroin, not even a taste, ok?"

"Sure. I swear." She gave his ear a little twist. "Ouch. That hurts. Seriously. I'm never going to try heroin."

"Good, because if I ever see you anywhere near smack, I'll kick your fucking ass."

Ian smiled as he rubbed his ear. It felt nice to have someone care about him. She tossed her half eaten toast into a grocery bag they used for garbage, then she snatched up her works and went in the bathroom. She was gone a long time. He ran water and started washing the dishes. When she came out he knew by her eyes that she had shot up again.

"I'm gonna crash."

He told her Larry has left some money and he was going to buy some groceries.

"Get me some smokes, eh? Craven A. And some ice cream, maybe chocolate." Her voice trailed off as she shut the bedroom door.

Ian finished the dishes, wiped the table and filled a garbage bag. He debated pulling the dried spaghetti off the wall but he knew Connie liked it. On the way to the store he dumped the garbage in a can in the back yard. It was a sunny day. People were out mowing lawns, working in their gardens, riding bikes, jogging. It felt good to be walking around, away from Larry and Wayne, seeing normal people doing normal things. He still felt fuzzy from all the drugs, but after a minute of concentrating he realized he had been in Vancouver almost two weeks, and he hadn't done any job hunting. Maybe tomorrow when he was rested up he'd get up early and go pound the pavement.

Watching street signs so he could find his way back, Ian walked to the same grocery store where he and Wayne had shoplifted. He worried the manager might recognize him but no one paid any attention to him as he circled with his cart. On the way back to the house, he stopped at a corner store and got cigarettes. There were bunches of flowers displayed outside in plastic buckets. On an impulse he bought a bunch of daffodils for Connie.

When he got back she was still in the bedroom. He put way the groceries. He didn't know what to do with the flowers. He found an old wine bottle under the sink and managed to jam the stems in there. He placed it in the middle of the table. The flowers seemed to glow. Ian realized that they were the only colour in this dingy basement world. Or maybe he was still tripping from last night's acid. He flopped on the couch and watched TV with the volume on low. Soon he drifted off…

When he woke an hour later, he heard Connie in the kitchen. He sat up, rubbing his eyes. This was the most rested he had felt since arriving on the coast. Connie was wearing a long pale yellow dress with little blue flowers on it. It was first time he had seen her in anything but her bathrobe or a baggy sweatshirt and jeans.

"Hey," he said.

"Hey yourself," She gave him a big smile. "Did you buy me these flowers?"

"Sure." he said. "I thought you could use some cheering up."

"You're sweet." She rushed over and grabbed him in a tight hug. He felt her belly against his. Except for the bump, she was skin and bones. She held him for a second. He felt a flash of heat between them. She kissed his cheek.

"Thanks for the flowers." She held both his shoulders and kissed him on the lips, just a peck but a split second longer than she should have. She broke off and put the kettle on. He felt awkward but glad he had bought the flowers. They decided to have soup and grilled cheese sandwiches. Connie kept up a constant steam of chatter about her family, her parents, her three brothers. Ian realized again, just how lonely she was. It occurred to him that she never left the apartment and never mentioned any friends in Vancouver. Much like him, she was trapped here with Larry. But at least he got out every day, even if it was just to watch Larry work the street.

After they ate, she jumped up and ducked into the bedroom. She returned with a small bag of grass and started rolling a joint.

"Private stash," she said. "Don't tell Larry."

As they toked Ian told her about his family and about running away. To his surprise he told her everything, about Julie, about the guy in Brandon, about how he hoped to find a job and buy a motorcycle. She was a good listener, laughing at things like him throwing the brick in Brandon and being crowned with his fedora as the King of the Road.

"I like that hat." She said. "It suits you." She stood up and touched his hair. "But your hair is getting too long for this side part shit. You ever tried it parting in the middle?"

Excited, Connie ran to the bathroom and grabbed her brush and comb. She wet the brush, and standing behind him, parted his hair down the middle, then brushed it to the sides. It hung down over his ears.

"There. Go look in the mirror."

Ian looked in the mirror, turning his head side to side. It was a cool. He no longer looked like such a nerdy bookworm.

"This will really go with your motorcycle." Connie said, taking a couple more puffs off her joint. "I dated a dude back in Lethbridge who had a Kawasaki. We used to buzz around the back farm roads." She smiled softly looking down at the table. "He was a really nice guy too. He wanted to marry me and have lots of kids, but I didn't want to settle down." She squeezed the burner off the joint.

"Oh well," she chuckled sadly. "Shit happens."

They sat in silence for a while.

"Wow. I'm being a bummer. Look, Ian, you really should get out of here. I love Larry, but he likes to use people. He'll fuck you over if he can."

Ian nodded and thought of Larry's frequent jokes about him turning tricks.

"Thanks." He said. "I really do need to find a job."

Connie stood up and patted her belly. "The kid wants to take a nap. I got no choice."

She shut the bedroom door. Ian stood up and took the plates to the sink. He washed the dishes, wiped the table and decided to go outside. He stepped carefully around the dog turds and crossed the yard to an old wooden kitchen chair in the back corner by the sagging fence. He sat down and leaned back against the fence. He watched the final moments of the sunset, glowing pink over the low rooftops. Darkness fell and one star appeared. Even with the glow of city lights he spotted a dozen more. It was a beautiful summer night. He wished Connie was out here to enjoy it. Addicted, pregnant, living with Larry, he was overwhelmed with sadness for her. She was right: he had to get out of here, find a job and get on with his summer. He had been in Vancouver long enough to know his lumber camp fantasy was just that. But there must be some other work he could do. He didn't care what is was, anything would be better than this. For the first time in two weeks he felt a burst of optimism that things would still work out.

Back inside he flopped on the couch to watch TV. He

drifted in and out of sleep. In the middle of the night Larry and Wayne came stomping down the steps.

"Hey," Wayne boomed. "There's the lazy fucker." He tossed his hat on the coffee table and scratched his curly hair with both hands.

"How was it?" Ian asked as he sat up.

"Fucking great." Wayne said. "Larry let me roam around and sell pot." He pulled a clump of money from his jeans and waved it in Ian's face.

"Look at that, a hundred bucks just for walking around. And look what I got today."

He fished in his shirt pocket and pulled out some mirrored sunglasses. He put them on and struck a serious gun fighter pose.

"Far out, eh? I picked them up in a store. Five finger discount. Just put them on and walked right past some lard-ass clerk."

Meantime Larry put the kettle on for tea. The three of them settled at the table while Larry rolled one of his wiry joints. As he was rolling, he nodded at the flowers.

"Where'd those come from?"

Nervously, Ian said, "I bought them for Connie when I went to get groceries."

"So you're fucking buying flowers for my woman?" As Larry stared hard at him, Ian felt his heart racing.

"I... I thought they might cheer her up."

Larry flicked his lighter and toked. He blew smoke through a thin smile. "I'm just jerking your chain. She needs cheering up. Since she got knocked up she's been a fucking crazy bitch."

Even though Ian sat closer, Larry handed the joint

across the table to Wayne. Judging from their eyes Ian knew they had dropped acid on the way home. Wayne started telling stories about his pot sales. He stood up while he talked, acting out some of his encounters. Occasionally he would lose his train of thought, side tracked with some detail in the room. He suddenly noticed the hum of the fridge "sounds like a train, way off in the distance" or he stopped talking and waved his hand around under the kitchen light amusing himself with the strobing. When he finally sat down again, he pointed at the flowers.

"Wow, look at that yellow, man, look at that." He touched one of the flowers and held his finger out to Ian. "Look, they are bleeding." He tugged on a petal and it fell off on the table.

"Oops." Wayne giggled. "I broke a flower." He played with another blossom until more petals fell off.

Larry reached out with his lit cigarette and burned a hole in one of the petals. It took a second and he nodded thoughtfully after he did it, like it was some kind of science experiment. He did it again. This time he moved his cigarette slowly down the petal leaving a long scorched mark.

Ian sat helpless, watching them ruin Connie's flowers.

Wayne continued to flick his finger at the other flowers, laughing as petals fell on the table. Finally, he grabbed a whole bunch of blossoms in his hand and squeezed his fist.

"Look at that," He pointed to the stained table top. "I squeezed all the colour out."

Larry pulled a stem out of the wine bottle. He held the flower in front of his face and plucked petals, one at a time.

"She fucks me. She fucks me not. She fucks me." This put Wayne into hysterical giggles. Larry kept mumbling. "She fucks me. She fucks me not."

The bedroom door opened. Bleary eyed, Connie emerged.

"Sounds like a party," she started to say, then she saw the flowers. "Jesus, guys, did you have to ruin them?"

"Sorry." Wayne looked guilty. "I dropped a couple of hits of acid. I'm really fucked up."

"You're an asshole!"

"Calm down," Larry said. He nodded at Ian. "Your boyfriend can buy you more flowers the next time he goes shopping."

"Aw, fuck you, Larry." Connie picked up the bottle with the remaining flowers and hurled the whole thing into the corner. The bottle bounced around but did not break. It rolled and spun, splashing water on the floor. Connie ran back to the bedroom and slammed the door.

"Bitch." Larry shrugged. He glared at Ian as if this was his fault. Wayne stood up and grabbed the bottle, scooping up the flowers. He sheepishly placed everything back on the table.

"I'm gonna crash." He said and staggered out of the kitchen. Ian stood up to follow Wayne. As he did, Larry grabbed his wrist in his boney fingers.

"See what happens when you fuck around with my woman!" Ian tried to pull his arm free, but Larry squeezed even harder. "Don't fuck with me, choir boy."

Larry let go, stood up, and went into the bedroom. Shaken, Ian turned off the kitchen light. He felt his way into the darkened living room and found his bedroll on the floor. He could hear Larry and Connie in the bedroom, shouting at each other. He lay there feeling helpless. He had to get out of here. Stoned and restless, Wayne kept getting up, wandering to the kitchen and back, talking to himself, but finally he settled down and Ian slept.

Ian had slept so much the day before that he woke up early for the first time since arriving in Vancouver. It was quiet. Around eight, he went to the bathroom, peed and washed his face. He wanted a shower, but was afraid the noise would wake up Larry. Overnight his hair had returned to the side part. He wet it down and parted it in the middle again. Connie was right, it looked much better this way.

Back in the kitchen he made tea and toast. The burnt and crumpled flower petals lay on the table, as did Wayne's wad of cash. Ian poked it with his finger – over fifty dollars. Like the day, before he pondered grabbing the cash and getting the fuck out of there. He peaked around the corner at Wayne, belly down on the couch, in a deep sleep, mouth hanging open. Ian would have to sneak over, roll up his blankets, get his gear and make it out the door without anyone waking up. He hesitated, terrified of getting caught by Wayne. Or worse by Larry! Besides where would he go? If he stole the cash, they would come looking for him. No, first he needed to find a job. Then, in a week or two he'd get some pay and he could get his own place. He downed the rest of his tea. He decided to head downtown to that employment office he had seen.

Ian walked slowly past Wayne, picked up his hat and tiptoed up the stairs. It had been raining hard. Everything was soaked. Low grey clouds filled the sky. In between the houses, Ian slipped past the window. The dog didn't come barking. As soon as he was clear of the broken gate, he walked quickly to the bus stop. He used the change left from yesterday's grocery run to pay his bus fare. On the ride downtown, he grew excited. He was finally getting back on track. He figured Larry would be upset when he got a job, but if he offered some money for rent that would smooth things over. If that was no good, fuck it, he'd head to a beach and sleep outside until he got his first pay.

The city looked so different in the morning that it took Ian almost an hour to find the youth employment office located in a store front. When he finally spotted it, he got nervous. He paused outside to look through the window. There were a few people working at desks, a couple of filing cabinets and two long banquet tables surrounded by stackable plastic chairs. On one wall he saw a large bulletin board under a long sign printed in bold letters: Job Opportunities.

Ian suddenly felt self-conscious of his dirty jeans, one knee worn through, still dirty and rust-stained from jumping the freight train. He took off his hat, patted his hair and put it back on. He took a deep breath and entered. Rock music played softly from a radio on one of the desks. He crossed directly to the bulletin board. It was dotted with file cards for each job, posted in different categories. There were a few cards under the label, Restaurant: places looking for line cooks, chefs and experienced wait staff. There were cards for trades people, welders and carpenters. Ian slowly walked the length of the board with a sinking feeling; there was nothing posted that he was qualified to do.

Finally, he went over to one of the staff. A pleasant woman in her thirties looked up from her desk.

"Anything I can help you with?"

"I'm new in town and looking for work."

"Well, you've come to the right place." She had a friendly smile. She handed him a clipboard and pen and told him to fill out the form, then he could see an employment counsellor.

He sat down at one of the tables. The form was only one-page long. He printed his name, then paused where it said address? He heard Larry's voice in his head, saying to never tell anyone where they lived. He left it blank. He had no telephone number to list. Under highest level of education, he wrote grade 11.

He stared at the area labeled Employment Experience. He had none. Zero. He had never worked, not even a part time job when in school. There was nothing he could put down. He felt useless. At the bottom was a place the date and a signature. He signed his name, but he wasn't sure of the date. He was not even sure what day of the week it was. He fought the urge to walk out.

Ian went over to the desk and handed the clip board to the woman.

"Oh." She said after seeing the empty page. "Josh" She called to one of her co-workers. "Josh, maybe you can talk to this guy."

Josh was in his late twenties. He had short curly hair and thick sideburns. He wore a short sleeved white shirt and a wide paisley tie and large aviator style glasses. He gestured Ian to a seat across from him. He looked over the form for quite a while, tapping his pen randomly on his desk top. He looked at the bottom and quickly filled in the date.

"Okey-dokey, Ian." He finally said. "So tell me a little about yourself and what kind of work you are after?"

Ian explained that he was from Ontario and had come out west to work for the summer. He stopped himself from saying in a lumber camp because he knew how stupid that sounded. "I'm really willing to do anything. "

"Good. That's a good attitude. Really good." Josh nodded. "But unfortunately the students snatched up most of the summer jobs back in June. Not sure why you waited so long to come in."

"Well," Ian said. "It took me a while to get settled. But I'd be up for any kind of work. I really need a job."

"I hear ya." Josh looked over the blank form as if he was reading it again. He leaned back and rocked in his chair. "To be honest you don't have much to offer. I mean in terms of actual experience. But we do get requests from time to time for casual labour, things like moving companies. Sometimes home renovation companies need some extra hands to knock down walls. No skills required. And we have companies that delivery flyers door to door. On foot. Of course, none of these jobs are steady."

"That's ok." Ian said. "I'll take anything."

"Well," Josh said. "I'll tell you what we can do. We keep you on file and call you when some general labour positions come in." He frowned at Ian's form. "You have not listed a phone number."

Ian hesitated. "Well, I'm crashing with some people I met. They don't have a phone."

"Ok. Ok. Well, that makes things a little difficult." Josh clicked his pen a more couple of times. In the address area that Ian had left blank he wrote: No Fixed Address. In the top right corner, he printed in large block letters: NFA.

He stood up. Ian stood up too.

"The best I can suggest under these circumstances is that you come here each morning when we open. That's at 8 am. Casual employers drop by between eight and nine. They hire on the spot. You might have to hangout for an hour waiting, but we always have coffee and doughnuts too. How does that sound?"

"Good," Ian said. "That sounds good."

"See you tomorrow morning?"

"Sure thing." Ian said but he knew it was bullshit. He could never make it here at eight. Staying with Larry and Connie he was lucky to get to sleep by four in the morning. He'd never get downtown that early.

"These are very helpful too." Josh handed him some brochures on how to write resumes, how to job hunt, and what to do at a job interview. Ian took them awkwardly. Josh walked him part way to the door. He patted him on the shoulder.

"Ok, Ian we'll see you tomorrow morning."

Outside Ian stood clutching the brochures. He

glanced back and saw Josh, holding Ian's form, talking to the woman at the desk. He shook his head. She seemed to be laughing.

Fuck this! He stuffed the glossy brochures into a nearby trash can and walked away.

Ian wandered aimlessly through Gastown. It was so different in the morning, largely empty. It started to rain, at first a light sprinkle, but gradually a steady downpour. Soaking wet, he slouched towards the business district. He bumped elbows with well-dressed men who glared at him. At a corner he turned his head. At the end of the street he saw the tops of large ships in Burrard Inlet. He walked down towards the water. Soon he was meandering along the docks where several huge freighters were unloading. He walked past metal shipping containers stacked four high. Then huge pallets of lumber and other building materials.

Finally, Ian came upon a massive bundle of huge logs encircled by large chains. He stopped by the logs. He reached out and touched the thick wet bark with both hands. He thought of his dumb fantasy of working in a lumber camp. How could he be so fucking stupid?! He was such a loser. He walked on, hands shoved in his pockets, water dripping off the brim of his hat. The cold breeze of the bay made him shiver. A man driving a fork lift truck nearly hit him. A couple of men in stained overalls and hard hats walked by. They did not look his way. It's like I'm invisible, he thought, like I don't even exist. He stopped near the bow of a huge ocean going ship. Massive black chains angling down to the pilings. Ian stared up at the towering ship. He longed to climb on board, to go somewhere, anywhere but here.

At the stern of the ship he noticed a weathered set of wooden stairs leading down to a small dock at water level. He climbed down the slippery steps to the platform. It rocked and swayed with the waves. Under his feet, the boards were stained white and yellow by bird shit. A thick grey mist covered the harbor and hid the mountains. Ian stepped to the edge and looked down at the ocean. Oily water slopped over the shit-stained wood, licking at his torn sneakers. A large dead fish floated there on its side, half eaten, eye sockets empty, guts dangling out. A seagull dropped from the grey sky and perched on the nearby pilings. Its small beady eyes reminded Ian of Larry's hard stare.

For a year he had fantasized about Vancouver, about living on some white sand beach with friendly hippies, about camp fires and swimming in crystal blue water. But he had fucked it all up. Here he was, broke, alone in the city. He looked down into the black water. His chest was tight. He wanted to cry but he could not. If he took one step forward, he could slip into the ocean and disappear. All this would be over. No one would know. And no one would care.

"Hey." Someone shouted at him. Ian looked up. A man in a red hard-hat scowling down from the wharf. "You aren't allowed down there." He waved at Ian to come up, then cupped his hands and yelled. "Get the hell off that dock." Ian hauled himself up the rickety stairs, expecting to be in trouble, but by the time he reached the top, the man was walking away towards a warehouse.

Ian turned his back on the ocean. *Fuck my plan*, he

thought, *fuck Vancouver.* His stupid fantasy was over.

Wet, cold, tired and hungry, he wandered aimlessly around downtown. Intuitively he found himself circling around the same route he followed with Larry and Wayne. The streets were ugly now, the gutters full of wet garbage. People's faces loomed as they passed him, angry, sad, dead-looking faces. When he finally decided to grab a bus back the basement apartment, he had to ask strangers for change to pay his fare. It was early afternoon by the time he trudged down the back steps into the apartment. He hoped everyone would still be sleeping. He opened the door a crack. Wayne was no longer on the couch. Ian slipped in, quietly closed the door and hung his wet hat on a hook. The kitchen light was on. He heard movement but no voices.

Larry, Wayne and Connie sat at the kitchen table. As he walked in, Larry shouted.

"Where the fuck have you been?"

"I went for a walk."

"A walk?" Larry jumped up, knocking over his chair. "You've been gone for fucking hours." He grabbed the front of Ian's sweater. "Where the fuck did you go?"

"I went downtown."

"Why?" He slapped Ian's on the side of his head. His ear stung. "Who did you talk to?"

"Wha- no one." He struggled but Larry still held his sweater in his fist. "I just walked around."

"In the rain?" Larry slapped him again. "You just fucking walked around in the rain?

"Yeah." Ian stammered. "I, I was bored."

"Larry." Connie tugged on Larry's arm. "Come on.

He's not shitting you. Look at him. He's soaked."

Larry slammed Ian back into the counter. He stepped to the table and reached for his smokes. His hands were shaking.

"We were worried." Connie stood up and patted Ian's shoulder. "We thought maybe you got busted."

"Well, I didn't. I just went for walk."

"Did you talk to anyone?" Larry paced and dragged on his smoke. "Anyone at all?"

"No." Ian repeated. "No. I just walked around." He knew better than to mention job hunting. Larry continued to scowl at him. Wayne stared at Ian too.

"Come on, Larry. Lighten up." Connie said. "He's too smart to talk to anyone."

Wayne finally piped up. "I believe him, Larry. He knows better than to talk to anyone, right buddy?"

"I just went for a walk." Ian repeated.

'Yeah, sure," Larry said but he still sounded skeptical. He stepped close again and jabbed Ian in the chest with one finger. "Don't you ever pull this shit on me again. You never ever go anywhere again without talking to me first. Got it?"

Ian nodded. Larry went the bedroom. He slammed the door.

"You're lucky." Wayne said as he lit a joint "He thought you were a narc."

"A narc?" Ian laughed nervously. "That's stupid."

"Yeah. Right." Wayne laughed. "You a narc!" He shook his head. "Man, I have never seen Larry that pissed off. You are one lucky fucker."

Wayne handed him the joint. Ian took a really long

toke. He was shivering; because of Larry or his wet clothes, he wasn't sure. Connie handed him a cup of tea. He added lots of sugar and slurped it down.

Larry came out of the bedroom with his shoulder bag.

"Ok, Let's get going. I got people to see."

Ian wanted to change out of his wet clothes but he knew better than to say anything. Connie looked very serious as she handed him a slice of toast. She patted his shoulder as he followed Larry and Wayne up the stairs. He wolfed down the toast on the way to the bus stop, wiping his greasy fingers on his jeans. The mood on the bus ride was ominous. Even Wayne said nothing. Ian snuck a peek at Larry. Does he really think I'm a narc?

Downtown Larry handed off some pot to Wayne and told him what time to meet at the doughnut shop. Ian hesitated.

"You're with me now. I want to keep an eye on you." Larry said and started walking. They did the usual route, the girls first, then some regulars. Larry never spoke to him except to say "wait here" and "let's go".

As the night went on it became just another night, except Ian couldn't shake the bad feeling. The first time they cut through a dark alley, he tensed up thinking Larry might kill him. But nothing happened. Walking around in wet clothes he kept shivering. Maybe he was catching a cold. As the night dragged on his early morning caught up with him. He could barely keep his eyes open. Coffee and doughnuts did nothing. As Larry and Wayne smoked and chatted, he laid his head on the table, using his arms for a pillow. He immediately dropped into a weird dream. He woke when Larry yanked on his hair.

"What the fuck is your problem?"

"Sorry," Ian rubbed his face. "I didn't get enough sleep."

Larry looked disgusted but fished into his shoulder bag. He pulled out a little pill bottle.

"Here," he shook a couple of dull red pills into Ian's palm.

"What are these?" Ian said.

"Bennies." Larry said. When Ian looked blank, Wayne said, "Benzedrine. Try it. You'll like it."

Ian still hesitated.

"Just fucking take them." Larry stood up. "We gotta get back to work."

Ian washed the two pills down with the last splash of his coffee.

Wayne headed off to sell more pot on his own. Ian followed Larry. By the time they had walked a few blocks, the bennies started to kick in. Ian felt awake and alert, like he had just downed a whole pot of coffee. He noticed that he was walking faster, so fast that Larry told him to calm the fuck down. When Larry went off to make a deal, Ian found it hard to stand still. His heart was racing. The deals took too long. He liked it best when they were moving, when his legs were pumping. The time flew by. His mind was clear and sharp for the first time in days. Why had he been so uptight before? It wasn't so bad walking around Van on a warm summer night.

A couple of hours later they met up with Wayne again. His sales had gone well and he wanted to grab a beer. To Ian's surprise Larry agreed. He noticed how those two were getting along better and better. Wayne acted more and more like Larry: wearing his shades at night, cultivating the same poker face, developing contempt for the weekend hippies who bought pot. Over beer he told them about roughing up a guy who tried to rip him off.

"Little pussy tossed me a five and started to walk away. I fucking slammed him into the wall and told him if he ever did that again I'd take off one of his nuts." Wayne pulled his jacket back and flashed his hunting knife as he talked.

"Be cool." Larry nodded at the knife. Wayne quickly covered the knife, glancing around to see if anyone noticed, but Ian could see that Larry was pleased with Wayne.

After a couple of beers, Ian's energy and mood dropped suddenly. He crashed down thinking again what a mess he had made of Vancouver. Watching Larry and Wayne buddy up left him feeling even more alone. He drummed on the edge of the table and finally worked up the nerve to ask Larry for a couple more bennies.

"Sure, I can give you more." Larry said. "But they aren't freebies. I'll have to take them out of your pay."

This made Wayne laugh.

"Ok," Ian said. "Give me more to do. I can do more. Let me sell some pot, at least. I can sell pot."

Larry squinted. "Naw, you're too straight looking. Everyone will think you're a narc." He stubbed his cigarette. "Don't worry. I'll figure out something to do with you."

Ian got that weird creepy vibe off Larry like when he

had joked about pimping him out. Still, Ian was relieved when Larry slid more pills across the table at him. He washed them down with beer. Back on the street, as they walked around, Ian felt the buzz come back. The three of them circled around the core but weekday nights were slow. Finally, Larry said fuck it and they grabbed a bus. As usual Ian and Wayne dropped acid. Tripping on top of the bennies, Ian found his hallucinations were fragmented. A couple of times he blinked and realized a block of time had passed, but he had no memory of doing anything. One minute they were on the bus, the next he was in the kitchen watching Wayne eat. He blinked and he was in the bathroom, close to the mirror examining his chin stubble and his pimples. He tossed and turned all night. Over breakfast he found himself asking Larry for a couple more bennies before they hit the streets again.

Now Wayne took over most of the random pot sales. Larry started dealing more speed and heroin which meant they were meeting with serious addicts. They went to more squats in abandoned buildings, in houses with broken windows, and in tents clustered beneath concrete overpasses.

"Stay sharp." Larry reminded him. "These guys will bash your head in for a buck."

Everywhere they stopped, skinny twitchy people gathered around Larry. Ian stood close, his heart racing, his hand resting on the butt of his knife, wondering if he would have the nerve to use it. He was always relieved to get away, to smoke a joint with Wayne or drop acid on the way home.

One night Ian followed Larry through a dark

laneway in Gastown. They were on their way to meet
Wayne and grab a coffee. Someone tumbled out of a
doorway and fell at Ian's feet. He rolled on his side, one
hand reached out and clutched at the air. Ian stopped.
Even in the dim light he recognized the guy as one of their
regulars. In fact, he was pretty sure the guy had scored
heroin from Larry earlier that night. Ian leaned closer and
saw a line of pink foam seeping from the man's lips.

"Larry." He called out, but Larry was already at the
end of the lane, waving at him to hurry up. Ian ran to
catch up. Larry looked really pissed off. Ian had broken
one of the rules: using Larry's name when they were
downtown.

"What the fuck are you doing?"

"That guy," Ian gestured back down the alley. "He
looks like he's in trouble. I think he's ODing."

Larry stared at him. "So?"

"Maybe we should call an ambulance."

Larry just turned and walked away. Ian trotted after
him.

"I'll find a pay phone and call an ambulance. I won't
say who I am."

Larry grabbed his wrist and yanked him up short.

"Look asshole. Other people's shit is not our
problem. Especially some lame-ass junkie." He gave Ian's
wrist as hard twist. "Now shut the fuck up."

Rubbing his arm, Ian trailed after Larry. Wayne
waited for them on the next corner. He was obviously
stoned. He handed Larry some cash and started to babble
about how his sales had gone. As they doubled back,
headed to the doughnut shop, an ambulance crept by,

siren off but lights flashing. Ian saw the driver peering around. He stopped the vehicle, backed up and turned down the alley. Ian broke away from Larry and Wayne. He followed the ambulance down the narrow space. The two medics jumped out, gear in hand. They had to elbow through the small crowd that had already formed.

Ian stepped into the semi-circle.

"What happened?" He asked no one in particular.

"Dead junkie." A man said. He said it casually, like someone would say, "I think it's going to rain."

Ian pushed forward and peered over someone's shoulder. It was the guy he had seen collapse. He was right where he had fallen. His eyes were still open. One medic was on a walkie-talkie. The other was chatting with a bystander. A cop car appeared the other end of the alley and drove slowly towards the circle of people.

"Cops." Suddenly Wayne was beside him, grabbing at his arm. "Come on. Come on. You can't be standing around here with the cops." He dragged Ian away.

Larry stood half a block away, smoking.

"What the fuck was that about?" He glared at Ian.

"Some guy snuffed it." Wayne said.

"Yeah," Larry spit on the sidewalk. "Shit happens. Let's head down to Stanley Park. This whole area will be crawling with pigs."

By the park, Larry and Wayne split up to sell pot to people partying on the beach. Larry told Ian to sit on a bench.

"Don't you fucking move and don't fucking talk to anyone."

Ian sat there. He could hear the waves in the

distance. He kept thinking about the junkie. He had seen him around, just a young guy, maybe nineteen or twenty. Now he was gone.

Ian waited so long that he wondered if Larry had cut him loose? Soon Wayne came back, complaining that he had only sold a couple of joints. He pulled a half a doobie from his jacket and they toked in silence.

Finally, Ian said. "That junkie who died. I think he scored from Larry."

"So?" Wayne exhaled a huge cloud of smoke up into the night air.

Ian shrugged. "I feel bad. I saw him crashing. If I had called 911 then, he'd probably be alive."

"So what?" Wayne handed him the joint. "They're fucking dumb-ass junkies. Some of them are going to OD."

Ian hesitated. "Connie is a junkie."

"That's different." Wayne was angry. "She's not in some fucking alley getting wasted."

But she could be, Ian wanted to say. She could be.

"Besides," Wayne added, "She's pretty much kicked it now."

Ian knew that was bullshit but there was no point in arguing.

When Larry finally returned he was in a slightly better mood. He had made some good sales. They walked back downtown but Larry was paranoid about getting near Gastown.

"That OD will fucking ruin the night. One dead junkie and the cops will be all over the place."

He sounded more upset about losing sales than someone dying. So they headed home earlier than usual.

On the bus Ian kept flashing on the junkie's face, that line of foam between his thin lips. He impatiently waited for Larry to pull out the acid. They each took a hit. Larry smoked in silence while Wayne babbled, as usual, about his night. Ian drummed his fingers on his knees, waiting for the first rush. Nothing happened. He could not stop thinking about the dead guy.

"I'm not getting a buzz." He said to Larry. "How about another tab?"

Larry shrugged. He tossed the little envelope over to Ian. He opened it and licked the end of his finger to pick up a tab. But when he pulled out his finger he saw four little micro dots stuck there. Larry was not looking, so Ian licked all four into his mouth. He handed the envelope back to Larry.

Shit happens, he thought, shit happens.

The bus moved slowly. Ian kept looking at his hands, waiting for some sign the acid was kicking in. The bus seat was hard. He shifted his legs. As he looked down he saw right through his blue jeans into the muscle and veins of his leg. He had X-ray vision. As he flexed his leg, he saw blood pumping. The corpuscles crawled up his thighs like insects. He brushed at his legs. He sat up straight and took a deep breath. He saw his lungs expand inside his chest, then noticed his spine was just wires inside a pipe. He saw electricity flowing up his spine, wave after wave, pulsing up and bouncing around in his skull like one of those Van der Graff electric generators. Afraid the sparks would crack his skull open, he grabbed the top of his head to hold the bones together. But when he touched his hat he smelled smoke. He snatched the hat off and waved it around.

"What the fuck are you doing?" Larry said.

"My hat's on fire."

Wayne laughed. "You're so fucking funny when you're stoned."

Ian felt another wave of sparks flying out of his skull. He grabbed his head with both hands.

"Oh wow." He blurted out. "Wow."

"I know." Wayne said. "It's fucking righteous acid."

Ian nodded. Righteous Acid? Was Wayne seeing the same sparks as he was? How was that possible? Had the acid made them psychic? He turned and looked at Wayne who was staring out the window. Ian concentrated: look at me, look at me, look at me. Wayne turned to look at him.

"Made you look," Ian said smugly. "Made you look."

Wayne just shook his head. "Oh man, you are so fucked up."

Back home Connie came out briefly to have a sip of Larry's beer and take a toke. She smiled at Ian and Wayne.

"You boys are really fired up." She said.

"Choir Boy doubled up," Larry said. "Two hits of acid."

Five, Ian wanted to brag. I took five hits, but instead he decided to demonstrate his new powers.

"Watch this," he said, "Watch this." He pointed his finger at a dirty coffee spoon on the table. "I can make it move." He concentrated. Where ever he pointed the spoon slid all around the table. "Pretty cool, eh?"

Connie and Wayne laughed. Ian looked back at the

table. The spoon was sitting where it had been.

"Did you see how I moved it around?" He asked excitedly.

"Poor Ian," Connie said. "Completely fucked up on acid." She stood up. "Ok, I'm crashing. You coming to bed?" She tugged Larry's arm and he followed her. "Have a good night boys." She pointed at Ian. "And you, don't be jumping off any tall buildings. You cannot fly."

Wayne said he was hungry. He decided to make a grilled cheese sandwich. As he cooked Ian stared at the cheese. He wanted some. He picked up the knife to cut a slice. He saw the edge of the blade touch the cheese, suddenly he zoomed in at a microscopic level and saw carbon steel atoms whirling through yellow cheese atoms. Delighted he realized he had shrunk to the size of an atom himself. It was unbelievable to watch the atoms whirl around him. He could hear them too, a deep hum that soon became a low mooing sound.

The cheese was mooing. This made him giggle uncontrollably.

Wayne grabbed Ian's wrist, his hand holding the knife.

"What the fuck are you doing?"

Ian looked down and saw that he had shaved the entire block of cheese into tiny shreds.

"It was mooing." He started to giggle uncontrollably.

"You are so fucked up." Wayne said. He plunked a sandwich in front of Ian. "Here, eat something. Maybe it will slow you down."

Ian took a bite and chewed it. It was hot and gooey and he liked the taste but when he went to swallow he knew it would stick in his throat and he would choke to death. He leaned forward and spit it on the table.

"That's fucking gross." Wayne said, who was eating just like he always did.

Ian took another bite. The same thing happened. No matter how much he chewed, he had to spit it out. Meantime Wayne ate with no problem. Ian didn't know how he could do it. He was like a robot. As he had that thought Wayne's skin turned tin grey; his forehead and jaw squared off, sharp corners formed and rows of rivets popped out.

"You're a robot." He said to Wayne.

"And you're a fucking loser. I'm going to crash." Wayne, still a robot, turned and with heavy metallic steps clumped to the living room.

Ian stared at the kitchen table. There was spilled sugar, crusty ketchup, bread crumbs and three wet balls of well-chewed sandwiches. Ian wondered where they had come from. He looked up and realized he was alone. He had no idea how much time has passed. He stood up, turned off the light and staggered into the living room. It was hard to walk. His bones had grown soft and spongey. He could feel the floor sucking at his feet with each step he took, like he was walking in a thick mud that tried to pull him under. In the dark he could see Wayne on the couch, a cloud of red heat pulsing from his body.

Ian lowered himself to the floor, fully clothed, and lay flat on his back. Between the bennies and the acid, he was too wired. He could not stop thinking about the junkie who died. He was overwhelmed with sadness. What was it like to die? To feel your heart stop? He became aware of his heart in his chest. Not only could he feel it but he saw it floating free in his rib cage, a red muscular fist. As he watched, it slowed down, slower and slower. Terrified, he watched it stop completely.

He was dead!

He knew it was impossible, yet he was dead. His heart sagged there inside his empty rib cage. He wanted to cry out but he could not. Suddenly he was standing over his own dead body. He seemed to float up towards the ceiling. He saw Wayne wake up and discover Ian on the floor. He was shouting and slapping his face. But Ian was dead. He saw Connie crying. He saw Larry looking down at him, very annoyed, then lighting a smoke. Ian heard a siren. As it came closer, he floated up through the roof of the house. Hovering over the street he saw and heard the ambulance approaching. It stopped at the curb. Curious neighbors wandered out of their houses to watch his body being carried out.

Ian floated higher still. As he did he felt less and less sadness and panic. So he was dead. So what? Shit happens. He looked down on the city as if from a low flying plane. All those thousands of people scurrying about their daily routines. They would all die too. They were so busy, so serious, so determined to do things, but they were all going to die. Ian heard himself laughing, even though he had no body. Now he was so high the people were just dots, frantic little dots circling around each other like atoms. He continued to float up. Soon the city was just a patch on a colorful map. He saw the curve of the earth. He floated higher.

Now the earth was a blue ball floating in black

space. He wanted to touch it but he had no body. He was a ball of light moving across the solar system. His light grew bigger and bigger, flowing out to the edges of the universe. He had never felt this happy before, this peaceful. Just ahead of him, in the darkness, he sensed something, a presence, an energy. But no matter how hard he tried he could not see it clearly, but he knew it contained The Answer. Desperately he wanted to touch it, to grasp The Truth. He concentrated really hard and his hand appeared before him, floating in space.

Ian struggled to reach out with his hand...then he crashed back into his body as if dropped from a great height. He twisted sideways on the floor, gasping for air. He felt like he had been punched. What had happened? A second ago he had been dead. He had left his body behind. He had seen the light at the edge of the universe. He almost touched it. But in a blink it was gone. *All gone.* He felt tears rolling down his cheek. They burned his skin. He was alive but he could not move. Everything was made of tiny dots spinning around each other. Whether his eyes were open or closed, all he could see were dull grey atoms.

Ian was still awake when sunlight crept in the little windows. He heard the kitchen light snap on. Connie was up, moving about. Ian felt like he had super-sonic hearing. He heard the scratch of a match, a needle tap in a spoon, the sucking sound as Connie prepared a fix. He heard her inhale sharply as the heroin entered her vein. Then he saw her dead in an alley, foam between her thin lips. He curled up and pulled the blanket over his head. He wanted this nightmare to end.

When Ian woke up, he was face down on the dirt carpet, some drool running down his chin. The others were already up, he could smell toast and hear Wayne and Connie's voices. He stood up, a little woozy and realized he was still stoned.

As he staggered into the kitchen, Wayne said, "Look, he's alive. He's alive." Connie laughed. Ian smiled shyly. Their faces twitched and melted, day-glow colours bled through their skin.

"Seriously dude." Wayne said. "I tried to wake you up a couple of times. I even slapped your face, but you were dead to the world."

I was dead, Ian wanted to say, but he knew they wouldn't understand. How could anyone understand what he had seen?

"Want something to eat?" Connie said. She waved a plate under his nose. It was covered with half chewed balls of grilled cheese. He felt wave of nausea and pushed the plate away.

"Oh fuck," he said. "I forgot about that. Sorry."

"You get seriously fucked up when you are stoned." Wayne said. "Seriously fucked up, dude." He said this like it was a good thing.

"Some people should never do acid." Connie laughed.

Larry came out of the bedroom, brushing his long hair. "Good, you're finally up. Get your shit together we need to get downtown."

Connie pushed Ian towards the bathroom. "Grab a quick shower. I'll make you some toast."

Ian striped down. He saw in the mirror how skinny he was getting from endless walking and rarely eating a real meal. His ribs were visible. He ran one finger down the bones. He remembered his heart stopping. For a second, as he touched his rib cage, it stopped again. He staggered against the sink. He looked at his eyes in the mirror. His pupils were very dilated. The irises looked cracked, like glass that had been hit with a hammer. He leaned closer. A weird light shone through the cracks. Behind his eyes he saw a field of stars and strange glowing planets but when he blinked they vanished. Now he saw pimples across his forehead and chin. A steady diet of doughnuts, fries and toast was doing in his complexion.

Larry pounded on the bathroom door. "Come on, space cadet, let's get going."

Ian stepped in and out of the shower. He half dried himself, fingered his hair into place and slipped back into his jeans and t-shirt. Connie handed him a cup of tea and toast with margarine and sugar. But as soon as he took a bite, the greasy sweetness made him nauseous. He pushed the plate away. He was so tired. He just wanted to lay down again. He hesitated, then asked.

"Hey, Larry? Can I have a couple of bennies?"

Larry looked annoyed.

"I didn't get any sleep last night."

"And how is that my fucking problem?" Larry said but he went the bedroom. A minute later he returned and handed Ian a brown pill bottle

"Here," he said. "Now you can stop fucking bugging me." The bottle was a drug store prescription bottle, made out to a P. Kelly. Benzedrine. Take as per your doctor's orders. Ian twisted the cap open. It was filled to the brim with small red pills.

"Thanks." Ian knocked two into his palm and washed them down with tea.

"Here's the thing." Larry said. "If you get spotted by the cops, ditch this. If they find it on you, tell them it's not yours. Say you found it on the sidewalk and picked it up. Hopefully they won't bust you. And what's the rule?"

"Shut the fuck up."

Larry smirked at Wayne. "Maybe the choir boy is learning, eh?"

"He's a smart guy." Wayne nodded.

"See," Connie tousled Ian's hair. "I told you he was a good kid."

But then Larry added: "Don't be thinking these are fucking freebies. You owe me."

"Sure thing." Ian nodded, thinking again of Larry's comment about pimping him out. As they headed out he wondered how long before the bennies would kick in.

Gastown was buzzing from last night's OD. Everyone had different theories: some knew the dead junkie and said he had just fucked up. Someone suggested that it was a murder, that he had been injected by someone who hated him. Others had wild theories that the police were deliberately distributing tainted smack to kill all the junkies. Larry, Wayne and Ian heard all the theories as they worked the lower Eastside. Larry met all the gossip with the same line: "Shit happens."

One thing was certain: the OD did not hurt sales; all

the regulars still ponied up for their fix. After making the
rounds to see Larry's girls, they split up. Wayne went off
with some pot and Ian followed Larry to all the usual
spots. Every time his energy flagged he took another
bennie. He quickly learned to dry swallow the small pills.

Later, they waited at the doughnut shop for Wayne.
He was late. Larry was nervous and kept looking at his
watch. He snapped at Ian.

"Stop fucking doing that."

Ian had been drumming the edge of the table with
his fingers. He reached for the sugar cubes and popped
one in his mouth. He had an endless craving for sweets.

Finally, Wayne rushed in. He tossed his hat on the
table and ran his fingers through his curly hair. His
forehead was wet with sweat.

"I almost got busted." He blurted out loudly.

"Shut up and sit down." Larry said. Wayne sat,
wiping his face with the sleeve of his jean jacket. Larry
looked around, leaned closer and whispered. "What
happened?"

"I was in that alley off Hastings by Main. Guy was
buying a dime bag from me when I see a cop car drive by
the end of the alley. It fucking backs up and the cop in the
passenger seat gives us the eyeball."

"Did he make you?"

"No way. I mean, I don't think so. It was dark and
we'd already handed off. But then the fucking cop car
turns down the alley. We just fucking booked it. We ran
out the other end and split off left and right."

Wayne lit a smoke. His fingers shook as he blew out
the match.

"Did they catch the other guy?" Larry asked.

"I don't know. I didn't stop to look back."

"Who was he? Do you know him? Was he a regular?"

"No." Wayne thought for a second. "I never saw him before. Shit! Do you think he was a narc?"

"Could be." Larry squinted. "No way to know." He looked out, scanning the passing traffic. "And you're sure you didn't get followed here?

"No way." Wayne insisted. "That's why I was late. I did a lot of zigzagging. I went through a couple of pubs and out the back before coming here." But he started looking around nervously too.

Getting busted, Ian thought. This was serious shit. He fingered the pill bottle in his pocket. If the cops stopped him, he could play stupid, but would they buy it? Would they believe he had just found it on the street? What if all three of them were arrested at the same time? They'd all get charged with dealing. They'd go to prison. Ian reached for another sugar cube, thinking for the millionth time that somehow he should get the away from this shit. But how?

Outside they started walking. Larry kept grilling Wayne, repeating the same questions. A complete stranger stopped them to ask where he could score some MJ. Larry shrugged and said he had no idea. The stranger walked away, but Wayne twirled around to look back at him.

"Narc?"

"Could be." Larry nodded.

Ian clutched the pill bottle in his pocket, ready to toss it.

Larry had a smoke and picked at his front teeth with his thumb nail.

"Ok." He announced. "You two split. Go home." He looked around nervously. "Here's some cash. Take a cab, get off a few blocks early and walk the rest of the way."

They flagged a cab. On the ride, Wayne babbled nervously. "I don't think the cops made me. I mean I ran as soon as they turned into alley. But maybe that guy was a narc. I should have fucking known something was up. This is a drag."

"Yeah," Ian agreed. "A fucking drag." He turned the pill bottle over and over in his hand. His heart was racing. He had taken over a dozen pills since waking up.

When they got back to the house, Connie was drinking tea. Ian noticed her works rested on the table. He figured was taking little hits all day while they were out.

"Who died?" She asked when she saw their faces.

"Wayne had a run in with a narc." Ian said.

"Where's Larry? Did he get busted?" Her voice was shrill. "If he gets busted, I'm fucked."

"Naw. He's fine." Wayne patted her shoulder. "Larry's way smarter than the fucking pigs."

"Shit!" She reached for her smokes. "You ok, Cuz?"

"I'm still here, aren't I?" He sounded defensive.

"How about you?" Connie asked Ian.

Ian shrugged. "I was with Larry. No problems."

They smoked a joint while Wayne repeated the details. The more he told the story the more it sounded like he was trying to convince himself everything was ok.

"I mean if the guy was narc, why didn't he just bust

me right there when I handed him an ounce?"

"I don't know, cuz." Connie said. "Maybe he didn't want to blow his cover. Maybe they're after Larry."

Ian reached over for the baggie. He had never rolled a joint before. He managed to make a fat, lopsided one, spilling some crumbs on the table. He fired it up and inhaled deeply. He needed something to take the edge off the bennies.

An hour later Larry got home looking troubled. Connie rushed over and gave him a hug. "I heard about the narc."

"Not sure he was a narc." He didn't sound confident. He opened a beer and sat at the table to smoke a doobie. After a long silence, Wayne spoke.

"So, what do you think? Is it safe out there?"

Larry took a long toke, squinting through the smoke.

"Maybe. Maybe not." He explained the buzz around Gastown: the kid who had ODed was the son of someone important, a university prof. Shit was flying at city hall about Vancouver's heroin problem. So the mayor told the cops to come down heavy on the Eastside.

"Well," Wayne said. "Even if he was a narc, he can't make me. It was dark when I met him and even darker in the alley."

Larry shrugged. "I think maybe tomorrow I'll go solo. You two can take a day off."

"Aw, come on, man," Wayne said. "I'm cool."

"I'm not getting busted because you fucked up."

Before Wayne could argue, Larry stood up and went to the bedroom. He slammed the door. The three of them sat in silence.

"Fuck." Wayne shook his head.

"Don't sweat it, cuz," Connie said. "Larry gets in these fucking moods."

"What the fuck did I do?" Wayne said. "I didn't get busted."

"It's Larry, babe." Connie patted his arm. "He's been on the street too long. He's paranoid all the time now." She butted her smoke. "He'll be better in the morning." She kissed the top of Wayne's curly hair and went to bed.

In the dark Wayne flopped on the couch and sullenly watched TV. Ian lay on the floor, on his side, head propped on his elbow and watched too. Long after Wayne was snoring, he tossed and turned, wishing he had not downed so many pills. Larry had gone to bed without offering them any acid. It felt weird to not be tripping. He was stuck with reality: sleeping on a basement floor, living with pimps, dealers and addicts, broke and trapped. In the dark, Ian stared at the ceiling, recalling the previous night's wild acid trip. But instead of floating up into the sky, the ceiling seemed to be sliding down, pushing him into the earth. The apartment was one big coffin he could not escape from. When he finally slept it was broken and filled with images of the house collapsing on him, burying him alive.

In the morning everyone had tea and toast in silence. Ian woke up with a really bad headache. While he was in the bathroom, he washed down a benny with a handful of tepid tap water. They waited for Larry to see if he would make them stay home, but as usual he came out of the bedroom with his shoulder bag.

"Ok. Let's go."

Wayne grinned at Ian as if to say, 'see, everything is ok'.

Downtown Larry was extra cautious. He had them stick together as they made the usual rounds. But he took a completely different route, going by the squats and rat holes at different times. At every corner he stopped to scan the crowd. In city parks, if he saw anyone he didn't know hanging out, he'd turn around, saying "let's come back later".

When night fell they went for a coffee, going to a greasy spoon Ian had never seen before, blocks from Gastown. Larry leaned over the table, looked around and said Ian would be a spotter for Wayne from now on.

"I don't need a baby sitter." Wayne protested.

"Shut the fuck up." Larry snarled. He nodded at a passing waitress. "I don't think the cops made you, but an extra set of eyes never hurts. It's just until things blow over."

"And you," Larry poked at Ian with one of his boney fingers. "Keep your fucking head on straight."

Ian nodded.

"What about you?" Wayne asked.

"I'm good. I know everyone. Besides," His eyes narrowed. "They know better than to fuck with me." He told them a time and place to meet. "If you think you're being followed, don't show up there. Keep walking. Later go sit on a bench by the beach and I'll find you."

Ian popped another bennie, his fifth or sixth, he wasn't sure. They helped with his fatigue and he liked how they made the time fly by. When he was wired he didn't feel so down about the situation.

Wayne and Ian headed back to the eastside, walking side by side. Now he stood guard for Wayne instead of Larry. The early part of the night was mostly high school and college students looking to score a couple of joints or a hit of acid. Handoffs where fast and discreet, almost like a handshake. Occasionally someone wanted to buy more or sample the goods. When Wayne went into an alley, Ian got nervous. Wayne could handle himself, but Ian worried that he would over react and stab someone. He remembered how fast that knife appeared in Revelstoke. If a fight did start, Ian would more likely be stopping Wayne from killing the other guy.

Occasionally they would smoke a joint as they strolled. Wayne bummed a bennie from Ian and became even more chatty than usual. He talked about Larry a lot.

"He's really got his shit together, man." Wayne said as they pounded the pavement. "He's working on some bigger deals so we can stop fucking around with this little shit." Wayne stopped walking. "Hey, I shouldn't be fucking telling you this. Don't tell Larry I told you. He'll be really pissed."

"No problem."

When they met up for coffee later that night, Larry directed all his conversation to Wayne, never making eye contact with Ian. Ian wondered if Larry still thought he was a narc. Or maybe, he thought, I'm just being paranoid? Still he couldn't shake the feeling that he was being shut out. Coming back from the john, he heard Larry saying something to Wayne about a delivery, but as Ian approached the table they fell silent. Ian sucked on a sugar cube and tried not to drum the table. He was relieved when he and Wayne headed out again.

To Ian's surprise, the next night Larry started sending Wayne to collect from some of his girls. They headed down to hooker row. All the women were familiar faces now. They seemed to like Wayne with his big smile and goofy flirting. Although Larry said to never give the girls freebies, Wayne occasionally smoked a joint with one of them. Wayne said to Ian, "That's bullshit. We work hard, gotta party a little." One night Wayne went behind a building to the toke with one of the girls, leaving Ian standing on the corner with the other hookers.

"He's cute." One of the older ones said as she stood near him. Ian felt his face grow warm.

"Oh you're right," Another reached out and brushed Ian's hair back from his cheek. "Shy too."

"Watch out for the shy ones," Someone called out. "They always want to fuck you in the ass."

"Hey, little boy." One teased, "Stand here much longer and you'll be getting offers."

"What's Larry doing now?" The older one asked. "Working the boy trade?"

"Larry'd pimp his own mother if she made him a buck."

The girls laughed and spread out again. This talk made Ian nervous. He noticed some of the passing drivers did slow down to stare at him. Where the fuck was Wayne?

Ian walked down the alley. He saw Wayne beside a dumpster, leaning against a wall. The hooker he had gone to toke with was standing next to him yanking on his dick.

286

Ian turned his head away but just then Wayne let out a little groan and came in her hand. The hooker turned and looked blankly at Ian. She shook the cum off her fingers and grabbed some paper towels from her purse. She tossed one to Wayne, then wiped her hands.

Wayne zipped up and grinned at Ian. "Hey man, you want some?"

"No." Ian was embarrassed. "I'm ok."

"Come on, man, relieve your stress. Clear up your acne." He turned to the woman. "Hey, will you give my friend a blow job for a couple of bennies?"

"Fuck off," The hooker said and headed back out to the street.

With a steady diet of bennies, pot and acid, Ian's days flew by. He always woke up wasted and fuzzy from doing acid. He took one bennie as soon as he woke up to relieve his headache. Anytime during the long day if his mood or energy slumped, he took more. He knew Benzedrine could be addictive, but he was only taking a few a day. The acid trips were almost routine now. The acid took the edge off the bennies, but he still tossed and turned long after everyone else was sleep. Laying on the floor in the dark he tried again and again to recreate the vision he had that one night. But nothing like it ever happened again.

Downtown the bennies made him hyper-alert as he walked around, aware of every little detail on the street. He was restless and fidgety when forced to stand lookout. He preferred to be on the move, walking. Even stopping for coffee or beer made him impatient. He lost his appetite but his craving for sweets kept growing. He loaded his coffee with sugar and bummed money off Wayne to buy candy bars. The greasy spoon they frequented had sugar cubes on the table. Ian sucked on them as Larry and Wayne made small talk. Before leaving he scooped up a handful of cubes and put them in his pocket.

"You're gonna rot your teeth." Wayne said.

"Fuck my teeth," Ian said.

Each day Ian grew more impatient. He hated waiting for a bus, for a waitress, or for Wayne to finish one of his long-winded stories. One night the three of them ran into one of their regular junkies in Chinatown. He launched into a long story about how he had been roused by the cops earlier that day. This was not news. He was always getting hassled by the cops because he was too fucked up to run away when they raided the park, which they did now two or three times a week for show. Annoyed, Ian watched the guy gesture wildly as he talked. Larry had already handed off the smack. The guy started to repeat the whole story.

"I mean what gives? I'm just sitting on a bench catching some rays when this big pig comes up-"

"Ok, ok." Ian grabbed the junkie's arm and slapped his face. "We get it. Shut the fuck up and give Larry his money."

The junkie looked crestfallen, like a little kid who has been scolded.

"Oh yeah, sorry man. Here." He slipped Larry some cash. "Sorry I'm rambling. You know how it goes. I was just minding my own business…" He wandered off still muttering about the cops.

"Fuck," Ian said. "I thought that guy would never shut up."

"Way to go." Wayne slapped Ian on the back. "See?" He said to Larry. "He's not as nice as he looks."

"Whatever." Larry shrugged. He didn't seem impressed.

Later, sitting in the doughnut shop, Larry looked at his watch and stood up abruptly.

"I got to make a call." He spoke to Wayne as if Ian wasn't there. He left and crossed the street to the pay phone.

"What's up?" Ian asked.

"Mind your own business." Wayne said. He tossed some money on the table. "Here. Go get us some more coffee."

Ian hesitated. Now he was Wayne's fucking gopher? But he picked up the money and went to the counter. Fuck Wayne. He treated himself to a jelly doughnut. When Larry returned he looked excited. He nodded at Wayne.

"Soon." Larry said. "Soon."

Wayne grinned and nodded. They said nothing else. Ian ate his doughnut, wondering what was up?

Two nights later Wayne and Ian were waiting for Larry at the doughnut shop. Usually he was there first, but tonight he was late. It had been a long slow night. Ian had lost count of how many pills he had downed. He had a bad headache, like his brain was pressing on his skull – it felt like any second his head would explode. He drummed on the edge of the table. Where the fuck was Larry? Wayne went to the counter to get more coffee and a couple of doughnuts. He just sat back down when Larry walked in. Even across the room Ian could see something was wrong. As he got closer he saw that Larry had a long welt on his forehead and a raw-looking scrape across his boney chin.

"Let's go." Larry said.

"I just got my coffee," Wayne said.

"Fuck that." Larry turned and started for the door. Ian jumped up. Coffee in one hand, doughnut in the other, Wayne ran after them.

"What's up?" Ian said.

Larry paused under the awning of a porn theatre. "You know Honey, the little blond from Newfoundland?" The boys nodded. "This dip shit college boy ripped her off. She gave him blow job and then he slapped her around and took his money back."

"Is she ok?" Ian asked.

"Yeah sure," Larry shrugged. "She's a tough chick. But he fucking took all her cash from the whole night. So she walks me around and points this shit out to me, drinking in the Oak Room. When I go in to get the money back, the asshole sucker punches me and takes off."

"Fucker." Wayne tossed his coffee on the ground. "What's the plan?"

"I know this guy. I mean I don't know his name but he's definitely local. I think he's copped from me before. We're gonna find this shit and teach him a lesson."

They swept around to all the bars where Larry regularly dealt. He knew the bartenders and waitresses and asked about the guy. Some thought he sounded familiar but they had not seen him that night. After a half an hour they found out he had just been seen watching the stripers at the King. The bouncer there said the guy had left about five minutes earlier, walking east. He was pretty sure he lived in the area.

"Come on," Larry walked really fast.

On top of the bennies, Ian had an incredible adrenalin rush. He felt like he could walk through walls. He had to hold himself back to not break into a run and get a head of the other two. Larry led them down a side street, then on a short cut through an alley. They popped out on the street, walking so fast they were almost trotting. At an intersection, they doubled back, pushing their way through all the weekend hippies. Larry paused to scan the crowds on either side of the street.

"Maybe he got away." Wayne said.

"Fuck that." Larry snapped. "We'll get him."

A minute later he pointed across the street at a man. "That's him. There. See the guy in the swede jacket? Get ahead and cut him off."

Wayne and Ian split left and right, dodging through traffic. A car almost hit Ian. He slammed his fist on the hood and screamed fuck off. The driver's eyes loomed large. Ian made the sidewalk ahead of the guy, who swaggered towards him. Tall and thin, the long fringes on his jacket swayed as he turned his head to ogle a woman in a mini-skirt. He spotted Larry behind him and broke into a run. Ian crossed his arms over his chest and stepped in front of the guy, slamming him sideways into the wall. It reminded Ian of one time in gym class when he was playing soccer and spun around, inadvertently body checking another boy who fell flat on the ground. This guy hit the wall, stumbled, and instantly regained his footing. Ian grabbed for his sleeve. The guy twisted and lashed out with his other arm. But Larry and Wayne were on him, dragging him into a narrow alcove between two buildings where garbage cans were kept. Wayne grabbed one arm. Instinctively, Ian grabbed the other. They pinned him against the wall.

"You fuck." Larry leaned into the man's face. "Where's my money?"

"I spent it. It's all gone." He had long thin hair. He wore a silver earring with a little skull on it.

"$200 bucks in an hour? Bullshit." Larry gave him a short hard punch in the stomach. Wayne added a quick punch in the side of the guy's head.

"Ok, ok." His eyes rolled wildly. "I spent some of it. The rest is in my wallet."

Larry grabbed at the man's jeans. "Where is it?"

"In my jacket. In my jacket." Larry frisked him and pulled out a large black wallet. He rifled through it, dropping paperwork and photos on the ground. He took the cash and stuffed it in his bag.

"You fucking asshole." He leaned into the man's face. "You ever fuck with one of my girls again and I'll kill you."

Suddenly Wayne's huge knife was in the guy's face. He started to whimper.

"Oh man, I'm sorry, man, I'm sorry."

"Why don't I cut him?" Wayne said, his blade an inch from the guy's eye.

Ian grabbed Wayne's wrist. "Don't. This is fucked

up."

"Yeah." The guy said. "Listen to your little buddy."

"You shut up." Ian punched the guy's face. "Just shut the fuck up." He punched him again.

"Don't waste your blade on this piece of shit." Larry said. He reached out and grabbed the guy's earring. With one hard yank he tore it out of his earlobe. The guy doubled over, grabbing his bleeding ear.

"You fucking asshole."

"Asshole?" Larry kneed him in the crotch. Wayne rabbit punched him two-three times in the head. As he fell to the ground, Ian kicked him: in the stomach, in the head, in the back when the guy curled up. He couldn't stop. *This asshole slapped Honey! This asshole ripped off Larry! This asshole caused all this bullshit!* Ian was so fucking sick of all this.

Now it was Wayne's turn to drag Ian away. They left the guy by the garbage cans, curled on his side, clutching his bleeding ear, crying like a baby. Back on the street they moved quickly putting as much distance as possible from the alley. Ian's fist hurt. He licked his knuckle and tasted blood.

"That fuck." He said.

"Fucking, eh?" Wayne shouted and slapped Ian on the back. "We should have offed that shit head."

"No," Larry said. "Last thing we need is more pigs down here. We got the money and that fucker got what he deserved."

Far away from the Eastside Larry took them for beer. Once the waitress returned with their drinks, Larry turned to Ian and said. "Nice body check there. I didn't think you had it in you."

Ian smiled. It was the first time Larry had ever given him a compliment. Still, he couldn't believe what he had just done. This was truly fucked up.

"You guys did good." Larry pulled out the cash and tossed a twenty to each of them. He went to take a piss. Wayne leaned back in his chair, hands behind his head. He grinned.

"Pretty cool, eh?"

"Yeah." Ian mumbled. "Pretty cool." He rubbed his knuckles. They really hurt. He wondered if he had broken any bones? When Larry returned he noticed Ian massaging his knuckles. He rifled through his bag and slid a few little white pills across the table to him.

"Take those." Larry said. "Pretty soon you won't feel a thing."

Ian didn't even ask what they were. He washed the pills down with beer.

"What about me?" Wayne said. Larry gave him a couple of pills too. They finished their beer and headed back out on the street. Ian's hand stopped hurting but soon he felt sleepy, so he took another benny. On the bus home they all dropped acid. Wayne was pumped up and kept chattering about beating the guy up.

"See what I have to put up with?" Larry said. "This small-time dealing is a pain in the ass."

"That's gonna change soon," Wayne said. Larry nodded. Ian wondered what they were planning.

Connie was waiting up. Wayne told her about the guy ripping Larry off.

"You ok babe?" She rubbed Larry's shoulders.

"Shit happens," Larry ignored her and rolled a joint.

"You should have seen Ian," Wayne said. "He fucking slammed that prick into a wall."

"Yeah." Larry nodded. "Blondie did good."

"Way to go." Connie patted Ian and Wayne on the shoulders. "You boys did good, taking care of my guy."

Larry slipped her a little smack and she went to the bathroom to shoot up.

Shit happens, Ian thought, dragging hard on the joint. Between the bennies, the white pills, the acid and the pot he was feeling no pain. He had done good. Larry wouldn't kick him out now.

But later, laying on floor in the dark, Ian could not stop his heart from racing. Blood pounded in his temples. He kept seeing that guy on the ground, clutching his bleeding ear as they kicked him. When he finally drifted off, he had nightmares again about the basement ceiling crushing him.

In the morning in the bathroom, Ian splashed water on his face. He refused to look at himself in the mirror. He cupped water from the tap and downed a couple of bennies. The sooner he got a buzz on the better. He wanted to forget about last night.

The night started like all the others. For hours Ian trailed after Wayne, spotting. Things went smoothly. Nothing weird happened. They smoked pot and took bennies. Around midnight they met up with Larry at the doughnut shop. Larry seemed a little distracted. He kept checking his watch. Then he went outside to use a pay phone. He rushed back.

"Ok. Let's go."

"I was going to grab another coffee." Wayne said.

"Fuck that. Let's go." Larry headed out. They scrambled to catch up with him. As they walked Ian noticed that Larry was jittery. He kept stopping and looking over his shoulder. A block later he flagged a cab. Larry sat in the front seat. He muttered an address to the driver. Wayne leaned forward.

"Where we headed?"

"To see a man about a horse." Larry said.

"Cool." Wayne laughed. He leaned back in the seat and gave Ian a huge toothy smile.

After a long cab ride, Larry had the driver drop them at the end of a quiet tree-lined street. They walked past a few large Victorian houses. Larry stopped in front of one. An old van and two big Harleys sat in the driveway. He adjusted his pony-tail a couple of times and pushed his bag around to the back. Ian had never seen Larry nervous before. He turned and scowled at Wayne and Ian.

"Be very cool, ok? Don't say a fucking word about anything."

They followed him up the walk to a wide veranda. Even in the dark there was something odd about the place. Ian noticed all the windows were covered with dark curtains. There was a single blue lightbulb overhead that gave their faces a weird pallor. Ian saw an iridescent glow from Wayne's big teeth. There was no screen door - it looked like someone had literally torn it off the hinges. There was a thick door with wide steel bands running side to side. There was no window, just a peep hole dead-centre. They heard muffled music and voices from inside. Larry knocked. The music dropped in volume. Larry knocked again. There were heavy footsteps on the other side of the peephole.

"Who's there?"

"Larry." He leaned close to the hole. "It's Larry. I'm here to see Buster."

Some latches clicked and a big man with a shaved head opened the door a crack. He gave Larry a hard stare, then peered suspiciously at Ian and Wayne.

"What's with these two?"

"They're my guys. They're cool."

The man swung the door open, turned sideways and gestured for them to enter. He was so big that Ian had to turn sideways to squeeze between the man's chest and the door frame. He smelled whiskey and pot on the man's breath. They stepped into a living room crowded with over-stuffed, high back chairs, all facing a large slab of a coffee table, littered with ash trays, beer cans, shot glasses, roach clips, and half eaten slices of pizza. In the centre was a huge candle the size of man's thigh. Wax puddled across the dark wood. Besides the candle, the only other source of light was two giant ornate floor lamps. The base of each was decorated with naked gold painted cherubs. The lamp shades were draped with thin red veils that gave the room a pale rosy glow.

"I'll let him know you are here." The big man stepped through some beaded curtains. He returned a moment later, said nothing, and sat down in a big chair by the coffee table.

As Ian's eyes adjusted to the dim glow, he saw three

women in the chairs. A young blonde wearing only a bra and panties. She smoked a cigarette. An Asian woman wrapped in a silk embroidered robe, one leg dangling over the arm of the chair. An older black woman in a short white teddy sat on a big arm chair, her legs spread, drinking a beer. The three women looked at Larry, Wayne and Ian with a mix of curiosity and boredom.

A short gaunt man came through a curtain. He had the slow confident movements of someone who was in charge. He hooked Larry's thumb in a quick shake.

"Hey, man, long time no see." He gestured around the room. "Welcome to the pussy palace."

"Thanks, Buster." Larry jerked a thumb at Wayne and Ian. "These dudes work for me now. Remember I said I was expanding my paper route."

Buster nodded. "Make yourselves at home, boys. Have a beer." He nodded at the woman. "Get laid. If you have the dough." He snickered. "Larry and I have to go in the back and talk business." The two of them disappeared through the curtain and down a hall.

The big man looked up from rolling a joint, then concentrated again on the thin papers in his thick fingers. He had the bulging muscles of someone who pumped iron. A long mullet cut hung over his torn jean vest. In the ring of tattoos on his thick neck, Ian spotted a swastika. A baseball bat leaned against his chair. A heavy chain ran from the leg of his chair to the spiky collar of a large Doberman. The dog stood up when Wayne and Ian took a seat, but the man gave the chain a hard jerk. The dog circled once and lay down by his feet. With teeth protruding through thin pink lips, it watched the newcomers with beady eyes.

Wayne stared openly at the three women. Ian sat on the edge of his chair, watching the big man roll another joint.

"So boys," the black hooker said. "You want to go upstairs with a real woman?" She gripped her large breasts in her hands, jiggled them and laughed.

"How much?" Wayne asked. She stood up and walked closer.

"Fifty bucks for a straight up fuck." She nodded at the big man. "Pay Arnie there and I'll show you a little bit of heaven. For another twenty-five, you little friend can watch and jerk off."

Ian was glad for the dim lights -he knew he was blushing. To his surprise, Wayne stood up, dropped fifty dollars on the table and followed the hooker upstairs.

The man swept the cash up with a big hand.

"How about you?" He gestured at the other women. "Wanna fuck?

"I'm broke." Ian said.

Arnie shrugged. "Wanna beer? It's on the house." He reached sideways, flipped the lid on a cooler and handed Ian a cold beer. He took one for himself. He fired up one of the huge joints that lay on the table.

"Toke?"

"Sure."

Ian took a hit. Arnie did not offer the joint to the women. The young blonde looked like she was already stoned on something; her leg rocked rapidly over the high arm of the chair. She seemed transfixed by her bobbing foot. The Asian woman browsed through a magazine, staring at the photos as it they were complicated road maps.

The joint came back to Ian again. He pulled his chair closer to the table. When he moved the dog jumped up and growled.

"Killer." Arnie scolded. "Shut up, you dumb mutt."

Ian lower his hand. The dog stepped closer and sniffed his fingers. Cautiously, Ian scratched it behind one ear. It immediately settled down by his feet.

"Ha ha. He likes you." Arnie laughed through a cloud of smoke. "Killer don't like many people." The dog rolled on his side. Ian leaned over and patted its stomach. Arnie smiled.

"Some fucking watchdog, eh?" He reached out a giant arm and patted the dog's rear. "You're big fucking baby, aren't you?"

A couple more tokes and the black hooker came down the stairs. Wayne trailed after her, tucking in his shirt.

"That was quick." Arnie said. Wayne looked annoyed but didn't reply.

"Hey," the hooker said. "The man has places to be, things to do, right? How about you, blondie?" She asked Ian. "You look like you could use a good fuck."

"Do it, man." Wayne lit a smoke. "She's a great fuck."

"Like you would know." The hooker teased. She walked over to Ian. She grabbed his hat and ran her fingers through his hair.

"What do you say, blondie?"

Ian shrugged. "I'm broke."

"Sorry, no freebies here." She laughed. "But you can

look for free." She lifted her skirt and spread her legs. It was hard not to stare.

"Look at that face, girls. I bet he's a virgin."

Before Ian could reply, she laughed and made a little flourish to cover herself. As she went back upstairs she yelled over her shoulder.

"Arnie, these boys are cute, but call me when some real men show up."

Arnie picked up a plastic bag. "Wanna do a line?"

"Coke?" Wayne said. "Sure thing."

"Hey man?" Arnie said to Ian.

"No, I'm cool." He petted the dog while Arnie and Wayne snorted. It was his first time watching someone do coke but after seeing people shoot up it looked pretty tame. The coke seemed to have no effect on Arnie. He did a couple of lines, sipped his beer and started to roll another joint. Wayne, on the other hand, snorted, then slapped his hands on his thighs.

"Fuck yeah." He shouted. He stood up and paced in a circle.

"That's some great shit." He rubbed his nose with the back of his hand. "I want to score some of that."

"You'd have to ask Buster." Arnie said. "This bag is for house use only. Keeps the girls from getting too bored, right girls?"

The Asian hooker gave a half smile and went back to her magazine. The blonde was still watching her own foot bounce.

Larry and Buster emerged from the back room. Larry looked very pleased.

"Ok," Buster said. "Call me when you are ready to

rock and roll."

Larry nodded and hitched his thumb at Wayne and Ian. The girls didn't look up as they departed.

Outside Wayne, coked up, kept touching Larry's arm "So man, what's up?"

"We worked out a deal." It was the first time Ian had ever seen Larry smile. "I'm going to expand my business a little."

"So cool, so fucking cool." Wayne was so hyper that he was walking backwards in front of Larry. "I want in on that action."

Larry paused to light a smoke. "Oh, don't worry I have plans for you." Then he gave Ian a mysterious little smirk. "I got plans for both of you."

Once they got back to a busy street, to Ian's surprise, Larry flagged a cab and they headed home early. This time Wayne sat up front, coked out and babbling at the driver. Ian looked over at Larry on the seat next to him. His shoulder bag rested on his lap but it bulged more than usual. Ian noticed how Larry gripped it tightly with both hands. At home he did not offer up any acid, but headed straight to the bedroom with his bag.

The next morning Wayne was the tired one. He had tossed all night from the coke. Ian felt relatively rested after his first acid-free night in a while. The three men drank tea in silence. Connie was still asleep when Larry announced he had to make a phone call. He left. Ian and Wayne ate toast and waited. When Larry returned he said nothing. He went into the bedroom and came out with a shoulder bag. Ian thought it was Larry's usual bag, then he saw it was a different one, it had a multi-coloured peace sign embroidered on the flap. Larry pushed aside the plates and placed the bag on the table. He sat down and stared at Ian.

"Ok, Blondie, I got a job for you."

"Sure thing." Ian stirred some extra sugar into his tea.

"I want you to deliver this bag to a friend of mine. He'll give you something to bring back to me."

"Ok." Ian said.

Wayne didn't seem at all surprised, as if he and Larry had already talked about this.

Connie emerged from the bathroom. "What's up?"

"Blondie is making a run for me."

"Oh wow." Connie bit her lower lip. "Are you sure, Larry?"

"Fuck, yeah." Larry said. "It's perfect. Whose gonna suspect this guy?"

"That's true." She laughed and walked over to Ian, patted his hair and adjusted his shirt collar over his sweater. "I mean, fuck, just look at him! He looks like he's on his way to church." She leaned in and kissed his cheek like his mother used to do. Her breath smelled really bad.

Larry handed the bag to Ian. It was heavier than he expected. He hefted it with both hands. He knew better than to ask what was in it. He stood up and worked the strap over his head. The bag hung by his hip. He rested his hand on it. He felt a rush of nerves and excitement, the same way he had felt standing on his parent's porch. He sat back down. The bag was heavy on his lap. He took a deep breath and exhaled slowly.

"Don't be nervous, man," Wayne said, handing him a joint. "It's a piece of cake."

Ian took a long toke. Larry wrote an address on the inside of a match book and handed it to Ian. He told him which bus route to take and where to get off. Ian stuffed the match book in his jean pocket. He kept touching the bag, then pulling his hand away.

"Now listen." Larry leaned close to Ian's face. "If the pigs stop you, do not say a fucking thing, you hear me?"

"Don't worry." Ian smelled Larry's cigarette breath. "I won't say anything."

"I mean it." Larry said. "You tell the cops anything about me or where I live and I'll find you and fuck you up so bad you'll wish you were dead."

"Larry." Connie patted Larry's shoulder. "Ian would never say anything. Would you, sweetie? Besides nothing will happen. Look at him." Connie giggled. "It's Sunday. The cops will think he's on his way to church."

In silence Larry stared at Ian for a long time. Ian felt the palms of his hands grow damp.

"Yeah, shit." Larry finally nodded. He waved his hand in front of his face like flies were bothering him. "You're right. No one will ever suspect this guy." He reached for a smoke. "OK, kid, hit the road."

Ian stood up. He put on his fedora. The other three watched him in silence. He hesitated at the door.

"Ok," He tried to sound casual. "See you later."

After the dark basement the bright sunlight was jarring. As he passed the side window the big dog spotted him. Fangs protruding, it gave a low growl. Ian felt a wave of fear sweep up his spine. As he walked to the bus stop, he thought, What the fuck am I doing? But what choice did he have -how could he say no to Larry? Even Wayne was afraid of Larry.

Waiting at the bus stop he fantasized about going straight to the police, turning himself in and telling them all about Larry, the drugs, the pimping. But he knew this would backfire. Larry and Wayne would get arrested but so would he. They would know he had done it. If they beat up that guy for a couple hundred bucks, they'd kill him for sure. And what about Connie and her baby? She'd end up in jail too, or on welfare, or back on the street. He fingered the match book in his pocket and ran the directions over and over in his head. The sweater was too warm but he didn't want to take it off now; like Connie said, he looked like he was on his way to church.

Even though the bus was almost empty, Ian sat at the back out of habit. He placed the shoulder bag on his lap. He wiped his palms on his jeans. He ran his fingers over the bag like a kid feeling a Christmas present. Whatever was inside, it felt thick and square.

One old lady boarded and sat near him but she paid no attention to him. He loosened one strap and tugged it out of the tarnished brass buckle. He lifted one corner of the flap. He saw the edge of a plastic bag. He lifted the flap more. There were several hard packed, plastic wrapped bricks of white powder. He slapped the flap down and looked around. The old lady still gazed out the window. His fingers shook so hard he could barely get the strap re-buckled. That was a lot of smack, at least ten pounds, maybe more, he guessed. People went to jail for having a few joints in their pocket. If he was caught now, he'd go to prison for a long, long time.

Anxious that he'd over-shoot his stop, Ian moved up to the front of the bus to watch for cross streets. He was light headed and bumped into seats as he walked. Sitting near the driver, he watched for his stop. Finally, it came. He rang the bell and said way too loudly, "Here. I have to get off here." The bus grunted to a stop.

Ian stepped down. He stood across from a strip mall. There was a McDonalds on one corner, across the street a gas station. Sweat covered his upper lip. He wiped his face with the sleeve of his sweater. He took his hat off and rubbed his hair. It was soaked too. Larry had said to cross at this corner, then turn right and walk a few blocks.

Ian stood waiting for the red light to change. He fingered the match book in his pocket for the thousandth time. Then a police car pulled up beside him. He looked quickly and saw two cops. Their windows were down because of the heat. Ian looked away. Blood pounded in his temples. He willed himself to stare straight ahead and fought the urge to run. In the edge of his vision he saw the police car creeping forward. They were waiting for an opening in the traffic so they could turn right. The light was taking forever. Trying to act casual, Ian glanced in their direction. The cop in the passenger seat was staring right at him. Ian looked back at the light. Ian felt sweat leaking from under his hat, running down his forehead.

Change, god-damn it, change.

"Hey," the cop in the passenger seat called out. "Hey kid."

Stomach twisting, Ian turned his head.

"I like your hat." The cop grinned. "It's very Bogart."

Ian managed a frozen smile. He nodded once. The light changed and the police car turned in front of him. The cop who had spoken flicked his wrist at Ian in a casual peace sign. Then they were gone.

Hysterical laughter bubbled out of Ian as he darted across the road. He stopped and looked down where his hand had rested on the bag. His palm and fingers were clearly printed in sweat. Ian turned right and started walking, fast, jerky, adrenalin-driven steps. He came to the street name written on the match book. He turned up the street, checking the house numbers. Probably a block or two to go.

Larry had told Ian to act normal, to not draw attention to himself, so he willed himself to slow down. He inhaled and exhaled deeply as he walked, but he could not shake the knot in his gut. The houses were mostly bungalows, ranch-style places, probably build in the fifties and sixties. Big front lawns with a few scrawny trees. Wide, paved driveways with car ports or attached garages. It was Sunday afternoon. A man washed his car, kneeling by the front tire, circling the hub cap with a sponge. Another man cut his lawn, pushing a very loud gas mower. It sprayed grass cuttings on the sidewalk. The man half nodded at Ian as he meandered past. A young boy and girl road their bikes in circles in the street while a woman watched them from her front step, holding a tall glass in one hand, a smoke in the other. She stared at Ian as he walked by. Two boys his own age shot hoops; the basket mounted above a garage door. The ball got away from them and rolled down the driveway. They stopped and looked at Ian. He snagged the ball with his foot and kicked it back up the drive.

"Thanks," one shouted, but Ian did not look back. He kept walking until he came to the number on the matchbook.

The house looked the same as all the rest. A panel truck dotted with rust occupied the car port. A small motorcycle was parked next to it. The front blinds were pulled tight. Nervously Ian walked up the sidewalk to the low front porch, wondering if he had somehow got the address wrong. He located a small doorbell button and pushed it. He didn't hear anything except his own labored breathing. He looked up and down the street. He touched the button again. Maybe it was broken. He tried the screen door. It was not locked. He opened it and knocked lightly on the door. He thought he heard movement inside, but no one came. He reached up to tap on the small diamond shaped window, when the door jerked open. A heavy set man grabbed Ian's wrist and yanked him inside. He pushed Ian face first into the wall, kicking the door shut. He grabbed the back of Ian's neck in a big hand and leaned close.

"Who the fuck are you?" He snarled in Ian's ear.

"I'm Ian. I've got the package for you."

"What package? Who the fuck are you?"

"From Larry. The package from Larry. Larry sent me."

"Larry who?" The man pinched his neck even harder. Pain shot up into his skull. Ian realized, even after all these weeks, he didn't even know Larry's last name.

"Check my bag. It's in the bag."

The man yanked at the shoulder bag. Seeing it was

slung over Ian's chest, he let go his grip for a second and dragged the bag over Ian's head. The fedora tumbled to the floor. Ian heard the man yanking at the buckles. Then he resumed his vice grip in Ian's neck, pressing his face right against the wall.

"Stay the fuck here." He snarled in Ian's ear. "Don't look anywhere but at that wall."

The man's heavy footsteps clumped down the hall. A door slammed. Ian blinked. The wallpaper was cream colour with tiny pink flowers. Ian bent down quickly and scooped up his hat. As he did this, he saw a pile of shoes by the door, including some little kid's sneakers. He rubbed the back of his neck. It really hurt. He heard a TV somewhere. Then a door down the hall opened. Ian saw the hulking shadow of the man coming back.

"What are you looking at?"

"Nothing." Ian leaned closer to the wall. He felt his own sour breath blowing back on his face.

"See this?" The man waved a bulging brown paper envelope in front of Ian. "I'm putting this in your bag." Ian heard him grunting and fussing with the bag. He looked sideways and saw the man had a skull tattooed on the back of his hand, in the fleshy part between the thumb and fingers.

"Here." The man yanked on Ian's shoulder and shoved the bag into his hands. Ian looked up. The man slapped his face. Hard.

"Don't fucking look at me. What did I just tell you?"

Ian stared at the floor and mumbled, "Sorry."

Hands pushed Ian to the door and opened it.

"Get the fuck out of here." The man shoved him out

on to the porch. "And forget my fucking address."

"Sure thing." Ian said, but the door had already slammed behind him.

He ran down the driveway, almost turning the wrong way. He ran past the boys playing basketball, past the man mowing his lawn, past a woman working in her rose bed, past the kids riding in circles, past an ice cream truck with its jingly ice-cream truck song.

He could not stop running!

When he reached the corner by the gas station, he doubled over, panting, waiting for the light to change. He saw the bus coming and ran across the road, dodging traffic. Once he was on the bus Ian went right to the back seat. He was soaked in sweat and still breathing hard. He clutched the bag tightly to his chest.

He had done it!

He did not have to look inside this time. He knew it was full of money. He ran his fingers over the bundles. What if he took this cash and made a run for it? He could ride this bus right downtown. But where would he go? He didn't know anyone on the west coast. He could jump on a bus or a train, or take the ferry to Vancouver Island. But where to? Larry would come after him. Maybe even Buster and his man Arnie. They'd kill him if they caught him. He kept touching the bundles through the canvas bag. There must be thousands of dollars. Then Ian thought of Connie. This money would really help her and the baby. Larry was an asshole, but Ian figured Connie was better with him –and this money- than back out on the street.

Still, he thought, his hands resting on the bag, it was

tempting.

The second Ian came downstairs into the kitchen, Larry leapt up.

"How did it go?"

"Great," Ian said. "Great." He flopped on a chair.

Larry grabbed the bag and disappeared into the bedroom.

"Hey man," Wayne patted him on the shoulder. "You look like you could use a beer." He looked at Ian with a new respect as he handed him a cold beer and fired up one of his fat joints. Ian had never toked so hard. His heart was still pounding, worse than when they had jumped the freight train.

Larry came out of the bedroom with a big smile.

"Good work, blondie."

Ian nodded. He was so relieved that it was over. Connie came out of the bathroom.

"So how did it go?"

Ian told them about the cop car at the red light. When he said the line about nice hat, they burst out laughing.

Wayne gave him a high five. "Excellent, man, fucking excellent."

"My little choir boy." Connie said. She ruffled his hair. "Didn't I say he'd do a good job?"

"How about the house?" Larry said. "Everything go ok?"

"Very smooth," Ian said. He said nothing about getting slammed against the wall and having his face slapped.

Larry said he had to go make a phone call. When he returned he looked very pleased. He sat down and opened a beer. Connie leaned against him and kissed the top of his head. He hugged her hips.

"See, babe," she said. "Things are getting better. We need to celebrate. How are we gonna celebrate?"

"What about a party?" Wayne said.

Connie laughed. "Sure, let's throw a party."

To everyone's surprise, Larry said yes.

"I deserve a fucking party," he said.

"You do, babe." Connie kissed his cheek.

Between the beer and the pot, Ian was already feeling better. It was great to see everyone so happy. And he had finally earned his place here.

"Hey Larry," he said. "When do I get paid for making that run?"

"Paid?" Larry started laughing. "I'd say this makes up for living here for free and all the drugs I've given you." He looked at Wayne. "Paid," he repeated, like it was a punch line of a really stupid joke.

Ian laughed too. He had hoped maybe, just maybe, to get a chunk of cash so he could split. Wayne passed another joint his way. Connie suggested they throw a party that night.

"What the hell?" Connie said. "It's Sunday night. Come on, Lar, take a night off."

But Larry said he would head downtown anyway, solo, but only for a few hours.

"I'll just see my regulars and get back by ten." He said he would invite some people while he was out. He gave Wayne a wad of cash and the number of a bootlegger to get booze delivered. After he left, Connie grabbed Wayne.

"Wait, wait." She grabbed some paper and wrote down some names and numbers for Wayne to call. "I want you to call some of my old friends. These are some gals I used to work with." She shot Ian a look. "No. Not that. Waitresses I knew before I got so fucked up."

Wayne left to make the calls. Ian helped Connie clean the kitchen. He was about to pull down the spaghetti mosaic from the wall when Connie stopped him.

"Shit no. Leave that up. It's a work of art."

She threw some Beatles on the record player, cranked the volume and danced around the living room, holding her protruding belly with both hands. It was nice to see her so excited. It was the first time since Ian had been there that Connie would have someone to talk to besides the three of men. He was happy for her.

Ian went to the corner store to get snacks. He had bad munchies already and grabbed all kinds of chips, cheese puffs, pretzels and Doritos. By the time he got back, Wayne had returned. Shortly, the bootlegger –a cabbie- dropped off two cases of beer and a big bottle of whiskey. The three of them drank more beer, toked and ate chips while they straightened up the rest of the apartment. Ian stuffed his gear into the bottom of the closet. Wayne announced he would be the DJ for the party and started sorting the small collection of LPs.

A little after nine, Larry came home. He had also scored beer and booze from someone he knew. Now that the fridge was nothing but beer, the shelves sagged from the weight. Larry fired up one of his thin joints and insisted they all have a shot of whiskey. Connie dug out an odd assortment of drinking glasses.

"To a big fucking sack of cash," Larry said. They all clinked glasses. The whiskey burned on the way down. Ian had not drunk anything but beer since last winter when he shared a bottle of rum with other students during a high school dance.

Connie went to the bedroom to change. She came out wearing a powder blue dress that hung just above her knees.

"Remember this dress, Larry?" He grunted. "I think I was wearing this when we first met." She turned sideways and cupped her belly. "Glad I can still wear it."

"Looking good, cuz," Wayne raised his beer. "Here's to the baby."

"To the baby." Ian said.

Larry raised his glass half-heartedly, but said nothing.

Connie opened another beer. She said beer gave her gas but drinking calmed the baby down. "I'm gonna get this little fucker too drunk to kick me."

Ian was pretty high by the time the first guests arrived. He had been drinking and smoking dope for a few hours. The first people to show up were two women who used to waitress with Connie at a bar downtown. When they learned she was pregnant they shrieked and hugged her. They congratulated her, and Larry too, who seemed pleased with the attention. They opened a bottle of wine and everyone sat in the living room and chatted. Whenever someone walked between the houses the dog upstairs barked and jumped around, so they always knew when the next guests were arriving. Wayne and Ian took turns opening the door. Most of the party guests were strangers to Ian. Some were people Larry and Connie had known for years but rarely saw any more. Three guys from a band that played in Gastown showed up with a case of beer. Ian recognized a few regulars from downtown, mostly pot-heads. A few people shook Larry's hand and congratulated him on being a father to be. Ian guessed the word was already spreading that Larry was moving up the dealer ladder. They wanted to stay on his good side.

Wayne also seemed to know a lot of the partiers from his street dealing. Soon he was in full party mode, always firing up a joint or taking a slug from someone's mickey. As it got more crowded he kept cranking the music until it was so loud they could no longer hear the dog barking or new arrivals knocking. Since it was a warm summer night, they propped the door open and let guests find their own way in.

Ian went to get another beer. He was drunk and clumsy, bumping into a chair as he walked. He decided to take a couple of bennies. He went to the closet and dug in his duffle bag to find his pill bottle. He washed two down with beer. The bennies woke him up but they also made him very restless. He'd start to talk to someone but mid-sentence he could not follow the conversation. He couldn't stand. He wandered around, hovering on the edge of a group, trying hard to join the conversations, but he'd get impatient and walk away. He started to feel disconnected and lonely in the crowd.

He went to the kitchen and drank another beer, hoping it would take the edge off the bennies. Connie was there with her girlfriends, smoking some weed. She introduced him again, telling them he was her cousin's buddy from Ontario. With great effort Ian managed to piece together a few sentences. When he returned to the living room it was even more crowded.

After midnight Buster from the whore house arrived. He pushed his way through the crowd. Arnie, the whore house bouncer, towered behind him, ducking his shaved head to clear the low ceiling. Two women in short skirts and plunging necklines trailed along too, their pupils extremely dilated. In the kitchen, Buster bumped fists with Larry and whispered something in his ear. Then from under his leather jacket, he pulled out a huge slab of hash wrapped in plastic. It was the size of a big hardcover book. He tossed it on the table.

"Here's a little something for the party." He hooked a thumb at the two women behind him. "They're on the house too."

Larry introduced Ian to Buster.

"This is the guy I told you about. He did the run."

Buster nodded at Ian and smiled. "I see what you mean." He grabbed Ian's chin in one hand and turned his head left and right. "Innocent as school girl. Maybe I can borrow him sometime."

"Sure thing." Larry nodded. "But it will cost you." He gave one of his little mirthless chuckles.

Ian pulled his head away. He didn't like this, Buster talking about him as if he wasn't there. It was exactly the way Larry talked about "his girls". Ian went back to the living room. He drifted past Wayne who was arguing with some guy about who was a better guitar player, Hendrix or Santana. Ian noticed some partiers wandering out the door. Ian followed them outside. A few people stood around in the dark backyard, drinking and smoking. Ian nodded hello. They all seemed to know each other. He concentrated hard, trying to join in, but by the time he figured out something to say, they had moved on to a new topic.

Then he saw a movement near the back fence. It was the crazy dog from the main floor, loose in the yard. It came running towards him barking loudly.

"Don't worry," The guy next to him said. "That's my dog. He acts fierce but he's cool."

When it reached Ian, the dog stopped barking and sniffed his hand.

"See? He likes you." Ian cautiously patted the dog's head. The guy was the upstairs neighbor. He explained that he rode a big hog but didn't actually belong to a bike gang. He worked in a factory and loved the Beatles. He gave the dog several hard pats on the side.

"I named him Ringo because he's always drumming the floor with his tail."

Ringo sat down on Ian's feet. He leaned over and patted the dog. It was nice to pet a dog. Maybe, once he got his shit together and had his own place, he'd get a dog. It would be nice to have someone around for company. The guy took his dog and went into his apartment. Ian staggered back down stairs. He pushed through the crowded living room, bumping into people, stumbling over the legs of people sitting on the floor. In the kitchen, people had started in on the huge block of hash. They took turns around the stove, doing hot knives. Ian had a few tokes. The smoke was thick but sweet and very easy on the throat compared to the home grown he had been smoking.

"Too bad we don't have a hookah." Someone said.

"Hookah?" Ian repeated.

"Yeah. A water pipe. That's really the best way to smoke hash."

"Or opium." Someone else said. "That's how they smoke opium in the middle east. I got some zebra stripe hash." A guy fished in his jacket pocket and brought out a foil ball. He unwrapped it to show them a dark chocolate coloured lump of hash laced with white stripes of opium. He and Ian smoked some on the end of a pin. After a couple of tokes Ian felt a weird flatness descend on him, like someone had removed the front part of his brain. It was even harder to follow conversations now. He didn't like the thick feeling and went to the closet to get more bennies. He washed three down with beer. Some guy he didn't know watched him dig the bottle out of this duffle bag. Feeling paranoid, Ian took the bottle into the bathroom and hid it under a stack of towels.

Back in the living room, people stood shoulder to shoulder, shouting in each other's ears to be heard over the music. A few people danced. Others sprawled on the floor, drinking and passing joints. Ian spotted Wayne standing by the stereo shouting in the ear of some skinny blonde woman.

"Hey!" Wayne shouted when he saw Ian. "There's my buddy." He threw his arm over Ian's shoulders.

"Candy. This is my bud Ian. He's my bodyguard when I'm downtown."

Being called a bodyguard made Ian laugh.

"Seriously," Wayne continued. "He lookd so nice but he's a fucking madman. He'd kill you just like that." Wayne snapped his fingers.

Candy had a nice smile. She offered her bottle of Jim Beam and Ian took a snort. She said things to Ian but even watching her lips moving he couldn't make out a word she said. Meantime Wayne changed LPs and cranked the volume.

"Hey, Wayne." Ian shouted in his ear. "You got any acid?"

Wayne shook his head but dug a few pills from his pocket. He dropped two in Ian's palm. He shouted in Ian's ear. "Mesc."

"What?"

"Mescaline." Wayne grinned. "Just take it. You'll thank me later."

Candy waved her bottle in his face. Ian washed the pills down with liquor. He staggered back to the kitchen to see what was going on. Now a few people were sitting around the kitchen table shooting up. Arnie seemed to be in charge. He sat, dwarfing one of the kitchen chairs, setting up fixes. Ian had seen a lot of people shoot up but it was weird to stand in the brightly lit kitchen watching people take turns. They rolled up their sleeves and tied off with a belt. Some people Arnie injected, others did it themselves. Ian felt like he was watching some strange movie through a thick plate of glass.

Connie took the chair next. She saw Ian watching

and smiled at him.

"Don't worry, choir boy." She giggled. "I'm just having a titch to get me through the party."

She took the needle from Arnie and quickly found a vein. As she leaned over her bare arm, Ian turned away. This was fucked up. Her baby would be born fucked up. They'd be stuck living with fucking Larry. His mood plummeted. He pushed a couple of people out of his way and headed back to the living room. Things went black, like he had blinked, it seems like only a second, but then he was talking with the blond, holding an album and babbling about the cover art. Ian blinked again and he was in the backyard with Wayne. They were watching the neighbour's dog chasing its tail.

"Ringo. Ringo. Ringo." They chanted. They doubled over in hysterical laughter. They couldn't stop. Ian started to tell Wayne about the dog he had when he was a kid.

Then he blinked and he was back in the kitchen inhaling deeply while someone held a smoldering ball of hash under his nose.

"Fucking Christ." Ian shouted as he staggered back against the wall. Everyone was watching him, laughing, big open jawed, haw-haw-haw as he bumped into the dried pasta glued to the wall. A large clump of it shattered and fell to the floor. He knelt down and scooped up handfuls of broken spaghetti. He tried to stick it back on the wall. No matter how hard he tried he could not make them stick. People kept laughing at him, but Ian felt overwhelmed with sadness because he had destroyed Connie's art.

"You are so fucked up." Someone shouted at him

over the music.

"I am fucked up." He shouted back. "So fucked up."

He blinked and was outside again standing with a couple he had never seen before. They were sharing a cigarette. He was telling them about jumping the freight train in Calgary. He was very animated, acting out the running and climbing. The man kept nodding and saying "Far out, man, far out."

Then Ian was in living room again. A woman danced in the centre of the room. She only wore her bra and panties. Several men watched her. Their eyes reminded Ian of snake eyes. Pink forked tongues slithered in and out between their wet lips.

Then he was standing next to Connie by the kitchen sink. She grasped her tummy in one hand and a smoke in the other. There was a horrible burnt plastic smell in the air.

"Some asshole tried to cook the frozen steaks." She pointed at a burnt mess floating in the sink. "Put them in the oven with the plastic on, then wandered off."

Ian stared at the scorched plastic. Had he done that? Maybe he had. He really didn't know. He wanted to say something to Connie, warn her about having a baby with Larry. He leaned close. She had massive tea bags under her eyes and a rim of pale sweat around her dry cracked lips.

"You look like shit." Ian said.

"Thanks," she said, "just what a girl wants to hear." She pushed him away.

Ian blinked. Blackness again. Then he was in the narrow hallway between the kitchen and the bedroom standing behind a man. The man looked over his shoulder at Ian but said nothing. Ian wondered why he was lined up for the bathroom. He didn't think he had to pee. He turned around. Another man stood behind him.

"Short line," he said to the man.

"Yeah." The man grinned. "Worth the wait I hear."

"Yeah," Ian said but he had no idea what the man meant. He noticed they were standing in front of the bedroom door.

"That's the bathroom there." Ian pointed at the bathroom door. The man nodded and said, "You look pretty fucked up."

"Yeah," Ian said. "I'm pretty fucked up."

"You sure you are up for it?" The man leered.

Up for what? Ian thought. Peeing? The idea that peeing would be hard made him giggle.

"Sure. I'm up for it." He said but he could not stop giggling. The man looked at him and shook his head in disgust.

Ian faced forward again. The man who had stood ahead of him was gone. There was the bedroom door covered with Larry's poster of Frank Zappa. Zappa was staring at him. When he moved his head, Zappa's big cow eyes followed him. Ian leaned against the wall, wondering why was he standing here? He should go get another beer. Then a man stepped out of the bedroom, tucking in his shirt tails. He pushed past Ian, his head down. The door was open a crack. There were no lights on. Ian was confused. *What was going on?*

"Go ahead," The man behind him gave him a push. "Knock yourself out."

Ian stepped into the dark and the door clicked shut behind him. When he blinked rainbow colours sparked off his eyeballs like fireworks. He had never been in Larry and Connie's bedroom before. The darkness scared him like when he was a kid in a dark hallway.

As his eyes adjusted, he realized there was someone on the bed.

"What are you waiting for?" A woman's voice said. "Get your ass over here."

Ian walked towards the voice. He bumped into the edge of the bed. The only light was a faint glow from the clock radio. He could see the numbers, crisp and white, floating in the blackness. He saw a number flip over. 4:00. It took a lot of effort to find and say the words.

"It's four am." he finally said.

"Yeah. I know." The woman said. "It's a long night." He felt her hands on his hips. She pulled him closer. Fingers grabbed at his belt buckle. Two swift tugs and his pants were around his ankles.

"Come on." She laid back in the bed and grabbed his wrist. He fell on top of her. She was naked. He felt the mash of her breasts against his chest. Heat rose from her thighs. She grabbed his flaccid cock.

"What's wrong? Cat got your tongue?" She chuckled deep in her throat.

"I'm pretty fucked up," he mumbled into her shoulder.

She brought her hand up to her face. In the glow from the clock he saw her shining red eyes for a split second. She licked her hand, then wrapped her wet fingers around his dick. It sprang to life as she stroked him.

"Come on." She guided his cock into her. "There you go." He plunged in, a deep wet hole. A sensation of pure joy shot up from his dick into his spine. A multi-coloured light show exploded in his head. He bucked uncontrollably and a second later came inside her. He moaned loudly, feeling embarrassed. His breathed heavily on her shoulder. He had drooled there. He smelled her salty skin.

"Ok. Ok." She pushed him away. He staggered up right, his wet dick flopping against his thigh. He realized he was dribbling on the sheets. He stood there awkwardly, swaying, his pants still around his knees.

"Here," she handed him a towel. He dabbed at his crotch, repulsed by the damp and crusty edges of the cloth. Meantime she patted the end table and found her cigarettes. For one brief second, as she flicked her lighter, he saw her face: an older woman with big fake eyelashes, her bleach blond hair permed into a huge afro. He had not seen her before at the party. He dropped the towel and pulled up his pants. He fumbled with his belt buckle, too stoned to close it.

"I have to go." He said.

"You sure do." She blew smoke. It formed a glowing cloud over the bed. He was so fucked up. The clock ticked again and he looked: 4:04.

Ian bumped into the wall. He felt for the door in the dark. When he stepped into the hallway, the leering man asked. "So how was she? Was she good?"

Other men waited in line. Their eye balls protruded from bloody sockets, fat scaly tongues dangling from their open mouths. Ian pushed past them and ducked into the bathroom. He slammed the door and locked it. A candle stub sputtered on the back of the toilet. The darkness here felt soft and enveloping. He dropped his pants and splashed cold water on his cock and thighs. It felt good but he could not get clean. He splashed more water. He tried to dry himself, then pulled up his jeans. He had thrown lot of water in the floor. He tossed some towels down and used his foot to try and mop it up.

"Hey," Someone rattled the door knob. "What the fuck, you drowning in there?" He froze hoping they would leave him alone. They pounded on the door. In the darkness, he fumbled with the doorknob, not sure how to unlock it. They pounded again. He yanked on the knob. "I'm trapped," he shouted.

Ian blinked. He was sitting in a kitchen chair across from Arnie. Arnie was heating a spoon with his lighter. Ian looked down at his forearm. He clenched and unclenched his fist. The blue veins wiggled like little worms. His fist was far away, as if he was watching someone else's arm on a distant TV screen.

"Pull that tighter." Arnie said. Ian held one end of a thin leather belt. It was looped around his scrawny bicep. He shook his head, confused.

"Whose belt is this?" He asked. People laughed.

"Must be a virgin," Someone said. More laughter.

I'm not a virgin, Ian wanted to shout, I just fucked a hooker. But he could not get his mouth to respond. He looked around at the small circle of people watching. Larry was there too, leaning against the stove, smoking a cigarette; his small blood stained eyes reminded Ian of the dead fish in the harbor.

Arnie sucked liquid from the spoon into a hypodermic. Ian saw some dried blood on the needle. Arnie looked up, his eyes big and soft like a dog. He pointed the needle at the ceiling and tapped the hypo with a tobacco stained forefinger. Ian held out his arm over the cluttered table top.

"What the fuck are you doing?"

Connie loomed over Ian. She slapped his arm down.

"What the fuck did I say about doing smack?"

Ian smiled at her.

"Don't smile at me, you dumb fuck." Connie grabbed at the belt and pulled it off his arm. She tossed it on the table.

Arnie shrugged. "Sorry. I didn't know."

Connie shook her finger at Larry.

"Fuck, Larry, he's just a kid"

Larry blew smoke out of the corner of his mouth. "No one's forcing him. He wanted to try it. "

"Fuck." Connie shouted. She grabbed one of Ian's ears and lifted him from the chair.

"Ouch. Fuck. Connie. That fucking hurts."

She pulled him from the kitchen into the living room. People laughed as she towed him past by his ear. She dragged him over by the back door. He tripped on a pile of shoes and boots and nearly fell down.

"Stop. Connie. Stop."

She let go of his ear and leaned close to his face. He could see the pores in her nose and tiny brown cracks in her big front teeth.

"Didn't I tell you to never ever try junk?"

"Ok." Ian mumbled. "I won't." He tried to step around her but she doubled fisted him in the chest. He stumbled back against the wall.

"Connie stop."

"You are so fucked up." She pushed him over the bottom step. "Get outside. Get out of here until you sober up." He started to reply but she slugged him in the chest again. "You do not want to fuck with me, choir boy. Now go."

Ian stumbled and fell going up the steps. She was right. He was so fucked up. He needed to get some fresh air. Outside a small circle of people stood around with drinks and smokes. Ian mumbling apologies as he pushed between them, bashing elbows and stepping on toes. He staggered on an angle across the dark yard until he collided with the back fence. He leaned heavily on it, head spinning, thinking he was going to throw up, but he didn't. He fell on his hands and knees, rolled over and leaned back against the fence. He heard music and voices but when he looked back at the house it was like he was looking down a long tunnel that was filled with water. Everyone was so far away. He had no friends. Even Connie hated him now. He was alone, all alone in the world and so sad. He tilted his head back and saw a few stars. He recalled his mystic acid trip, the feeling of floating in space, of seeing the Truth or God or whatever the fuck he thought he had seen. That's the problem, he thought. He should have taken acid tonight. If he just dropped some acid, he might have made that mystical trip again. Maybe someone had some acid he could take. He stood up, reaching for the top of the fence, but the earth turned sideways beneath his feet and he fell down again. He lay on his back, staring at the stars. He felt the earth moving under him. It was just a ball of dirt in a huge empty universe and he was a speck of dust hurtling through space. He was nothing, really, *nothing.*

Ian woke at dawn under a pale blue sky, covered in a thin cold dew. He heard the faint sound of birds. He sat up and wiped the moisture from his face. Hoisting himself up, he held onto the fence for a second. Images of the party flickered through his addled brain like a slide show. The last image he saw was his veiny forearm and Arnie preparing a needle. He had come within seconds of doing heroin. Then he remembered Larry, watching him, looking so pleased.

I have to get the fuck out of here.

He stumbled towards the house. There were a couple of broken beer bottles by the back door. He descended the steps. The door was unlocked. He pushed it open slowly and peered inside. Once his eyes adjusted to the dark he saw Wayne on the couch, naked, laying under the blond who had been dancing. She was also naked. They were half covered with Wayne's sleeping bag. Some guy Ian had never seen before was passed out on the floor by the coffee table.

He tiptoed to the closet and pulled out his duffle bag, bedroll and canteen. He went to the kitchen to fill the canteen. The light was still on. There were empty bottles everywhere. The floor was sticky from spills, broken bits of spaghetti crunched under his feet. Ian pushed aside some dirty dishes and ran the water until it was cold. He filled the canteen and screwed the cap on.

Connie came out of the bathroom, rubbing her eyes. "What's up, dude?"

"I'm splitting," he said. "I'm headed back east."

Connie sighed. "Can't say I blame you." She fished in an ashtray, found a butt and took a couple of shaky drags. Neither of them mentioned last night.

"I'll miss you, choir boy." She looked very sad and tired.

"You take it easy." He nodded at her belly.

"Don't worry. As soon as this monster pops I am going cold turkey."

Ian nodded and forced a smile.

"Ok," Connie yawned and butted the smoke. "I gotta crash."

They did not hug. She turned and slipped back into the bedroom. Ian peed and splashed a little water on his face. He was terrified that Larry would wake up. Back in the kitchen, he paused to stare at the table covered in empty bottles, chip bags, pizza crusts, and ashtrays. The belt Connie had pulled off his arm was draped over the back of a chair. Leaning closer he saw several dirty hypodermics needles in the clutter.

Then he spotted the plastic bag with the hash. He picked it up. One end was ragged where people had pulled off chunks to smoke, but two-thirds of the huge brick was still there. Ian looked once at the bedroom door. Fuck Larry, he thought. He ducked into the living room and stuffed the hash in his duffle bag.

Wayne was still sleeping, his mouth half open, one arm over the blond, who had slipped sideways, one exposed breast pointing nowhere. Ian was tempted to wake Wayne, to say goodbye, but he knew Wayne would be loud. He'd try and talk Ian into staying because he loved it here: the dealing, the drugs, the hookers, the bullshit.

Ian shouldered his bedroll and canteen and grabbed his duffle bag. By the door he saw Wayne's faded jean jacket on a hook. Without a moment's hesitation, he grabbed it and darted up the stairs. In the backyard, he peeled off his infamous sweater and stuffed it into the duffle bag. To his surprise Wayne's jacket fit him well. He had lost a lot of weight the last few weeks. He put on his fedora. Ian walked quickly between the houses, afraid the dog would bark and Wayne and Larry would come chasing after him. But Ringo stood silently in the window and watched him walk by.

Ian caught the first bus he saw that went downtown. It took him a while to figure out where to transfer buses and how to find the highway east. He asked around and someone directed him to an overpass where they said he would find an eastbound ramp. He trudged along, severely hungover, pausing twice to lean against telephone poles, on the border of vomiting. He saw some flattened cardboard boxes leaning against the wall by a corner store. He decided to make a sign and tore off a long rectangular strip of cardboard. He dug a ballpoint pen out of his duffle bag. He sat down on the curb and stared at the cardboard. His head was pounding. He needed to put as many miles as possible between him and Vancouver before Larry woke up and realized he was gone and had stolen hundreds of dolars in hash.

What should he write? The next big city was Calgary, but today he would take any ride anywhere. Should he write Alberta? Ontario? Madanon? What about just East? Then he had an idea.

Clutching the pen in a shaky hand he outlined four big block letters, then he scribbled hard to fill in the squares. He had to stop a couple of times to shake the pen and flex his cramped fingers. When it was done he held it at arm's length; short and easy to read. When he reached the highway he went up the ramp and turned to face the traffic. He stuck out his thumb and held up his new sign.

HOME.

Ian smiled bitterly, yes, he was going home.

Five days later Ian woke up somewhere in Northern Ontario. He was snoozing in the passenger seat of a car. His head rested awkwardly on the window. He sat up, rubbing his stiff neck. The car was turning off the highway. He sat up and asked the driver.

"Where are we?"

"White River," the driver said. "I'm stopping for gas."

As he filled the tank, Ian stepped out of the car and stretched. He looked around. This was the very parking lot where his trip had begun. Over there he had hopped off that school bus. When was that? Six, seven weeks ago? So much had happened since that day, it seemed like years ago. He looked across the highway. Over there he had stuck out his thumb for the first time, his head filled with a fantasy of life in BC.

What a fucking idiot he had been.

The driver, whose name he had already forgotten,

returned from paying for the gas. Ian climbed in the front seat. Less than two hours to Madanon. Thumbing around the clock he had made it from Vancouver to Ontario in record time. His first ride out of Vancouver had headed off the main highway into the Okanagan Valley. Ian didn't care, he just wanted to get out of town before Larry and Wayne woke up and Connie told them he was headed back east. When they saw the hash was missing they'd come looking for him. Every minute he waited in Vancouver, he was in danger. So when a car finally stopped, Ian jumped in without even asking where the driver was headed. Turned out he was an airplane mechanic on his way to a job in the valley. He was very chatty, telling Ian his life story in immense detail. Ian was so tired he barely heard a word. He reached around inside his duffle bag and realized that he had left his bennies in the bathroom, buried under the towels. By late afternoon, on top of the severe hangover and lack of sleep, a temple-crushing Benzedrine withdrawal descended on him. As soon as he was dropped off on the side of some country road, he used his hunting knife to scrape slivers of hash from the brick. He sucked on them like leathery cough drops. The buzz dulled the pain but he still felt like shit.

As evening turned to night, Ian kept thumbing. He only had the vaguest idea where he was. He got a series of short rides from locals, from one crossroad to the next, sometimes just to someone's driveway. Finally, after midnight, getting dropped off in the dark, he laid down in some weeds by the roadside. He saw the lights of a farm house not far away. He woke early to the sound of a gas engine. He sat up and realized he had been sleeping in a huge front yard. The farmer circled around his property on a massive riding lawn mower. As Ian grabbed his things and walked away, the farmer raised his hat and gave a half-hearted wave.

The second day was long waits between short rides. Ian had nothing to eat. He continued to suck on little strips of hash that reminded him of apple peels. By night fall he was somewhere in the Rockies. It was cold here. He wore his sweater under Wayne's jean jacket. A man with a pick-up truck stopped to pick him up. The man had his two sons with him in the cab, so Ian rode in the back, laying on some dirty canvas tarps with two big dogs who insisted on laying on his legs. Each time the truck hit a pot hole, he bounced up and down very hard, banging his head on the truck bed. Just before dawn they dropped him on the eastern side of the Rockies. They turned down an unmarked dirt side road. He was on the main highway but in the middle of nowhere.

Ian thumbed all morning, numb and hungry. Finally, another pickup truck stopped. The driver just grunted when Ian thanked him for stopping. The cab was very warm and stank of body odour. Ian noticed some Playboy magazines on the seat between them and a couple of trashy porn novels laying on the dirty dashboard, but he was too tired to care. After his sleepless night in the back of the truck he fell asleep immediately. He popped awake, wondering why it was so quiet. They were parked on the side of the road. The man's zipper was down, his cock in one hand. He was staring at Ian and jerking off.

"You fucking perve." Ian shouted. He grabbed at his

hunting knife, fumbled with the sheath, then pointed the knife at the man. Sweaty faced, his cock still in his hand, the man stared blankly at Ian, who scrambled sideways out of the truck, dragging his stuff to the ground. Before he could slam the door, the man started the engine and stomped on the gas. Gravel popped and spewed as the truck fishtailed down the shoulder and around a sharp corner. Ian was shaking with rage and fear. If he hadn't woken up when he did, he might have ended up in a shallow grave somewhere. He gnawed on a big chunk of hash to calm his nerves.

After a couple of hours, he snagged one long ride to Calgary. From the eastern edge of that city, several short rides carried him into Saskatchewan. But near Gull Lake he got stuck at another country sideroad. There was nothing there. Night fell. Traffic died down. It started to rain. It was not a hard rain but Ian knew it would not take long for him to get soaked. Before dark, he had spotted an old abandoned barn off in a field. He decided to check it out. He climbed over a wobbly wire fence and walked across the field in the dark, tripping and stumbling over the hard rutted ground. By the time he reached it, the barn was just a dark rectangle looming against a darker sky. The big door hung open. Inside he struck a match. Not much to see. Some old loose hay and broken barn boards. Rain dripped here and there through wide cracks in the old roof.

Ian decided to build a small fire in the centre of the room. Using his foot, he cleared hay and debris away, making a circle in the hard packed dirt. He gathered some old straw in a pile and lit it. It flared up quickly but went out just as fast. He piled up more straw, then added some twigs and old fragments of wood that were laying around. But the straw still burned too quickly to light the wood. By now he was shivering. To start a fire, he'd need something else to burn. Then he remembered: in his duffle bag he still had Jack Kerouac's On the Road. All these weeks and he had never read it. He dug it out, kneeling next to his straw pile. Bending the cover back, Ian tore out the first few pages. He crumpled them up and added them to the straw. This time the fire lasted long enough for Ian to feed in some small twigs and bits of barn board. It still wasn't much of a fire. The flames would gutter and go out but some wood smoldered and caught fire. Ian kept reworking it, tearing more out more pages to insert under the planks, blowing until the wood lit up again. He worried someone on the highway would see the fire and call the cops. He worried even more that sparks would float up from the fire and set the barn ablaze. But still it was a fire. He spread his blankets on the dirt floor, very close to the fire, and lay down half curled around the flames. He felt a little warmth on his damp clothes. All night he drifted in and out of sleep, adding more pages and bits of wood to keep the fire going. Just before dawn, as the birds began to chirp, he burned the last few pages. Soon as he could see he would get back on the road. The last thing he laid in the glowing coals was the book's cover. It smoldered for a second, then black holes appeared in the painting. Small flames rose, swallowing the beatniks, the fast car and the dancing woman. On the Road, he thought, as the cover flared up, turned black and crumbled to ash, at least you kept me warm.

As soon as the eastern sky started to glow, Ian kicked the remaining embers apart. He splashed some water from his canteen over the coals hoping a passing driver would not notice the rising smoke and steam. He shouldered his gear, hurriedly crossed the field and climbed the fence to the highway.

Another day of short rides and long hours in the hot sun. The headaches finally stopped. He lived on hash and warm canteen water. He made it to Brandon but he did not want to stop at the hostel where he had lost Julie, so he kept thumbing. Luckily a young family picked him up. They were going as far as Ontario. At first Ian sat in the back seat with their young son, a kid of about eight, who seemed to find Ian fascinating. But when they stopped for gas, the mother insisted on switching seats, getting Ian to ride in the front. He had a feeling she did not like a dirty hippie sitting in the back with her son. But her husband was nice. He listened sincerely to Ian's adventures. For the first time in a long time Ian told his story, or at least the version he could tell in front of a little kid and his mother. He talked about hitchhiking, about Julie, about jumping the freight train, about running out of money and crashing with Wayne's cousin. Of course, all he could say about Vancouver was that he couldn't find work and had to get back to Madanon.

East of Thunder Bay the man spotted his turn off. He pulled over to the shoulder. As he got out of the car, Ian said thanks to the man's wife. She nodded but said nothing. Her son knelt on the back seat and watched his father opened the trunk. The man lifted out Ian's things and sat them on the ground.

"Thanks," Ian said.

"My pleasure. I enjoyed hearing your stories. You've had quite an adventure." He pulled out his wallet and handed Ian a twenty-dollar bill. "Take this, you might need some cash."

"I can't take your money." Ian said.

"I insist." He pushed the twenty firmly into Ian's hand. "Look, some day in a few years, my son might be out here doing what you are doing. I'd like to think someone will help him out too."

"Thanks." Ian said, choking up.

"Good luck." The man gave Ian a firm hand shake. He slammed the trunk down and got back in the car. As they drove off, he beeped the horn. The boy in the back seat waved. When the car was out of sight, Ian looked around. Rock cuts, pine trees, and a cold wind off Lake Superior. He had come full circle.

This last ride took Ian right to the Madanon exit. He thanked the driver, slung his gear and started walking into town. The sun shone brightly in a vibrant blue sky. He was very excited to see his high school friends and tell them about his adventures. He was curious what people had thought when he disappeared. What had his parents done? Had the police been looking for him? Mostly Ian wondered what his friends would think of him now. He had left town a nerdy bookworm but he had changed; into what he didn't know. He wanted to tell people about his trip, but he doubted anyone would understand what he had experienced. Still, he was excited to be back.

Ian walked past the long strip of gas stations, fast

food places and cheap motels on the edge of town. He thought Madanon would be different, but everything looked the same as the day he left. He didn't see anyone he knew, but he noticed a few locals staring at him as they drove by. They probably thought he was some stranger wandering into town.

Downtown, Ian stopped: he wasn't sure what to do now. Most of his school chums would be at work or away at their family cottages. Seeing the grocery store across the street, he thought of Joe from his physics class. He stocked shelves, part-time during school, full-time in the summer. Ian crossed the street and went around back to the loading dock. Sure enough, there was Joe having a smoke.

"Hey Joe." Ian shouted. Joe looked over and smiled.

"Ian. How's it hanging?" He jumped down from the dock and shook Ian's hand. A normal handshake.

"Excellent." Ian said. "How've you been?"

"Aw, same old shit. Working here for the summer. Hey man, that's a cool hat."

"I got it out west."

"Out west?"

"Yeah, I just got back from Vancouver."

"What?! You're shitting me."

"No. Remember, during exam week? You saw me by the buses. I said I was headed out west to work?"

"Aw," Joe laughed and shook his head. "I thought you were just kidding me."

"No," Ian said a little defensively. "I hitchhiked to Van and back."

"I didn't see you around," Joe nodded. "but I've been

working a lot of hours. All the full-timers are taking vacation. I haven't seen much of anyone since school got out."

"I was in Vancouver for almost two months." Ian bragged. "Just hanging out, smoking a lot of pot, doing acid." He said doing acid very casually, waiting to see how Joe would react. He was dying to tell someone the whole story, about Julie, about Wayne, about the freight train, about Connie and Larry, about the hookers and heroin, about the whole insane trip.

But Joe looked at his watch. "Hey, sorry man, my break's over. I gotta get back to work." He flicked his smoke down the alley and swung back up on the loading dock. "Let's grab a beer sometime. Where are you staying?"

Ian hesitated. "I don't know. I just got back."

"Fucking hippie," Joe teased. "Ok man, see you around."

Back on the main street, Ian walked into the Adanac, the diner where he used to go after school. A few people paused their conversations and watched as he hauled his duffle bag and bed roll to a booth. The waitress barely nodded as she took his order for a burger and fries and a cup of coffee. After five days of not eating, the smell of hot grease overwhelmed him. When his order came he ate so fast that he felt a little nausea. He put a lot of sugar in his coffee but he still felt tired. He ordered a refill. The waitress brought more coffee and the bill. Before he finished the second cup, she came, removed his plate and wiped around his elbows. He could take a hint. He paid up and counted his cash. He had less money now than when he left home in June. He smiled bitterly - so much for The Plan.

Outside, Ian slung his gear and started walking. At the next corner he heard a motorcycle and turned to look. He recognized the driver, Jason, a tall athletic guy, a year ahead of him at school. The girl, who sat behind Jason, her arms around his waist, was Mary from his home room class. He always had a bit of a crush on her. They were stopped at the light. Mary smiled and shouted something but Ian could not hear what she said over the revving engine. He started towards them but when the light changed, Jason popped the clutch and they roared off. Mary looked back over her shoulder and threw Ian a peace sign. He stared after them for a minute, then started walking again.

Almost unconsciously he found himself approaching his parent's house, although it had not been theirs since June. He stopped on the sidewalk. There were no curtains on the windows. Stuck in the middle of the patchy lawn was a short white pole with a For Rent sign. Ian walked up the narrow path to the porch. He leaned close to the living room window, shaded his eyes and peered in. The house was empty. No sign of his family, not a hint of his old life was left.

Ian dropped his gear and sat down on the top step. He had done it, hadn't he? He had run away from home but nothing had changed. He was back but with no money, no job, and nowhere to sleep. Now what? The weight of the summer, of everything he had seen and done on the road hit him. He crumpled forward, cupped his head in his hands, and started to cry.

ABOUT THE AUTHOR

Neil Muscott is a writer, photographer and visual artist based in Toronto, Canada. He has published articles, fiction and poetry in literary and commercial magazines. After earning his living for two decades performing, directing and teaching comedy, he returned to his first love, writing fiction. NFA is his first novel. You can learn more at www.neilmuscott.com or follow him on Facebook, Twitter, and Instagram.

Made in the USA
Monee, IL
06 June 2021